The Missions of
Indian Territory
Book 2

LOOK UNTO

the

FIELDS

Enjoy!

Jonita Mullins

JONITA MULLINS

ISBN-13: 978-0-9789740-4-6

ISBN-10: 0-9789740-4-2

First Printing May 2015

Published by Jonita Mullins

Printed in the U.S.A.

Look Unto the Fields

CHAPTER ONE

Union Mission, Arkansas Territory
Late May, 1822

Clarissa Johnson woke with a start in her cabin at Union Mission but quickly settled back on her down pillow hoping for a few more moments of sleep. The day before had been hot and it had taken a long while for the temperature to cool enough for sleeping. Now that it was cool, she wanted to sleep as long as possible before beginning this Monday.

Closing her eyes, she listened to the familiar sounds of the awakening prairie. A too-eager rooster crowed in their chicken coop and birdsongs drifted up from the stand of scrubby trees and thick cane growing along the nearby Neosho River. In the barn, one of the cows informed the farm apprentice Robbie Bake that she was ready to be milked. Soon the mission compound would stir to life.

But Clarissa's cabin remained quiet, for today she was its only occupant. How strange it seemed to have the place to herself. After traveling from New England on a squat, little keelboat and then settling at the mission outpost in a cabin she had shared with four other missionaries, Clarissa had grown used to crowded conditions.

She smiled drowsily to herself, remembering her longing once for her own bedroom back home in Colchester, Connecticut. Now she felt lonely in a room to herself and missed her mission sisters. What a difference the last two years had made in her life.

In that time, Phoebe Beach, the mission's house-mother, had married Abraham Redfield and moved out of the cabin.

Amanda Ingles, their cook, was now on her honeymoon with her new husband Stephen Fuller. Susan Comstock had transferred to the Harmony Mission in Missouri to serve as a housemother there. And Eliza Cleaver was visiting Harmony, hoping to recover from a very bad fever.

So the cabin seemed rather melancholy today. Or perhaps this feeling came because it was the last week of the school year and she would soon be saying goodbye to her Osage students for the summer.

Her mind began to spin with all the things she wanted to accomplish in this final week of school. With a sigh, she realized she would not be able to drift back to sleep now and so threw back the light muslin sheet and put her bare feet on the rag rug beside her bed. Beyond the rug, hard packed dirt served as the floor. What would her mother think of her padding around barefoot on the dark prairie soil?

 Emily Johnson would be aghast at the primitiveness of her oldest daughter's surroundings. Clarissa had almost felt that way too, when she had arrived at the mission the winter before last. Now it seemed perfectly normal and compared to the living conditions of others in the "neighborhood," the mission actually had quite comfortable accommodations.

Except for the children who were part of the mission family, the students at the school were Osages who lived in pole and grass lodges or in makeshift trapper tents and log cabins. Their Indian neighbors were fascinated with the stone fireplaces in the mission's buildings.

Frequent visitors from the nearby fur trade community of Three Forks enjoyed the mission's hospitality with a meal prepared at their kitchen hearth. Three Forks, about 25 miles to the south, was an ideal location for a fur trading post and several outfits were located on the banks of the three rivers that joined there.

Considering that Union Mission had been built at the edge of civilization in western Arkansas Territory, the living conditions weren't as bad as Clarissa had expected when she volunteered to teach the girls at this outpost.

As she poured tepid water into her wash basin, she

reached for one of the few luxuries she enjoyed at the mission – a bar of rose-scented soap she had bought in St. Louis on the journey out to Arkansas Territory. Clarissa washed up quickly, then scrubbed her teeth vigorously with a rough cloth and a bit of salt, for she hated the woolly-sock feeling of dirty teeth.

She heard the cry of an infant coming from William and Asenath Vaille's cabin, two doors down from her own. She listened carefully to identify whether the cry came from Joseph Vaille or from her own adopted baby Thea. Mrs. Vaille was acting as wet nurse for the little girl who was Osage-Pawnee and had been left at the mission when her mother died in childbirth.

Clarissa dressed carefully and braided her long brown hair before twisting it into a knot at the crown of her head. She made a quick run to the outhouse and then joined Phoebe and Rachel Chapman in the kitchen where she washed her hands again, this time with the lye soap made at the mission last fall. After breakfast she'd spend a little time with Thea before walking over to the schoolhouse.

"Morning, Miss Johnson," Phoebe greeted her when she stepped into the spacious kitchen which adjoined the dining hall and shared its massive fireplace. Clarissa had never been able to convince her mission sisters to address her by her first name. One's station in society still mattered, even out here on the frontier.

"Good morning, Phoebe, Mrs. Chapman," she returned the greeting and then smiled at herself. She couldn't bring herself to call Mrs. Chapman by her first name either.

Rachel Chapman came from one of the wealthiest families in Connecticut and was by far the best educated and most cultured of all the missionaries serving the United Foreign Mission Society. Her husband, Rev. Epaphras Chapman, was the mission director. Even here in the kitchen, Rachel was the epitome of style with her pale blonde hair and garnet-colored dress dusted with a bit of biscuit flour.

"Well, Miss Johnson," Rachel said, "are you ready for the school year to end?"

"No, not really," Clarissa admitted. "I don't feel that I've made nearly as much progress as I would have liked."

"Well, you have valiantly fought a difficult battle just in getting the Osages to send their children to school on a consistent basis," Rachel said as she settled the big metal cooking oven onto the fireplace grate to bake the biscuits she and Phoebe had prepared.

"I had to teach every lesson at least twice and sometimes I went over the same thing every day for two weeks just to be sure every girl heard it," Clarissa agreed as she tied on an apron. She began to slice a slab of salted bacon from their smokehouse.

Phoebe, who had received little formal education herself, patted Clarissa's shoulder. "I admire that you taught everything in French and English," she said. As an exact opposite to Rachel, the housemother's dark hair was already falling from the haphazard bun she had pulled it into. She was wearing a loose maternity dress borrowed from Mrs. Vaille.

"With just a little of my garbled Osage added in," Clarissa laughed. "It's a good thing most of the Osages understand French."

"Do you think you'll have many parents attend the closing exercises?" Rachel asked as Alice Spaulding arrived to join them.

"I don't know," Clarissa admitted. "Every day I remind the girls of how many sleeps there are until the final day so they can remind their parents. I'm glad it falls at the full Strawberry Moon. That helps with communicating a date to all the students."

"That's just what John says," Alice responded. Her husband taught the boys at the mission school. "He doesn't expect very many parents to attend, though."

"I know one person who'll be here for sure," Phoebe said.

"Who?" Alice asked as she worked to capture her abundant honey-blonde hair into a kerchief.

"Star-That-Travels," Phoebe said with a smile. "He

4

never misses a chance to come to the mission if Teresa Revoir is here. Not since they have decided to marry."

Teresa was a young Osage widow who had two children in the school and lived in a lodge on nearby Flat Rock Creek. Her French-Osage husband had been killed in an altercation with Cherokees the summer before. Now that her time of mourning had passed, she would "share the blanket" with Star-That-Travels, a man from her clan's village near Three Forks.

As Rachel peeked into the oven to check the biscuits, the tow-headed farm apprentice stepped into the kitchen carrying two pails of frothy milk. He emptied them into the big metal creamer while greeting the women. Phoebe would skim the cream later and churn it to make butter.

The sisters tried to hide their smiles when the fourteen-year-old young man's voice cracked a little and his face went red. "Thank you, Robbie," Phoebe said. "Will you check on the girls to see if they're gathering eggs, please?"

"Yes, ma'am," he said, looking grateful for a chance to escape the women's domain of the kitchen.

There were ten children at the mission whose parents worked for the United Foreign Mission Society. Shortly the four oldest girls stepped into the room all carrying cane baskets filled with eggs.

They set their egg baskets on the work table and quickly moved into the dining hall for a chance to play with the babies, Joseph and Thea. The Vailles were settling the two infants into their cradles and the other men at the mission were finishing up morning chores to join them in the dining hall.

Clarissa took a quick glimpse into the dining room to check on Thea before taking her place at the fire to fry the bacon in a huge skillet. She was almost as eager as the girls to scoop up her black-haired baby and coax a smile to her sweet but solemn little face.

Phoebe did a quick count of the eggs and set aside a dozen for baking later in the day. The rest she would scramble for breakfast after the bacon was cooked. "Looks like the hens are slacking off in their egg laying," she commented.

"It's the heat," Alice agreed. "It seems to always slow down the eggs."

"Might have to send the boys down to the river on an egg hunt," said Martha Woodruff, the mission's midwife. She had joined the ladies in the kitchen and was reaching for the stacks of enamelware to set the tables for breakfast. "My Alexander says the turkeys are roosting down there."

The Woodruffs, a couple their fifties, were the oldest members of the mission group. He served as blacksmith and Martha acted as mother to all of them.

"Turkey eggs are good as hen eggs," Phoebe agreed.

As the bacon sizzled, it sent its aroma out the open windows along with the fragrance of the coffee boiling in the heavy enamel pot nestled into the fireplace coals. There would be no need to call anyone to the meal on this warm morning. Most everyone was already gathered in the dining room, visiting quietly and waiting for morning prayers and generous helpings of a hearty breakfast.

Clarissa removed the bacon from the fire and she and Alice worked to quickly fork the thick slabs onto a serving platter. Phoebe took her place working over the fire with another skillet to quickly scramble the eggs. The smooth efficiency of the kitchen operation came from long practice and the great organizational skills of the mission cook, Amanda, who was away on her honeymoon.

"Wonder if the Fullers will be back today?" Martha said as she took up a pitcher of milk for the children.

"I hope so," Rachel stated. "I love you all dearly, sisters, but none of us comes close to cooking like Amanda."

The others smiled and nodded their agreement.

Phoebe heaped two large bowls with the eggs, Rachel used her apron skirt to carefully pull the coffeepot from the fire and they all carried the food into the dining room, including crocks of butter, pitchers of cream and honey, and Amanda's strawberry preserves.

After Rev. Chapman, the mission superintendent, offered

a prayer over their meal, everyone passed the platters and bowls of the hot and hearty breakfast. Quiet conversation and laughter filled the room over the long wooden tables. When she had finished eating, Clarissa went to Thea's cradle and picked up the five-month-old baby. She still marveled and thanked God every day for the chance to mother the quiet little girl looking so pretty in the pink gingham gown Asie had made for her. Clarissa rocked Thea gently at the table while Rev. Vaille read the morning scripture.

Following the devotions the pastor asked Will Requa, their stonemason, to lead a prayer. He did so, remembering to include the Fullers, his younger brother George, Eliza Cleaver and Dr. Marcus Palmer in his request for health and protection. All of these had taken the three-day journey to Harmony Mission, Missouri, but they were expected back soon. Hopefully George and Eliza were recovered from the fever that had plagued the mission since the weather turned hot.

After the prayer, each of the mission family rose to continue the day's work. The school and 1,000-acre farm operation kept everyone busy, especially the women. Two of their number had died on the journey out to the mission site so they always felt as if they were behind in the numerous chores required.

Rachel had convinced her husband to send a request to the mission society in New York for another woman to be hired as seamstress and housekeeper. But with the slowness of transportation, it would be several months before such a request could be met.

"Will you need more firewood today, ma'am?" Paul Gillard, the blacksmith apprentice asked Rachel as he prepared to head out to the forge. Keeping firewood stocked was one of his daily chores.

"Only for the laundry fire," Mrs. Chapmen told the young Negro. Though 16 years old, Paul was small for his age and also an orphan like Robbie.

Clarissa handed Thea to Phoebe who would feed the little girl some thin gruel now that everyone else had finished breakfast. Then with two of the girls holding her hands, she and Mr. Spaulding and the other mission children made the short trek to the schoolhouse to begin this last week of classes.

Their Osage students, they had learned, would arrive at various times throughout the morning, depending on how far they had to travel to reach the school. For a people who kept time by the sun and dates by the moon, punctuality had an entirely different meaning than what these New England missionaries knew. Clarissa had long ago learned not to fret at the all-morning arrival times of her students.

Martha and Alice worked to clear and wash the breakfast dishes and put a venison haunch and root vegetables in Amanda's huge roasting pan to slow simmer over the kitchen fire. Asie Vaille and Phoebe fed the babies and settled them down for naps.

Then all the women gathered the week's laundry and with water hauled by Robbie and Abraham Redfield, Phoebe's husband, they started the task of washing clothes and hanging them on the rope clothes lines strung between t-poles near the kitchen. The men set to work in digging rock from the river bank for the gristmill they were constructing.

Clarissa spent the day helping her girls with the short recitation pieces she had chosen for them for the closing school exercise. Most were saying simple Bible quotations, but her three oldest girls had been given more challenging assignments.

Elizabeth Vaille, her most dramatic student, was reciting a Shakespearian sonnet, Abigail Chapman was singing a hymn and Marie Lombard was reading a story of her own composition. It was an interesting mix of French and English, but Clarissa could not fault her for that since that was the way she taught.

Mr. Spaulding was likewise helping his male students prepare for the final day of classes. Since John did not speak French, Will Requa would often spend time in the class to help with translation. Will, along with Rev. Chapman and Dr. Palmer, had often visited Claremont's Town, the nearby

Osage village, with the goal of learning their language. Will and his brother George had learned French from their grandparents.

Clarissa found that her students were having a hard time in concentrating on any lessons. The pretty day was calling them to recess and she was hard-pressed to keep their eyes and minds focused on the chalk board. She didn't want to start any new lessons, but drilling them on past studies held about as little appeal to her as it did to them.

She gave them ten additional minutes of play time following their dinner break, hoping the extra time of jumping rope would settle some of their restlessness. The blond and youthful looking Mr. Spaulding stood with her at the schoolhouse door watching the students at play.

"I don't know if I will get Jean Revoir or Bearpaw to come back for classes tomorrow," the teacher noted. "As far as they are concerned school is over and they're not enthused about recitals of multiplication tables and European capitals."

"I know Mrs. Revoir will keep Jean in class, but I understand what you're saying," Clarissa said. "And if Bearpaw doesn't return, neither will his sister. I had hoped final exercises would give the parents a reason to spend time among us here at the mission. We have such little interaction with them otherwise."

"That is the hazard of trying to reach children from such a wide area," John stated. "When we had some of them board with us this winter we had a semblance of order. But the spring hunt and spring planting blew them all away like dandelions."

Clarissa smiled at his imagery. It was certainly true. Life on the prairie was one of constant work for survival and education was a luxury few parents felt they could afford.

"I just hope Amanda is back before the closing exercises," Clarissa said. "She has a well-established reputation for her wonderful cooking. If nothing else will entice the parents to attend, perhaps the food will."

"It would certainly bring me to the mission," John smiled. Then he lifted the school bell from its resting place on the open window sill and called the children into afternoon class.

CHAPTER TWO

Union Mission
Late May, 1822

Later in the day, the mission sisters set the roast and vegetables, along with cornbread and strawberry shortcake on the tables for supper. Small, wild strawberries were abundant this time of year and Teresa Revoir had brought several pints she had picked.

Clarissa mashed a few of the turnips and carrots to let them cool to see if Thea might be interested in trying them. So far she had spit everything out but her gruel.

Everyone was gathering in the dining hall when Robbie called out, "Wagon on the trail."

The mission family smiled and turned toward the west windows. They often teased Robbie by calling him the "town crier" because he always seemed to notice first when visitors arrived.

Turning off the road known as the Osage Trace was an oxen-drawn wagon they recognized as belonging to the mission. The two occupants of the wagon were the Fullers – Amanda and Stephen – returning from Missouri. Clarissa felt a twinge of disappointment that neither George Requa nor Dr. Palmer had also returned.

Robbie hurried to open the corral gate while the others made their way to meet the wagon. Stephen helped his wife step down, using the wagon wheel, and then he turned the wagon into the corral. He and Robbie unyoked the oxen while the women all gave Amanda a hug of welcome.

"Oh, it's so good to be home," Amanda said, trying to hug everyone at once. "Me backside is right tired of that wagon seat," she whispered so the men couldn't hear. Phoebe and Alice giggled at the redheaded cook.

"Well, come to supper, you two," Mrs. Chapman said. "I imagine you'll welcome something hot after a week on the trail."

"Aye," Amanda agreed with her Irish brogue evident. They all made their way to the dining hall. "Though Mrs. Chouteau fed us bison tongue at La Saline last evening," she said.

Everyone took their seat at the tables and after grace was offered began to enjoy the frontier supper.

"How are Eliza and George faring?" Alice asked Amanda as soon as everyone was served. Eliza was Alice's younger sister and it was she who had insisted that Dr. Palmer take her to a cooler climate, hoping that would alleviate her symptoms. "Have they not yet recovered from the fever?"

"Both were doin' better," Amanda quickly assured Mrs. Spaulding. "It is cooler at Harmony, but they too have had a lot of sickness there."

"Dr. Belcher at Harmony has found that quinine is helpful with the fever," Stephen added. "Dr. Palmer took the Osage Trace on up to St. Louis hoping to be able to get some proven medicinals. He hadn't returned before we left."

Clarissa felt her heart constrict a little. She was glad to hear that Eliza and George were better, but now she would worry about Dr. Palmer traveling alone to St. Louis. Though the Osage Trace was a well-traveled road in Missouri, Colonel Chouteau had told them it ran though some sparsely settled areas.

"And how was everyone at La Saline?" Rachel asked.

Located some ten miles north of Union Mission, the Chouteau trading post La Saline was one of their closest neighbors. Colonel Auguste Chouteau was a member of the wealthy St. Louis fur trading family. He and his wife Rosalee, an Osage, lived at La Saline near a salt spring.

12

"The colonel is making considerable changes to his home," Stephen replied. "He's added a second story to the house and planted several trees which he had imported all the way from France."

"So he is in Arkansas Territory to stay then?" William Vaille inquired. "Mrs. Revoir told us that, but I wondered that he would leave his trading post in St. Louis."

"According to the brothers at Harmony, the Osages are feeling some pressure from settlers in Missouri to move further west," Stephen said. "We may see some of Pawhuska's band move down into our area. Colonel Chouteau plans to encourage them to bring their furs to his trading posts in Arkansas Territory rather than taking them to St. Louis."

"That might be good news for our mission except that the Cherokees are feeling the same pressure to move west," Rev. Chapman mused. "Some are already settling at the mouth of the Illinois River near the Bean brothers."

"We may see more clashes between Mad Buffalo and Walter Webber," William Vaille added quietly so the children at the next table with the Redfields and Spauldings would not hear. These two tribal leaders had a long-running feud that had more than once resulted in death among the Osages and Cherokees, including Teresa Revoir's husband Joseph.

"But on the other hand," Will Requa put in, "it may open some opportunities to develop our demonstration farm. The Osages from Pawhuska's village may be ready to consider the farming life. More so than Chief Claremont's band."

Chief Claremont, father to the warrior Mad Buffalo, had his village near the Verdigris River twenty-five miles northwest of Union Mission. The Verdigris and Neosho Rivers followed a somewhat parallel southward flow to empty into the Arkansas River at Three Forks. Abundant game in the Three Forks area meant the Osages here were little inclined to take up farming. Raising the crops was work left to their women.

The two missions – Harmony and Union – planned a collaborative demonstration farm located somewhere between them. Will Requa and Rev. William Montgomery from Harmony would head up the project.

They could not start the farm without receiving authorization from the Mission Society and permission of the Osages who claimed the area as their hunting grounds. They had also sent their request to the Arkansas territorial governor. It could be several more weeks before they could move forward with their plan for a new mission.

"Well, we won't be building any cabins for the smaller mission, just yet," Abraham Redfield stated. "So shall we begin on your cabin in the morning, Fuller?"

"Sounds good to me," Stephen said with a smile at Amanda. "We don't mind sleeping on the ground for a time, but it does get hard on my old bones."

The group laughed, for Stephen was hardly old. But having suffered an attack by a panther last spring, they knew he needed to rest in one of the rope-strung feather beds in a cabin. Until their home was completed, the Fullers planned to sleep in the storage lean-to next to the kitchen. Their cabin would be built on the other side of the large kitchen garden Amanda and the other women tended.

When the men had constructed the first buildings at Union Mission, they had created a longhouse with seven cabins under one sod roof. The Fullers' cabin would be the first individual home built and the men had spent the last few weeks felling timbers in the "*spavinah*" – a young stand of pine trees a few miles north of the mission.

The next day was cloudy and a little cooler and Clarissa feared they might see thunderstorms which could keep their students away. The missionaries had learned to respect the fierce prairie storms that came roaring out of the west. They had never seen a cyclone yet, but they had heard stories about them from their friend and veteran trader Joseph Bogey. They knew to keep a watchful eye on the sky when the dark clouds built along the western horizon.

The clouds proved benign today, however, and provided some respite from the heat. The men worked to lay out the rock footings for the Fullers' cabin and took the oxen down to the river to haul up the logs and stones collected for the project.

Clarissa let her girls read quietly for most of the morning and then drilled them again in their recitations for the following day. She hoped the weather wouldn't become another reason for parents and students to stay away from closing exercises.

"Can we decorate our classroom?" Abigail Chapman asked that afternoon. "So it will be pretty when everyone is here tomorrow."

"That's a wonderful idea," Clarissa said, inwardly scolding herself for not thinking of it. Though paper was scarce, she gave each girl a sheet and allowed them to use old copies of the *Arkansas Gazette* to cut out pictures and words to create their individual welcome to their visitors. She borrowed some flour from Amanda to make a paste for their creations.

The afternoon session flew by with the creative endeavors. After the four mission girls said goodbye to Louisa Revoir, Marie Lombard and Bearpaw's little sister Deer-in-Water, they secured permission from their mothers to walk down the Trace with their teacher to pick wildflowers.

Carrying their egg baskets, the girls chattered excitedly while dashing off the road here and there to pluck the pretty Black-eyed Susans and Crown Vetch. The Indian Blanket flowers grew in such profusion they did indeed look like a colorful orange blanket that had been spread across the prairie. Clarissa had brought Thea along and she clutched a flower in each hand, her bright, black eyes seeming to delight in their color.

When their baskets were full, Clarissa insisted they return to the mission. The Trace was empty now, but she didn't want to be out too far from their home should someone come along.

The missionaries were not fearful of the Indians, for none had ever molested their work. But the frequent mule skinners who hauled freight along the Trace looked as rough as the boatmen who had brought them to Arkansas. The women kept their distance from them and let the men deal with them when they would sometimes stop to replenish their water canteens or seek a repair for a wheel rim at the blacksmith shed.

"We have enough flowers to share with Mr. Spaulding's class," Leah Chapman said, holding up her basket to her mother when they arrived at the dining hall. Her older brother James rolled his eyes over the molasses cookie he was eating. "We don't need no flowers in our class," he stated.

"Any flowers," his mother and Clarissa corrected at the same time.

Clarissa smiled apologetically at Rachel. It wasn't her place to correct him; it just came out automatically.

Mr. Spaulding was sitting at a nearby table, grading final exams. "I think a pitcher of flowers will be a nice addition to our class," he said with a smile. "You can tell the parents what their Latin names are."

James groaned, but at his mother's warning look, he became quiet and finished his mug of milk without saying anything more.

The children were quite excited over breakfast the following morning. The last day of school was a momentous occasion in their young lives. Elizabeth confessed to being nervous about her recitation and Clarissa assured her she would be fine.

"I'll be right there to prompt you should you forget your lines," she said. "But I doubt that you'll need my help at all."

Amanda was putting the final touches to the platter of cookies and three pies she had made for the event and the other women helped her carry them into the dining room. A hot pot of coffee and cool cider would be set out later. Then they joined Clarissa and the girls in setting out the flowers they had placed in water in every jar and pitcher that Amanda could spare.

The classrooms looked quite gay and inviting and a gentle breeze through the open windows kept them from being too hot. The men worked at the Fullers' cabin but would stop for the closing exercises when all the other students had arrived. Everyone knew to keep busy and wait patiently for their Indian neighbors.

Teresa Revoir came first on horseback with her children Jean and Louisa. Following close behind was her sister, Mrs. Lombard, with Marie and a younger son, Antoine. Her husband, a French trapper, was away checking his trap lines.

Star-That-Travels rode up the Trace from Three Forks. He was already proving to be a kind father to Teresa's children. Like Teresa, he was a Christian who had been baptized by the Catholic priest Pierre Menard who kept a cabin on a bayou near Three Forks. Last to arrive were Bearpaw and Deer-in-Water with their father, an Osage warrior named Bird.

Though the school had seen other students come on occasion through the school year, these were the only ones who came consistently. When everyone had settled in the boys' classroom, Rev. Chapman welcomed all and opened with prayer. Then Rev. Vaille read a scripture and gave a brief devotion. At last it was time for the children to demonstrate what they had learned this school year.

Clarissa felt her palms getting wet. She was as nervous as her students and she could tell that Mr. Spaulding was feeling some anxiety as well. His nervous habit of pushing up his spectacles gave him away.

The children performed well, though not without a few stumbles. Even the five-year-olds, Sarah Vaille and Billy Spaulding, managed to repeat the alphabet in unison and then each quote a short scripture verse.

They ended the ceremony with a hymn. Clarissa had little talent for singing, but Mr. Spaulding had a beautiful voice and led the children in the hymn "Love Divine." He had even taught them some harmony so the pure sweet voices of the children sounded lovely. It was a wonderful ending to the event and Clarissa felt a few tears in her eyes.

While they all gathered in the dining hall for refreshments, Marie came to her teacher and gave her a hug. "*Merci*," she said, then remembered to practice her English. "Thank you for what you help me learn."

"You are so welcome, Marie," Clarissa responded, feeling teary again. She bent down to the girl's level. "You come and see me some this summer please. We'll keep working on your English."

"I will try," Marie said, "but I will have to work in the garden." Then pointing to her brother, she added, "Antoine will get to come next year."

"Good," Clarissa said, looking at the handsome little boy. "I'm sure he will be as good a student as you."

As Clarissa suspected, Amanda had made far more food than could be eaten at the reception. So she sent cookies and pie home with the students and their parents. The treats were the best gift the children could have received. Except for wild honey, they had few sweets in their usual diet. No wonder the mission's neighbors looked forward to a visit whenever food was going to be served.

The missionaries bid their visitors goodbye with reminders about church services on Sunday. Each of their Osage students gave their teachers hugs and Mrs. Redfield got a hug too. Her love of children and ability to create fun for them made her a favorite among the students.

Mrs. Revoir reminded Rachel that she would be moving her lodge to Three Forks to begin her marriage to Star-That-Travels. They had waited until school was out so the children would not have far to ride to class each day.

Now Clarissa wondered if Jean and Louisa would even attend classes next year. Unless they boarded at the school, the distance from the Osage village at Three Forks would be too great for them to travel each day. It was one of the discouraging aspects of trying to bring education to this untamed prairie.

With a sigh, Clarissa joined Amanda and Martha in cleaning the dining room. The men resumed their work on the Fuller cabin and Rachel sent her boys to gather hoes from Mr. Woodruff. She and the children would tackle the never-ending weeds in the garden until dinner time. The rich river bottomland brought an abundance of corn and vegetables, but it also meant plenty of weeds.

"Oh, Leah, dear," Mrs. Chapman said, looking at her youngest daughter's arms while they waited for Thomas and James. "You are just covered in mosquito bites. They must like you because you are so sweet."

"They liked the flowers we picked yesterday," Leah said, scratching at the red spots.

"Try not to scratch them, dear," her mother gently scolded. "You'll make them bleed."

"It will be alright," Leah said. "I know Jesus."

All the women smiled at the little girl's trusting words, but Clarissa felt a little prick of fear that she couldn't explain. *Please, Lord, let it be alright*, was the prayer that lifted from her heart.

CHAPTER THREE

Union Mission
June, 1822

The mission family settled into their summer routine in the days that followed the close of school. Besides working on the Fullers' cabin, the men were also building a grist mill. Stephen had nearly fifty acres of land in corn production, far too much to grind by hand.

The missionaries knew if they were going to encourage their Osage neighbors to turn to farming and grow larger amounts of corn, they would need to provide a means to convert it to meal or it might instead be converted into alcohol. The Osages were not inclined to drink, but other tribes in the region did not share such scruples.

"We'll need two more yoke of oxen for the mill," Stephen stated at supper one evening. "There just isn't enough water from the spring to run a waterwheel."

"You'll have to travel to Fort Smith for them," Rev. Chapman agreed. "You're the best one of us to be choosing farm stock."

Stephen was quiet for a moment and Clarissa knew what he was thinking about. His first wife Lydia had died at the fort on the journey to the mission. She was buried at the garrison's cemetery and Stephen had never had the chance to visit her grave. He had been a part of the advance group of men who had come out earlier to build the mission.

Amanda gently stroked her husband's arm, sharing the moment of remembered grief. She had become good friends with Lydia on the journey and her death had been hard for her as well.

"I've wanted to go to Fort Smith," the farm director said with a catch in his voice. He had taken Lydia's death very hard last year. "I never really got to say goodbye to Lydie." He smiled almost apologetically to Amanda.

She patted his arm with understanding. 'You need to go," was all she said.

"Now would probably be a good time for travel," Rev. Vaille stated. "The spring rains are past, the corn is all planted and we finally have a break in this heat. You might ask Mr. Bogey when he's planning his next trip to Little Rock and see if you can join him."

"Mr. Bogey is due for a visit," Rachel observed. "He always brings the mail up when the packet arrives at Three Forks and we have an order of supplies coming as well." Keelboats regularly navigated the Arkansas River in the spring and fall when water levels were high enough for their draught. Steamboats traveled regularly to Dwight Mission near Dardanelle, but none had yet to reach Three Forks. The sandy Arkansas River was a difficult passage for the larger vessels as well as a seven-foot drop in elevation at a spot known as La Cascade.

Though the mission was mostly self-sufficient they still imported staples such as wheat flour, some sugar, molasses, dried beans, candles, and tools, especially plowshares. Rachel managed the household accounts and most everyone knew that it was her own personal finances that paid for much of what the mission purchased.

"Our cabin should be complete in a few days," Stephen laughed as Amanda quietly clapped her hands in delight. "I'll ask Bogey if I can travel with him when he brings the supplies."

Two days later, the women were helping Amanda move furnishings into her cabin. The fragrance of the pine logs and wood smoke from the fireplace made it seem warm and inviting. Will, their brawny stonemason, was testing the fireplace he had built to be sure the smoke would pull up into the chimney as it was supposed to.

"Works perfectly, Mr. Requa," Amanda complimented him after he doused the fire. It was too warm to need the blaze going for long.

Will grinned and nodded his thanks. "It will keep you two lovebirds cozy this winter," he winked.

Amanda blushed slightly, but smiled and returned his teasing. "Too bad you lack a lovebird of your own," she said, knowingly.

The smile left Will's face. "Yeah," he agreed glumly. "I guess I messed that up."

He was referring to the blossoming romance he had once shared with Susan Comstock. She had come to Union to serve as a housemother, but had transferred to the Harmony Mission because their school was larger and in need of her assistance.

"It's never too late, Mr. Requa," Amanda said quietly so the other women wouldn't hear.

"I'm not so sure," Will said. "She didn't care enough to stay."

"She thought you didna' care enough to ask her to stay," Amanda corrected.

"Well, I guess I'll never know," Will concluded, dusting his hands and then standing to go.

Amanda resisted the urge to roll her eyes. Mr. Requa was too stubborn for his own good.

"They're back!" Robbie's voice called out.

Clarissa paused from hanging curtains at a window. She felt a flutter in her throat and her hands flew to tuck in any stray hairs from her braided knot. She hoped the other women didn't notice her sudden need to look her best.

Everyone left their various work stations and went to greet the three men on horseback turning off from the road. So many travelers made the turnoff that a hard packed trail from the Osage Trace to the mission compound now cut through Stephen's cornfield.

Dr. Palmer, George Requa and Harmony minister

William Montgomery rode up to the split rail fence of their corral and then dismounted. It was clear they had been in the saddle for some time for they seemed stiff. George, who looked like a younger version of his brother Will, stomped his feet to return some feeling to them.

"You must have ridden hard this morning," Abraham Redfield commented, as he took the horses reins and led them inside the fence.

"We only stopped briefly at La Saline," Dr. Marcus Palmer confirmed. "George and I were anxious to get home."

"But where is Eliza?" Alice asked, concern evident in her voice.

"She wanted to spend the summer months at Harmony," Marcus replied. "But she is much improved in her health."

Alice did not look happy that Eliza was still in Missouri. Though Eliza was now nineteen, she was still Alice's little sister and the woman felt responsible for her. John slipped an arm around her shoulders and gave her a brief squeeze of reassurance.

"The Austins will be traveling down in a few weeks," Rev. Montgomery said. The stocky young minister had light brown hair and hazel eyes. "They will bring Miss Cleaver with them when they come. I'll travel back with them and return these horses."

"Well, I want her to have enough time to be fully recovered," Alice said reluctantly.

"Dr. Belcher administered quinine to Miss Eliza and George. It greatly aided in their recovery," Marcus explained as everyone walked toward the dining hall. Amanda and Phoebe hurried ahead to put out some coffee and biscuits for the men.

"Were you able to get some quinine at St. Louis?" Stephen asked as the adults took seats in the dining hall. The gathering gave the children some time away from garden chores so they headed for the barn to play with a new litter of kittens.

"I secured a small amount," Dr. Palmer confirmed. "And placed an order for more to be delivered on the next riverboat.

This medicine is not a cure, but it certainly helps alleviate the worst of the symptoms."

"So we may continue to see the fevers come?" John asked.

"I am afraid so," Marcus said, running his fingers through his dark, curling hair. It was a habit of his whenever he was frustrated. "Until we can determine the cause and remove it, we will have to deal with this intermittent attack. Harmony has been dealing with it as well."

"The Indians don't seem to have as much trouble with it," Abraham observed.

"They have probably developed some type of resistance to it," explained the doctor. "We are vulnerable because of our limited exposure."

The missionaries quietly absorbed this information while sipping the coffee Phoebe had poured all around. Unlike Mrs. Vaille who had stayed hidden in her cabin during the last months of her pregnancy, Phoebe was less concerned with such social niceties. She had blossomed with impending motherhood.

"Any news from St. Louis?" Rev. Chapman asked after a moment.

"I dined with Governor Clark while there," Marcus said. "Though he is happy to be out of politics now, he still meets frequently with Indian delegations. There was a group of Sioux dining with us. Their language is quite similar to the Osages and I found I could actually understand some of the conversation."

Dinner with the famed explorer, William Clark, was always an honor for visitors to St. Louis.

Palmer took a sip of coffee and then went on. "Governor Clark told me we can expect some changes in U.S. relations with the eastern tribes in the next few years. There are a number of new treaties being drafted that may bring them out west."

"The Osages won't be happy to learn that," Vaille noted. "They already resent the movement of the Cherokees and Chickasaws into their hunting grounds."

"Have you heard if Colonel Arbuckle at Fort Smith has succeeded in getting the Cherokees and Osages to sign a peace treaty?" George asked.

"As far as we know he's still working on it," Chapman said. "He hopes to have something concluded this summer. It has to include Mad Buffalo, or it won't work."

"Have you visited Claremont's Town to discuss the demonstration farm?" Rev. Montgomery asked. "I'm anxious to get started on it."

"To Claremont, a farm is a farm whether it's has a thousand acres or ten acres," Chapman explained. "He has no use for 'field makers,' and doesn't think any of his band will be a part of our effort. But perhaps a few from the other clans will. We will still need authorization from the mission board and that may not come for some time. But we can make our plans and be ready when it arrives. We have yet to hear from the Arkansas governor as well."

"I'd like to ride out to look for a site while I'm here this summer," Montgomery said.

"We can head out tomorrow," Chapman agreed. "You and Will and Abraham can decide on the best location and I'll tag along to make it all seem official." The men laughed and agreed to the outing for the next day.

Before the men could leave the next morning, the family heard a familiar voice call out, "Hello, the house."

It was Joseph Bogey, their friend from Three Forks who had established the first trading post in the region back in 1806. He knew every grove of trees, every bend in the Arkansas River, and every friendly farm between Three Forks and Little Rock.

Bogey always timed his arrival to join them for a meal so after securing his pack mule at the corral, he hefted a large sack into the dining hall to join them all for breakfast. His white hair and long white beard revealed his age, though he had no trouble carrying the heavy pack.

"Welcome, Bogey," Rev. Vaille greeted him. "We haven't seen you in a while. How are things at Three Forks?"

"'Bout the same as always," Joseph replied, while taking a seat at one of the dining tables. He hungrily eyed the fried cornmeal mush, ham and gravy being set out by the women. "Getting too crowded around here," he issued his standard complaint, "especially with the Cherokees moving in around La Cascade."

"You always say that Bogey," George laughed, "but you still haven't moved further west."

"Getting too old to traipse around the mountains like Father Menard does," the man said.

The missionaries smiled. Bogey might be in his seventies, but he remained as spry as a man much younger than him.

"Got your mail in my pack," the trader said as everyone passed the breakfast dishes. "You have an official looking envelope from the governor's office in there." Bogey loved being the bearer of neighborhood gossip so no doubt he had examined every letter in the pack quite closely.

Rev. Chapman started to rise to get it, but a small shake of Rachel's head, settled him back into his chair. Clearly mealtime was not for reading letters or conducting business in Rachel's mind.

"Hopefully it will grant us approval to start the demonstration farm," he said. "And hopefully such providential timing will mean we have the Lord's blessing as well."

"You really think you're going to teach the Osages to be farmers?" Bogey asked around a mouthful of ham.

"We believe their fate on the prairie will depend upon it," Rev. Vaille replied. "Though the massive herds of buffalo and elk would suggest they can live on the hunt forever, we have seen that prove untrue for the eastern tribes. Settlement will come here eventually and if they are to survive as a people, they must learn to adapt."

"Change comes hard to the Indians," Bogey countered. "They are proud of their traditions."

"Tradition has value and we respect that, "William Montgomery entered the conversation. "But we're trying to help them survive."

"They're hunters," Bogey argued. "Nothing wrong with that. You turn them into farmers and you might just put me out of business."

The missionaries had heard this argument from Colonel Chouteau as well. While concerned with the Osages welfare, the Chouteaus made their living trading for the furs and hides the Indians took in the hunt. It created a certain tension between the mission and the trade community.

"Adapting is something we all have to do," Dr. Palmer inserted quietly. "Those who adapt survive, and those who adapt while preserving their values will thrive."

His thoughtful observation sent a little shiver down Clarissa's spine. Dr. Palmer had a depth of spirit that she had come very much to admire. She wished she knew how to tell him that. But private moments for conversation were nearly non-existent at this crowded mission.

"Well said, Doctor," Bogey conceded. "I've moved westward across this country my whole life and seen the changes come. Can't stop change any more than you can stop an ocean tide."

"So, we must be about the business of preparing the Osages for the inevitable," Montgomery stated as breakfast concluded. "Let's go scout out a place for our farm."

Will asked his brother George to come along on the scouting trip so he joined the two ministers and Abraham Redfield, their carpenter and building superintendent. After the men had helped Bogey unpack the supplies from his mule, they started out following the Neosho River northward.

They were looking for a good water supply and wanted a location closer to the *spavinah*. Hauling logs from the pine grove was an arduous task they wanted to lessen if possible.

Roughly half way between the mission and La Saline, they found a sweet water spring that fed into Pryor's Creek about a mile above where it joined the Neosho. Captain Nathaniel Pryor's home was located a few miles upstream.

The ground along the creek was level and the soil dark and heavy. It sat only about a mile east of the Osage Trace.

All agreed that this location would make a good location for a farm.

"Pretty place to bring a wife and start a homestead," William Montgomery noted as they walked around the area.

"You thinking of bringing a wife here," Will asked, somewhat sharply, his eyes narrowing. Montgomery was a widower. His wife had died shortly after they arrived at Harmony Mission in 1821, along with an infant daughter. He also had a two-year-old child named Mary.

"My daughter needs a mother," the minister replied with a sad smile. "I don't plan to build a cabin here unless I can bring a wife with me."

George gave Will a questioning look. There were few Christian women out on the prairie. Only Miss Johnson and Miss Cleaver were unmarried at Union Mission, but there were four single women at Harmony. Susan Comstock was one of them. Did Montgomery already have a wife in mind? George saw Will's hand curl into a fist.

Unaware of the sudden tension between the two Williams, Rev. Chapman asked, "What shall we name this mission?"

"Something about a field," Montgomery suggested. "The Osages hold field work in derision, but I would like to speak of it as something positive."

"How about adding hope," Redfield suggested. "Hopefield Mission or something like that."

"Hopefield," Montgomery repeated. "I do like the sound of that."

"Then Hopefield Mission it shall be," Chapman stated. "Let us *hope* the mission board doesn't keep us waiting long for approval." The men smiled at his pun.

"We'll likely miss a fall planting season and may not get to put anything in next spring either," Montgomery sighed. "I come to understand why the Indians have developed such stoic patience. Nothing seems to move quickly out here in the wilderness."

"There is no point in getting in a hurry," Chapman agreed as they remounted their horses to ride back to the mission.

As they rode the Trace south, Will deliberately slowed his horse and held up a hand to get George to do the same. When the other men were far enough ahead to be out of hearing, he spoke to his brother.

"Is Montgomery keeping company with Miss Comstock?"

"Not that I saw," George responded. "But she does help take care of his little girl."

"Did she ever ask about me or anything?" the stonemason then inquired.

"She asked if you were well when we first arrived," George answered. "But I was so sick for most of the time I was there I didn't speak much to anyone."

Will frowned. "I guess I should have said something to keep her from moving to Harmony," he concluded.

"You mean you never asked her to stay?" George asked. When Will shook his head, the younger brother said under his breath, "Stupid."

"Well, you're a fine one to talk," Will responded, showing his frustration. "Have you have ever spoken to Miss Johnson?"

"Miss Johnson?" George responded. "No. She's an educated lady. What could I ever offer her?"

"I think she would be receptive to you," Will argued.

"I don't," George replied glumly. "Besides I think Palmer has feelings for her."

"Well he better speak up then," Will said. "Montgomery wants a wife and he won't be shy about asking for the hand of one of the unmarried women at our missions. It just better not be Miss Comstock."

"Then you should go talk to her," George urged. "If you have feelings for her, she ought to know."

"I don't know what to say," Will slumped in the saddle. "I don't know how she feels."

"You'll regret saying nothing if Montgomery convinces her to marry him."

"I know," was all Will could say.

CHAPTER FOUR

Union Mission
June, 1822

A few days later, Rachel noticed that Leah had crawled back into the bed she shared with her older sister. She had gotten up and dressed, but now lay listlessly on the down-stuffed mattress.

"What is this, Miss Leah?" her mother asked as she went over and sat on the bed. "Time to pick those eggs or the hens will be squawking." She gently smoothed the little girl's pinafore, trying to prod her to wakefulness.

"I don't feel well, Mama," Leah said, brushing her strawberry blonde curls away from her face.

Usually the Chapman children addressed Rachel as "Mother," but in moments of trouble they all called her "Mama." It told Rachel something was wrong.

She placed a hand on her daughter's forehead.

"Oh, dear," she said, a brief look of fear crossing her face. "You are burning up with fever."

Rev. Chapman had already left the cabin but Thomas and James were still up in the half-loft where they slept.

"Thomas," Rachel called to her eleven-year-old.

His face appeared over the side of the loft. "Yes, Mother?"

"Come down quickly and go find Dr. Palmer," she instructed. "Tell him Leah has a fever. Then find you papa and ask him to come."

Hearing her urgency, the boy clambered down the ladder and hurried out the cabin door without pausing to question anything. He was a mature child and had already proven his astuteness in understanding the dangers of life on the frontier.

"Abigail, dear," Rachel reached a hand for her oldest daughter. "Pour a cup of water from the pitcher and bring it here for your sister."

The girl set down the doll she had been playing with and hurried to do her mother's bidding.

"Can I help, Mother?" James asked as he descended the ladder.

"Help me pray, son," she said, not able to disguise her fear. "Your sister is very ill."

James was the mischievous one of the four Chapmans, and he liked to tease his sisters. But his eyes filled with tears and he nodded solemnly at his mother's request. He came to stand at the foot of the bed. "I'll pray hard, Mama," he said.

"Thank you, dear," Rachel replied, drawing in a deep, steadying breath. She took the cup of cool water from Abigail and lifted Leah's head to help her drink.

It seemed to take forever for Dr. Palmer to arrive. At last came a quiet knock at the door and Abigail opened it to admit the tall doctor. He carried his medical kit with him.

"I'm afraid it's the fever," Rachel said as the doctor stepped inside. "She's terribly hot to the touch."

Marcus moved toward the bed and Rachel stood to give him room to examine her daughter. He knelt at the bedside and felt her forehead and then counted her pulse. He gently pressed her neck and then asked her to open her mouth so he could peer down her throat.

"Could you bring a candle closer?" he asked, glancing up at Rachel.

She hurried to light one and stood at his shoulder so the light would illuminate Leah's throat.

"Do you hurt anywhere, Miss Leah?" he asked while opening each of her eyes wider for a closer look.

Leah shook her head at first, but then said, "All over."

"The fever causes muscle aches," the doctor said. "Her throat doesn't look inflamed."

About that time Rev. Chapman stepped into the room.

He came immediately to Leah's bedside and pressed a hand to Rachel's back.

"Has she taken the fever, Doctor?" he asked. Chapman had experienced the illness himself having already had two bouts with it.

Before answering, Marcus turned the little girl's arms and felt along them. "Did you see any red spots on your legs or tummy when you dressed this morning?" he asked.

"No," Leah said. She held up an arm to look at it. "All the 'squito bites are gone now."

"She had several mosquito bites about ten days ago," Rachel explained. "That wouldn't have made her sick, would it?"

"I know of no reason to think so," Marcus responded. "We've all been bitten." Then to Leah he asked, "Did you feel cold before you got hot?"

"Yes," she said. "I was shaking hard last night."

Hard chills were one of the symptoms of the mysterious fever.

Marcus sighed. "I was hoping it was a common childhood malady," he said. "But I'm afraid it is the fever."

"What should we do?" Rachel asked.

"Fever can spike very high in children," he said. "Bathe her with cool water, but don't let her get cold. The chills will increase the muscle pain."

He stood and started to open his medical kit to leave the quinine but then changed his mind. He only had a limited supply of the medicine and needed to be the only person to administer it.

"I will ask Mrs. Fuller to brew some willow bark tea. That will help with the achiness. After she has drunk that we'll wait about an hour and I'll give her some quinine. It's very bitter so we'll have her take it with some tea and honey. Make sure she drinks plenty of liquids."

Rachel nodded and pressed a hand to her mouth as if to quiet the trembling of her lips. No one had died of the fever while at the mission, but their seamstress, Sally Edwards, had succumbed to it while they traveled west by boat. That seemed never far from anyone's mind, especially the doctor. He blamed himself for Sally's death.

Rev. Chapman squeezed his wife's shoulders. "I'll ask Robbie to bring some cooler water from the spring house," he said. Then he and the doctor left the cabin.

Thomas had followed his father into the room and was sitting quietly in one of the cane-bottomed chairs by the fireplace. Rachel sat back down beside Leah and patted her hand to comfort her. Then she turned to her oldest son.

"Thomas," she said and he jumped to his feet. "Take Abigail and James to breakfast and then do your chores."

"Yes, Mother," Thomas said. "But you'll send for me if you need me, won't you?"

"Absolutely, Thomas," Rachel smiled at her strong young man. "Thank you for offering."

The mission family gathered in the dining hall and spent extra moments in prayer for Leah. It was especially hard to know that one of the children was suffering.

Amanda and Martha went to the Chapman cabin, carrying the willow tea and a supply of muslin rags for bathing the child. They both promised to return with some food for Rachel and to help with the girl's care. Rachel smiled her gratitude, but the worried look never left her eyes.

Throughout the day, Dr. Palmer checked on Leah. Though her fever still raged, the girl slept fitfully. She had made a face at the taste of the quinine, but had obediently swallowed two small doses.

In the afternoon Clarissa knocked at the cabin door. She came with some trepidation and had scolded herself for her fear all the way from her cabin to the Chapmans'. Clarissa had been with Sally when she died of the fever. That fact made Clarissa fearful of stepping into a sickroom where the fever was present. But she was determined to offer her assistance even if she was afraid.

She put her head in the door and spoke quietly, "I've come to see if you would like me to sit with Leah for a while, Mrs. Chapman," she said. "You should take some time to exercise a little."

"I thank you, Miss Johnson," Rachel said. "But I just can't bring myself to leave her."

Clarissa held up one of the Bible story books her students read from. "I thought I might read her one of her favorite stories."

Leah turned her head toward the door. "Hello, Teacher," she said in a thin little voice.

Rachel looked at her daughter. She knew Leah adored her teacher and Miss Johnson was the one person beside her parents that Leah would quite welcome sitting with her.

"Well," she said reluctantly. "I could take a quick moment to visit the outhouse and get more tea from the kitchen. I'll only be gone a few minutes." But she remained seated as if torn about leaving.

Clarissa nodded. "You need a break to keep away the strain," she said to encourage her decision. "You'll want your strength if you need to sit up through the night."

"Yes," Rachel said and finally stood and moved toward the door. Clarissa took her place in a chair by Leah's bed. With a final look back, Rachel stepped out into the sunshine, leaving the door ajar.

Clarissa was just finishing the story of Esther when Dr. Palmer ducked into the cabin. "Oh, Miss Johnson," he said, stopping suddenly.

Startled by his presence, Clarissa snapped the book shut and nearly dropped it. She felt the heat of embarrassment rise into her cheeks and fought the urge to check her hair.

"I was giving Mrs. Chapman a short break," she said, rising from her seat. "She'll be back just any minute."

The two of them stood awkwardly for a moment. Clarissa could not remember a time when she and the doctor had been alone in a room together. Propriety said they shouldn't be so now, even though Leah was present.

"How is she doing?" the doctor asked. He wanted to check on Leah's fever, but doing so would put him in dangerously close proximity to the pretty schoolteacher. So he just stood there, feeling stupid.

"She's drifted off to sleep," Clarissa replied, edging away

from the bed. Slowly the two of them stepped around each other in a cabin that suddenly seemed very small.

Dr. Palmer sat down and laid a practiced hand on the girl's forehead. Clarissa watched, quite taken with the gentle way that he brushed back her damp curls.

She was about to ask his assessment of his patient when Rachel returned.

"Oh, Dr. Palmer," Rachel said as she set down a tea tray and then hurried to her daughter's bedside. "Can you tell if the fever is down?"

Marcus hesitated but then shook his head. He tried always to be honest with those in his care, even when the news was difficult. "It does not seem to be," he said. "But it takes time for the quinine to have an effect. Miss Cleaver and George saw no improvement for a day or two after receiving it."

Rachel nodded her understanding. "Is there anything more we can do?"

"Just continue as you are," the doctor stated. "And let the other women help you," he reminded her, knowing a mother never wanted to leave a sick child. "You'll be no good to her if you exhaust yourself."

Just then Rachel's husband stepped into the cabin and Clarissa took that moment to excuse herself. She wanted to stay just because Dr. Palmer was there, but she could not intrude on the doctor's need to privately visit with the Chapmans.

She walked toward the dining hall where she had left Thea with Phoebe. She suddenly felt a great need to hold the little girl very close.

That evening Phoebe helped the older Chapman children gather their nightclothes and she took them to the Redfields' cabin. It was warm enough that they could sleep on buffalo robes and blankets spread out on the floor. The Redfields helped them say their prayers and settled them in for the night. Then they stood together just outside the door to their cabin watching the stars alight in a clear evening sky.

"It's a frightening thing," Phoebe said just above a whisper, "to think of losing a child."

Abraham brushed a kiss against her temple and gently massaged the small of her back. "I wish I could promise you that we will never face such a thing," her tall sandy-haired husband replied. "But I can't."

"I don't expect you to make such a promise," she said, protectively rubbing the swell of her belly where their own child grew. "Just promise me that no matter what we face, we will always face it together."

"That I can and do promise," he said.

From the Chapmans' cabin they could hear the low murmur of voices. A long vigil would be held there tonight.

Rev. Chapman helped Leah take a drink of tea and then eased her back onto her pillow. Rachel hovered above him, seeing the loll of the little girl's head as if she were too weak to hold it up. Her fever still raged and she gave no response to their ministrations. She had steadily grown weaker throughout the day and her breathing was raspy and labored.

The young mother covered her face with her hands. "I cannot lose her, Chapman," she said. "Don't ask that of me."

"It is not me who asks it," he responded, resting his arms across his knees in an attitude of defeat.

"Then is it the Lord who asks?" Rachel said with bitterness in her voice. "Heaven has seen me bring my children to this wilderness to follow you. Because you had something to prove to my parents . . . to all of Connecticut society who said I was wrong to marry you."

"That is not what this mission is about," Chapman said, his jaw tight. "And you could have said no."

"I can never say no to you," Rachel shook her head and paced beside Leah's bed. "And you well know it."

"I did not know until this moment that you regretted coming out here," he said, looking up at her with pleading in his eyes.

"I did not regret it," she whispered, looking down at her daughter, ". . . until this moment." She wiped away tears streaming down her cheeks.

Outside the half-full Green Corn Moon rose late that night and cast its silent silver over the fields of cornstalks with tassels waving in a soft breeze. The death angel might have passed through the mission compound that night, but a little boy was praying hard and so he passed on by.

Rachel woke the next morning from where she had laid beside her daughter. Immediately she felt her forehead. "Still so hot," she murmured and kissed her baby, "but at least we made it through the night."

Rev. Chapman lifted his head from where he sat across the room with his Bible in his hands. The look of love he sent to his wife and daughter was followed by a whispered "thank you," sent heavenward.

He rose and stiffly crossed the dirt floor to help Rachel stand. Together they held each other as if drawing strength for another day of battle.

They could hear the mission stirring to morning life and soon a knock came at the door. Chapman opened it to admit Dr. Palmer.

"How is she today?" the doctor asked as he stepped inside.

"No change that I can tell," Rachel said. "But she doesn't seem to be worse."

Marcus went through his usual examination and then laid his ear against the little girl's chest. "Have her sit up some today, if you can manage it," he instructed. "We don't want her lungs filling up."

Rachel nodded.

"I think the fever is down slightly," Marcus said, knowing this would encourage the girl's parents.

"Do you?" Rachel asked hopefully.

"We'll follow up today with two more doses of the quinine," the doctor said as he prepared to leave. "I'll check on her often, but send for me if there is any change."

"Yes, we will," Chapman said. "Thank you so much, Doctor."

Leah's recovery was slow and even after a week, her

mother kept her in bed most of the time. It was a great relief to all the mission family that she was on the mend and many thanks were expressed in their prayers each day.

Stephen prepared to join Joseph Bogey on a trip to Little Rock, planning a stop in Fort Smith to visit Lydia's grave.

"I almost dread going," he told Amanda as they said their private goodbye in their cabin on the morning of his departure. "A man doesn't like to show his tears, especially not at a fort full of soldiers."

"They will give you your privacy," Amanda assured him. "Mostly because they don't want to see you cry for fear it will make them cry. Those soldiers are young men missin' their mamas and sweethearts, you know."

Stephen smiled. "God blessed me with an understanding wife."

"Just don't be gone too long," she said with a quick kiss and then walked with him to join Bogey at the corral where a saddled mustang stood by the trader's mule.

"Bogey isn't sure I can find oxen at Little Rock," he said regretfully. "We may have to go to Arkansas Post or even Memphis."

"You have two weeks until the corn is ready," Abraham said, as he handed the horse's reins to the farmer.

"I'll be back by then," Stephen promised. "Even if I have to return without getting the oxen."

Stephen would not miss the corn harvest. All the men were needed for the task. But it would be good to have the oxen to grind the corn once it had dried.

With a last smile at Amanda he mounted the mustang given to the mission by Chief Claremont and joined Bogey for the ride to Three Forks. From there they would paddle a pirogue down the Arkansas River to Fort Smith.

Stephen had been gone two days when the mission received a visit from the commander at Fort Smith. Colonel Matthew Arbuckle, head of the Seventh Infantry, had been at the post since February. A veteran of the recent Seminole Wars, he had transferred to Fort Smith from Fort Gadsen in Florida.

With the commander were Nathaniel Pryor and the U.S. Agent to the Cherokees, Colonel David Brearley. Pryor was serving as a guide and advisor to Arbuckle as he toured the Osage lands for the first time since his appointment to the Fort Smith post.

Extending their usual hospitality, the missionaries invited the officials to a meal, eager to learn news from the world beyond the prairie.

"So you feel like you can get a peace treaty signed this summer?" Rev. Vaille asked the men after the children had been dismissed from the table. The adults were lingering over cups of coffee and sour cream cake.

The Secretary of War will settle for nothing less," Colonel Arbuckle replied in crisp tones. A man in his mid-forties, he had thinning hair with grey at the temples. He had an air of authority and self-possession which would likely make him a formidable negotiator of treaties.

"Arkansas politicians are being bombarded with complaints about these Cherokee-Osage conflicts," he went on. "They all want something done about it. I was brought to Fort Smith for the primary purpose of maintaining peace on the frontier."

"You have a challenge ahead of you," Chapman stated.

It's not as great as most people think," Colonel Arbuckle countered. "I have fought beside the Indians as well as against them. While a lust for power may be the motivation of the men who start wars, most men on the battlefield just want to defend their homes and their families. If you don't give your enemies a reason to hate you, then you can negotiate with them."

The men of the mission seemed impressed with the colonel's perspective.

"I think you are the right man for this job, Colonel," Chapman said. "Chief Claremont and Walter Webber both say they want peace. A man in your position of authority should be able to secure it."

David Brearley spoke up then. "For Webber this conflict is personal and he is adamant that it be Skiatook who signs the treaty, not just his father, Chief Claremont." Skiatook was the Cherokee's name for Mad Buffalo. As the Cherokee agent, Brearley seemed more familiar with this name for the Osage warrior.

"It's personal for Mad Buffalo, too," Will Requa said, thinking of the death of Joseph Revoir.

Some thought Walter Webber was responsible for shooting Mad Buffalo's friend. The Osage had vowed revenge for that death. But Webber claimed he was only avenging the death of his cousin killed by Mad Buffalo. It was a tangled situation that had kept the Three Forks area on edge for months.

"Will Webber sign, if Mad Buffalo does?" Dr. Palmer asked.

"I want both Webber's and Skiatook's mark on the treaty," Arbuckle responded. "But don't confuse signing a treaty with actual peace," he advised. "Peace is determined by what happens after the treaty is signed."

The three men took their leave of the mission family after this and mounted their horses to travel north on the Trace. They would stop at La Saline and ask Colonel Chouteau to join them in visiting Claremont's Town.

The missionaries watched them ride northward with hope that the good sense of Colonel Arbuckle could indeed bring peace to this portion of the prairie.

CHAPTER FIVE

Union Mission
Early July, 1822

Abraham pulled back the husk from a corn cob and tested the ripeness of one of the dark golden kernels. It would be hot work bringing in the harvest, but it promised to be a bountiful one.

No wonder that for centuries the native people had lived and farmed these rich river bottom lands. The many ancient mounds along the three rivers were testament to the long use of the land by ancestors buried there.

Abraham tossed the corn into one of the bushel baskets Robbie had set at the end of the row. Stephen hadn't yet returned, but the corn would not wait. Even the older boys would be helping by carrying the full baskets to a wagon that George would drive to their corncrib by the barn.

Amanda walked out to the south field where the men were beginning their work. "Robbie," she called to the farm apprentice.

He ran down the corn row to reach her.

"Yes, ma'am?"

"Bring me one of the first bushels," she instructed. "We'll have fresh corn on the cob tonight for supper."

"Yes, ma'am!" he said, licking his lips in anticipation of the roasted ears slathered in butter.

Amanda laughed and then turned back to the kitchen with a wave. The only thing that would make this day better would be for Stephen to return home.

It was almost dark that evening when Amanda's prayer
was answered. Stephen rode up just as most of the
missionaries were leaving the dining hall where they had
spent the hours after supper with small chores done by hand.
Their cabins were hot so no one was in a hurry to retire for the
night. The larger dining hall with its windows in the east and
west walls allowed a breeze to drift through, making it a more
comfortable location to spend the evening.

The sound of the approaching horse made them all turn
toward the trail and then make their way to meet Stephen at
the corral.

"Welcome home, Fuller," George said, taking the reins of
the mustang.

"It's good to be home," Stephen responded as he
dismounted, his eyes searching for Amanda. They shared a
smile.

"Any success with the oxen?" Chapman asked.

"Took some time, but I finally found two pair at Pine
Bluff," the farm director said. "Saw them loaded on a
keelboat that should be at Three Forks in a day or two."

Amanda slipped her arm through his and his fingers
curled around her hand. They walked together toward the
kitchen with most of the adults trailing along. The mothers
among them took their children on to bed. Phoebe had
already retired for the evening as well, complaining of painful
swollen ankles.

"Any news from Fort Smith?" Will Requa asked Stephen
when all had settled in the dining hall. Amanda was
scrambling eggs and heating some ham for her husband.

"Colonel Arbuckle had just returned when Bogey and I
got back there," Fuller said. "I take it he had a successful tour
of the Osage lands. I didn't speak with him directly, but
Lieutenant Bonneville told me he had secured Mad Buffalo's
mark on a peace treaty. Arbuckle is planning a trip to
Dardanelle to meet with Walter Webber and the Cherokee
chief John Jolly."

"That is good news," Chapman stated. "We've been
invited to attend Claremont's green corn feast at full moon. I

hope to reinforce to him and Mad Buffalo how important this treaty is for all involved."

The south field had been harvested three days later and the men were moving on to the west field. Chapman, Montgomery, Will Requa and Dr. Palmer were going to travel to Claremont's village for their summer feast. The Indians in most tribes celebrated the corn harvest with a gathering that included songs, drums, dancing and a bountiful array of food.

The men found the Osages in animated spirits, happy with an abundant harvest, believing this meant *Wah-Kon-Tah* – the Great Spirit – was pleased with them. They joined the villagers in a large circle around the bonfire and enjoyed a supper of roasted ears of corn along with venison and dried buffalo pemmican, squash and beans, berries, pecans and wild honeycomb.

After the meal, several of the men rose and spoke. The Indians prized oration and their Little Old Men, the teachers of the tribe, shared many stories. Some were serious and mystical; some were filled with superstitions, others were humorous and even a little ribald. The missionaries shared rueful looks, but did not speak up. Sometimes understanding the language had its disadvantages.

Chief Claremont politely extended an opportunity to Rev. Chapman to address the gathering. He had expressed a hope to the other men that he would have a chance to speak and planned a brief sermon about Jesus being a Prince of Peace.

When he stumbled a little with the Osage words, Bird, the father of Bearpaw and Deer-in-Water, helped with translation. The people of Claremont's Town listened attentively as was their custom. Even an enemy had the right to be heard, according to their traditions. But their faces remained passive and it was hard to tell what their thoughts were of Rev. Chapman's sermon.

After oration, the young men of the tribe danced around the fire. The Old Men sat around a large hide drum, beating out the rhythm and singing an ancient chant. Some of the women added a counterpoint rhythm by shaking hollowed out gourds filled with small pebbles. The firelight threw strange shadows across the lodges and gave the dance a shiver-inducing surrealism.

At first Dr. Palmer worried that the dance might be frightening to the children, for he noticed several of the young ones inching closer to their parents. But he supposed it was not unlike the reaction he had seen from children when hearing Mr. Washington Irving's story of the headless horseman.

The tale had been hugely popular in New England when the missionaries set out for Arkansas Territory two years earlier. Perhaps children in every culture didn't mind being a little frightened. It gave them an excuse to climb into parents' laps.

When the fire had died down and the women and children had left the circle to settle on buffalo robes beside their lodges, the men passed the pipe. It was an age-old tradition to smoke together at the end of a meal, particularly one of importance.

The missionaries had learned from Captain Pryor that refusing to smoke would be taken as an insult so they took their turn with the pipe. Dr. Palmer only pretended to pull a draught from the long, painted pipe and hoped no one would notice in the growing darkness.

After the pipe had passed completely around the circle, Chief Claremont lifted it toward the sky as though offering it to the Great Spirit, *Wah-Kon-Tah*. This signaled the end of the feast and the men began to drift away from the waning fire.

Buffalo Woman, wife to Mad Buffalo, brought robes for the missionaries to spread out beside the dying embers. The men thanked her and she smiled shyly at them. Buffalo Woman had been their first convert when she had attended church at the mission earlier in the spring.

Though she rarely was able to attend their Sabbath service, the missionaries considered her a sister and friend to the mission. There was no doubt in Dr. Palmer's mind that Buffalo Woman's acceptance of Christ had made her a positive influence on her husband. He knew it was likely at her urging that the warrior had signed the peace treaty.

The missionaries stretched out on the robes for the night. The communal nature of living outdoors in the summer months would have been regarded as "uncivilized," back in New England, but it was a practical way to live here on the southern prairie.

Probably healthier, Dr. Palmer thought as he lay staring up at the darkened sky where the bright stars looked as if they were being lit one by one by the unseen hand of God. *And certainly cooler*, he concluded to himself before drifting off to sleep with the pleasant scent of wood smoke and roasted corn wafting on a gentle breeze.

The men rode back to the mission the following day to find that the west field was harvested and all that remained was the north ten acres. While the men went about the hot and dusty work of picking the ears of corn, the women were shucking the husks and cleaning mounds of ears to be canned. The girls carried piles of the husks to a stack beside the barn.

Most of the corn would be ground into meal, but some would be dried for fodder for their farm animals. Some would be soaked in lye to make hominy. It was a task Clarissa dreaded for rinsing the lye from the swelled corn kernels would leave the women's hands dried and chapped. She wanted to make hominy as little as she wanted to participate in soap making in the fall.

The men were emptying a wagonload of corn at the corncrib when Paul tapped Robbie on the shoulder. "You lettin' down on your job, Robbie," he said, pointing to the west. "We got company comin'."

Robbie lifted his gaze to where Paul pointed. A wagon was turning off the Trace and making its way toward the mission.

"Wagon coming!" he yelled.

The men all laughed then quickly finished tossing the last of the corn into its pile. They watched the wagon approach until it was close enough to recognize who was aboard.

"It's the Austins from Harmony Mission," Rev. Montgomery stated. Also in the wagon was blonde-headed Eliza Cleaver.

George turned their own wagon toward the corral and the men all jumped to the ground. In response to Robbie's call the women were washing their hands and brushing off corn-spattered aprons before joining everyone at the corral.

Daniel Austin, the stout millwright from Harmony, halted their oxen team well away from George's team which consisted of two of the newly acquired animals Stephen had purchased.

When Alice saw her sister, riding in the wagon with the Austins, she quickened her pace from the kitchen.

"Eliza, just look at you," she exclaimed as the young woman was helped down from the wagon by Mr. Austin. "I almost didn't recognize you."

It was as if a metamorphosis had occurred in Eliza in the months that she had been away. She had left as a very sick and somewhat spoiled girl. But now as she alighted from the wagon, she clearly had become a mature young woman.

No longer wearing her hair in long, silky blonde ringlets, she had arranged her tresses in a braided coronet while wispy curls played around her face and neck. Her sapphire eyes competed with the new cornflower blue dress she wore. Clarissa had known that someday Eliza would be a beautiful woman and clearly that day had arrived.

She noticed that every man at the mission had also noticed Eliza's transformation. They were looking at her like a calf at a new gate. Clarissa suddenly felt as frumpy as she had once thought Phoebe.

"Well, I've hardly changed that much," Eliza laughed as Alice folded her into an embrace.

"Oh, I'm so glad you're home," Alice said, seeming reluctant to let go of her sister.

"It's good to see you too, Alice," Eliza replied, trying to disentangle herself from the prolonged hug.

She did not say that she was glad to be home Clarissa noted. She had rarely complained aloud, but they all knew that Eliza did not much care for life on the frontier. She had probably been reluctant to return to Union Mission.

Why had she returned?

Clarissa glanced at Dr. Palmer and saw that he seemed as taken with Eliza's new beauty as all the other men. She turned back to the kitchen with the other women feeling sick in her heart.

"What you need is a sawmill," Daniel Austin told the Union Mission family over supper that evening. "We've put one in at Harmony and it's providing income for the mission."

"But that points out one of the main differences between our mission and Harmony," Rev. Vaille responded. "We are located on a treeless prairie. Hauling logs to a sawmill makes it impractical for us."

"Have your customers haul their own timber here," Austin advised.

"We might consider that in the future," Abraham said. "But right now we would have few customers interested in sawn logs. The Osages still prefer their lodges – they're easily moved for the hunt. And we don't have many settlers yet this far west."

"They'll soon come, though," William Montgomery said with confidence. Then he thoughtfully added, "It would be good to have a plank cabin for our farm. We could demonstrate the advantage of it over raw logs."

"True," Will Requa agreed. "Our cabins here are only two years old, but they're already showing some wear."

"Tell you what," Austin said. "You plan on one plank cabin for your Hopefield Mission and I'll help you haul the lumber for it."

"That would be wonderful," Rev. Montgomery said. But Abraham looked skeptical.

The conversation turned back to the main purpose for Daniel Austin's visit. The gristmill was now built and it was time to wrestle the grinding stones into place and test them with some corn from last year's harvest.

"Let's get to it first thing tomorrow," Stephen proposed,

eager to get started. "We may not have enough timber for a sawmill, but we have plenty enough corn to run a gristmill business. It'll be the first one in the neighborhood and I don't think we'll lack for customers." Everyone in the area grew corn.

With that, the missionaries all finished the last of their coffee and began to take care of final chores for the evening before retiring to their cabins. The Austins and Rev. Montgomery were staying in the divided loft above the classrooms.

Clarissa changed Thea's diaper and then with a kiss gave her to Mrs. Vaille for the night. Thea was mostly sleeping through the night, but she still slept in the Vailles' cabin, her cradle alongside baby Joseph's.

Soon Clarissa hoped to bring Thea to her cabin for the night, but she wondered how Miss Eliza would feel about that. Even a quiet baby like Thea could be fussy at times and she'd be teething soon. She hoped the baby would not be a source of contention with her returned roommate.

When Clarissa arrived at the ladies' quarters, Eliza was already in her pink nightdress and was sitting on her bed, brushing out her long hair. She looked up when Clarissa entered the cabin but said nothing.

Determined to be friendly, Clarissa said, "It's good to have you back, Miss Eliza."

"Thank you," Eliza said, continuing her count to 100 strokes. When she reached the required number she set down her hair brush on an upturned half barrel that served as a bedside table. "But I don't plan on staying too long."

"Oh?" Clarissa questioned in surprise, as she began to unpin her own tresses. "Are you going back to Harmony?"

"No," Eliza shook her head. "I want to go back to New England."

"Will Mr. and Mrs. Spaulding take you?"

"Alice doesn't want to leave," Eliza sighed and drew her knees up under her chin and hugged her legs close. "She says there is no reason to go back there. But I don't see any reason for me to stay."

"It would be difficult to get back to New York on your own," Clarissa tried to gently point out.

Eliza laughed rather bitterly. "Oh, Alice would never let me travel alone," she agreed. "But I think I can get someone from here to return to New England with me."

Clarissa cast through her mind for someone among their family who might wish to travel back East. No one readily came to mind. She knew Mrs. Vaille frequently expressed homesickness, but doubted that the minister's wife would want to travel with a small baby. Eliza would have to travel with one of the married couples for it would be inappropriate for her to go in the company of one of the single men.

She said as much to Eliza. The young woman stretched out her legs and plumped up her goose down pillow. "It wouldn't be inappropriate if we were married," she said. Then she settled down on her pillow and closed her eyes, signaling the end to the conversation.

Clarissa was left to brush out her own hair in silent contemplation as dusk deepened the shadows in the room.

Clarissa awoke the next morning at the rooster's crow. She rose and dressed quietly while Eliza slept on in the bed across the small room. The schoolteacher laced up her boots, wishing she didn't have to wear such heavy shoes in the summer heat. But the girls had spotted a large snake skin near the hen house last week so everyone had been advised to don heavy shoes until the snake was found and killed.

Clarissa kept a watchful eye as she made her way to the outhouse and then walked back toward the kitchen. She was washing her hands when Amanda stepped into the room. She carried a water bucket from the spring house which she set on her work table. It was then that Clarissa saw tears streaming down the cook's freckled face.

"Amanda, what's wrong?" Clarissa asked with concern as she quickly dried her hands.

"It's Phoebe," she said, swiping at her tears. "She lost her baby. Mr. Redfield just told me. He asked me to make a breakfast tray for her."

"Oh, no," Clarissa gasped. "What happened? I thought everything was going well with her."

"I don't know for sure," Amanda said. "The baby was stillborn sometime in the night. Mrs. Woodruff is with her."

"Phoebe must be devastated," Clarissa said, thinking about how happy the housemother had been to share the news of her pregnancy. She had so looked forward to being a mother to her own child.

"Mr. Redfield said she was holding up well," Amanda told her. "But he seemed quite upset himself. He and Mr. George were going to try to fashion a coffin from the staves of one of the flour barrels."

Their lack of sawn lumber had meant that the two burials they had already undertaken at the mission had been without coffins. Joseph Revoir and Thea's mother Whitestar had been buried wrapped in the wool trade blankets used by the Indians.

It was a common practice here on the prairie, but Clarissa could understand why Phoebe would want a coffin for her tiny baby. She felt sick at heart to think of the sorrow her sister must be feeling right now.

"I wish I knew what would help Phoebe," she said in a quiet voice.

"I know what you mean," Amanda agreed. "You feel so helpless in situations like this."

Just then Mrs. Chapman joined them in the kitchen. Seeing the somber faces of the two young women, she said, "I suppose you have heard about Phoebe."

"Mr. Redfield just told me," Amanda explained. "We're gettin' some breakfast ready for her. Is there anything else can be done?"

"I just visited with her briefly," Mrs. Chapman said. "And the Vailles are with her now. Just keep her in your prayers," she advised. "There simply are no words that seem adequate at a time like this. It's so frightening to think about losing a child."

"Aye," Amanda agreed and Clarissa nodded. They both knew that Mrs. Chapman had faced that very prospect just recently. They were never far from reminders of how fragile life was.

Silently the women went about the breakfast chores, each pausing occasionally to wipe away quiet tears. When the girls brought in the eggs, they were quick to notice the sadness that permeated the room.

"What is wrong, Mother?" Abigail asked.

Rachel hesitated a long moment. Things like pregnancy and childbirth were not discussed with children. Finally she said, "Mrs. Redfield isn't feeling well and we're concerned about her."

"Does she have the fever like I did?" Leah asked, her tender heart making her own eyes well with tears.

"No, dear," her mother responded. "But she still needs our prayers. You'll pray for her, won't you?" she asked all the girls.

Yes, Mother," Abigail said and the other girls nodded.

Shortly afterwards the Spauldings entered the dining room carrying Joseph and Thea. Eliza was helping Billy along. The five-year-old boy still seemed sleepy and out of sorts. Clarissa hurried to take Thea from Alice and spend a few moments holding her close with her in the kitchen.

Martha Woodruff came in shortly and with slumped shoulders made her way to the wash basin. No one said anything at first, though Clarissa knew they all wanted assurances from the motherly woman that Phoebe would be alright.

It was Martha who broke the silence. "Phoebe is a strong young woman," she said, with admiration in her voice. "She is far more concerned for her husband's grief than for herself. She wanted so much to give him that little boy."

"It was a boy, then?" Amanda asked.

"Yes."

"She doesn't blame herself, does she?" Rachel asked. "Misplaced guilt can be a terrible burden."

Martha nodded, but said, "Phoebe has a practical faith. She has placed her baby in her Father's hands and speaks of meeting him someday in heaven."

Clarissa understood Martha's admiration of the young housemother. She wasn't sure she would not feel anger or bitterness should she lose a child. She smoothed down Thea's thatch of black hair that she had sleep-wallowed into all directions. Thea wasn't even a child of her own womb, but she couldn't have loved her more if she were.

Gradually the dining hall filled as the mission family quietly gathered for breakfast. Amanda and Martha had carried food to the Redfields' cabin for the grieving couple and their pastors, the Vailles. The rest shared a prayer for solace for Phoebe and Abraham and then ate in mostly a grief-filled silence. Even the boys, who usually were full of laughter and boyish energy, were quiet. They finished the meal and went to the never-ending summer chores.

The men gathered at the round, stone gristmill they had built near the spring house. They hitched four of the oxen to the drive shafts that would turn the huge limestone wheels to grind their corn. Will Requa and Alexander Woodruff had spent many hours fashioning the wheels, gears, axles and shafts for the mill.

Under Daniel Austin's instructions they soon had the oxen turning the shafts while Stephen steadily poured dried corn into the feed hopper. As the coarse meal spilled slowly from the grinding stones, the men gave a whoop of satisfaction. Assembling the mill had taken months of effort, but it now seemed worth each hour of work.

They were slapping each other on the back in congratulations of their accomplishment when the women and children came from all directions to see the mill in operation.

"I finally feel that we have met one of our primary objectives," Rev. Chapman stated with obvious pleasure. "This day has been a long time coming."

"You'll bring your neighbors from far and near for this service," Austin assured them. "It will make Union Mission a gathering place for this part of Arkansas."

"You have a good road, too," Rev. Montgomery added. "That will bring folks in."

"Food will bring folks in," Amanda stated softly to the women. They smiled at the cook in agreement. Amanda had long ago proven her prophetic words that food would be the mission's best outreach to their neighbors.

"Mr. Fuller," Amanda said more loudly to get her husband's attention.

"Yes, Mrs. Fuller?" Stephen replied, looking up at her with a twinkle in his eye. He was sifting the cornmeal into a small barrel.

"Bring that first barrel to the kitchen," Amanda said. "We'll have warm cornbread with butter for dinner today."

"Yes, ma'am," Stephen responded.

Everyone grinned at the exchange. Cornbread was a staple served at nearly every meal. But it would taste particularly good today.

The jovial mood shared at the gristmill continued through dinner that day, but the Redfields were never far from everyone's mind. Phoebe and Abraham had requested a brief committal service at the little cemetery located on the highest ground of the mission's acreage. George had finished the little coffin and Mrs. Woodruff lined it with a soft square of white flannel.

Dr. Palmer had suggested that Phoebe remain in bed, but she was insistent that she attend the service that afternoon. Her husband was equally insistent that she ride in the back of the wagon on a bed of buffalo robes. The Spauldings kept all the children at the schoolhouse, but the adults walked slowly alongside the wagon to the cemetery.

Rev. Vaille spoke quietly about the hope of heaven before the tiny coffin was lowered into the resting place Alexander had prepared. Phoebe and Abraham stood with arms around each other. It was hard for Clarissa to tell which of them was holding up the other. Both had tears quietly streaming down their faces.

She noticed that Rev. Montgomery too was crying freely. This solemn duty must be a difficult reminder to him of his own lost wife and baby. They all had known so much grief out here on the frontier, but Clarissa supposed it was really no different here than anywhere else. She was grateful for Rev. Vaille's closing words from the Messianic prophesy in Isaiah.

"He hath borne our griefs, and carried our sorrows."

"Amen," the group all quietly said.

CHAPTER SIX

Union Mission
September, 1822

"Good morning, children," Rev. Chapman greeted the students who had gathered for the first day of school. Including the eight mission children old enough for school, there were fifteen students altogether sitting in the boys' classroom for first day exercises.

It was a good beginning, Clarissa thought, frankly surprised that Louisa and Jean Revoir had been able to attend. They now lived at Three Forks at Big Tracks' village. She supposed they would stay at the Lombard cabin on Flat Rock Creek with their aunt and cousins. Here they would be close enough to make the five-mile ride to and from school most days. Also present for the first time were Francis Chouteau and his younger sister Masina, the children of Colonel Chouteau and his Osage wife Rosalee.

The missionaries had learned that Rosalee was of French ancestry as well, for her father was a wealthy fur trader who had done business with the Chouteaus in St. Louis for years. The Chouteau home at La Saline was a long ride to Union Mission though, and Clarissa wondered if the Chouteau children would board with them during the school months.

As she ushered her girls into their classroom, the young schoolteacher smiled to herself at the irony that most of her Indian students were French speakers. No wonder she had been asked about her fluency in French when Rev. Vaille had interviewed her for the position here. At the time, she had not

55

expected she would be conducting her classes in French and English.

It was mid morning when Clarissa glanced out the west window and saw two mustangs making their way toward the mission from the Trace. She recognized from the traditional dress they wore that the riders were Osage. As they neared the corral, Clarissa could tell that one of the riders was Buffalo Woman. She had four children with her.

Hope made her heart pound a little faster. If Buffalo Woman was bringing her children – the children of Mad Buffalo – to their school, it was a show of approval from the Osage leader. It might be the very thing to bring the mission greater acceptance among the two nearby Osage villages.

She saw that Mr. Spaulding had stepped out of his classroom and made his way toward the corral to greet the woman and the three boys and one girl who rode with her. Will Requa, who was assisting John today with Osage and French interpretation, also joined them.

Robbie offered to lead the two horses into the corral, but Clarissa saw Buffalo Woman shake her head. She wondered if the woman had some reservations about being at the mission.

"Elizabeth, will you finish our reading while I go greet our new student?" Clarissa asked.

"Yes, Miss Johnson," Elizabeth readily agreed.

All the girls had been watching the approach of these new children with as much interest as their teacher.

Clarissa dusted chalk from her hands and then stepped outside. As she approached the corral, she saw John extend his hand toward the oldest of Buffalo Woman's children, but the boy did not respond. There was a sullen look of resentment on his face. He clearly did not think he needed to attend classes.

Will and Buffalo Woman were speaking in Osage and Clarissa could understand a few of the words they exchanged. The woman wanted her children to learn from the "talking leaves" – especially the one about *Wah-Kon-Ta-Izke*, the Jesus-God. She gave a little nudge to the two older boys who looked to be about twelve and ten years in age. Neither seemed enthused about school.

Buffalo Woman touched each boy's bare shoulder as she gave their names. The older boy was Black Beaver and he looked like a young version of his father Mad Buffalo. The other boy was Six Bulls and he seemed to follow his older brother's lead in attitude and posture.

The girl was named Red Corn and Clarissa estimated her age as eight. She wore her raven black hair in tight braids wrapped in intricately beaded leather. She looked frightened and Clarissa couldn't blame her. The first day at a new school was an overwhelming experience for any child, but it must seem especially so for one who was just being introduced to the concept of a classroom.

The youngest boy was Little Rabbit, about three years in age. He would not be attending school. While Buffalo Woman was speaking he had managed to climb up her back and was clinging to her neck while peeking around her braids at the missionaries. His mother ignored his antics, but Clarissa couldn't help but smile at his inquisitive little face.

She then turned to Red Corn and spoke a welcome to her in what she hoped was passable Osage. Clarissa extended her hand to the little girl, but she made no move from clinging to her mother's deerskin dress. Buffalo Woman pushed her forward toward Clarissa, speaking to her softly but firmly.

With a last glance backward at her mother, Red Corn reluctantly placed her hand in the teacher's and allowed herself to be led to the girl's classroom. Her brothers obeyed their mother's quite firm words to them and followed Mr. Spaulding into his class. Buffalo Woman told Will that she would return for the children later in the day.

Using the lower rail of the corral fence as a mounting step, the woman grasped the mane of her mustang and with practiced ease leapt onto its back with Little Rabbit still on her own back, his arms and legs tightly wrapped around her. Then taking the reins of the second horse also, she made her way along the cornfield path toward the Trace.

As they stepped into the classroom, Clarissa asked Red

Corn if she spoke French. Expecting a *"oui"* in the affirmative, she was surprised that the girl simply looked at her and gave no indication that she understood the question.

Oh, dear, Clarissa thought. This would be the first real challenge to her limited knowledge of the Osage language. Even little Deer-in-Water, who was also full-blood Osage, was quite fluent in French. Her father, Bird, was a trapper who had dealt with French fur traders for many years and had passed his knowledge of the language along to Deer-in-Water and her brother Bearpaw.

Hopefully she, Louisa or Marie would be helpful in translating for Red Corn.

To her surprise, Red Corn's face lit up with happiness when she saw Louisa Revoir. She ran to the girl and the two hugged like long-lost friends. Clarissa remembered that Louisa's father Joseph had been good friends with Mad Buffalo, a fact that sadly led to his death. Apparently the children had been friends as well.

The teacher also noted that Red Corn did not even acknowledge Deer-in-Water though they both were from Claremont's clan. When she asked Deer-in-Water if she knew Red Corn, the girl shrugged and said in her limited English, "She Sky People," as if that explained everything. Then seeing her teacher's puzzled look, the girl pointed to herself and said, "I am Earth People."

"Oh, I see," Clarissa said. She guessed that really did explain everything.

To help her Osage students learn English, Clarissa had devised a game. She would write on each girl's slate a name of something in the classroom in either English or French. Then the girls would take their slates and place it on or in front of the item in the room. Clarissa had borrowed several items from Amanada's kitchen for the game today. They were enjoying the game with many giggles and wild guesses when Dr. Palmer knocked briefly and then stepped into the room.

The giggles abruptly stopped at the breach of the classroom walls by a man. The girls all looked up at the tall, dark-haired doctor and Clarissa suddenly felt like a girl herself. Aware of her chalk-covered fingers, she tried to wipe them clean on her apron. But the stirred dust made her suddenly sneeze.

"Bless you," the doctor said with a smile. "Are you coming down with something, Miss Johnson?"

"Uh, no," Clarissa said, though she felt her face flush. She was very aware of the watchful eyes of her students, especially the speculative look of nine-year-old Abigail Chapman.

"Can we help you with something, Doctor?" she then asked.

"I was just checking to see if you might need some assistance," Marcus said. "With Osage translation, I mean. I heard you had a new student." He smiled at Red Corn and the little girl responded with a shy smile of her own.

Dr. Palmer had developed a friendship with Buffalo Woman after leading her to a Christian faith earlier in the year. He had visited in Mad Buffalo's lodge from time to time and knew the children well.

"That's very kind of you," Clarissa said, feeling torn about his offer. Having him in the classroom might prove to be too intimidating for her students . . . and if she were honest with herself, she might find it a distraction as well.

"Louisa has been doing a very good job of helping me so far this morning," she said reluctantly.

"Of course," Marcus said, looking at Joseph's daughter. "She is blessed to know three languages, isn't she?"

"Yes."

"Well, I'm sorry for the interruption," the doctor said, reaching for the door. "It sounded like you were having great fun."

Clarissa felt embarrassed then. Many people did not think fun should be had in a classroom. Quiet and sober study was to be the rule. But she saw no condemnation in the doctor's kind eyes.

"You're welcome to interrupt any time," Clarissa said, feeling very bold in the offer.

"Would I be?" Marcus asked, pausing from walking out the door.

"Yes," was all Clarissa had breath to say.

"Thank you," the doctor said and then stepped out of the classroom and quietly closed the door.

Clarissa heard a dramatic sigh from all of her students and then had to suppress a laugh when she realized one of those sighs was her own. This would never do.

"Now, girls, we must get back to our studies," she said in as stern a tone as she could muster.

But she couldn't resist a glance at Abigail and she saw a knowing twinkle in the girl's brown eyes.

During the noon break, after enjoying soup and cornbread in the dining hall, the students spent a few moments in play in the school yard. Black Beaver and Six Bulls stood stoic and somber at the classroom door, refusing to be drawn into the game of tag the other boys were playing.

From time to time, Clarissa saw Black Beaver turn his head to look toward the little hill where the cemetery stood. She wondered if he was curious about the burial ground. Will Requa must have noticed also for he said something to the boy. Black Beaver responded in Osage.

At Clarissa's questioning look, Will quietly explained the boy's words. "He says their mother is there. She is watching them."

Clarissa looked toward the cemetery and at first saw no one. But as her eyes swept across the hill, she caught just a glimpse of movement among the tall grasses. Buffalo Woman, like her people, had the finely developed ability to blend into the environment so as to be almost invisible. But Little Rabbit hadn't yet learned such complete stillness. It was his movement that Clarissa saw.

No doubt, Black Beaver could see his mother for keenness of eye was a trait Clarissa had noticed in all the Osage students. The teacher wondered if it was his mother's silent vigil that kept Black Beaver at school.

At the end of the day, Black Beaver led his brother and sister along the path toward the Trace. Soon their mother rode up with the second horse and the children all mounted and turned toward Claremont's Town.

Buffalo Woman lifted an open-palmed hand toward the teachers who stood watching from the mission yard. It was the universal symbol of peace and acceptance among the Plains people. Black Beaver might not like it, but Clarissa was sure the children would return to school again.

A week later Robbie gave the call that riders were approaching the mission. The men had been working at the grist mill and the women were harvesting rows of carrots from the fall garden in the late afternoon. Everyone paused to see who was turning off the road to reach the mission compound.

"They're military," Rachel said as she pulled her bonnet brim forward to shade her eyes.

Amanda had an apron skirt full of carrots, but she dumped them quickly into a nearby basket and brushed furiously at the bits of dirt that clung to her.

"I'll start a pot of coffee," she said.

All the women, except Phoebe who watched the babies at her cabin, followed Amanda's example of trying to brush up and be presentable for their guests. Leaving their baskets and trowels, they made their way toward the corral where guests were always greeted. The children were granted permission to go and play before supper.

Four men in uniform and one civilian were the riders who turned their horses toward the mission and pulled up at the corral. Clarissa recognized Hugh Glenn, who was a retired colonel and now had a trading post at Three Forks. Like Captain Pryor, another Three Forks trader and veteran of the War of 1812, Glenn often served as a guide for military expeditions throughout the southwest.

Rev. Chapman reached the corral as the men began to dismount.

"Welcome to Union Mission," he stated, offering a hand to Colonel Glenn.

"Thank you, Reverend," the portly Glenn said, shaking

the proffered hand. "I'm giving General Gaines here a look around the territory. He's inspecting forts in the area."

"Then you've come from Fort Smith, I take it," Chapman said, as he shook hands with the general. The man was tall and stood sharply erect, with a full head of steel gray hair and bushy chin whiskers.

"Yes," the general said. "And this is General Atkinson and you know Major Bradford. Colonel Arbuckle at Fort Smith assigned Lieutenant Charles Summers here as my aide-de-camp. The colonel also asked me to tour this area with the idea of placing another fort out this way."

"We would be very happy to see that happen, General," Rev. Vaille stated and then gestured for the men to move to the dining hall. Here Amanda and Asie Vaille were setting out coffee and biscuits with fresh churned butter and strawberry preserves.

"Lieutenant, we're glad to have you visit," Vaille said. Then he made introductions of everyone as they took seats in the dining hall.

"A pleasure to be here," the young, wide-shouldered lieutenant stated, making sure his smile took in all the ladies. He was not tall, but quite handsome with dark wavy hair and deep brown eyes.

While the men occupied one table, the women sat at another, out of the conversation, but able to hear everything that was said. Amanda and Martha remained in the kitchen working on supper preparations.

"That's General Edmund Gaines," Rachel said softly to the other women as the men spent a few moments of helping themselves to the food. "He's commander over all the frontier forts."

Clarissa nodded, remembering reading something about the man in the *Arkansas Gazette*. Gaines was one of the military's top officials along with Winfield Scott and Andrew Jackson. She'd had the impression from the newspaper article that Gaines and the other two generals did not always agree on frontier military strategy or Indian relations.

"So you are considering Three Forks as the location for a

new fort, sir?" John Spaulding asked the commanding general.

"It would seem a logical place for one, what with the accessibility by the rivers," Gaines responded as he buttered a biscuit. "And that will likely be my recommendation, unless Glenn shows me something better."

"We find Fort Smith is a bit too far away to be truly effective in overseeing this area," Chapman said. "I'm sure Colonel Arbuckle has reported the conflicts between the Osages and Cherokees."

"Yes, he has," said the general. "That is why I agree with him that we need a fort further west. But I'm not sure I can convince those desk soldiers in Washington City that the need is genuine and not just the posturing of a few Arkansas politicians." It was clear that General Gaines had little patience for the politics in the nation's capital.

The men spent some time discussing frontier conditions and the treaty of peace just signed by Mad Buffalo and the Cherokee leaders John Jolly and Walter Webber. The summer had been quiet and all were hopeful that conflict would not be stirred up again when the fall hunting season began. It was the chase of the buffalo by well-armed men that seemed to bring about the clashes over hunting territory.

At a lull in the conversation, Amanda stepped in to the hall and spoke to Mrs. Chapman. "We're ready to serve supper, with your leave."

"Certainly," Rachel said and then stood and walked over to the men's table. "General, we hope you and your party will join us for supper. We're ready to serve you if that is agreeable."

"If these biscuits and coffee are any indication of what you serve here, I understand why everyone at Three Forks urged me to take a meal at Union Mission. You folks should be charging for your hospitality here."

Rachel smiled at the compliment and sent a look to Amanda to let her know it was to her credit.

"Perhaps you gentlemen would like to take a few moments to freshen up before the meal?"

"Another excellent suggestion," Gaines agreed and the men all stood. While the visitors took turns making use of the outhouse, Eliza tarried over setting out a second wash pitcher and basin at the little table that stood outside the dining hall door.

She was arranging the towels for a third time when Lieutenant Summers approached. "How kind of you, ma'am," he said with a little bow when she offered him a towel and bar of soap for washing up.

"It's Miss . . . Cleaver," Eliza gave a flirting smile. "Eliza Cleaver."

"Miss Cleaver, it's my pleasure to make your acquaintance," the young man stated with a matching smile as he began washing his hands.

"Do you visit this area very often, Lieutenant?"

"Very rarely, I'm afraid," the officer said. "Colonel Arbuckle keeps me quite busy with writing reports. Rather dull duty, but he seems to think I'm good at it. He only sent me with General Gaines because he knows I agree with his assessment of the need for a fort out here and he wanted me to make that point with the general."

"If a fort is built here, will you be serving at it?" Eliza asked.

"Most likely," Charles said. "Colonel Arbuckle would transfer the Seventh Infantry to the new location."

"Well, I hope that happens soon," Eliza said.

"Don't expect it soon, Miss Cleaver," the young man countered ruefully. "Nothing happens quickly in Washington City."

"Do I detect that you are from New England?" Eliza then asked.

"Yes," Summers answered. "From Boston."

"Oh, I love Boston," Eliza gushed. "Will you be traveling back there any time soon?"

"It isn't likely," the officer stated ruefully. "I am at the disposal of the Army and Colonel Arbuckle for the time being." He dried his hands and with another bow made his way into the dining hall.

Amanda stepped out to call everyone to supper by banging a spoon on a tin pan.

The children came running from the school where they had played for the last half hour. The two apprentices along with Stephen and Alexander Woodruff came from the grist mill. Asie and Phoebe carried the babies from the cabins.

Phoebe brought Thea to Clarissa and the teacher gladly took her little girl and settled the baby in her lap. She had been concerned, at first, when Phoebe resumed caring for the nine-month old girl when school started up again. She feared it would be a painful reminder of the housemother's loss.

But Phoebe had assured her she was fine and from all appearance this was so. Phoebe might be a simple young woman with little education, but she had a strong faith and a pragmatic nature. She assured Clarissa that she hadn't given up on her dream of having a child of her own.

"I plan on having a whole passel of children, if God blesses me," Phoebe had told her. "Even if they all ain't my own, I think of every child I care for as a gift from the good Lord."

Clarissa smiled at Phoebe as she sat down beside her. They were soon joined by Abraham, the Spauldings and George Requa. Their guests resumed their seats and the women served the chicken and rice, stewed turnips, fresh steamed carrots and peas with cornbread.

Once all had helped themselves to the steaming food, the conversation turned to the trip Colonel Glenn was planning to Cincinnati to pick up trade goods. Glenn had family and several business ventures in that town.

"Anything I can bring you folks?" the trader asked.

"Bring us a seamstress," Rachel replied, half joking. "We can't keep up with the mending and sewing that needs to be done out here."

Rev. Chapman smiled at his wife. "You know the mending is piling up when that is all my wife would ask for," he teased.

Glenn looked thoughtful. "You know, I might be able to help you with that," he said. "My sister has been widowed and is struggling to support seven children. But she's awfully proud and doesn't want charity from me."

"Does she take in sewing?" Rachel asked. "What are the children's ages?"

"Well, it wasn't my sister that I was thinking of for the job," Glenn clarified. "Her oldest daughter Sarah is working now at my meat packing plant, but it's really not the best place for a young lady. I've been trying to find something more suitable for her. I think she's a fair hand at sewing and she's of age."

"Is she of a strong Christian faith?" Rev. Vaille asked.

"Oh, definitely," the colonel responded. "My sister has raised all the children in the fear of the Lord. They are in church every Sunday."

Clarissa saw the Chapmans exchange a look.

"Then if your niece is interested in the position, please extend an offer from Union Mission," Rev. Chapman stated. "We really do need additional workers here and we already have the salary for a seamstress in our budget set by the mission society."

"I'll speak to Sarah when I arrive in Cincinnati," Glenn assured them. "I know my sister would rather she didn't work at the packing plant."

Rachel looked very pleased at the prospect of hiring a seamstress. Clarissa would never had guessed that such a position would be so needful, but life on the prairie was rough on clothes and the children were growing and always in need of hems let out or new clothes sewn. She had stitched two gowns for Thea, but had been almost embarrassed to let anyone see her needlework.

Colonel Glenn went on to tell the missionaries about the steamboats that were now regularly plying the western rivers. Travel times were being reduced and larger loads of goods could now be moved by the new riverboats. He hoped to return from Cincinnati before the end of the year.

Their guests spent the night at the mission, using the dormitory rooms above the school's classrooms. The following morning, after a breakfast of ham, biscuits and gravy, the men continued north on the Trace to visit Claremont's Town.

CHAPTER SEVEN

Union Mission
October, 1822

In mid October, the school took a break since most of their Indian students would not be attending during the fall buffalo hunt. When the migrating beasts reached the southern plains, the Osage villages followed the herds for a few weeks to lay in their supply of meat for the winter. Abraham and Will Requa had taken two of their mustangs and had joined the hunt to bring back meat for the mission.

Following the hunt, everyone in the region would gather at Three Forks for the annual Pumpkin Moon Rendezvous. All of the missionaries were looking forward to traveling to Three Forks for the event. It was one of the few times each year that the women and children left the mission. Travel was arduous and there was usually little reason for them to venture far from home.

A few days before the planned trip, Amanda asked Clarissa to gather some of the last heads of cabbage from the garden for dinner. The teacher reached for a basket and knife and made her way to the large patch of tilled earth. Most of the harvest was in already and Stephen had turned under about half of the kitchen garden.

Clarissa hummed softly to herself as she collected the cabbage heads. Just as she had finished filling her basket, George Requa approached the garden. In one hand he carried a brace of ducks he had shot from among the thousands that were migrating southward. In the other hand he held his loaded musket, the barrel pointed downward for safety.

"Fresh duck for supper," he said to the teacher as he held up his take for her to appreciate.

"Excellent, Mr. Requa," Clarissa smiled. "And there'll be more down and feathers for our flattened pillows once they have dried."

It was a joke among the missionaries. A few mornings earlier Billy Spaulding had declared over breakfast that he could hardly sleep because of his "mushed" pillow.

Compacted by a year's use, all their mattresses and pillows would be opened and re-stuffed through the fall months as the men brought in their catch from the massive flocks of migrating birds. It was one more reason why a seamstress was needed at the mission.

George smiled at Clarissa's remark and started to comment but suddenly the smile left his face.

"Miss Johnson," he said, keeping his voice low so as not to cause alarm. "Please stand perfectly still."

"What?" Clarissa asked. What an odd request. But something about his tone of voice penetrated her puzzlement and Clarissa froze in place. "What is it?" she asked again.

"Snake," George replied tersely as he eased the string of ducks slowly to the ground at the garden's edge. "Just a few feet away from you."

Clarissa felt a shiver run up her spine. It was all she could do to contain the desire to run from the garden. Moving her head slowly, she caught a glimpse of what seemed to her an enormous copperhead hiding among the foliage of the fall potato patch.

"Just keep still," George reminded her. "It hasn't coiled to strike yet and we don't want it to feel threatened." Carefully he circled around the edge of the garden, raising his gun as he stepped closer to his target.

Clarissa held her breath, her skin crawling with the thought of the snake slithering near her.

"Please hurry," she said, though in reality she knew she didn't want George to make a sudden move that might cause the snake to strike.

The blast of the musket made her jump even though she

had been expecting it. She nearly dropped the basket of cabbages she held.

Now her feet would not be still. Stepping high she hurried to leave the garden and stand behind Mr. Requa.

"Did you get it?" she asked, just then realizing her movement might have been a terrible mistake if he had not succeeded in killing the poisonous snake. She peeked around his shoulder.

"I rarely miss," George assured her with a hint of a smile as the teacher clung to his arm. She was not even aware of her action. "You're safe."

Suddenly others at the mission were hurrying toward the garden, alerted by the gun's report. Clarissa then became aware that she had practically thrown herself onto her rescuer's back and she pulled away as embarrassment heated her face. She hoped no one had seen her.

Rev. Vaille was the first to reach the garden. "What happened?" he asked, seeing no one but Miss Johnson and George.

"Killed that snake we've been on the lookout for," George explained. Then with the barrel of his musket he reached down and scooped up the copperhead. Its long length draped over the barrel and caused Clarissa to step back even further.

Next Dr. Palmer arrived, carrying his medical kit. It had become a habit for him. Any sound of alarm in the compound and he automatically searched for the medical bag, all the while praying he wouldn't need it.

He gave a low whistle as he joined Rev. Vaille at the garden and saw the snake.

"Are you alright, Miss Johnson," he asked, seeing how pale the young schoolteacher looked.

She nodded mutely, but resisted the urge to go and stand behind the good doctor.

Alexander Woodruff arrived then, coming from his blacksmith shed where he had been sharpening tools. He carried his own musket which he always kept close at hand. Life on the edge of civilization meant always being prepared.

Clarissa caught sight of Amanda and Martha peeking out from the kitchen door. The women and children had all been advised to stay inside should gunfire be heard. From the cabins, the other women also opened doors cautiously to see what had caused the one shot to be fired.

"All is well," Rev. Vaille announced in his preaching voice.

With that assurance, most everyone made their way to the garden. Paul and Robbie along with Thomas and Richard wanted to hold the dead snake. The girls gave squeals of fear, but were pulled into the garden for a closer look all the same.

George pretended to throw the copperhead in to the direction of the girls causing more squeals. Even the women instinctively took a step backward. The men all laughed.

"Stop that, Mr. Requa," Rachel scolded, but with a smile on her face.

"Well, you have a trophy now," Martha stated. "That snake's skin will look good on your cabin wall."

George laughed, but turned to Clarissa and gallantly bowed. "But I'll offer it to Miss Johnson instead," he said. "Would you like a pair of boots made from this beast?"

George had taken on cobbler duties at the mission. Though not trained in the art of sewing shoes, he had learned the skill at the mission out of necessity.

"No thank you, sir," Clarissa replied. She still felt a little shaky from the incident, but didn't want it to show. "You may keep it for yourself."

"Let's measure it," Robbie suggested and the boys raced to the barn for a yard stick. Everyone else made their way back to their morning chores.

Clarissa turned toward the kitchen to deliver the cabbages in the basket she still held.

Dr. Palmer fell into step beside her. "You look a little pale, Miss Johnson," he said in a low voice. "Are you sure you're alright?"

"Yes," Clarissa assured him. "It was a bit frightening, but I'm fine."

"Have Mrs. Fuller fix you some hot tea," Marcus

recommended. "With a bit of honey," he added with a wink. "That's my prescription for you and you must follow doctor's orders."

Clarissa smiled and felt a blush warm her cheeks. "Yes, Doctor," she said.

When they reached the kitchen door, he briefly squeezed her hand and then parted from her to return to the grist mill where he had been working.

Clarissa took a moment to steady the pounding of her heart before she stepped into the kitchen. The curious eyes of Amanda Fuller would discover her secret if she wasn't careful.

At dinner, the snake was the subject of discussion and George was lauded as a hero for removing it as a threat.

"How fortunate we are, Miss Johnson," Eliza said with what seemed a false sweetness to Clarissa. "If George hadn't come to your aid, you might have been bitten and would have required the services of Dr. Palmer."

Clarissa looked at Eliza, trying to discern the motive for her words. She was the picture of innocence, but she did not return Clarissa's look. She was gazing at Marcus.

Dr. Palmer looked back and forth between the two women. He decided the best thing to do was keep his mouth shut.

Early the next morning before sunrise, the mission family loaded into the wagons for their trip to Three Forks. Almost everyone was going, but the Redfields and Vailles remained behind to care for the babies and see to regular chores. The children were nearly beside themselves with excitement. A trip to the Pumpkin Moon Rendezvous was a highlight of the year.

They reached the little fur trading community late in the afternoon, weary from the long ride but eager to explore town and mingle with the interesting menagerie of neighbors and visitors. Besides the many trading posts located on the banks of the Verdigris River, there were dozens of tents pitched along the dirt trail that made up the main street.

Games of chance were being hawked by gaudily dressed hucksters from some of the tents. The women averted their eyes when their wagons rolled past a tent advertising "Baths 5 cents." At the Pryor-Rutherford Trading Post, George and Will steered their oxen teams into an open field beside it. Everyone was eager to exit the wagons and begin an exploration of all that the Rendezvous offered.

Across the trail from Pryor's post, Mrs. Lilla Bradley had set up a table and was selling gingerbread and apple cider. Her two daughters were helping serve their customers.

The Creole woman was known for her cooking and her cabin was often called upon by visitors who were looking for a neighborly meal. Mrs. Bradley's Scottish husband was a trapper who spent much of the year in the western mountains but always made it home in time for Rendezvous.

Several of the missionaries, including the children, quickly made their way to Mrs. Bradley's table. The children were eager to spend the few pennies they had been given for the outing. Hungry from their long journey, almost everyone chose a generous square of the dark and fragrant gingerbread and were soon enjoying the treat.

"Mrs. Bradley, this is wonderful," Dr. Palmer complimented the woman. He had enjoyed a meal at her home when the men first arrived at Three Forks two years earlier.

"Thank you, sir," the woman replied. "'Bout as good as your Mrs. Fuller's?" Amanda's reputation for setting out a fine meal was known far and wide.

"I think you have me beat," Amanda responded. She was enjoying the gingerbread just as much as the rest of them.

"You Mrs. Fuller?" Lilla asked.

"Yes," Amanda nodded and then wiped her hand on her apron to offer to Mrs. Bradley.

"Good to know you," the dark-skinned woman said. Then she added, "Which of you is the teacher for the girls?"

"I'm the girls' teacher," Clarissa responded. She also offered a hand shake and gave her name.

"I'm pleased to meet you," Mrs. Bradley said. "My girls

have been asking me 'bout going to school. Now that the garden's all in, I thought I might send them. You let dark children come?"

Clarissa smiled ruefully to herself, remembering her reluctance at one time to be a part of teaching a Negro student while the missionaries had spent a few months in Little Rock. She had learned to overcome her fear of defying the social conventions that would deny a child an education.

She almost answered Mrs. Bradley, but stopped herself. This was really a decision to be made by Rev. Chapman as mission superintendent.

"I'll ask our director," she said, hating that it made her sound reluctant. "We'll let you know before we leave Three Forks."

Clarissa made a point of presenting Mrs. Bradley's request to Rev. Chapman when the missionaries met at their wagons a short time later for a light supper that Amanda had packed.

"Mrs. Bradley would like for her daughters to board with us through the winter months so they can get some schooling," she explained as everyone sat on blankets spread out under a towering cottonwood tree.

The teacher saw the minister exchange a look with his wife. It had always been Rachel's position that offering education to Negroes might cause conflict here in a territory where slavery was legal and commonly practiced.

Some slave states had outlawed education for blacks, even free blacks. But their mission society supported the abolition of slavery and took a position of equality in education and religious expression. How to put these beliefs into practice without running the risk of being shut down by the territorial government was a concern the missionaries had debated more than once.

Looking around at all the missionaries gathered over their meal of cornbread, boiled eggs and dried pemmican, Rev. Chapman seemed to be seeking consensus among the group.

"We can't deny a child an education," John Spaulding said quietly, but with a conviction he had long and fearlessly held. In fact, the only opinion against it he seemed to fear was that of his wife Alice. He studiously avoided looking at her.

"You know these children are of mixed race," Mrs. Chapman said. "That seems to inflame prejudice even more."

"Most of our Osage students are of mixed blood," Clarissa pointed out, surprising herself with her boldness.

Rachel seemed surprised at her boldness too for she gave Clarissa a sharp look. Then with a softer tone of voice she said, "You are right, of course."

"I think we are far enough removed from Little Rock that we need not fear government interference," John added. There were nods all around by the other missionaries.

"Then we shall open the school to Mrs. Bradley's children," Rev. Chapman concluded. "I'm sure Rev. Vaille will be in agreement. It's a shame we even have to debate this issue. We will lead by example and hope our Southern neighbors will see that we are acting in Christian charity."

The missionaries retired for the evening shortly after finishing their cold supper. They were tired from the early start and long drive from the mission. They settled on blankets and buffalo robes in and around the wagons, listening to the horse races being held further up the river. Because gambling and guzzling free-flowing rum always accompanied this event, the missionaries chose to avoid it.

The following day, the children were first to rise, eager to enjoy their school holiday and spend the last of their pennies. Clarissa and Rachel agreed to take the children to Colonel Chouteau's trading post on the west side of the Verdigris River. It would mean taking the ferry across and the boys in particular were eager for the experience.

With George, Marcus and the Fullers, they walked to the river's edge and signaled for the ferryman by raising a flag to the top of a post at the landing site. A long rope cable was strung across the shallow river between posts on each side. They waited for a few minutes for the ferry to leave the western bank and begin its slow pull across the river.

The flat wooden boat was operated by two men. One

kept the small vessel from drifting downstream by holding the guide rope and pulling hand over hand. The other man used a long pole to muscle the boat across the stream. With a hard final push, they forced the boat onto a sandstone outcropping where the bank was shallow. Deep ruts revealed where wagons were driven on and off the ferry.

"Ya'll crossing over?" one of the men asked the group. Dressed in bib overalls and a slouch hat, he had a thick red beard and a thick southern drawl.

"Yes," Dr. Palmer answered. "Can you take all of us at once? There are fourteen of us."

"Surely can," the other man said. "Cost is two bits."

Mrs. Chapman started to open her reticule, but Dr. Palmer was quicker in reaching into his pocket and flipping a coin to the ferry operator.

"Thank you, Doctor," Rachel said as the children eagerly scrambled aboard.

"Now stand in the center," the red-bearded man directed. Then he reached a hand to help Clarissa, Rachel and Amanda step aboard. George, Marcus and Stephen also assisted from the shore and then were last to board.

Standing on the boat proved challenging, especially with wiggly children trying to take in every aspect of the crossing. From a distance upstream, they could hear the Falls of the Verdigris though they could not see them because the river made a bend just north of the ferry crossing.

The white water falls were a popular fishing and swimming spot and was the location Paul and Robbie had set out for first thing this morning. It was too cool for a swim, but they had brought fishing line and would cut some cane for poles and catch crickets for bait. If they caught enough fish, Amanda had told them they would have a fish fry for supper this evening.

The crossing took longer than Clarissa had expected for the ferrymen moved slowly so as not to toss anyone into the river. At one point the boat hit a piece of driftwood and sluiced sideways a bit. The girls reacted with high-pitched screams causing the ferrymen to grin. They all steadied themselves and Clarissa found both George and Dr. Palmer taking her elbows to ensure she didn't fall.

"Thank you," she said, looking at both of them in turn, feeling rather awkward at the attention. Dr. Palmer had also taken Rachel's elbow to steady her.

"Stand still, children," Mrs. Chapman admonished them. "I don't want a dunk in the river and I'm sure your teacher doesn't want one either." She gave Clarissa a smile at her reminder of the unplanned swim Clarissa, George and Marcus had taken in the Mississippi on their journey from Pittsburgh.

Shortly they arrived at the west bank of the river and the men assisted the women again as they de-boarded the ferry and made their way up the well-worn slope. On this side of the river stood the Chouteau trading post and his boat-building enterprise. A little further upstream was the post and cabin of a man named Seaborn Hill. Skin lodges of the visiting Osages were set up around the Chouteau post for the week-long Rendezvous.

The missionaries made their way toward the Chouteau store, reaching its dirt front porch just as a man was exiting. He was tall with shoulder-length brown hair and a neatly trimmed goatee. He was dressed in the garb of a mountain man with a fringed leather jacket. He had pinned up one brim of his large hat with a feather giving him a rakish air. The pearl-laid handle of a pistol peeked out from his coat and his gun belt was studded with silver and turquoise. He tipped his hat to the ladies and said, "Mornin', folks," but did not stop for conversation.

The mission family stepped into the dim interior of the trading post which also served as a general mercantile. Since the colonel kept the furs he traded in a back room, the smell of them was not as overwhelming here as it was at most of the trading posts. That was one reason the women preferred to shop at Chouteau's.

Colonel Chouteau kept his post well stocked with the cloth, blankets, glass beads and metalware his trade partners sought. There were a few Osages inside the store, including Yellowbird, the wife of Chief Claremont.

Dr. Palmer greeted the woman and she gave him a smile and spoke in Osage. His knowledge of the native language was proficient enough that the two conversed for a time while the others looked around the mercantile.

The children immediately migrated to the jars of hard candy set on a side counter. Deciding exactly which of the peppermint, horehound and molasses pieces they would purchase would keep them happily occupied for a while.

Abigail made her way to the rolls of ribbon stacked alongside bolts of fabric. Clarissa joined her in looking over the bright colored silk, wondering which color would best suit Thea. She planned to purchase fabric to make some new dresses for the growing girl.

George struck up a conversation with the clerk behind the counter. Clarissa overheard the man introduce himself as Paul Liguest Chouteau, a half-brother to the colonel. Like his older brother, Liguest had dark hair and sharp beaky features. He seemed happy to field the questions George threw at him.

"Who was that trader we saw as we came in?" George asked.

Liguest sent a look of disdain toward the door the man in question had just existed. "That's John McKnight," he said. "He fancies himself an empire builder like the Chouteau family. He's building a trading post down on the Canadian River."

"I've heard of McKnight," George mused. "The *Gazette* says he's led expeditions all the way to Santa Fe. So he's going to settle in the area?"

"That's what he says," Chouteau responded. "But he won't have much success on the Canadian. It's barely navigable and most of the Indians in these parts already do business with the Chouteaus or one of the other outfits here at Three Forks. He seems to think a road will develop out of Fort Smith to Santa Fe and will cross the Trace right where he's going to put his store."

"Could happen," George said.

"Not for many years," Liguest countered. "There is no reason to cross miles of Comanche land to get to Santa Fe.

The trade is not worth it and the land is nothing to desire. More folks will be traveling the Trace from St. Louis down to Texas. A man named Stephen Austin is starting a colony around the Mission de San Antonio. He has advertised free land in the New Orleans newspapers."

Dr. Palmer entered the conversation then after bidding a goodbye to Yellowbird who left the store with her purchases. "We've noticed more traffic on the road by our mission," he said. "We'll sometime see a dozen wagons together all heading south."

"Free land is very enticing," Chouteau said. "Mexico wants more people now that they've gained their independence from Spain."

Clarissa carried two bolts of pastel calico to the front counter and asked Liguest to cut a yard of each for her. The clerk pulled a marked measuring string from his pocket and quickly measured and cut the fabric. Then with a practiced hand, he wrapped the lengths in brown paper and tied it neatly with string.

"I'm going to get ribbon instead of candy," Abigail declared and with her teacher's help decided how much of the pink ribbon she would need for a bow for her hair.

Clarissa smiled at her, knowing that Abigail was on the verge of young womanhood and was already concerned about her appearance. Though Elizabeth Vaille was only a few months younger than her best friend Abigail, she still preferred peppermints and lemon drops to hair ribbons.

After all of them had looked the store over and completed their purchases, they made their way back to the ferry landing. The boat was already on their side so they were quickly heading back to the east bank of the Verdigris to the area known as French Point.

The young men returned from their fishing expedition later that afternoon and all the men helped with cleaning their catch. Joseph Bogey had provided a sack full of apples from a Tontitown orchard.

"Your old guide Jean Baptiste brought over several bushels," Bogey explained to the group. Tontitown was a small community about three day's journey northeast of Three Forks.

Amanda had brought corn meal and a tin of hog lard for the fried corn dodgers she prepared along with the fish. It was a fine meal after an enjoyable day.

Following supper, the group all walked down the trail to Father Pierre Menard's brush arbor service. They met Teresa and Star-That-Travels and sat together on the blankets they carried with them.

As the Pumpkin Moon rose over the river, the French priest and trapper spoke of Jesus as light of the world. In his typical fashion, he wove the sermon with words in English, French and Osage. Clarissa noticed that Star-That-Travels listened intently as if committing the words to memory. As she watched him, she wondered if he might not become a preacher himself someday.

The mission family spent one more night at Three Forks and then rose before dawn for the long trip home. It had been a good holiday away from the never-ending work of the mission.

CHAPTER EIGHT

Cincinnati, Ohio
Late October, 1822

Sarah Clapp removed the heavy canvas, blood-stained apron she wore and tossed it into a large laundry hamper at the Glenn Meat Packing Plant in Cincinnati. She pulled a kerchief off her dark curls and stuffed it into the pocket of her jacket she took from a rack near the plant office.

Then taking her time card from its slot on the wall, she handed it to the plant manager to stamp her out time. Bone weary, the petite young woman stepped out into the dusk having completed another 12-hour shift at the plant.

Only a mile's walk home and she could then put up her feet and enjoy her mother's cabbage soup before heading off to bed. She had learned that if she could get to sleep before her two sisters came to bed, she would not have to listen to their childish chatter or be kept awake by their snores. She needed every minute of sleep before rising ahead of the sun and beginning another day of dreary work.

Sarah hated the job at the meat plant; hated the blood, hated the smell, hated the fact that she was one of only three women working there. She wished she were a man and could work at Uncle Hugh's boat building enterprise instead. She'd even gladly work at his trading post somewhere out in the Indian Country if it would get her away from the plant. In fact, the romance of the uncharted west sounded wonderful in comparison to her life in Cincinnati.

Feeling tears of self-pity sting her eyes, Sarah gave

herself a mental shaking. *Don't start feeling sorry for yourself*, she scolded. *You know you're blessed to even have work.*

She knew this to be true because she had been criticized often enough for "taking a job away from a man." Apparently this "man" needed the job to support his family. Never mind that she was supporting her mother and six younger siblings. At least her brother Leonard had just been given work sweeping sawdust at the boat shop. His income would ease the tight finances just a bit.

"Why couldn't Uncle Hugh run a mercantile here in Cincinnati?" she said in a wishful prayer. "I'd be happy to work there, God." It was almost a daily prayer for Sarah.

Arriving home, she stepped into the warmth of the house and was surprised to see Uncle Hugh sitting at the small dining table. She felt a bit guilty at the resentful thoughts she had been sending the colonel's way on her walk home.

"Here she is," her mother smiled and hurried to help Sarah out of her wrap and then placed a bowl of soup in front of her after she took a seat.

"Your uncle has some news of a job," her mother said.

Sarah looked at her uncle with a sharp sense of hope and a silent thanks sent up to God. Then she noticed that though her mother was smiling, there was a sad look in her eyes. Perhaps she shouldn't be too hopeful until she learned more about this job.

"Your mother has been showing me some of your needlework, Sarah," Uncle Hugh said as he fingered an embroidered doily as if he wasn't quite sure what it was. "You do very pretty work."

"Do you have a need of doilies, Uncle?" Sarah asked, getting the ludicrous picture of an Indian woman setting one out in her lodge. The colonel had described the homes of his Osage trading partners to the children. Doilies didn't seem to fit the picture she had in her mind.

Glenn chuckled. "No, there is not yet much demand for them on the frontier," he said. "But I was telling your mother about the Christian mission located north of Three Forks.

They are in need of a seamstress and I thought you might like that work."

"A seamstress?" Sarah repeated, feeling hope once again. "I love to sew; I've asked all over town for sewing work." Then she felt embarrassed that she had admitted out loud her desire for work somewhere beside the meat plant.

"I thought you might," Uncle Hugh said gently. "I know work at the plant is not very pleasant for you."

"But we're grateful for it," her mother said. "Aren't we, Sarah."

"Yes."

"But you'd rather be doing something else, wouldn't you?" Glenn went on. "Would you have an interest in this sewing job then? It would mean leaving home."

Now Sarah understood the sadness in her mother's eyes. Could she leave her mother and siblings? Should she?

"Would I be able to send my salary home?" she asked.

"I believe so," her uncle replied. "In fact, I'd be willing to advance you your first six-month's pay which you can leave here with your mother. Then when the mission society pays you, you can just pay me back. How would that be?"

Tears of gratitude filled her eyes, but still Sarah hesitated. Traveling west seemed an answer to her prayers, but she didn't want to be selfish. Her mother might prefer she remain in Cincinnati. Looking at her mother she said, "What do you think, Mama? Should I do this?"

She saw her mother square her shoulders as if stiffening her resolve. "I'd miss you terribly, Sarah, but it seems like a good opportunity for you. And Hugh tells me the folks at this mission are good and kind people and there are several women there, some your own age. Some nice young men, too. If you don't like it, you don't have to stay. Your uncle can always bring you home."

This truly felt like an answer to prayer. "Then I think I would like to give it a try," Sarah said. They discussed the job at Union Mission for a time and then Uncle Hugh told Sarah he planned to leave Cincinnati at the end of the week and head back downriver to Three Forks.

"Why don't you take that time to make preparations to travel with me," he said. "No need to go back to the plant. I'll see to any pay you're owed there."

Sarah felt as if a weight had been lifted off her shoulders. She had come to dread the meat plant to such a measure that she had often contemplated running away. Only her obligation to her mother had kept her plodding to and from work each day. Now she would be free from it.

As she settled into bed that night, her mind was whirling with thoughts of this new opportunity.

She felt a mixture of hope and excitement. She wasn't exactly sure where Three Forks and Union Mission were located out in the middle of the vast American continent. But she had always thought it would be grand to travel out there as Uncle Hugh had done.

She knew she ought to be concerned about Indians and primitive conditions and wild animals. But instead she couldn't stop smiling to know that she was free from the meat plant and would soon get to see some of the world beyond her hometown.

It would be hard to leave her family, and that thought put a little bit of doubt in her mind as she drifted off to sleep. But when she awoke the next morning without the usual feeling of dread, she knew she had made the right decision.

At the end of the week, Sarah walked with her family down to the wharf. Uncle Hugh was to meet them there to board a steamboat called *The Comet*. Sarah had told herself that she would not cry as she said her goodbyes, but she found her resolve crumbling as everyone gave her a hug in farewell. Even a few friends from church were there to see her off.

Colonel Glenn did not own *The Comet*, but knew her captain well and had traveled aboard the paddlewheeler more than once so he was quite familiar with it. He saw to the loading of Sarah's small trunk. He had a handsome leather valise which he would carry with him.

The trunk had been a gift from her mother's good friend Ada McKinley who with her husband ran the largest inn in

Cincinnati. A guest had left it at the inn over a year ago and never returned to claim it. Sarah felt blessed to receive it. She couldn't have afforded to purchase one herself.

Her mother had tearfully helped her pack and seeing her mother's sadness had almost changed her mind about traveling so far from home.

As they waited at the wharf for the boarding call, Sarah turned to her mother for a final time. "Are you sure you want me to go?" she asked, searching her mother's face for the truth.

Mrs. Clapp took both of her oldest daughter's hands. "We will all miss you, Sarah," she said. Then lowering her voice she added, "But I want something better for you than working at Hugh's meat plant. The Lord will go with you and I just believe he has something good for you at that mission."

Giving her hands a final squeeze she said, "Just write as often as you can so I know you are doing well, will you?"

"I will, Mama," Sarah promised.

The boarding call came at last and the colonel stepped over to say his goodbyes to the family. Then taking Sarah's arm, he walked with her up the gangplank to the middle deck of the large boat. They stood at the rail while the boat's crew cast off the lines and fired up the wood-fueled boilers.

Other passengers lined the rails as well and the dock was crowded with well wishers sending off friends and family into the American frontier. After what seemed a very long time to Sarah, they finally felt the boat pull away from its mooring. A bright toot of the whistle seemed to give a cheerful farewell to Cincinnati.

Uncle Hugh walked Sarah down to the passenger deck to locate her tiny quarters. His was down the starboard hall on the other side of the boat. Sarah wondered with a feeling of guilt how much passage aboard this modern boat had cost her uncle. She had not even thought to ask. She would have to add that to amount she owed him. A private room had to be expensive. Most folks traveled in steerage and slept in dormitory style rooms for women and men.

Sarah had tried to give Uncle Hugh her pay from the

plant, but he told her to keep it until they reached Three Forks in case she might need to make a few purchases along the journey. Sarah was determined to be as frugal as possible. She hated the thought of being in debt, even to her kind uncle.

After her trunk was delivered to her room, Sarah shook out two of her dresses and hung them on pegs lining the wall opposite the narrow bunk. Despite growing up in a river town, she had never traveled any distance by river. It would be a new venture for her and one she was looking forward too. She couldn't wait to discover what lay beyond the next bend in the river.

Not confident of her ability to find her way around the steamboat, she sat on her bunk and waited for Uncle Hugh to come and escort her to the dining room for dinner. Located on the upper deck, the dining hall gave passengers a good view of the river and the passing shoreline which seemed to fly by to Sarah.

"How fast are we going, Uncle?" she asked as a boat's mate set their plates before them.

"Oh, probably six or seven miles per hour," the colonel replied, smiling when Sarah gasped.

"How long will it take us to arrive at Three Forks?"

"That depends on weather and river conditions; how many stops we make at ports of call," Hugh replied as he began to carve the ham that had come from his own packing plant. "It could take anywhere from six to ten weeks." Then noticing that Sarah hadn't yet touched her plate, he added, "Better enjoy this ham," he smiled.

Sarah looked ruefully at the meat and grinned. "I don't know if I can," she said. "I think I met this pig personally."

Hugh threw back his head and laughed, causing the other diners to look at the pretty girl with deep dimples traveling with the grey haired gentleman.

When their laugher subsided Sarah asked, "Will I have a chance to mail a letter to mother along the way?" In truth, she could hardly eat; she felt so full of questions.

"Certainly," her uncle answered patiently. "We'll definitely make stops at Louisville and Memphis. Hopefully at Little Rock too. River conditions will determine whether we can make it all the way to Dwight Mission on *The Comet*. But from there, or from Fort Smith, we'll then be traveling by keelboat. That will be the slowest part of the journey."

Sarah nodded as if she fully grasped her uncle's answer. She knew what a keelboat was, for she had seen plenty in Cincinnati. But the names of towns they were to pass on the journey were completely new to her.

"You've traveled a great deal haven't you?" she asked.

I've seen quite a bit of the west," Glenn smiled. "Just got back from a ride out to Santa Fe."

"Where is that?"

"In the western section of Mexico. An old friend of mine named Jacob Fowler and I led an expedition out that way. Checking on trade opportunities. We got permission from officials at Santa Fe to trap beaver along the river as we came back to Three Forks. Had our pack mules loaded down by the time we arrived at my trading post."

"Beaver is popular in European fashion, isn't it?" This was something Sarah did know about. She loved looking through old copies of the *Saturday Evening Post* to get ideas for her sewing.

"Quite popular," Hugh confirmed. "It's proven a lucrative venture for me."

Sarah was quiet as they finished their meal. She had heard the whispers about Uncle Hugh once having financial troubles. It was one reason he had left Cincinnati. But he had certainly rebounded over the last few years.

"The good Lord has blessed me," Hugh said, as if reading where her thoughts had wandered.

Sarah blushed slightly and her uncle smiled.

"Don't feel in any hurry to pay me back, Sarah," he said as he pushed away his plate. "This is my way of helping your mother. She's too proud to accept it otherwise."

"I know," Sarah nodded. "She doesn't want to be a burden."

"You are my only family," her uncle countered. "You are not a burden."

Long having served in the military, Glenn had moved from post to post from a young age and had never married or had children of his own.

"I appreciate you, Uncle Hugh," Sarah said as they pushed back their chairs and prepared to leave the dining room. "I'm ever so grateful for the chance at this new job."

"I think it will be good for you, Sarah," he responded and slipped her hand through the crook of his arm. "Now let's get you familiar with this boat we're going to be on for next several weeks. You'll want to find ways to occupy yourself while I'm having a cigar with the captain."

Weeks and weeks, Sarah repeated in her mind. *How far from home am I going?*

At Union Mission, the family prepared for their Sabbath service. They had seen more and more of their Osage neighbors attend the meetings on occasion, but they never knew from week to week who might arrive for the service.

Usually the Lombards and Revoirs would ride up from Flat Rock Creek. Star-That-Travels had become an interpreter for the church service because he had a very good grasp of English.

The Bradley girls – Tassie and Lena – were boarding with them now as were Bearpaw and Deer-in-Water so Clarissa always sat with her students in the worship service. Buffalo Woman's children had not returned to school since their break for the fall hunt and Clarissa did not expect them to attend classes after the weather turned cold.

The little congregation had completed the final hymn when the chapel door opened to admit Teresa Revoir and Star-That-Travels. Rev. Chapman greeted them warmly as they took the seats Paul and Robbie pulled out for them.

While Chapman preached, Clarissa observed again that Star-That-Travels seemed held in rapt attention. Occasionally he would assist the minister with the words he needed in Osage. She appreciated his clear desire to learn from the scriptures and be of assistance in the preaching.

Their Osage guests joined them for dinner following the

worship service. As everyone enjoyed the soup that had simmered all morning, Star-That-Travels spoke up. "Mr. Bogey told us you are planning a new field place. Will it be close for school?"

"Yes, about five miles away," Rev. Chapman responded. "We expect to begin building in the spring."

"Teresa and I would like to build a log lodge there so the children can stay to school and not have to live here away from their mother. Maybe that be possible? Maybe you help us build such a place? Teresa has never built a log lodge."

The missionaries smiled at the remark. The Osages were accustomed to home building being the responsibility of the women.

"We would be happy to help you build a log cab . . .uh . . . lodge," Chapman stated. "It's very heavy work and we always help one another with buildings. Do you want to learn farming?"

Star-That-Travels hesitated but finally said, "Teresa grows the food."

His guileless response showed again why teaching farming among the Osages was proving to be such a challenge. The missionaries could not imagine a woman pushing a plow. The Indians could not imagine a warrior doing so. The two cultures were far apart on the idea of "field making."

"We can travel to the Hopefield site soon and help you begin you new lodge," Will offered. "We should start before the snow falls."

"Yes," Star-That-Travels agreed. "Maybe sunup tomorrow?"

"Sunup tomorrow," Will nodded. It would be a chilly start to the day.

The following morning, Star-That-Travels arrived at the mission just as the sun was peeking over the river. Will, George and Abraham were making coffee in the kitchen, hoping Amanda would not be annoyed at the spilled grounds and unwashed dishes. She had left biscuits and cold slices of ham for them both for breakfast and to pack for their dinner at the farm site.

After their quick morning meal, the men mounted their mustangs and set out as the rest of the mission family was rising. The morning was cool but promised to be clear and pleasant once the sun was at its highest. The breath of the horses huffed visibly in the crisp air.

The tree line along the river was awash in fall colors of orange, brown and burnished gold. Not the blazing crimson of New England's sugar maples, the oak, pecan and cottonwood trees were nonetheless quite pretty in their autumn finery. The blue haze of distant hills to the east provided a beautiful backdrop.

George pulled his wool cap down over his ears and tugged his gloves higher. "Going to be a good day," he said. His mustang must have agreed for it pranced along the trail as if enjoying the cool morning. It must have been a welcome relief from the summer's heat and torment of flies.

They made good time in reaching the Hopefield site. Since selecting it with Rev. Montgomery, Will and Abraham had traveled up on occasion, scouting out the best possible locations for cabins, and outbuildings.

They had planned to begin with a cabin for Will. It was a pleasant and hopeful turn of events that the first cabin would be built for an Osage family.

They hobbled their horses and walked the area through which Pryor's creek flowed. To the men from the mission, the best locations for a cabin were level ground some distance from the creek to avoid flooding. Star-That-Travels, however, walked through the site and would occasional squat to ground level while his eyes searched the distant horizon. For him the best location seemed to be one that gave him a clear sightline to every point on the compass.

The mission brothers watched respectfully, giving each other a quirked eyebrow now and again as the Osage warrior took his time in considering the location for his family's new home. Finally he stood from his crouch and pointed to the spot. "Here is where we will put our lodge."

"Good choice," Will said.

Abraham added, "You might want to bring your wife up to see what you've chosen. I know my wife would want to have some say where her home was going to be."

A speculative look came across Will's face. He seemed to be making a mental note of that information.

"Teresa will like what I chose," was all Star-That-Travels would say.

The men built a small fire to make coffee and unpacked the ham sandwiches they had brought for their dinner. Conversation centered on plans for felling the logs they would need for the cabin and the possibility of snow before they could finish it.

"Will it snow soon, do you think, Star?" George asked.

Star-That-Travels looked amused. "White man always thinks Indian knows when it will snow. You know the Maker of snow. What you think?"

The brothers laughed. "I think we'll all just have to wait and see what the Maker of snow will bring us," Will said.

Abraham smiled at the banter, but then sobered and asked their Osage friend. "Star-That-Travels, how did you come to the Christian faith?"

The warrior tossed out the grounds at the bottom of his coffee mug and then adjusted the blanket he wore over one shoulder. His eyes were thoughtful as he answered.

"I heard the trapper priest tell a story many years ago," he began. "He say that when God's Son was born a star traveled to the lodge where his mother held him. The star led the Old Men to find him and they brought him gifts to honor him."

The brothers leaned forward with interest as they heard the nativity told from a new perspective.

"I mocked the priest for his story," Star-That-Travels admitted. "I was young and did not understand. I did not believe a star could move alone across the sky. The stars move together like the buffalo. But the story would not go away from my heart. So I asked *Wah-Kon-Tah* to show me if this story was true. If it was true, I would believe and would honor his Son like the Old Men in the story.

"A few nights later my uncle came to me and said I must prepare for my naming ceremony," he continued. "So he led me out to the prairie to spend the night alone."

"What is the naming ceremony?" George asked.

"When you reach manhood, you are given an adult name," Star-That-Travels explained. "The name is something of bigness in your life. But I did not know what my name would be. My uncle would decide."

"So he left you alone to see if you could spend the night out in the wild?" Will asked.

"To see if I would be afraid," Star confirmed. "But I was not afraid. I had slept often out on the prairie, but never alone before. It was cold but uncle had left some coals for a fire. So I built the fire and sat beside it. I did not want to fall asleep because I was afraid uncle would find me sleeping and would say that I was not a man. I decided to count the stars to help keep me from sleep. And I remembered the priest's story.

"I asked again for *Wah-Kon-Tah* to show me the truth. And then I saw a star fall across the sky. And then another and another and another. I could not count them all. And I believed.

"When my uncle came for me in the morning, I told him what I saw. He said that stars fall sometimes, but I knew that *Wah-Kon-Tah* had showed me this to tell me the story of the star that traveled was true. So that is the name my uncle chose for me."

The Osage warrior paused and looked at the dying fire for a time. The other men must have sensed that there was more to the story for they waited quietly.

"I told the priest later about what happened and he water sprinkled me. Then I asked him what gift I could give the God-Son, like the Old Men in the story. He told me to give him myself, for that was the only thing that he didn't have and was what he wanted most in the world." Star-That-Travels voice was husky with emotion. "So that is what I gave him."

CHAPTER NINE

Hopefield Farm
December, 1822

The men from the mission spent the next few weeks working to get Teresa and Star's home completed before cold weather set in. The Osage couple worked with them, with a little uncertainty about the process of raising a cabin.

Putting up a traditional lodge usually took only a day's labor. The work of felling logs, trimming the branches, notching them for a cross-fit, lifting them into place and then daubing the walls with a mud and grass mixture was a much more lengthy process. In the meantime, they lived in the skin lodge that Teresa had erected near the cabin site.

When the final square of sod was laid on the roof and Will had tested their fireplace, the Osage family prepared to move inside. Here Teresa had the say in the arrangement. No beds or chairs were placed in her home. They would sleep as they did in the lodge, on layers of shaggy buffalo hides. Colorful blankets provided seating.

Though there were Cherokees in the neighborhood who lived in cabins, few Osages did so. The group had received visits from friends and family of Teresa and Star-That-Travels, curious about this new living arrangement. Many were derisive of the log structure.

Star-That-Travels bore their remarks in stoic silence. But it was clear to the missionaries that the man might pay a high price for his decision to embrace a new way. Change came hard for many of the Indians.

After he wrapped their saw in a leather pouch and set it into the mission wagon, Abraham walked over to where Star-That-Travels stood looking up at the smoke rising from the chimney of the cabin.

He rested a hand on the warrior's shoulder. "Will building this cabin cause problems for you, Star?" he asked quietly.

Star-That-Travels smiled ruefully. "Yes," he answered in his bluntly honest way. "But Teresa and I knew this when we made our decision. It is why we chose to build here instead of near your mission. We do not wish to cause problems for you as well."

"We appreciate that consideration, Star," Rev. Chapman stated. "But please understand that we have made our decision to work among your people. We knew it might cost us something as well. If you ever face trouble up here, don't hesitate to come to the mission."

Will nodded his agreement as he and George walked by with the horses, ready to hitch them to the wagon for the trip back home.

"I'll be starting my cabin up here soon, I hope," Will said. "Got to take care of something before then, but hopefully I can get it completed this winter."

George gave his brother a questioning look, but nodded when Will gave him a wink. Montgomery's remark about bringing a wife to his cabin seemed to have built a fire in the mission's stonemason.

The day after the men completed the cabin, everyone at the mission rode up in wagons to see it. The women all brought gifts to share with Teresa – jars of canned vegetables, down pillows and a patchwork quilt they had all helped stitch together.

Rev. Vaille offered a prayer of blessing over the Osage family's new home. Then they shared the dinner Amanda had packed before returning to the mission. Clarissa was pleased that Louisa would continue to live close enough to attend school. And, if she had observed correctly, Teresa would have a new little one soon who might be a future student in her class.

The women were discussing Teresa's apparent condition that afternoon as they worked in the kitchen to prepare not only supper for that Saturday evening, but also Sunday's dinner. "I'm so happy for Teresa," Rachel commented as she chopped potatoes for tomorrow's meal. "She endured such sadness when Mr. Revoir was killed. I'm glad she's found happiness again."

"Nothing like a new little one to bring joy to a home," Martha Woodruff agreed.

Phoebe was keeping Thea and Joseph in the dining room so the women felt free to talk about Teresa's pregnancy. Though she had assured them she was fine, they all were sensitive to the time of sadness Phoebe had also endured.

Amanda finished rubbing some dried sage from her herb garden on the three prairie chickens she would roast on a spit over the fire. A little giggle escaped her lips.

"Alright, Amanda," Asie Vaille said, placing hands on her hips. "Out with it. Will you need to borrow my maternity dresses after Mrs. Spaulding has finished with them?"

Clarissa and Eliza both turned to look at their former roommate who was blushing. "Aye," Amanda smiled. "Mr. Fuller and I will be welcoming a wee little one come spring."

The women offered hugs of congratulations to the cook. Two more babies would become a part of their mission family in the coming months. Clarissa might have felt a twinge of jealousy had she not been blessed with baby Thea. But as she too offered a hug to Amanda, she noticed a stricken look on Eliza's face.

Eliza quickly masked it with a look of cool indifference, but it gave the school teacher a rare pang of sympathy for the beautiful young woman. Dragged unwillingly to this prairie outpost by her sister, Eliza must truly feel trapped with an uncertain future ahead of her.

Clarissa's feelings changed abruptly after supper, however, when she observed Eliza hurrying to catch up with Dr. Palmer as he walked toward his cabin.

"A lovely evening, isn't it, Doctor?" Eliza said as she fell into step with him.

He slowed his pace and moved toward the path that led to the schoolhouse. It would never do to have Eliza visit with him in the bachelors' cabin.

"Yes, quite nice this evening," he agreed.

"We've just heard Mrs. Fuller's joyful news," Eliza added. "I do hope neither she nor my sister have troubles. It's such an uncertain thing for women out here in these primitive conditions."

Marcus felt uncomfortable with the topic of conversation and wondered where Eliza was taking it. "Yes, it can be, unfortunately," he said.

"I know you felt so badly for poor Sally's death," Eliza pushed forward as their steps took them past the schoolhouse and back around toward the dining hall. "And that poor Pawnee girl, Whitestar. Do you ever wish you hadn't come out here? I mean, it's a difficult place to practice medicine."

"I knew I would be facing such conditions when I came," the doctor stated. "I don't have any regrets."

"But don't you miss New England?" Eliza pressed. "I know I certainly do."

Marcus stood still for a moment but resisted the instinct to pat the young woman on the shoulder in sympathy. "You miss your friends back home," he stated.

"I want to go home," Eliza said, her lips forming a pretty little pout. "But Alice won't let me travel alone." She placed a hand on the doctor's arm. "I need someone to take me." She looked up into his eyes and a tear seemed to glisten in her own bright blue ones.

Marcus understood then where the conversation was going. He knew the disapproval and even dangers an attractive young woman would face if she attempted to travel alone. But he was not prepared to make the offer he knew she wanted from him. To travel home with her without a chaperone would require that he marry her. And his heart belonged to someone else.

Gently he removed her hand from his arm and gave it a

sympathetic squeeze. "I don't plan to return to New England, Miss Cleaver," he said. "But I do hope you'll find a way to get back home if that is what you desire."

"You care not at all about what I desire," Eliza said in a disappointed huff. Then she turned on her heel and hurried to her own cabin leaving the doctor standing in the growing dusk.

On Monday Will announced at breakfast that he planned to travel to Harmony Mission. "With Rev. Chapman's permission, I'll be heading up there today," he told the group after their devotions had been completed.

Most of the mission family seemed surprised at his decision, but Amanda had a knowing look on her face. "Oh, you must send our greetin's to Miss Comstock," she said with a smile.

Will ducked his head slightly and his face flushed a little. "Yes, I'll be sure to do so," he said. "I'll be visiting with Mr. Austin about the sawmill he has operating at Harmony."

"Then you'd better send your brother's greetings to young Mary Austin," Mrs. Woodruff laughed. The missionaries loved to tease George about the 11-year-old girl who had once declared her intention to marry him. They had never let him forget it.

George grinned good naturedly. "No need for that now," he returned, with a shake of his head.

"Let me pack you some food, Mr. Will," Amanda offered as they all stood to leave the breakfast tables and get to the work of the day.

"I'd appreciate that, Mrs. Fuller," Will said and followed her into the kitchen.

The teachers and students walked to the schoolhouse and the other men went to their daily chores of chopping wood, seeing to the livestock, and making needed repairs around the mission compound. The women began to clear the dishes from the tables and straighten the dining room while Asie and Phoebe fed the babies.

Amanda began to assemble a basket of food for Will. He

stood watching her, clearly wanting to say something, but hesitating.

"Well, what is it, Mr. Will?" Amanda asked, looking up from her work.

"What should I say to her?" Will spoke softly so no one else could hear his query.

"Just be honest with her," Amanda advised, careful to keep her voice low as well. "If her feelin's are the same as they were last year, she'll welcome your words."

"Do you think so?"

"Yes, I do," Amanda confirmed as she cut a generous wedge from a wheel of cheese.

"I'm afraid Rev. Montgomery may be paying her call." Will sighed.

Amanda handed the husky man her basket filled with good things from her larder. "Then you best not be lettin' any grass grow under your feet," she said. Then she pointed to the door. "Now be off with you," she said, "and don't come home until you've settled things with Miss Susan."

"Yes, ma'am," Will grinned, grasping the long handle of the basket that he could loop over his saddle horn. He made his way to the barn where Robbie was currying the mustang Will would ride to Missouri. Together they saddled the horse and Will tied on his bedroll, saddlebags and the food hamper. He led the horse to the corral where George awaited him.

"So you're gonna do this?" George asked.

"I'm gonna try," Will returned. Others of the mission family were gathering at the fence to say goodbye. "Safe journey, Requa," Rev. Vaille said as he shook Will's hand.

"Thanks," Will said. "I'll stop and check on Star-That-Travels."

"You'll probably pass the children on their way to school," Marcus said. Though now December, it still hadn't turned so cold that they children couldn't ride to school. Star-That-Travels always accompanied them. The conflict with the Cherokees meant most of the Osages were hesitant to let their children travel alone.

"Yes, I suppose so," Will replied as he mounted the mustang. Then with a final wave, he headed toward the road that would take him across the Neosho to La Saline and then on to Harmony.

A few days later, Robbie announced that visitors were turning off the Osage Road and heading to the mission. "Riders comin'," he called from the corral where he was working with a young colt.

It wasn't a surprise to see a stranger approaching for more and more traffic on the road leading to Texas meant the mission frequently had visitors. They stopped for water from their spring, or have a wagon wheel repaired or to let the doctor look at an injury or treat an illness.

Travelers heading out from Missouri on the road to Texas were advised to "make a stop at Union Mission," a location with a good source of water and hospitable accommodations. It was not unusual to have a small wagon train pull into their yard to spend the night.

On this day, two men approached on horseback, coming up from Three Forks. Usually visitors from the south were associated with the government or the military and had followed the Arkansas River up from Fort Smith.

Rev. Chapman met the two riders as they dismounted at their corral. Recognizing one as Lieutenant Summers who had visited earlier with General Gaines, he greeted the young officer.

"Welcome, Lieutenant," he said, extending a hand. "What brings you back our way?"

"Colonel Arbuckle has sent me out with Mr. McCoy here," Charles answered, indicating his traveling companion. "He's to do some government surveying in this area."

The other man appeared to be in his early thirties and was tall and thin with dark hair. He extended his hand to the mission director. "Rev. Isaac McCoy," he said.

"Reverend?" Chapman repeated.

"Baptist Mission, from Kentucky" McCoy explained. "But I'm out here working as a surveyor."

"Well that sounds interesting," said Rev. Vaille who had joined the group. Others of the family were also gathering around their two visitors.

"Come join us for some coffee in the dining hall," Vaille invited. "We'd like to hear about your project."

Those who weren't engaged in work sat down with their visitors to enjoy some coffee and molasses cookies. Rev. McCoy removed his dusty wide-brimmed hat and took the seat offered him.

Allowing the surveyor a moment to enjoy his coffee, the missionaries made conversation with Lieutenant Summers, asking about conditions at Fort Smith.

"Colonel Arbuckle has expanded the fort and brought in a new sutler from Fort Jesup, Louisiana." Charles told them. "But he's still waiting for word from Washington about a more western fort. There's some debate about whether it should be located on the Arkansas or on the Red River. Now that Mexico has secured its independence, Washington wants to be sure the boundary to the Texas territory is well established at the Red."

"It has been quiet out here since the treaty was signed," Abraham observed. "But we still would like to see a fort closer to us. I think even the Osages would prefer that as well."

"Colonel Arbuckle still wants it, but some other things have to be settled first," the lieutenant said. "Like boundary lines. That's why Mr. McCoy is here."

"So tell us about your work, McCoy," George said. As always, he seemed eager to learn about anything having to do with the West.

"It all goes back to an agreement the last Cherokee agent worked out between the Osages and Cherokees," McCoy explained. "His name was William Lovely and he negotiated a hunting outlet for the Cherokees in this area. The Osages were to be paid for the land by the federal government. It was never officially agreed to in Washington, however, and so it never actually went into effect."

"I remember reading something about it in the *Gazette*,"

Abraham said. "Called it Lovely's Purchase. From the article, it sounded like our mission was just inside this supposed buffer zone between the two tribes."

"Yes, well that is what I am here to determine," said McCoy. "The government is considering making the purchase a legal reality. But they want an established boundary line for the territory. I suspect that the eventual goal is to move the Cherokees now settled around Dardanelle out here to Lovely's Purchase."

"Seems like the government is always trying to induce the tribes to move further west," Chapman said ruefully. "When will it end?"

"I am of the opinion, as are many others back east, that the government should set up a territory just for Indians," the surveyor said. "Move them once, and don't ask them to move again. Create enough distance that the conflicts in the states can come to an end."

"And you think Lovely's territory would be enough for the Indians?" asked George.

"No, hardly so," McCoy replied. "I think all of the Kansas and western Arkansas Territories should be set aside for the Indians. There are few Americans out here yet and it's such a dry climate that most farmers won't wish to settle here."

Clarissa noticed that Mr. Fuller started to say something, but appeared to change his mind. After all, their farming operation was proving to be quite successful. Farming the land of the prairie was the very thing they were hoping to demonstrate to the Osages.

"I would like to use your mission as a base of operation," Rev. McCoy went on to say. "If that is agreeable to you. I will gladly pay for board and supplies."

"Certainly," Chapman stated. "You're welcome to come and go as you need to. We'll be very interested in learning exactly where you set the boundary line. It may impact our mission."

"You may find that once the boundaries are set that the western line of Lovely's Purchase will become the western boundary of Arkansas Territory," McCoy replied as he finished his coffee. "And you may find that this mission is now in Cherokee lands rather than Osage lands."

CHAPTER TEN

Harmony Mission, Bates County, Missouri
Christmas Season, 1822

"You'll stay through Christmas, won't you?" Mary Austin asked Will as he led his horse into the barn at Harmony Mission.

Will laughed at the red-haired girl's eagerness. "I have just arrived, Miss Mary," he said. "I don't want to presume upon your hospitality right from the start."

Mary gave the visiting stonemason a longsuffering look. "You would never do that," she assured him. Then she revealed her apparent purpose for following him into the barn where he unsaddled his horse. "Why didn't your brother come with you?"

Will hid his smile by turning to lift his saddle bags off the horse. "George has a great deal of work to do, keeping our mission stocked with firewood. You wouldn't want anyone at Union getting cold now would you?"

Mary considered this for a bit of time, her freckled nose scrunched in thought. "No," she finally sighed. "You have babies at Union. We have one baby here. Her name is Mary just like mine. We call her Little Mary."

"So I have heard," Will said with a tightness in his voice. Then more casually he asked, "Miss Comstock takes care of her, doesn't she?"

"Yes," Mary said, leaning against the wall of one of the stalls. "Either her or Miss Woolley."

"Mary, don't talk Brother Requa's ear off," her father scolded as he stepped into the barn.

"I wasn't," Mary protested, but she took that moment to make her exit.

"Welcome, Brother Requa," Daniel Austin said, offering his hand. Like Will, Austin was stocky and well-muscled. "What brings you our way?"

"Wanted to look over your saw mill," Will explained as the two men also exited the barn and made their way to the mission's dining hall. "I think we need one at Union, just as you suggested."

As they walked, Will's eyes darted about the Harmony compound. It was much different from Union. The structures here were constructed of sawn lumber and each family had a separate cabin. In fact, the mission looked like a small town with a neat row of whitewashed houses, a school, dormitory, church with a steeple and numerous other outbuildings.

When they stepped into the dining hall, Will stopped abruptly as if his feet had found a bog of mud. Across the room, Susan Comstock was feeding scrambled eggs to a chubby toddler. Susan looked up over the little girl's tight brown curls and her eyes widened in surprise.

"Oh, Mr. Requa," she said in her soft, little-girl voice. She had to grab Little Mary's hand to keep the girl from smearing eggs into her curls. But Susan's eyes never left Will's.

He quickly swept his wool cap off his head, unaware that the movement in the dry winter air made his straight brown hair stick out in all directions. Susan's smile was bemused, and very happy.

"Miss Comstock," Will nodded.

"That's right," Austin stated. "You two don't need introducing. You already know each other."

"Yes," both Will and Susan said together. But both seemed too tongue-tied to offer anything more.

Just then Rev. Montgomery entered from the opposite door, his arms loaded with kindling. Seeing Will, he quickly dropped the wood into a large basket beside the fireplace. "I heard you had arrived," he said, approaching Will. The two men shook hands.

Susan was working to clean Mary's hands, but the little girl threw them up toward her father, almost hitting the pretty blonde housemother in the nose. "Da," she said.

Montgomery turned to his daughter, smiling with fatherly pride. He walked over to where she sat in Susan's lap. Bending slightly, he tousled the girl's curls with one hand while he laid the other on the back of Susan's chair in a possessive gesture.

Will's hands strangled his cap.

By this time, Mary Austin had alerted others at the mission of Will's arrival. They began to gather in the dining hall to offer greetings to their guest. Like everyone on the frontier, they were eager for news beyond their own settlement and Will was pummeled with questions for a time. He was offered coffee and a seat at one of the tables across the room from Susan.

Throughout the afternoon's visit, Will and Susan continually looked each other's way, but both seemed caught across a chasm of social restraint that they didn't know how to cross.

When Martha Austin stepped into the dining room to announce that supper would be served, her husband stood from the table. "Let me show you where you can bunk while you're here," he offered their guest. "You can stow your bags and wash up."

"Thank you," Will said, standing also. "That would be good."

Supper might have been a pleasant affair, but Will ate with a tight jaw and jealousy in his eyes. Rev. Montgomery sat across from Susan at another table and they seemed to share an amiable conversation.

Harriett Woolley, the other housemother at Harmony Mission sat near Will and tried to draw him into conversation. But his answers were brief and he seemed preoccupied. Harriett followed his eyes with her own and saw the object of his interest. She smiled in pity for the young man whose shoulders slumped in defeat. How could a man who made his living with his hands hope to compete with a minister who made a living with words?

Later that evening Susan and Harriett made the rounds of the dormitory where girls slept on the first floor and boys on the second. Having tucked the students into bed, listened to their night time prayers and extinguished all candles, they settled into the room they shared.

"So this is your stonemason," Harriett said as the two women began to prepare for bed. Harriett was a plain, no nonsense woman of 25 who had cared for children for many years.

"He's not my stonemason," Susan protested, but her sweet voice made the protest sound rather weak. "He doesn't belong to me."

"Oh, but his heart does," Harriett said knowingly.

Susan shook her head, but then came to sit by Harriett on her bed. "Do you truly think so?" she asked.

"Listen, sister," Harriett said with affection. "I may be an old spinster, but I've seen the symptoms of love enough among my students that I recognize them. Your Mr. Requa is absolutely miserable and that's a sure sign of love."

"He's miserable?" Susan repeated, sounding uncertain about whether she should be happy or sad at his state.

"Miserable," Harriett affirmed. "But he's scared to say anything to you."

"Scared," Susan repeated again in disbelief. "Why would a strong, handsome man like him be scared of anything?"

"You don't know much about men, do you?"

"No."

"Well, let me tell you," Harriett said, patting Susan's hand. "Men, especially the strong ones, don't like that weak in the knees feeling that love gives them. It scares them to think that a woman can have that much power over them."

"But women don't have power," Susan protested.

"We don't have political power, or physical power," Harriett agreed. "But we have power of the heart and that's the greatest power of all."

Susan looked unconvinced.

"You have to encourage your stonemason to show you his heart."

"I don't think I can," Susan sighed. "I tried when I was at Union Mission, but it did no good."

Harriett looked thoughtful. "You just leave everything to me," she advised.

"Alright," Susan agreed, but she looked as if she might regret what Harriett might do.

At Union Mission, the family was preparing for another snowless Christmas. The mission children all remembered the holiday in New England and bemoaned the lack of snow. There was little greenery to provide decorations so Clarissa's students cut strips of newsprint from old copies of the *Gazette* for paper chains.

There was plenty of corn to pop and then string together, but without a Christmas tree there seemed little reason to do so. George promised that he would try to scout out an evergreen the next time he went elk hunting.

Teresa showed Clarissa and Amanda how to make a red dye with poke berries she had harvested in the summer. The girls soaked their newsprint strips in the dye and soon their fingers were as red as the paper. After the strips dried, they applied generous globs of flour paste to form the chains.

Then the girls directed Robbie and Paul in hanging their creation around the door and window frames and in long swags across the ceiling.

For the Osage girls, who knew little about Christmas traditions, the efforts brought many perplexed looks and giggles. But they entered into the preparations with enthusiasm.

Deer-in-Water and Masina Chouteau were delighted with the transformation of their classroom as it was festooned with the bright chains.

Tassie and Lena Bradley were boarding at the mission which may have been what prompted Paul to shimmy up a tall cottonwood tree at the river's edge to harvest a bunch of mistletoe. Twelve-year-old Tassie gave the apprentice a shy smile of thanks when he presented it to her.

The girls placed the bit of greenery on teacher's desk around a fat white candle. Clarissa decided not to tell the girls about the "kissing tradition" associated with the mistletoe.

A few days before Christmas, the mission received a visit from Richard Bean, one of two brothers who operated a salt mining operation on the Illinois River between Three Forks and Fort Smith. This shallow tributary to the Arkansas River flowed through flinty hills and was clear and cold. The Bean brothers had one of the most successful salt mining operations in the region. A salt spring provided them with gallons of briny water that they boiled in huge kettles to extract the salt.

Mr. Bean drove his wagon into the mission yard and was met by Stephen and Abraham. In the wagon he had two barrels of salt and several bushel baskets of shelled corn.

Setting the brake on the wagon, the bearded farmer hopped down from the seat and drew off his driving gloves.

"Welcome to Union Mission," Abraham greeted the tall, lanky man.

"Good to finally get up here to see you," Richard Bean replied as the men shook hands. "We heared you started a grist mill. Wanted to know if you'd take some salt in trade for grinding some corn for us."

"We'd be glad to," Stephen replied. "Pull your wagon around behind the barn and we'll help you unload."

With Paul and Alexander helping, they quickly hauled the baskets of corn into the grist mill while Stephen and Robbie led four oxen into the traces. After the cattle were secured, they started moving the huge stones that would grind the dark kernels.

Richard Bean grinned as he watched the mission brothers quickly set the grist mill into operation. "Ya'll been doin' this some, ain't you?" he said, clearly impressed with how smoothly the mill functioned.

"We harvested about 80 bushels an acre from our fields," Stephen replied. "We've ground about half of it."

Bean whistled. "Ya'll have good soil up here. Ours is a

little flinty. Wish we had a penny for every rock we've pulled out of our fields."

"Yes, we're blessed with rich soil," their farmer agreed. "But it's heavy, hard to plow. We go through plowshares wicked often."

"Same with us," Bean nodded. "But ours get beat up by the rocks."

"Good that you have your salt business," Stephen commiserated, watching Robbie slowly empty the first basket of corn into the hopper.

"Yep," Bean agreed. "We just got us an exclusive contract with the new sutler at Fort Smith. We'll be providing the garrison with all its salt."

Now Stephen looked impressed. "Congratulations," he said. "Salt's as good as gold out here."

"Yep," Richard nodded. "Few people on the frontier have much coin. We all use salt for trading. That's how we pay Mr. Bogey for all those plowshares," he laughed.

The men stood and watched the oxen slowly plod the circle for a while, then Stephen invited the trader to pull his wagon to the kitchen lean-to where they could unload the salt barrels.

"I'm sure my wife would be glad to offer you a cup of coffee," he said.

"Sounds good," their visitor agreed.

Mr. Bean was invited by Rev. Chapman to stay for dinner so he joined the missionaries in the dining hall for bowls of thick potato soup with cornbread and stewed cabbage. As with any visitor, they plied him with questions about conditions beyond the confines of the mission.

"We haven't heard about any conflicts between the Cherokees and Osages," Rev. Vaille said. "You're closer to Cherokee settlement; does it seem like they're going to honor the peace treaty?"

"Ain't but a few families down around us," Bean said. "But they seem like peaceable folks. Don't think anybody goes looking for trouble, but it does seem like it finds its way to us, don't it?"

"Yes, it does," Chapman agreed. Then he asked, "Are you a believer, Mr. Bean."

The man looked rather uncomfortable at the question. "Wa'll, yes," he said, stroking his long dark beard in thought. "Cain't nobody look up at the heavens and not be a believer in God, now can they? But me and my brother Mark ain't never been much for church, if that's what you're asking."

"I just wanted you to know that you and your brother are welcome to our special Christmas service this coming Sabbath," Chapman said.

"Oh, yeah," Bean said, "Mighty obliged for the invitation. I'll talk to Mark and see if he wants to ride up."

"We won't have your corn all ground today," Stephen said. "You ought to come up on Saturday and we'll load up your wagon. You can stay for the Christmas service and then head home on Monday." The missionaries were strong believers in not traveling on the Sabbath day.

"Wa'll that sounds like a possible plan," Bean drawled. He looked as if he felt caught in a missionary trap. His eyes darted around the group and then fell on Eliza who was absentmindedly running her spoon around her soup bowl. Feeling his gaze on her, she looked up and bestowed upon him a smile.

Richard returned her smile and said, "I think coming back for Christmas is a mighty good plan."

He failed to see the frown that Alice bestowed upon him.

After their noon meal was completed, Bean turned his wagon toward the Osage Road to head back down to Three Forks. Eliza walked Alice back to the Spaulding cabin and helped her get settled into a rocking chair with her feet up on a crate covered with a quilt. Soon to give birth, Alice needed help getting in and out of the rocker.

As Eliza fluffed a pillow to set behind her sister's back, Alice looked at her closely.

"Don't lead that man on, Eliza," she said after a moment.

Eliza looked genuinely surprised at her sister's words. "What man?" she asked.

"You know who I mean," Alice huffed, "that Mr. Bean."

"Why would I lead him on?" Eliza asked, a look of innocence on her face.

"Simply because you know you can," Alice replied. "I want better for you than some frontier farmer with half his teeth missing." The remark was not accurate, for Mr. Bean appeared to be missing only one tooth.

"Then you should have thought of that before you dragged me out here," Eliza returned archly. "There's little choice around this mission."

"Just don't lead him to think you would consider marriage to him," Alice softened her tone. "That would hardly be fair to him. You can turn the head of any man you want. Wait for someone of better quality than a country bumpkin."

"I can hardly have any man I want," Eliza countered with some bitterness as she made her way to the door. Stepping outside, she finished her thought out of Alice's hearing. Murmuring low to herself she said somewhat defiantly, "And I'll marry whoever will take me back to New England."

In the days leading up to Christmas at Harmony Mission, Will found himself with hardly a spare moment to attend to the real purpose for his visit. Mr. Austin kept him busy showing him the operation of their grist mill and saw mill for the better course of one day. Then he proposed they ride into the hills the following day to evaluate the possibility of harvesting lumber for the Hopefield cabins.

The two men were just preparing to ride out in the morning when Susan happened to walk by the corral. She was carrying Little Mary toward the dining hall, but she slowed her steps as she passed Will and Daniel Austin.

Will froze in place with his left foot already in the stirrup. He tried to quickly extract it and nearly fell. He face went deep red.

Susan hid a smile in Mary's curls.

"How are you today, Mr. Requa?" she asked when she could do so without laughing.

"Very fine, Miss Comstock," Will replied, again

sweeping off his cap. "Mr. Austin and I were just going to look at wood."

"How nice," Susan said, though she looked puzzled.

"For my cabin at Hopefield," Will further explained.

"Oh yes, *your* cabin," Susan repeated flatly. She shifted the squirming child to her other arm, but stood waiting, as if hoping for Will to say something more. When he didn't she sighed, bid the men good day and then continued on to the dining room.

Will's sigh matched Susan's as he mounted his horse. Austin had watched the exchange with a knowing look in his eyes.

"Tomorrow you might want to ride into Pappinville," he suggested as they pointed their horses toward the Ozark hills. "It's not much of a town, but it does have a mercantile there. You might want to do a little Christmas shopping."

"I wouldn't know what to buy her," Will mumbled. He seemed unaware that his words confirmed what Daniel Austin had just surmised.

When the men returned that afternoon, Harriett Woolley met Will as he walked from the corral toward the dining hall.

"Might I have a word with you, Mr. Requa?" she asked, falling into step with him.

Will looked at her in surprise, but said, "Yes, ma'am."

"It's miss," Harriett corrected the stonemason. "I'm not married."

Will got a wary look on his face.

"Oh, don't worry," Harriett rolled her eyes. "I'm not trying to drag you to the altar. I want to talk to you about Susan."

"Miss Comstock?"

"Yes," Harriett said with longsuffering patience. "Miss Comstock. I have every reason to believe that Susan has feelings for you. And if I have observed correctly, you have an affection for her as well. Am I correct in this?" She spoke in the crisp tones of a school teacher trying to help a rather slow student learn an important lesson.

Will's face reddened slightly, but he nodded. "I think she's wonderful," he admitted.

"Have you told her that?"

"I don't know how."

"You just told me how you feel," Harriett countered. "Why can't you tell her?"

"I just get all tongue-tied when she's around," Will tried to explain. "I'm afraid she'll laugh at me."

"Any woman who would laugh at a man for telling her she's wonderful doesn't deserve that man," Harriett stated firmly. Then she took Will's arm and steered him away from the dining hall where the students were enjoying toast and jam after school.

"Do you know where Pappinville is?" she asked as they walked toward the barn.

"Mr. Austin pointed out the road to me today," Will confirmed. "Just an hour's ride southwest, he said."

"Exactly." Harriett lowered her voice conspiratorially. "Now here is what you are going to do."

George had managed to find a somewhat straggly little cedar to serve as a Christmas tree for the Union Mission. It occupied a place in the corner of the boy's classroom which also doubled as the chapel on Sundays.

The girls had generously donated some of their red chains to adorn the little tree. Both the boys and the girls had strung popcorn, eating about as much as made it onto the long crochet threads Mrs. Woodruff had provided.

As the girls decorated the tree after class on Friday, they chattered excitedly about the upcoming holiday. The missionaries at Union did not exchange gifts except for providing small presents for the children's stockings. But the women had been cooking special dishes for the Christmas Day meal and the stockings were lined across the massive dining hall fireplace. It was enough to create quite a sense of anticipation among the children.

Abigail Chapman worked beside her teacher as they wound the popcorn strings around the tree.

"We always had lots of candles on the tree at Grandmother's house," she said to Clarissa.

"I imagine that would have been a lovely sight," Clarissa said.

"It was beautiful," Abigail confirmed. "But the biggest trees we ever had were at the mansion."

"The mansion?" Clarissa asked.

"The Governor's House," Abigail explained in a matter of fact tone. "I don't remember much about the house; but I remember the big tree that always stood in the front hall."

It was then that Clarissa remembered that Rachel Chapman's father had served two terms as governor of Connecticut.

"It's very different out here than back home, isn't it?" she asked, wondering if Abigail missed New England as much as Miss Eliza.

"Yes," Abigail agreed. "But we are doing a good work here and that's important."

Clarissa smiled at the girl's solemn tone, sure that she was repeating something she had heard her mother say.

"Do you miss it?" the teacher asked.

"No, not really," Abigail said, not quite understanding the question. "Grandmother never let us run or play in the mansion. Thomas was always getting into trouble. And Papa hated going there. He said he would rather visit the needy in the poorhouse."

The nine-year-old was too young to understand that she was telling things her parents wouldn't have wanted told.

Clarissa decided to steer the conversation in another direction.

"I think we are done here, girls," she said. "Who wants some of Mrs. Fuller's cookies?"

The girls were hurrying to don their coats before the teacher could suggest that very thing. She followed in their wake as they raced to the dining hall. She made a mental note to herself to explain to the girls that proper young ladies never raced to the table.

Their Christmas Sabbath service was well attended by several Osage families as well as the Chouteaus and Pryors. As Stephen had suggested, Richard Bean and his brother Captain Mark Bean had returned on Saturday and were in attendance also. Both appeared to have given each other haircuts and they had trimmed their beards and donned clean plaid shirts.

Mr. Spaulding led the children in singing a few Christmas songs to the solemn appreciation of the adults. Clarissa had a hard time keeping Thea in her lap while the songs were being sung. The little girl had learned to stand and could take steps as long as she held on to something. The bright little Christmas tree had caught her eye and oh how she wanted to touch it.

Following the sermon offered by Rev. Chapman, the worshipers moved to the dining hall for the special Christmas feast Amanda had worked on for days. Two big turkeys had roasted over a low fire overnight and ham from their smokehouse had been set to bake this morning. White and sweet potatoes, canned corn and peas, a big pot of beans with onion, molasses and bacon, light bread and corn bread, stuffing and three kinds of pickles, pecan pies and apple cobbler for dessert filled the serving table.

While the women set about getting the dishes assembled and the tables set, the children were allowed to check their stockings for gifts. Dr. Palmer lifted each one down for them and had them all giggling with wild guesses about what each stocking held. Clarissa smiled as she watched him interact with the children.

Even Thea had a little knitted sock that Martha had made for her. It was filled with soft molasses candy, bright ribbons for her hair, a rattle and carved blocks, even an Osage beaded bracelet made by Teresa. Of course, everything went into her mouth and Clarissa had to finally set her gifts out of reach for the time being.

Clarissa noticed that Eliza had found two admirers to sit with her during the Christmas feast. Though the Bean brothers seemed like nice enough men, they hardly fit her idea of the sort of gentlemen Eliza would allow to pay her court. But this was the frontier. Perhaps Eliza had decided to settle with a farmer from the neighborhood and build the best life she could for herself out here on the prairie.

At Harmony Mission, Will pushed back from the table after enjoying the fine Christmas meal the women had prepared. The school children had been dismissed to play in a light snow that was falling outside.

He sat for a time in conversation with Daniel and a few of the other men at the mission, discussing Missouri politics, the weather, plans for crops come spring, and preaching opportunities among the Osages. All the while, he sent glances Susan's way, watching as she helped the other women clear the tables and carry dishes into the kitchen to be washed and dried.

After a time, the dining hall began to empty as some slipped on coats to join the children in a bit of fun or to walk to their cabins for a nap. Across the room Rev. Montgomery sat in conversation with Dr. Belcher. At another table Miss Woolley and Miss Comstock sat with heads together perusing a magazine.

Will sat alone. Hands on his knees as if willing himself to rise, nevertheless he remained seated. His nervousness was evident. Finally Harriett sent him a commanding look such as she might give a wayward student. Will started to stand, but at that moment Montgomery also stood and made his way to the table where the two housemothers sat.

"Mighty fine meal today, ladies," the minister complimented them.

"Thank you, Brother Montgomery," Susan said looking up at him where he stood at her elbow.

Harriett speared Will with another look that any man would recognize as an "obey me right now or else!" command. He stood and walked across the room, hands stuffed in his big coat pockets.

"I was wondering, Miss Comstock . . ." Montgomery began.

"Rev. Montgomery, might I have a word with you?" Harriett interrupted.

"A word with me, Miss Woolley?" the minister repeated.

"Yes, about the students," Harriett responded. Then turning to Susan she said, "You don't mind if I join Brother Montgomery and Dr. Belcher for a moment, do you?"

"No," Susan said. Her sweet voice implied she had no idea what Harriett was about, but there was a twinkle in her eyes.

Harriett stood and gave Will one last look and a nod of encouragement. Then with Montgomery following behind, she crossed the room to Dr. Belcher's table.

Will stopped in front of Susan's chair. "Miss Comstock," he began, then hesitated.

"Yes, Mr. Requa," Susan encouraged.

"Would you care to take a walk with me?"

Susan's face was wreathed with a smile. "I would like that."

After helping the pretty young woman into her coat, Will opened the door for her and they stepped out into the winter afternoon. The snow had stopped but clouds hung low in the sky. It was not terribly cold though, so the couple began a leisurely walk away from the dining hall.

"Miss Woolley must be a good hand with the students," Will remarked.

"She certainly is," Susan agreed. "She is strict but fair. The students respect her."

"There is a verse in the Psalms that says God guides us with his eye," Will said. "I think he has bestowed this gift upon Miss Woolley as well."

Susan giggled, "Yes, she can issue commands without saying a word."

The housemother's laughter seemed to help her suitor relax.

"I owe you an apology, Miss Comstock," he said.

"I cannot think why you would," Susan said, looking puzzled.

"When you decided to leave Union and come work here

at Harmony, I should have told you . . . I should have asked
you . . ." Will's words seemed to logjam in his mouth. "I
thought you didn't care . . ."

"I thought you didn't want me to stay," Susan tried to
explain. They stood still and looked at each other in the eye.

"I'm sorry," both said at once. Then with widening
smiles, they resumed their walk.

Will reached into his coat pocket and pulled out a brown-
paper package tied with string. He had tucked a bit of pine
twig and a tiny pine cone into the string.

With a slight blush, he handed it to her and said, "Happy
Christmas."

Susan took it, her eyes widening in surprise. "How
pretty," she said of the package.

"I know you like pretty things," Will said, trying to sound
indifferent, but clearly pleased that she liked the gift wrap.

Susan hesitated to open it. "I'm afraid I haven't a gift for
you," she said with regret.

"It's alright," Will shrugged. "Besides I have something
in mind you might give me."

Susan ducked her head but looked up at him shyly
through lowered lashes. "Oh?"

Will laughed, but pointed to the gift. "Open it," he urged.

Carefully Susan removed the string, slipping the pine
cone and twig into her own pocket. Pulling back the paper,
she found six freshly sharpened colored pencils.

"How did you know?" she asked, delight in her voice.
Susan was an accomplished artist and loved to sketch.

"Miss Woolley told me you'd been looking at them at the
mercantile for months," Will explained. "She suggested I get
them for you. So I rode in to town yesterday."

"They are perfect," Susan sighed. "Thank you."

"I was hoping you might make a sketch for me," Will
said. "That could be your gift to me, if you want."

"Oh, I'd love to sketch something for you," Susan
agreed. "What would you like?"

"A log cabin," Will suggested. "I mean . . . our log
cabin. For Hopefield Farm."

"Our cabin?"

"Yes," Will said and there in the snow he went down on one knee. "If you would agree to be my wife and share a home with me." Looking up into her eyes he drew a deep breath of courage. "I . . . I love you, Miss Comstock. Will you marry me?"

Susan covered her trembling lips as tears filled her eyes. For a moment all she could do was nod, but finally said, "Yes, I will."

"Then can I get up now?" Will asked. "I'm freezing."

Susan threw back her head and laughed. "You silly. Yes, stand up."

Will stood and reached for Susan's hand. She allowed him to intertwine her fingers into the warmth of his own. They turned to walk back to the dining hall.

"But why do you want me to sketch a cabin?" Susan asked.

"Because Redfield told me that women like to have some say in their house," he explained. "I can't take you down to the Hopefield site until we're married. But I thought you could draw a picture of what you would like. And I'll do my best to build it for you."

CHAPTER ELEVEN

Union Mission
Winter, 1822-23

Clarissa woke on the morning after Christmas while the cabin was still dark. Something had awakened her and she lay in a sleepy fog trying to determine what it was. Prying her eyes open, she looked across the room toward Eliza's bed. From the soft ember glow of the fireplace she could see the young woman was clothed and pulling on her navy wool cape. On her bed was an overstuffed carpetbag. Clarissa had to muffle a gasp of surprise.

The schoolteacher lay quietly watching Eliza as she grasped the handles of her bag and walked to the door. The young woman threw a glance at Clarissa before opening the door to step outside. With extreme care, she closed it behind her.

Clarissa threw off her bed quilts and reached for a wool wrapper. Thrusting her feet into her boots, she hurried to the door and opened it slightly. There was a narrow rim of pink dawn on the eastern horizon giving enough light for her to watch Eliza make her way to the barn.

Clarissa's jaw tightened. The Bean brothers had bedded down in the barn and were planning to leave at sunrise this morning to travel back to their farm. It appeared that Eliza planned to join them.

What was the girl thinking, Clarissa wondered in alarm. And what should she do? She could follow and try to stop Eliza before the brothers pulled their wagon out of the barn.

But she was hardly dressed to head into a possible confrontation with two strange men. And it would take too long for her to dress properly.

Pulling on her own cloak and grabbing a hat to cover her disheveled hair, Clarissa made her way to the Spaulding cabin. She knocked lightly, hoping she could arouse her fellow teacher without wakening anyone else. It took a few moments for Mr. Spaulding to open the door. He looked quite surprised to find Clarissa standing there.

"I'm sorry to disturb you, Mr. Spaulding," Clarissa whispered. "But I felt I must tell you that I have seen Eliza carrying her luggage to the barn. I believe she is planning to leave the mission."

John looked beyond Clarissa and squinted to catch a glimpse of his sister-in-law as she reached the barn door. "Thank you Miss Johnson," he said. "I'll see to it."

Clarissa nodded and then walked slowly back to her cabin, her curiosity making her reluctant to simply go back to bed. She stood at her door and watched as John emerged from his cabin having pulled on his coat over his long nightshirt. He was carrying a musket.

Clarissa drew a sharp breath and began to pray. "Please, Father, don't let anyone get hurt."

Glancing down the row of cabin doors, she could tell that Alice was also watching.

All was quiet at the barn . . . no yelling voices and thankfully no gunfire was heard. Inside its confines, John walked toward the Beans' wagon, holding his musket across his chest. Having failed to put on his spectacles, he had to squint at the three people sitting on the wagon seat.

"What do you think you are doing?" the teacher asked.

Richard Bean threw up his hands. "Now, hold on," he said. "We didn't intend no harm to the girl. We just planned to get her to the steamboat landing at Dwight Mission."

Eliza stared at the man in disbelief. "You said you would take me to New England," she accused.

Bean looked shamefaced. "Now, a man will say just about anything to a pretty woman," he excused himself.

"What I said was that a man would be happy to take you anywhere you wanted to go. Didn't mean I'd travel all the way to New York with you myself."

"Get down from the wagon, sister," John said to Eliza.

Angrily Eliza pushed past Richard and clambered down from the high seat, ignoring the hand Mark Bean offered her. She tried to pull her valise from back of the wagon but was not tall enough to lift it over the side. John took another step forward and pulled the bag out himself.

"Let's get back to Alice," he said. "She'll be worried."

Captain Bean spoke up as the two walked toward the barn door. "We really didn't mean any harm," he said, seeming sincere in his apology. "We thought we were being of a help to the young lady."

"Yeah," his younger brother nodded.

John turned back and seemed to consider his words carefully. "Then have a safe trip home," was all he said. Then he led Eliza outside.

Clarissa saw John and Eliza emerge from the structure. John carried Eliza's valise and she walked with her head down and shoulders hunched. As they arrived at the Spaulding cabin, Eliza's quiet sobs reached Clarissa. She closed her door and hurried to get back into bed.

Clarissa stretched out under the quilts and silently prayed for poor Eliza. How unhappy she must be if she was willing to risk her reputation by traveling even to Three Forks with the two brothers.

Within a few minutes, Eliza slipped into the cabin and made her way to her bed. Through her lashes, Clarissa watched as the young woman sat down and began to unbutton her cloak. A forlorn sense of defeat surrounded her and she sniffled quietly.

In a little voice she said, "Thank you, Miss Johnson."

Clarissa was surprised by her words. She had expected Eliza to be furious with her. Giving up her pretense of sleep, Clarissa opened her eyes. "I am sorry you are so unhappy here, Eliza," she said quietly. "I promise to try to help you get home if that is truly what you want."

"It doesn't matter," Eliza shrugged, her words flat. "Having to live here is my punishment."

"Punishment?" Clarissa repeated, sitting up to look at her roommate. "Whatever for?"

"For being vain," Eliza said. "Alice says I think too much of myself."

Now Clarissa threw off her covers again and went to sit beside Eliza. Putting an arm around her, she pulled the girl close. Eliza did not resist but rested her cheek on Clarissa's shoulder and cried anew.

"You are not vain," Clarissa soothed with conviction. "It is not fair that people assume because a woman is beautiful that she is therefore vain."

"I try not to be," Eliza said.

"I know," Clarissa agreed and she had to acknowledge to herself that it was true. Though she had often felt resentment toward Eliza for her effortless beauty, the girl did not simper in front of the mirror endlessly. She took care of her looks, but no more so than Clarissa did herself and certainly not as much as Mrs. Chapman who always looked impeccably coifed as if she were about to serve high tea at "the mansion."

Clarissa smiled at her thought. Rubbing Eliza's arm she asked, "What were you thinking, girl?"

Eliza sighed. "I don't know. I've made a fool of myself."

"No," Clarissa countered. "No one else knows what happened this morning. I'll certainly not tell and I'm sure Mr. and Mrs. Spaulding won't either."

"Alice threatened to make me move back in with them so she could keep an eye on me," Eliza confided. "If she didn't have the baby coming, I think she probably would."

"Well, she needn't do that," Clarissa stated. "I'll be your big sister and look out for you myself. Just let me know if you get some idea to run off again and I'll talk you out of it." She smiled as she said it to let Eliza know she was just trying to lighten the mood.

"Thank you," Eliza said through a stifled yawn.

"You need to get some more sleep," Clarissa stated.

"You get back to bed and I'll ask Amanda for a breakfast tray. I'll tell her you're not feeling well. That's the truth, isn't it?"

"Yes," Eliza said. "That's the truth."

The prairie winter would have seemed rather cheerless if not brightened by the first birthday celebrations for Joseph and a few weeks later for Thea. Both were taking tentative steps and everyone had to keep a watchful eye that they didn't get too close to the fireplaces.

Will rode back from Harmony and showed the family a very pretty sketch of a log cabin with real glass windows that Susan had made. His news of their engagement was met with smiles all around. Amanda rolled her eyes at him and said, "Well, it's about time."

The weather had been dry and Stephen expressed concern over dinner one day about the lack of moisture. "The fields are turning hard," he said. "Going to be even tougher to plow come spring if we don't get rain or snow soon."

"Snow, please," James Chapman said as he finished a bowl of bread pudding. Everyone laughed at his eager request. "We want snow."

"Normally I might not agree with you," Stephen replied, reaching over to tousle the boy's hair. "But at this point I'll take anything. River level is getting low as well."

"That must be why we haven't seen Mr. Bogey in a while," Rachel mused. "River traffic has slowed our usual mail delivery. I am missing having a letter from my mother."

"And we still haven't received permission from the Society for Hopefield," her husband added.

Clarissa silently agreed with Mrs. Chapman. She usually received at least two letters a year from her family back at Colchester and she was hoping for one soon.

Their hope for mail and snow was met on the same day just a week later when a wagon turned off the road and made its way to the mission as a light snow fell. The children were playing outside for afternoon recess and Clarissa watched with interest as the unknown wagon approached from the south. A man and woman were on the wagon seat.

As the driver pulled it into the yard and removed the hat he had pulled low over his brow, the school teacher recognized him as Colonel Glenn. She wondered who the dark haired woman beside him was, then remembered he had said something about his niece coming for the seamstress job.

"Tassie, watch the girls for me a moment," Clarissa instructed her oldest student.

"Yes, Miss Johnson," Tassie agreed in a mature tone that was ruined when she stuck her tongue out at her sister.

Hiding her laughter, Clarissa joined everyone else at the corral to greet their guests.

"Welcome back, Colonel," Redfield greeted him. "You've returned from Cincinnati, I see."

"Yes, I had a good trip," the trader affirmed as he stiffly stepped down from the wagon seat, using the wheel's hub for a step. Then he helped his young companion down as well.

"I've brought your mail, some supplies left at Bogey's post and your new seamstress," he announced. "This is my niece Sarah Clapp."

To Clarissa the young woman looked no older than eighteen with coffee colored curls and deep green eyes. She was smiling brightly so the ride from Three Forks must not have been too daunting for her.

"Miss Clapp, we are pleased to have you here," Rev. Chapman greeted her.

"Thank you," Miss Clapp replied, making a little curtsy. "I am so grateful for the chance to work here."

George looked into the back of the wagon. "Does everything in here need to be unloaded?" he asked.

"Yes," Glenn said. "Most of it's your supplies, but Sarah's trunk is here too." He pointed to the luggage at the back of the wagon bed.

"I'll move that to the ladies' cabin, if you like, Miss Clapp," George said.

"Oh, thank you," she said. "That would be very good of you."

George looked at Clarissa. "With your permission, Miss Johnson," he said.

"Of course," Clarissa agreed. Then she extended a hand to the new girl. "I'm Clarissa Johnson, the school teacher. You'll be rooming with me and Miss Cleaver." She pointed to Eliza who waved a little at the girl. "We'll show you to your quarters."

"After you've helped her settle in, Miss Johnson, bring her to the dining hall so I can visit with her about her duties," Mrs. Chapman instructed.

"Yes, ma'am," Clarissa agreed and then the three women made their way to the end cabin with George following behind with Sarah's trunk.

Stepping into the dimly lit cabin closed up against the cold, Clarissa showed George where to place the trunk.

"Miss Clapp, this is our mechanic George Requa," Clarissa made the introduction. George doffed his cap, but didn't linger in the small cabin after Sarah had thanked him.

Sarah looked around as she drew off her gloves. "There are four of us here?" she asked, counting the beds.

"No, only three now that you're here," Clarissa explained. "There used to be more single women here, but some have moved and some have married."

"I see," Sarah said. "Which bed shall be mine?"

"You have your pick of these two," Eliza pointed out. "This is mine and that is Miss Johnson's."

"Well this one looks just perfect," the dark haired girl said as she sat on one and tested its feel. "Oh, it's a real feather bed," she sighed. "And I'll have it to myself?"

"Yes," Clarissa confirmed. "You're used to sharing, I suppose."

"With two younger sisters," Sarah said. "This will be a luxury." She clapped her hands in delight. "Oh, I am just thrilled to be here."

Eliza and Clarissa shared a bemused look. Since Eliza's embarrassment with the Bean brothers, the two had become much closer than before.

"You surely jest," Eliza responded.

"Not at all," Sarah enthused as she pulled several pins from her hat. "What an adventure this is going to be."

Clarissa smiled. While she had never detested the frontier living conditions as Eliza had, neither had she been delighted with the crowded, dirt-floor cabin.

"You'll want to freshen up a bit, I'm sure, after your long ride out here," Clarissa said. "Eliza can you show Miss Clapp around and then take her to the dining hall? I need to get back to my class."

"Sure," Eliza agreed as Clarissa stepped out of the cabin to make her way back to the schoolhouse.

"If you're ready, Miss Clapp, I'll walk you around the mission" Eliza said.

"Can you just call me Sarah?" the younger woman asked. "I'm not used to being real formal."

Eliza hesitated. "Here in the cabin I suppose we can," she finally said. "But be careful around Mrs. Chapman. She maintains a certain formality even out here."

"Oh, thanks for telling me," Sarah said. "I suppose I'd better put my hat back on then."

"Not unless you just want to," Eliza advised. "We won't be outside for long and there's no sun to worry with."

"Alright," Sarah said, tossing the unfashionable bonnet back on her bed. "Then lead on. I want to see everything about my new home."

After the two young women had walked around the compound, stopping for a brief respite at the outhouse, Eliza showed Sarah to the kitchen where she washed up a bit. Then smoothing down her travel-wrinkled skirt as best she could Sarah went for her interview with Mrs. Chapman.

Amanda stopped Eliza before she could leave the kitchen.

"I just got back from your sister's cabin," the cook told Eliza. "She asked me to send for Mrs. Woodruff and asked that I tell you to keep young Billy with you after school is out."

"It's time?" Eliza's eyes grew large.

"I'm thinkin' so," Amanda confirmed.

Eliza unconsciously wrung her hands. "I hope she'll be alright," she worried aloud. "She just told Billy a few days ago that he's to have a new brother or sister. He's ever so excited about it."

"Mrs. Spaulding seemed very relaxed," Amanda reassured her, patting her hand. "And Mrs. Woodruff is quite competent at carin' for mothers and babies."

"Yes, I know," Eliza acknowledged. "Still, we've had both a mother and a baby die out here."

"Bein' out here isn't to blame," Amanda consoled. "Give your fears to the good Lord. He'll see you through."

Eliza gave her a smile that didn't hide the worry that remained in her eyes. "I think I'll check on Alice and see if she needs anything."

"Yes, do that," Amanda agreed. "It will put your mind at ease."

Throughout the afternoon, all the adults at the mission were made aware of the impending arrival of the Spaulding baby. When classes were dismissed for the day, John alternated between pacing in front of the dining room fireplace and sitting at a table nervously sipping at a cup of coffee that Amanda kept hot for him.

Dr. Palmer also remained in the dining hall, his medical bag sitting beside him, but out of sight of Mr. Spaulding. The doctor had long ago learned that the sight of his kit made people more concerned not less. It made it seem more real that medical attention might be needed.

Mrs. Chapman introduced Sarah to everyone as they gathered for supper. When introduced to the doctor, the young woman said, "Just so you know, doctor, I've had some experience helping with birthings. I'm the oldest of seven and I helped the midwife with my mother several times."

"Thank you, Miss Clapp," Marcus said, smiling at the girl. "I will certainly keep that in mind. But Mrs. Woodruff rules the birthing chamber. I don't even dare enter without her permission."

Sarah laughed. "That's just the way Mrs. Hinckley was back home. Didn't think a man should ever be at a birth. But I always thought having to witness one might make men think a little more about the responsibility of making babies."

Mrs. Chapman looked shocked. George, who was seated nearby, started to laugh but turned it into a cough instead.

Sarah saw Mrs. Chapman's disapproving look and immediately was contrite. "Oh, I'm sorry ma'am," she apologized. "Didn't mean to say anything untoward. Sometimes things just slip out before I can stop them. I'll keep quiet from now on."

"You don't have to keep quiet, Miss Clapp," Rachel said, her voice cool. "But you should think before you speak."

"Yes, ma'am."

Clarissa wondered if the young seamstress had irreparably damaged her reputation with the director's wife. But Rachel was far too unflappable to be long bothered by ill-chosen words. When she introduced Sarah to Mrs. Vaille, she was quite complimentary.

"Miss Clapp made her traveling outfit," she said to Asie, having the girl give a little turn so Asie could admire it. "Her stitching is excellent."

Sarah beamed. "Thank you, ma'am," she said. "Sewing purely is a pleasure to me. I like to think it's my gift from the Lord. I am so looking forward to all the things I can do to help out the mission here."

Clarissa inwardly chuckled at Sarah's bubbling words. Her promise to keep quiet would certainly have been one she could not have kept.

Supper was just ending when Mrs. Woodruff entered the dining room, drying her hands on her apron. Everyone looked at her with expectation and concern.

"Mr. Spaulding," the midwife said. "You have a young miss who wants to meet her father."

John jumped up from his chair. "A girl?" he asked.

"Yes," Martha confirmed, he face wreathed in smile wrinkles. "She's a tiny thing, but healthy." The midwife might have said more to him, but the schoolmaster was out the door before she could.

Eliza turned to her nephew sitting beside her and tapped him playfully on the nose. "Well, Billy, you have a little sister now."

"I do?" Billy asked, pausing from forking another bite of pie into his mouth. "Can I take her fishing?"

Everyone at their table laughed at the innocent question.

"Not for a few years, Billy," Abraham Redfield said.

"Besides, she might not like going fishing. Some girls don't, you know."

Billy considered this information with a slight frown. "Then I'll take Joey fishing," he said. From his mother's lap nearby, Joseph Vaille gurgled his agreement to the proposition.

Martha walked over to Dr. Palmer and sat down across the table from him. "Far as I can tell, the little girl is fine," she said quietly. "But I told Mrs. Spaulding to have you check her over, just to be sure."

"I'll call upon her in the morning," Marcus agreed.

Amanda set a plate of chicken and dumplings in front of the midwife.

"You're next," Martha winked at the red-haired mother-to-be.

"I'm thinkin' mine will be a boy," Amanda said.

"You're carrying low," Martha said with a professional eye. "I think you're right."

"We shall soon be overrun with babies," Marcus observed dryly.

"Ah, but that's a good thing," Mrs. Woodruff smiled.

CHAPTER TWELVE

Union Mission
Early Spring, 1823

Almost exactly a month later, Amanda gave birth to her expected baby boy. He was premature by a few weeks and even smaller than Allie Spaulding. The Fullers gave the tiny lad with a head full of red hair the name of Ian Patrick. Sadly, he died within a month and on a windy March day the mission family attended his burial in their cemetery.

After the death of his first wife Lydia, Stephen had worked out his grief behind the plow. The loss of his son likewise drove him to the solitude of his farm work, alone in prayer and tears. Amanda cried more openly, advising her mission sisters to ignore her "cloud bursts" as she called the frequent moments of mourning.

They had been gathered in the kitchen following breakfast a few mornings after the graveside funeral. Amanda wiped tears with the dish towel she had just used to dry the morning dishes. Seeing her sisters' looks of concern, she said, "Don't mind me none. I'll be fine, just as Phoebe is."

The dark-haired housemother gathered her friend into her arms. "Yes, you will," she assured the young woman. "And I know there'll be other babies in your life. God will see to it just as he has for me."

Amanda pulled back from Phoebe's grasp. "Does that mean . . ."

"Yes," Phoebe laughed. "Dr. Palmer was right. We're going to be overrun with babies."

Amanda's smile was sad as a few minutes later she

walked to the west field with a pitcher of water and three enamel mugs. Besides Stephen, Robbie and Abraham were also plowing the fields, getting them ready for another year of corn production. With three yoke of oxen now, the work would be done more quickly and Stephen even planned to add a large field of potatoes. His Irish wife had convinced him that folks in the area would trade for the potatoes and they would be a good addition to the limited diets most of their neighbors knew.

She crossed the field with her eyes on her husband, hoping to see that his grief was finding healing. He whoa'd the oxen and stood waiting for her, watching her approach. When she reached him, they shared a quick little kiss since neither Robbie nor Abraham was watching.

Amanda poured a full cup of the cool spring water for him and he downed it quickly. Then he whistled to get the attention of the other men so they could join them for the water break.

Robbie stopped his team immediately and came bounding across the clods of dirt to get the water Amanda offered. Abraham finished his row, then withdrew his gloves, slapping them against his legs to free the straw and dust. He smiled his thanks when Amanda handed him a cup.

Robbie poured the last of his water over his head before slapping his hat back on. Then turning to get back to his oxen team, he spied a group of riders on the road.

"Riders . . ." he started to yell, but his voice trailed off. The riders were Indians, heading north and not turning toward the mission.

"Looks like Cherokees," Abraham commented.

"Spring hunt," Stephen nodded. "After that herd of elk we saw last week."

"I wish they didn't feel the need to hunt in the Osage lands," Abraham said. "I have a bad feeling about this."

"They aren't a war party," Stephen observed.

"No," Abraham said. "And I shouldn't borrow trouble. But it seems like every time the Cherokees come into the area to hunt, they end up in a fight."

"We best be prayin' then," Amanda observed.

Stephen handed his wife his cup, pulled on his gloves and took the handles of his plow. "Let Rev. Vaille know," he told her. Amanda nodded and turned toward the dining hall where the minister was visiting with the surveyor Isaac McCoy and Dr. Palmer.

Having finally received permission to develop the Hopefield Mission, Will was building the cabin Susan had designed. Today George, Chapman, Alexander and Paul were helping him with the work. Star-That-Travels was also there, but mostly he watched the progress. He was unaccustomed to this kind of work since manual labor was considered beneath a warrior.

The walls were up and Paul was mixing mud with the tough dry prairie grass for daubing between the logs. Will was on the roof, setting the upper stones of the chimney.

As they worked, they saw a group of Osage hunters approaching from the Trace. It was a fine day, good for hunting as well as building. The Osages were from Big Tracks town and knew Teresa and Star.

The hunters rode into the area of land that Will had burned off for his cabin and garden. Field work would have to wait until this fall, but he planned to get a garden broken for his bride.

Star-That-Travels spoke with the Osages and invited them to dine with him at his cabin about two hundred yards away on a little rise of ground. Teresa was cooking over a fire out of doors. Her baby slept in a cradleboard on her back.

The men from Union Mission greeted the warriors, but continued their labors. Star and the Osage men sat on the ground under the lone tree that grew between the two cabins. They talked of the hunt and of the movement of game in the region.

"Elk just across the creek," one of the hunters said.

From his perch on the roof, Will looked in the direction the warrior had pointed and could see the huge animals grazing the greening prairie just beyond Pryor's creek. He paused to watch the majestic creatures, spotting the lead bull with its tremendous antlers.

"Elk are closer than usual," Will commented to Alexander who was working just below him slapping mud into the wall's crevices.

"Bogey says it's been dry out west. The animals have moved closer to the rivers around here," the blacksmith observed.

Just then they all heard the crack of gunfire. The Osage men all leaped up and ran to their mustangs to withdraw their muskets from leather slings. Teresa hurried into her cabin.

Will stood to try to see who the shooter might have been. The sound had come from near the elk herd which was now bounding toward the tree line of the Neosho.

He spotted a group of about ten mounted hunters and could tell from their dress that they were not Osages.

"Cherokees," he called down to his work partners. Then he winced with regret when he saw the reaction of the Osages. Their faces hardened and they began to load their single-shot guns.

Rev. Chapman stepped closer to the men. "I'm sure they are just hunting the elk. They mean none of us any harm," he said.

He threw a look to Star-That-Travels as if to encourage him to try to keep the men from confronting the hunters of the rival tribe. But their friend only shook his head as if to say there was nothing he could do. A warrior was honor bound to defend hunting territory.

Will could see that the Cherokees were approaching the farm site. "They're heading this way," he advised Woodruff in a quiet voice.

The blacksmith nodded and with a jerk of his head told George to get the one gun they had brought with them from Union. George stepped over to their wagon and pulled the musket out of its bed along with a horn of powder.

"Better get down, brother," he warned Will as he returned to the cabin.

"I will," the stone mason said. But he waited to move,

watching the Cherokees as their horses splashed through the creek. They seemed unaware that they were approaching an Osage hunting party.

They did not remain unaware for long. As they crested the near bank of the creek, one of the Osages whooped a call to battle. All the warriors leapt onto their mustangs and the horses themselves seemed to come alive with the sound.

"No, no, no," Chapman yelled, but to no avail. The Osages urged their mounts forward and a blast of gunfire erupted.

Crouching low the minister dashed back to the cabin, grabbed Paul from where he stood frozen at the corner of the house and pulled him inside with him. Alexander and George also rushed to enter the cabin.

Will remained on the roof, watching in fascination as the two groups of hunters began the circular style of fighting they had developed on the prairie. He could tell that the Osages had chosen to wait until the Cherokees cleared the creek so that their enemy would have that obstacle at their back.

But the Cherokees were not driven back by the charging Osages. In fact, the battle was pushing ever nearer to the farm. The gunfire was sporadic for loading a musket on a moving horse was a challenge. In reality, the battle seemed more about who could make the most noise for the war whoops increased as the warriors dashed in and out of the whirling fight.

Will had waited too late to reach the ladder so he threw himself against the shingles beside the fireplace. Even in this defensive position, he couldn't resist watching the fight. Below him the other men peeked out the open window of the cabin.

Suddenly Will flinched and grabbed at his shirt sleeve with a stunned look on his face. A stain of blood began to seep across the torn fabric and the force of a slamming bullet drove him backward off the roof. He fell with a sickening thud onto the blackened ground. He moaned in pain.

George dove out of the cabin window and hugged the wall to reach his brother. Quickly he grabbed him under the arms and pulled him around the corner out of sight of the battle.

At the same time, the Cherokees had put enough space between them and the creek that they could whirl around to the northwest toward the road. The Osages gave chase and soon the battle cries grew distant.

The other mission brothers made their way around to the back of the house where Will lay moaning.

"Shot clean through the shoulder," George said as he carefully examined the bullet wound.

"Leg's busted too," Will informed them through gritted teeth as they all knelt beside him.

"It will be difficult to move him," Alexander said as he ran his hand over the oddly bent leg. "Need to set the leg first before we try."

"Should we ride for the doctor?" Paul asked. "I can do it."

The men all looked at each other, uncertain about the best course of action.

George gave the decision to his brother. "You want us to set it or wait for the doc?"

"I can wait," Will said.

"Don't trust us?" George couldn't help asking.

"Don't trust you, brother," Will tried to smile but grimaced instead.

"I'll ride down," Paul again volunteered. "I'm the smallest, be the fastest."

Rev. Chapman shook his head. "We don't know where that fight is headed. I would hate for you to encounter it on the road."

"I can outrun 'em," Paul asserted. "They horses don't have shoes."

"He's right," Alexander stated. "Our shod horses do better on the hard pack of the road."

Still the minister hesitated as if uncertain about sending the young apprentice into possible danger.

"Alright," he finally assented. "But get off the road if you see them and follow the river."

Paul nodded and then hurried to their hobbled mustangs. The horses were agitated from the recent melee, so it took him a moment to mount. But once he was astride, he found the horse needed little urging to run.

From her cabin, Teresa looked out the door. "You have been hurt?" she called.

"Just Requa," Chapman responded. "Took a bullet through the shoulder."

Teresa nodded and closed her door for a moment, then re-emerged while she pulled her cradleboard on her back. She walked to where the men gathered around Will.

"Palmer would pack the wound," George said. "To stop the bleeding."

Alexander nodded in agreement and started to tear at his shirttail to use it for bandages. But Teresa shook her head and held up her hand. She walked around to the enamel tub that held the mud mortar. Scooping up a large handful of the mixture she returned.

"Take off shirt," she directed. The men hesitated. It wasn't considered polite for a gentleman to be seen shirtless by a woman.

But Osage men rarely wore shirts so it would not be shocking to Teresa. With George's help, Will drew his shirt off the bloody shoulder.

The Osage woman knelt down and firmly packed the mud into the wound both front and back.

Will's expression was one of surprise. "That actually feels good," he said. "Cold. Takes the fire out of it."

Teresa nodded. "Your medicine man come?" she asked.

"Yes," Chapman said. "Paul went for him."

She stood. "Pray for *Wah-She-Hah*," she requested, her voice little more than a whisper. This was the Osage name for Star-That-Travels.

"You mean he went with them?" George asked, showing his surprise.

"He is a warrior," Teresa shrugged. "He could not stop them so he must help them."

"We will pray," Chapman assured the woman.

She nodded and then because her baby was beginning to fuss, she turned and walked back to her cabin.

Chapman knelt beside Will. "This has to stop," he said, shaking his head. "There was a peace treaty."

"Claremont and Mad Buffalo signed it, but did Big Tracks?" Alexander asked.

"I don't know," Chapman responded. "If not, then Colonel Arbuckle made a grave miscalculation. Every chief among both tribes needs to be party to these peace negotiations."

"Little late to consider that now," Will said ruefully. His face was taking on a gray pallor and a slow seep of blood continued from his shoulder wound.

The men shared looks of concern as they settled on the ground around their fallen brother to await the doctor and pray.

Clarissa had just dismissed her class for the afternoon and was walking in ladylike fashion with them to the dining hall for an afternoon cup of buttermilk with cornbread crumbled in it. They all paused when they heard the hoof beats of a rapidly approaching horse.

Paul on the dark gray mustang they called Thunder quickly came into view. The horse was in a lather and Paul barely waited for it to halt at the corral before he was sliding off its back.

The young apprentice hastily looped the reins around the upper fence rail. From the fields, the three workers were striding to the compound to learn the reason for Paul's abrupt arrival.

"Where the doctor?" he called.

Clarissa could see Marcus through the open dining hall window so she pointed and said, "He's here. What is wrong?"

Paul strode rapidly to the dining room. "Cherokees and Osages swappin' lead," he explained. "Mr. Will been hit."

Clarissa drew a sharp breath. Then seeing the frightened faces of her students, she said, "Let's go around to the kitchen, girls." She didn't want them to hear the details of what must have been a bloody conflict.

Dr. Palmer had heard Paul's inquiry and stood to meet him at the dining room door. All the men gathered around the young man as he explained what had happened at Hopefield. As the women became aware of the situation, they too gathered in the dining hall and listened to Paul's account of the fight between the Osages and Cherokees. Sarah stood with her hands over her mouth, her eyes large and filled with concern.

"The bullet went clean through Mr. Will's shoulder," Paul said. "But he broke his leg, too, when he fell off the house."

"Lord, have mercy," Martha breathed. "Was anyone else hurt?"

"Not of our folks," Paul assured her. "Can't rightly say about the Indians."

"Let's saddle some fresh horses," Abraham said to Robbie and the two of them departed for the barn.

"There's a wagon at the Hopefield site, isn't there?" Dr. Palmer asked.

"Yes, suh," Paul affirmed.

"Mrs. Woodruff would you put together a bedroll of quilts to bring Will back on. And Mrs. Chapman, bring me what bandages we have ready."

Both women hastened to comply.

"Can I do anything to help?" Sarah asked and her voice seemed a little high pitched.

Dr. Palmer shook his head but briefly rested a calming hand on the girl's shoulder. Then he turned to the apprentice.

"Paul, go to the wood pile. Pull out some long, straight pieces for splints." Paul turned and on a run went to the blacksmith shed where the wood rick was kept.

The doctor left also to get his medical kit from his cabin. Within a few minutes all met at the corral where two horses waited.

Marcus mounted one horse and by unspoken consent Abraham climbed into the saddle of the other.

"Where did the fighters head?" Abraham asked Paul.

"They was following the trail to Captain Pryor's cabin," Paul said. "I never saw a soul on the way down here."

Nodding, Abraham turned his horse and gave a look of assurance to Phoebe. Then he and the doctor followed the field trail toward the road at a fast trot.

The missionaries watched them go, concerned but calm. After all they had dealt with this type of situation before. Sarah, however, clearly didn't know how to respond.

"Do we need to get our guns?" she asked. "Does everyone have a post for shooting?"

Amanda looked at the seamstress in surprise. "You've read too many wild accounts about Indians, haven't you?" she asked.

"The Cincinnati paper was always telling about an Indian attack," Sarah admitted. "I wondered if they exaggerated a bit."

"More like a great deal," Asie said. "You don't need to worry about being attacked."

Sarah nodded, though she didn't look entirely convinced. "But I can get my gun if it's needed," she offered. "I know how to shoot."

"You have a gun?" Phoebe asked.

"Uncle Hugh bought me a little pistol," Sarah confirmed. "But I already knew how to shoot. My father, rest his soul, thought all his children should know how to defend themselves. Of course, I never thought I would need it for Indians."

"Well, you likely never will need it for Indians," Phoebe assured her. "The Osages have granted this mission the right to be here. We've never been under attack."

"But they were attacked at Hopefield," Sarah countered.

"No, they were caught in the crossfire between the Osages and Cherokees," Rev. Vaille explained to the girl. "That unfortunately is something we have on occasion had to deal with. But we have never been targeted here."

Sarah nodded, some of the fear seeming to leave her eyes.

"Let's gather in the chapel for prayer," Rev. Vaille suggested and all who remained at the mission were soon in the boy's classroom lifting their voices to heaven.

Abraham and Marcus reached Hopefield just as Star-That-Travels did as well. The Osage warrior was alone and appeared unharmed. His horse looked spent.

The missionary brothers dismounted and quickly made their way to the back of Will's cabin where he lay on the ground. Star hurried to his own cabin where Teresa waited in the open doorway. After they spoke briefly, Star-That-Travels also joined the men.

"You alright?" George asked him.

"No one was hurt," the Osage man said. "The Cherokees have been shown the way to leave the area." Then looking down at Will he said with regret, "I am sorry you were caught in this."

"My own fault," Will said, while Dr. Palmer carefully examined his shoulder. "George told me to get down; I just waited too late." He winced when the doctor pulled at his shirt that had stuck to the drying mud and blood on the red, swollen flesh.

"I'll need to clean and sanitize this," Marcus said to the stone mason as he pulled a flask of whiskey from his medical bag. "It's going to sting. You need something to bite on?"

"No, just do it," Will shook his head, but he sucked in a sharp breath and reared up slightly as the alcohol hit the wound.

"Man, did you need to use that much?" he asked through gritted teeth.

"Someone did a very thorough job of mud daubing your wound," Dr. Palmer smiled.

"Teresa," Star-That-Travels said. "I know her work. She is always generous."

Marcus began to wrap the shoulder in the long strips of muslin bandages. "Which leg is broken?"

"Can't you tell?" Will asked, sounding rather annoyed. "I mean, isn't it obvious."

The doctor tied off the bandage and looked down at his brother's legs. "The left one," he surmised from the way it bent between the knee and ankle. "At least it's the one you don't use all the time."

"Ha, very funny," Will replied, now sounding truly annoyed. The other men couldn't help but grin at the doctor's way of taking Will's mind off his pain.

After assessing the break, the doctor directed the men in how they would set the bone. "George and Redfield, hold his shoulders as still as you can," he said. "Woodruff, you grasp the leg above the knee and hold it steady. I'll do the moving."

The blacksmith nodded and took a firm hold. Marcus paused and looked at his patient who was now sweating profusely. "Reverend, look in my kit. I have a smooth piece of wood in there. Put it between his teeth. He's going to need it this time."

All of the men stiffened in sympathy to the pain their brother was about to experience. Working quickly, the doctor gave a sharp jerk on the lower leg and with an audible snap pushed it into proper alignment. Will bit at the wood, but said nothing.

Everyone let out their breath. George eased away from his brother. "I should have had that wood," he said. "I nearly bit my tongue." They all laughed and the tension of the moment eased.

"Will it heal straight?" the stone mason asked.

"It will if you stay off it as long as I tell you." Dr. Palmer returned.

Will looked up at the unfinished log cabin. "Miss Comstock is going to be furious with me."

Star-That-Travels stood with the other men. Glancing at his cabin where Teresa watched from the doorway with hands on her hips, he dryly advised, "Get used to it."

CHAPTER THIRTEEN

Fort Smith, Arkansas Territory
Late Spring, 1823

Colonel Matthew Arbuckle sat at his desk at the Fort Smith garrison. An array of papers was scattered across the desk's surface, but his attention was not upon them. Running his hands through his thinning gray hair, the colonel showed his frustration at the news being presented him.

Across the desk from him sat John Nicks, a retired colonel who now acted as sutler for the garrison. Though younger than Arbuckle, Nicks was a respected military strategist having been a part of the brilliant victory at New Orleans against the British in 1814. He was also a newly elected member of the Arkansas Territorial legislature.

"When the governor heard about this latest clash between the Osages and Cherokees, he was furious," Nicks told the garrison commander. "It might not have raised such alarm if an American citizen hadn't been injured. But the *Gazette* editor is calling for action and that's stirring up the general populous. Politicians can abide just about anything except scared and angry voters."

Arbuckle shook his head. "According to the report Captain Pryor brought me, that missionary accepted responsibility for his injury. Said the Indians never deliberately fired at the mission."

"Doesn't matter," Nicks responded. "The Osages and Cherokees are still fighting. Everyone thought we were past that. Now you're supposed to come up with a plan to calm things down again. The governor wants a report from me within the month."

The commander sighed. "I can only do so much from Fort Smith. My superiors have my hands tied as long as they wrangle over where to put a new fort."

Nicks leaned forward and spoke in confidential tones. "Just send over a show of force," he advised. "Tour them around this Lovely's Purchase as it's called. That should make everyone feel more secure. Then folks can sleep easier in their beds at night and the politicians won't have to worry about their re-election plans."

Arbuckle smiled at the cynical remark of his friend. "I suppose I could take a couple of troops around the region," he consented. "Your mention of Lovely's Purchase reminds me I need to meet with that surveyor to find out the exact boundary line. Then I can nail down where I'll put a new fort when Washington City gives approval for it."

At Union, Will Requa made an impatient patient for Dr. Palmer. The stone mason chafed at his forced inactivity and had to be constantly reminded to stay off the leg that had been broken in his fall. Though the other men were willing to continue the work on his cabin, Will wanted to be involved in the work as he had promised Susan.

George finally constructed a pair of crutches for his brother to hobble around upon. When Will complained about their roughness George asked Sarah to stitch some padding for the tops of the crutches.

Within an hour of his request at breakfast, Sarah had created the pads and sought out George where he worked with Alexander at the blacksmith shed. The men were sharpening plowshares, a constant chore during the planting season.

"Well, here you are, Mr. Requa," Sarah said as she stepped tentatively into the shop. This was a male domain and none of the other women had ever ventured into it. But Sarah was not one to worry with conventional boundaries.

"I used an old quilt, you see," the seamstress said as she held out the crutch pads. "I hope your brother will like them."

"That was very quick, Miss Clapp," George said as he hastily slipped an arm into his coat sleeve. There was no fire in the shed since they were only using the whet stone, but both men had removed their coats because the day was warm. Woodruff also reached for his coat.

"Oh, gentlemen, please don't worry with your coats," Sarah said, her smile showing her dimples. "I worked in a meat packing plant, remember. I have seen men without their coats on."

Still the two men hesitated to be seen in such an impolite state of undress. They both pulled on their coats.

Sarah sighed. Then turning her attention back to the crutch pads, she turned them about so George could see how they were fashioned. "All I need now is to have the crutches for a bit and I can slip the pads on and stitch them tight," she explained. "Your Mrs. let me cut up a quilt so they're nice and thick." She included Woodruff in the conversation to be polite. "I've just slip stitched a hem, but I can take that out easily enough if the size isn't right. I just estimated the size and I've taken a tuck or two so they'll fit snug."

George nodded and grinned as if he understood the seamstress' explanation of her design. In reality, it was obvious that he had no idea what she was talking about. Still, he seemed to enjoy listening to her chatter and appreciated her dark curls, bright eyes, and winsome dimples.

Alexander didn't enter the conversation, being a man of few words. But he watched the two young people with a bemused look on his face.

"I'll find my brother and get those crutches for you, Miss Clapp," George offered.

"Oh, he's in the dining hall," Sarah stated.

George looked confused. "Then why didn't you just take the pads to him?" he asked. "Since he's not in his cabin." It would not have been proper for Sarah to visit Will in his cabin.

"I wanted you to see them first," Sarah explained, blushing a little. "To be sure they met your approval."

"They're fine, Miss Clapp," George assured her. "Why

don't we walk over to the dining hall and see if they're agreeable to Will."

"That would be lovely," Sarah agreed, reaching out to take George's arm. "Good day to you, Mr. Woodruff."

Alex barely hid his grin. "Good day to you as well, Miss Clapp."

Colonel Arbuckle quickly followed through with the plans he had discussed with Nicks. Two units of the Seventh Infantry under Lieutenant Benjamin Bonneville and Lieutenant Charles Summers headed west from Fort Smith. There was no cleared road from Fort Smith to Three Forks so travel was slow.

"If we place a fort near the Three Rivers, we'll need to survey a supply road between it and Fort Smith," the colonel observed in the officer's mess tent one evening. "Slogging through this river cane is entirely too difficult."

"The fur traders don't even bother with overland travel," Summers agreed. "The Arkansas River is a much better 'road,' if you know what I mean."

"We'll get Lieutenant Butler working on a road survey when we return," Arbuckle said as he reached for a cigar from a box he kept close at hand. The military man did not drink, but he did enjoy a fine Spanish cigar after a rather unappetizing camp meal. It was a habit he had picked up while serving in Florida.

The Seventh troops continued westward over the next days, stopping briefly at the Beans salt works at the mouth of the Illinois. A week later the two troops, made up of twenty infantrymen each, set up camp at Three Forks on French Point. Using this location as his base of operation the colonel conducted a series of visits around the Lovely region.

He paid call upon Captain Pryor and Colonel Glenn at their trading posts. Then with Pryor acting as interpreter, he and his two lieutenants visited Big Tracks' village just north of French Point.

The Osage leader assured the commander that he and his warriors would not engage the Cherokees in battle, unless provoked. That little caveat always accompanied the professions of peace among the Indians. Then they could always place the blame for provocation on the other side in the conflict.

"Standard military strategy," Arbuckle stated to his officers and Captain Pryor as they ate together that same evening at Pryor's post. "I've used the exact same line of reasoning myself so I can hardly fault Big Tracks for it." But he shook his head in frustration as he carved the buffalo steak Pryor had served.

"True," Pryor agreed. "And the Indians understand it well, though too many people in the states underestimate their military prowess. I saw it frequently while out with the Corps."

Pryor's experience with the Lewis and Clark expedition many years earlier had gained him the respect of the military commanders working on the frontier.

"And I saw it during the Seminole War," Arbuckle agreed. "Jackson himself told me he would rather fight alongside an Indian as any other soldier."

Pryor nodded. "So provocation becomes the justification for most fighting."

I dislike using a heavy hand with the Indians," Arbuckle said thoughtfully. "But I'm going to have to make it clear that as the law on the frontier, the military will determine who provoked a fight and will hold those individuals to account."

Pryor nodded in agreement, but then stated, "I do not envy you that role, Colonel."

Two days later, Arbuckle with his lieutenants and a small force of ten men arrived at Union Mission. Invited to join the missionaries for supper, the officers sat down to Amanda's fried chicken, turnip greens, new potatoes and cornbread.

The soldiers camped near the corral and ate their usual hard tack, beans and biscuits but enjoyed molasses cookies from the mission kitchen.

"In your opinion," Arbuckle began after a prayer over the meal was offered, "who provoked the fight at your farm site?"

The men who had been present at Hopefield all hesitated to speak up.

"It would be difficult to say," Chapman finally responded. "I'm not sure what you would consider provocation."

"Who fired first?" Arbuckle prompted.

"The Osages," George said. "But they felt justified because the Cherokees were hunting in Osage lands."

Arbuckle nodded and stroked his mustache thoughtfully. "There always seems to be a justification for the conflict."

"I'm no expert on Indian matters, Colonel," Rev. Vaille stated. "But it seems to me that these fights are rarely meant to actually draw blood. They are simply the way the various tribes interact with one another, test each other's strength and push against the hunting boundaries. They are rather like two young men having it out on the school yard. Once the fight is over they step back, respect each other for the fight and work out some sort of acceptable truce. They seem to rather like these occasional scraps."

"You no doubt are right," Arbuckle acknowledged. "But the land has changed. The Indians now share it with others who don't want to be caught in the middle of a fight such as you were. I can't have the tribes working out their differences in battle."

"Yet you still haven't convinced General Scott and General Jackson to approve a fort for Three Forks?" John Spaulding asked.

"Not yet," the colonel said. "But the Arkansas governor is howling mad right now and Washington City will hear from him soon. Mark my words; you'll see a fort nearby within a year."

At the next table, Lieutenant Bonneville had managed to secure a seat next to Clarissa.

"I have thought of you often, Miss Johnson," Benjamin stated quietly to her as they ate. "It was quite a pleasure to visit with you when you arrived at Fort Smith two years ago."

"Thank you, Lieutenant," Clarissa said, feeling flattered that the young officer would even remember her from that time. It seemed so long ago. "I trust you have been well during your time at Fort Smith."

"Well, enough," the officer smiled ruefully. "But a bit lonely. Female companionship is woefully lacking at Fort Smith. Some of the soldiers spend their leave over at Dardanelle, hoping to catch the eye of a Cherokee belle."

"But not you?" Clarissa teased.

"My mother would frown upon my fraternization with Indians, I am afraid," Benjamin said. "She comes from the aristocracy, you see, and expects certain conduct from me."

Though Clarissa imagined that her own mother might feel the same way, she didn't like hearing it expressed aloud. It sounded too much like prejudice.

"I know my mother would want me to keep company with a fine lady," the lieutenant went on as if hinting at an interest in courting Clarissa. "Such as yourself."

Clarissa doubted that a French aristocrat would want her son paying call on a poor mission schoolteacher, but she didn't express that. She knew her mother would wish her to encourage the interest of the officer, but she couldn't mislead him. She was never one who could pretend an interest that didn't exist or play at the courting game that so many of her friends back home had enjoyed.

"You flatter me, Lieutenant," Clarissa said demurely, hoping she could communicate her lack of interest as gently as possible. Looking over at Dr. Palmer at the next table, she added, "But I am seeing someone right now." She turned back and smiled at the officer, trying to silence her protesting conscience. "Seeing" could mean many different things, couldn't it?

Clearly disappointed, the lieutenant gave a little bow. "Well, I thank you for your honesty," he said.

Clarissa almost told him she wasn't being honest, but she bit her tongue and kept silent. *Please don't let me regret this,* she prayed.

From across the room, Dr. Palmer had watched the young officer in conversation with Clarissa. He saw her smile at the man and it left him suddenly without an appetite.

I've waited too late, he thought. *How stupid to think I had time.*

Colonel Arbuckle and his men continued northward the following day. He planned a visit to Colonel Chouteau at La Saline and then to march west to Claremont's Town. He had sent a courier to find Isaac McCoy and requested a visit with him at Union before the troops returned to Fort Smith.

Rev. McCoy had arrived at Union by the time Colonel Arbuckle returned from his visit with Chief Claremont. In the growing heat, the commander had discovered that a few in the village were ill with the fever. It seemed to affect their elders and small children the most. The Indians were preparing to pack up their lodges and move away from the Verdigris River and out into the drier prairie.

After supper one evening in the dining hall, the missionaries were discussing conditions in the neighborhood. Teresa and Star-That-Travels had joined them for the meal. McCoy had produced a map with the boundaries for Lovely's Purchase. Union and Hopefield would fall within the designated area as would both villages of Claremont and Big Tracks.

"Colonel Nicks will propose that the territorial legislature make the area a county," Arbuckle noted as the men passed around the map.

"Will Three Forks become the county seat?" John asked, showing great interest in the map. Clarissa imagined he would copy it and incorporate it in future lessons for the boys. But geography was not a subject often taught to girls so there would be no map study for her students.

"I doubt Three Forks will get the county seat," Arbuckle responded as the map continued to pass from hand to hand in the dining hall. "The politicians in Little Rock hardly think of it as a true settlement."

"But there is little else in this area that is a settlement," Rev. McCoy countered. "Has anyone in the territorial legislature ever ventured this far west?"

"Several have visited Fort Smith," the colonel responded.

"But I don't know of a single one who has traveled to Three Forks."

"Perhaps you should suggest that to Colonel Nicks," Bonneville interjected. "Miller County is in his district." Miller County lay directly south of Three Forks with the Arkansas River serving as its northern boundary.

"Good suggestion," said Arbuckle. "I'll see to it when we get back to the fort in a few days." Then turning to Dr. Palmer he added, "And I might suggest to you, Doctor, that you visit Claremont's Town. The fever has taken hold up there."

Dr. Palmer looked surprised. "I've rarely seen any of the Osages with the fever," he said. "I assumed they had developed some immunity to it."

"Mosquitoes are bad already," Star-That-Travels remarked. "Black Dog, the great medicine man of the *Wahzhazhe*, says the mosquito gives the fever. He leads the people away from the water where the mosquito dwells."

Dr. Palmer looked skeptical. He had heard many of the moral tales and fireside stories of the Osages. They frequently gave human qualities to animals and assigned good and evil intent to their actions. A black cat was a guardian of a dwelling; a hooting owl portended death. Mosquitoes giving someone fever seemed nothing more than superstition to him.

"And does a journey to the prairie cure those who are sick?" Marcus asked.

"No," Star acknowledged. "But it keeps others from getting the fever."

"A sort of quarantine, I suppose," Lieutenant Summers interjected. "Dr. Russell at Fort Smith has tried that. The fever can get bad at the garrison during the summer."

"And does that control the spread of the disease?" Marcus pursued. He was eager to learn anything he could to combat the "intermittent" they had come to dread each summer.

"Can't say that it does," Summers replied. "Dr. Russell is quite baffled by the problem."

"As are we all," Marcus stated. "I should ask Bogey to get more quinine for us. If the fever is affecting the Osages, we may be in for a very bad summer."

"I pray you are wrong about that," Rachel said quietly.

"Amen," several among them added.

CHAPTER FOURTEEN

Union Mission
Summer, 1823

Clarissa sat outside the women's cabin in a cane-bottomed chair, hoping for a cooling breeze in the afternoon sunshine. She would have preferred the shady interior on such a warm day, but she was sewing a dress for Thea and she needed the light to see her stitches. With school dismissed for the summer, she hoped to get two dresses completed for Thea in addition to making a new one for herself.

With Sarah's help, she had cut eight yards of a soft green faille for a new gown. Not having seen a magazine in three years, she took Sarah's advice about the design for her new dress. The empire waist was out of fashion, Sarah assured her. A close fitting bodice and full skirt was the style of the day. For Thea, Clarissa had also cut the two calicos she had purchased at the Chouteau trading post last fall. She planned to cut down one of her old aprons to make a protective pinafore for the girl who loved to play in the dirt.

The teacher smiled as she watched her dark-haired daughter across the compound. The children had an hour's play away from their garden chores and were engaged in a game of Red Rover. Thea was too young to play, but she ran round and round Phoebe who was supervising the game. She rarely made her circuit without falling at least once, but the girl was never fazed by her falls. She seemed to almost bounce back up and continued her romp with two little braids flying out behind her.

153

"Oh to have such stamina," Sarah remarked as she stepped out of the cabin, bringing her own chair to join Clarissa. She was mending several pairs of pants, patching the knees for both the men of the mission and the boys. "I always felt that way with my six brothers and sisters. A whirlwind of activity, they were, never still unless they were asleep. I could never understand how my mother could remain so calm and serene around them all day long. And here I am now with ten children flying about."

"Yes, they make me tired just watching them," Clarissa agreed after Sarah's flow of words ran out.

She paused in her sewing to rub a spot between her eyes. Concentrating on making her stitches fine and even was giving her a headache. Or perhaps it was the bright sunshine hurting her eyes. She tugged at her bonnet, hoping to shield her eyes better.

"Are you alright, Miss Johnson," Sarah asked. "You look rather pale."

"It's a headache," Clarissa explained. "Although I haven't felt quite right for the past few days. Seems I am always tired lately."

"You overdid the other day when you and the girls went down to the river collecting them pussy willows," Sarah observed.

"I suppose," Clarissa agreed listlessly. "It was very hot that day."

"Well nothing sets me to right better than sitting and stitching," the seamstress said. "You'll be right as rain soon."

Clarissa knew sewing did not have such a soothing effect upon herself, but she suddenly had no energy to even respond to Sarah's remark. She felt flushed and oddly hot and cold at the same time.

"I don't . . ." Clarissa began, but couldn't think of how to finish her sentence. She was becoming rather fuzzy brained. "I think . . ." She slumped back in her chair, feeling faint.

"Miss Johnson," Sarah said hurrying to set her needle in the pants she held and rising to catch the teacher before she tumbled from her chair.

"You need to lie down," the girl gasped in concern. She took the teacher's sewing and set it in her own chair. "Here, let me help you to your bed."

With Clarissa leaning heavily against her, Sarah led the way into the cabin. Eliza was taking a rest upon her own bed in the dim interior. Having suffered badly from the fever last year, she had been advised by Dr. Palmer to rest during the hottest part of the day. But she sat up quickly when Sarah and Clarissa entered.

"What's wrong?" she asked with concern in her voice.

"Miss Johnson doesn't feel well," Sarah explained. "I'm helping her to bed."

Eliza came and took Clarissa's other arm to offer her assistance as well. She placed the back of her hand against Clarissa's cheek. "You have a fever," she stated.

"But I feel so cold," Clarissa said. She was starting to shiver.

"Oh, dear," Eliza whispered.

"What?" Sarah asked.

"It's *the* fever," the blond explained. "I know because I have had it."

"What should we do?"

"I'll help her to bed," Eliza said, taking charge. "You find Dr. Palmer and tell him we think Miss Johnson has come down with the intermittent. If you can't locate him, bring Mrs. Woodruff."

Sarah nodded and dashed out of the room. Eliza helped her friend settle on her bed, then poured some water into the wash basin and dampened a cloth. She removed Clarissa's bonnet and began to wash her face.

"Sorry to be a trouble," Clarissa murmured.

"We have all been someone's trouble some time in our life," Eliza said in soothing tones. "I've had my turn and now it's yours. Letting others help you is the lesson trouble teaches you. Then when someone else is a trouble, you better understand them and aren't so quick to judge."

Clarissa's green eyes met Eliza's bright blue ones. "Trouble must also make you wise," she said.

Eliza's smile held a look of irony. "Who would have thought it of me, eh?"

Clarissa smiled too, but found she could not hold her eyes open any longer.

Sarah hitched up her skirts higher than proper for a lady and raced to the dining hall. Only Rev. Vaille sat inside with his Bible open. He was preparing a sermon for Sunday service. He looked up as Sarah fairly tumbled into the room.

"What is it, Miss Clapp?" he asked.

"Miss Johnson has taken ill," she said. "Would you know where the doctor is?"

"No, but I will help you look for him," the minister said, closing his Bible. "I'll check his cabin."

"Thank you," Sarah said breathlessly. Then she hurried into the kitchen. Only Amanda, Rachel and Asie were there, just starting supper preparations. Sarah didn't even stop to explain but hurried on through the outside door and ran toward Phoebe.

"What on earth?" Asie said. "Is something wrong?"

"With Miss Clapp one never knows," Rachel said dryly. "Perhaps she has simply seen another deer."

The other women chuckled because Sarah frequently exhibited squealing excitement whenever she encountered prairie wildlife. But Amanda went to the door to look out just the same.

"I don't know," she said. "Seems like more than a deer this time. She looked more worried than excited."

"Well, I'm sure we will learn soon enough," Rachel commented and the three of them returned to their work.

Sarah reached Phoebe who was sitting with the girls in the shade of the school building. The boys had left for the haymow, a location where no girls were allowed.

"Do you know where Dr. Palmer is?" she asked without preamble.

"I saw him go to the blacksmith shop," Elizabeth offered.

"Thank you," Sarah said and off she dashed again with a ,whirl of her skirts.

"What's wrong, Aunt Phoebe?" Leah asked, her brow furrowed with concern.

"I don't know," Phoebe answered as she stroked the little girl's hair. "But I'm sure Dr. Palmer will take care of whatever it is."

The girls all sighed and nodded. They clearly believed tall and handsome Dr. Palmer could fix anything.

Sarah rushed to the blacksmith shed and stepped inside. As her eyes adjusted to the dim interior, she saw the doctor standing at the shed's one window. He was using the light to try to extract a splinter from Woodruff's finger.

"That's a wicked piece of timber there," he said and the blacksmith winced as the doctor probed with a needle. Both men looked up as Sarah entered.

"Is there a problem, Miss Clapp?" Marcus asked.

Sarah nodded, trying to catch her breath. "It's Miss Johnson."

"Clarissa?" Marcus breathed, feeling as if he had been punched in the gut. "What is wrong?"

"Eliza says it's the fever. She sent me to get you."

The doctor dropped Alexander's hand as if it was hot poker. "I'll see to her right away," he said and left the shop without a backward glance.

"Miss Clapp," the blacksmith stopped her before she could follow the doctor.

"Yes, sir?" Sarah turned back to look at him.

"You're good with a needle, aren't you?"

"Yes."

"Perhaps you could assist me then." Alexander held up his hand. "Dr. Palmer has left his with me, you see," the man grimaced.

The doctor's needle was stuck in his finger. "I'm too cowardly to pull it out myself," the man explained.

"Oh my," Sarah said, taking pity on the burly blacksmith. She walked over, took his hand and carefully eased the needle from his finger.

"Don't tell my wife," he smiled through his graying beard. "She'll laugh at me."

Sarah shared his conspiratorial smile. "Your secret's safe with me." Then with a little wave she hurried from the shed.

Woodruff watched her go with an inscrutable look of sadness on his face.

Sarah raced back to the cabin to find that Dr. Palmer had retrieved his medical kit and was already taking Clarissa's pulse as Eliza stood at the end of her bed. After completing his usual examination, he ran both hands through his hair with a look of deep concern on his face.

"It's the fever, isn't it?" Eliza asked, keeping her voice low. Even so, Clarissa opened her eyes to look up at the doctor.

"I'm afraid it is," Marcus confirmed.

"Don't let it scare you, Doctor," the teacher said in a voice barely above a whisper. "If Leah and Eliza can beat this, so can I."

Marcus smiled and squeezed Clarissa's hand. "That's the spirit," he said, but the worry did not leave his eyes. He had not felt this gut-clenching fear since Sally Edwards had languished with the fever on the journey out from Pittsburgh. Her death still plagued his mind at times.

Clarissa began to shiver again, bringing the doctor out of his reverie.

"Get a light blanket for her," he instructed Eliza. She crossed the room to a trunk and pulled a crocheted throw from it. Together she and the doctor tucked it loosely around the teacher.

Sarah had watched with concern from the doorway. "Is there something I can do, Doctor?" she asked.

Palmer turned to her as if just now aware of her presence. "Yes, Miss Clapp, if you wouldn't mind. Please ask Mrs. Fuller for a cup of hot tea with honey. I need to administer a dose of quinine and the honey will make it more palatable."

Sarah nodded and with a swish of her skirts turned and began another sprint toward the kitchen. She stepped inside to find that Mrs. Woodruff and Alice Spaulding were also assisting with supper.

"What is wrong, Miss Clapp?" Rachel asked.

"It's Miss Johnson," Sarah explained, feeling a parched need for some tea herself. "She's taken the fever and Dr. Palmer has asked for some hot tea with honey."

"I'll steep some now," Amanda said, moving quickly to dip water into a kettle and place it on the grate in the fireplace.

"When did she take ill?" Martha asked.

"She said she hadn't felt well for a few days, but it really hit her hard just a while ago," Sarah said, reaching for a mug and dipping some water for herself. "Eliza . . . umm . . . Miss Cleaver recognized it as the fever and sent me for the doctor. He was at the blacksmith shed taking out a splinter from Mr. Woodruff's finger but he went right away to check on Miss Johnson."

She swallowed down the water in one big gulp.

"Are you alright, Miss Clapp?" Asie asked.

"Just winded a bit," the seamstress said. "And worried for Miss Johnson. She seems quite ill."

"I'll take that tea and see if there's something more needs to be done," Martha volunteered as Amanda added a generous dollop of honey to the teacup. Then she pointed toward the dining room and said to Sarah, "You sit and rest. You've raced around enough for today."

"Yes, ma'am," Sarah agreed, suddenly feeling drained. She flopped into a chair near the kitchen door.

As Martha left, the boys all arrived from the barn, having caught the aroma of the molasses and pecan basted ham and sweet potatoes the women were spooning into serving platters. Thomas hurried into the kitchen.

"Mother, Robbie is sick," he said, while snitching a bite of pecans from the platter.

Rachel lightly slapped at his hand. "Sick, how?" she asked.

"Says he has a headache," her son responded. "He was laying down when we left the barn."

The women looked at each other with growing concern.

"I'll send Mr. Fuller to check on him," Amanda said.

The men were gathering at the wash stand outside in anticipation of another fine supper.

Will, George and Paul arrived from Hopefield where they had been working on the new cabin. Will could do little more than supervise, but he was too anxious to complete the work to let more idle days go by.

Before supper was completed Abigail and Elizabeth were both complaining of a headache and chills as well. Over the next days, George and Rev. Chapman also experienced a relapse from their previous bouts with the disease. The missionaries went into what Sarah called "battle array," taking turns in nursing the sick and watching for signs of new cases.

Joseph Bogey rode up from Three Forks, bringing supplies which fortunately included another precious bottle of quinine. He reported that there were several folks at the trading community also suffering with the mysterious fever.

"Miz Bradley's two girls has got it," Bogey told them as he ate dinner with them that day. "She's asked that you come and check on them if you can, Doctor."

Marcus looked up from the cornbread and beans he had been eating, fatigue written on his face. "I'll try to make it down there this afternoon," he promised.

As he saddled a horse after the noon meal to join Bogey for the journey down to Three Forks, Paul stepped into the barn. "Mr. Woodruff says I can be the one to go down with you," he told the doctor.

The missionaries made it their policy to never travel alone for safety. Panthers, mountain lions and occasionally black bears traveled through the region, not to mention the feuding Osages and Cherokees who hunted the area. As a matter of caution, everyone always carried a gun.

Dr. Palmer smiled at the apprentice. "Then get a horse saddled," he said.

Paul grinned and set to work. "I told Miss Tassie I would come down and see her sometime," he said as the men set out. "Wisht it wasn't for this reason though."

They arrived at Three Forks before sunset and found Mrs.

Bradley sitting on the front porch of her log cabin located west of the Chouteau trading post.

She stood when Marcus and Paul approached. "Glad you could come, Mr. Doc," the ample woman said. She looked Paul up and down as he dismounted from his horse. "Who's this raggedy taggedy fellow you brung with you?" There was a smile in her voice though she tried to look severe.

Paul smiled at her and tugged at his hat. "I'm Paul Gillard, ma'am," he introduced himself.

"Paul's my fine companion today," Marcus added. "Bogey tells me your daughters are taken with the fever."

"They gets it every summer," Mrs. Bradley said as she led the way into the cabin. "But it seems 'specially bad this year. Mr. Bogey said you had some new medicine so I thought to send for you."

Paul took a seat in a bent willow rocker near the fireplace while the mother and doctor stepped behind a quilted curtain into the tiny room where Tassie and Lena shared a bed. The doctor gently examined the girls while Mrs. Bradley held a candle close.

"I'll give them some quinine, but it's very bitter, Mrs. Bradley," the doctor said after he had satisfied himself that the girls did have the same fever being fought at the mission. "Do you have any honey?"

"My, yes, pounds of it," the woman said. "Liam found a honey tree last trip home and brought a hide full of it."

"Put some in hot water or tea and I'll add the quinine."

Mrs. Bradley went to do as he asked. After the girls had been ministered to, Mrs. Bradley said, "You'll stay for supper." It was not a question.

"We don't wish to impose," Marcus started to weakly protest. A meal at Mrs. Bradley's table would be as fine as at Mrs. Fuller's.

"No, 'pose to it," the caring woman said. "I can't pay you with coin, but I can feed you good."

The meal was, indeed, a fine one and Mrs. Bradley tied up several biscuit stuffed with ham and a jar of the honey in a large kerchief for the men to take with them.

As they stood to leave, Paul called softly, "Goodbye, Miss Tassie." There was no response from the bedroom.

"She's sleepin'," the girl's mother said.

"Would you tell her I stopped in?" Paul asked.

"You think she'd care if you come by?" Mrs. Bradley teased.

"I hope she do," Paul responded as he and Marcus stepped onto the porch.

"I hope she do, too." Mrs. Bradley's smile lit her rich, dark face.

The two men mounted their mustangs and started back toward Three Forks.

"I think you have received her blessing, Paul," Marcus observed when they were well away from the cabin.

Paul grinned at the doctor and started to whistle. Marcus smiled too, his worry momentarily lightened.

The fever seemed like a specter that haunted the mission. Though he gave the mosquito theory little credence, Marcus recommended that everyone stay away from the river or other areas where the mosquitoes bred.

As some of them recovered or improved, others found themselves in the fever's grip. The doctor was called to Three Forks and La Saline to look after patients. He was nearing exhaustion.

Through it all, his worry for Clarissa was never far from his mind. She seemed to grow weaker by the day. Eliza and Sarah were faithful nurses and the other women helped as well, but besides bathing her in cool water and keeping her comfortable there was little they could do. She ate very little and was wasting away. A deep cough had settled in her chest, so like the symptoms Sally Edwards had displayed just before her death.

Marcus sat at Clarissa's bedside one afternoon, slumped forward in the chair, one hand stroking hers while she fitfully slept. Across the room, Sarah sat in the open doorway with her never-ending sewing, acting as chaperone. Sensing the doctor's distress, her chatter was stilled.

The doctor chafed at propriety today; annoyed that he could not have even a moment alone with Clarissa. If this was to be how her life ended, he wanted to at least tell her goodbye as the man who loved her.

Instead he sat quietly and prayed. "Father," he whispered with eyes open, watching the labored breathing of his patient. "I know I have failed terribly so many times and I do not deserve your mercy. I ask it not for myself, but for Clarissa. Please let her live. She has a daughter who needs her."

His voice broke for a moment. Hardly caring that Sarah sat nearby, he swallowed down his emotions and continued. "She has a failure of a doctor who needs her too, though I may never have the courage to tell her so. I know that she may never love me, for she had dedicated her life to your service, but it will be enough for me if you will simply spare her life."

He closed his eyes to keep hot tears from spilling out. After a moment he opened them, hoping to see a miraculous change in Clarissa's condition. But she slept on, a frightening rattle in her lungs. He dropped his head and gave in to despair.

Marcus felt a hand gently squeeze his shoulder. Sarah had crossed the room and stood behind him, offering comfort.

"She won't die, doctor," Sarah said with a quiet certainty. "She told me she would fight this fever for Thea . . . and for you."

Marcus looked up at the seamstress, doubt and hope mixed in his expression. He nodded, then he stood and made his way out of the cabin; its walls seemed suddenly to close in on him. Ignoring his own advice, he walked down to the river and stood beneath a lone towering cottonwood tree.

As he cried his fear out, faith filled the void. It was going to be alright. With a certainly he could not explain, he knew she would live.

CHAPTER FIFTEEN

Union Mission
Late Summer, 1823

The long, hot, difficult summer passed slowly with the battle against the fever raging all the way from Fort Smith to Claremont's Town. Tassie and Lena recovered and George and Rev. Chapman were on the mend. Clarissa's cough continued, but she showed some improvement each day. Sadly Robbie Bake died.

The fun-loving, tow-headed farm apprentice was laid to rest in the little cemetery on the high ground. Only a few from the mission could attend the brief committal service, but everyone felt the sadness as they went about the task of nursing the sick. Paul was nearly inconsolable for a time. He and Robbie had come to the mission at the same time, both orphaned and alone. He had been like a little brother to the Negro apprentice.

Eliza was giving Clarissa a sponge bath a day or two later when the schoolteacher opened her eyes and looked about the room as if seeing it for the first time.

"How long have I been sick?" she asked, her voice a raspy whisper.

"Long time" Eliza answered. "We were afraid we might lose you."

"Thirsty," Clarissa said. Eliza poured a cup of water and helped raise her head to sip the cool liquid slowly.

She felt the teacher's forehead. "I think your fever's down."

Clarissa nodded and seemed drowsy still. "I had an odd

dream," she said. She stared out the open cabin door to the distant horizon, trying to recall the details of the dream.

"Tell me about it," Eliza said.

"I saw a man standing under a tree. It was Dr. Palmer, I think," Clarissa murmured. "The tree was so tall it reached all the way into the sky. And I decided to climb it like I used to do when I was a little girl."

Eliza smiled as she smoothed the rumpled bed clothes. "Did you climb it?" she asked to try to keep the teacher awake.

"I started to," Clarissa whispered, struggling for a moment to catch her breath. "But then I heard a voice tell me to come back down. Someone . . . needed me. So I started back down and that's when I woke up."

"Faith was calling you back to us," Eliza said. "We've all been praying mighty hard for you. And the others."

"Are others sick?"

"Almost all of us have had it this summer," Eliza confirmed.

"Thea?"

"She has been spared, thankfully," her friend assured her. "As have Billy and little Allie, but John was sick for a while." She chose not to tell Clarissa about Robbie.

But all are better now?"

"Most all are," Eliza said. "The fever seems to have retreated since it's gotten so dry. But we'll probably have to delay opening school this year."

Eliza stood then. "I'll run fetch some broth from the kitchen if you think you can eat it," she offered.

"That sounds good," Clarissa agreed.

Eliza walked toward the kitchen, but caught sight of Dr. Palmer exiting the Vailles' cabin where Elizabeth and Richard were still abed with the illness. She waited for him to approach the kitchen.

"Miss Johnson is awake," she told him as he came near.

His bowed head came up and a hope flashed into his eyes. "She is?"

Eliza's smile was bittersweet. The doctor had not looked

so happy at her recovery from the fever. "You might want to accompany me back after I get some broth for her."

"I'll do that," the doctor agreed.

After Eliza had fed Clarissa a few spoonfuls of the broth, Dr. Palmer took the seat by her bed and reached for her hand to measure her pulse.

"Heart rate is elevated a bit," he noted. Then while still holding her hand he felt her forehead. "But the fever is down." His sigh was one of great relief.

"I told you I would beat this," Clarissa said quietly. "Just didn't think it would be so hard a fight."

"It was a frightful fight," Marcus agreed. He still held her hand and she made no effort to withdraw it from his grasp. They looked into each other's eyes for a long moment.

Eliza cleared her throat. Dr. Palmer quickly withdrew his hand. To Clarissa, her hand suddenly felt very bereft and cold.

"Can I help her sit up for a bit, doctor?" Eliza asked.

"Yes, I think that will do her some good," Marcus agreed. "We want her lungs to clear."

Eliza moved around to the other side of the bed and the two of them help Clarissa into a sitting position. Eliza fluffed the pillows behind her back.

"My hair must look a mess," Clarissa said, self consciously.

"I'll brush it out for you," Eliza said.

Marcus fled the cabin again, an entirely different set of emotions in place this time.

It was well after the Persimmon Moon when school was able to resume. Phoebe hovered close in Clarissa's classroom, ever watchful that the teacher did not tire herself out. Mr. Redfield was doing the same in John's class.

Gradually life at the mission returned to normal, though everyone missed Robbie's cheerful presence. Will had fully recovered and finally completed his cabin. He had paid one call to Harmony Mission during the summer to make arrangements for his wedding with Susan. They planned to marry there in October and set up house at Hopefield before the Rendezvous.

Mr. Bogey brought their mail up from Three Forks after river levels began to rise with the fall rains. The missionaries were all enjoying letters from home in the dining hall before supper that evening. Clarissa smiled as she perused a letter from her sister Jerusha.

"Good news from home, Miss Johnson," Marcus asked from down the table.

"My sister writes that she has taken a teaching position at Cornwall," Clarissa explained. "There is a men's school there that is accepting students from among the Indian tribes. A benefactor named Elias Boudinot is providing scholarships. So she has met a few of these students and some are Cherokees . . . from Georgia, she says. It seems ironic that we are so far apart, yet both of us have had some connection with the Cherokees."

"I am glad to hear that schools in New England are opening for such students," John Spaulding commented. "It will do New Englanders good to accept and learn about men from other cultures."

John had once lost his own teaching position in New York because he was teaching Negro children.

"I don't know how much acceptance they are finding in Cornwall," Clarissa said as she carefully folded the letter. "Jerusha says they are quite adamant that the girls in her school have nothing to do with these Indian students."

"Progress comes slowly," Rev. Vaille observed. "If more of our fellow New Englanders had an opportunity to know Indians as we do here, much prejudice would disappear, I think."

The other missionaries were nodding in agreement. Then Rachel Chapman gasped suddenly and put her hand over her mouth. She too had been reading a letter from Connecticut. "Rachel, what is it?" her husband asked.

"Mother," Rachel said with a sound of dread in her voice.

"Is something wrong with grandmother?" Thomas inquired, looking up from the spoon spinning contest he and

167

Richard had been engaged in while waiting for supper to be served.

Looking at her son as if just becoming aware of his presence, Rachel drew a deep breath and put a bright smile on her face. "Nothing wrong, dear," she assured him. "She's coming for a visit."

"Your mother is coming here?" Chapman asked, disbelief in his voice.

"Yes." Rachel stuffed the letter back into its envelope, her hands shaking. She seemed more flustered than Clarissa had ever seen her.

"She expects to arrive sometime around Christmas," the minister's wife went on. "She's sailing down the coast and will take a steamboat from New Orleans."

"Is the governor coming too?" Abigail asked about her grandfather.

"No, he doesn't feel up to the journey," Rachel explained. "Mother will be traveling with Rev. and Mrs. Washburn at Dwight Mission. They will accompany her here because they also want to visit Union."

"How nice to have someone visit from home," Martha Woodruff said, but her voice trailed off as she looked at her husband.

"Well," Rachel said, looking around at the dining hall as if seeing it through her mother's eyes. "You'll need to get the sawmill finished, Mr. Chapman. Mother will want a real floor to walk upon."

"Yes, dear," her husband agreed.

Getting the sawmill running was proving to be a challenge for the men. None had experience at this sort of operation and though Will had studied the mill at Harmony, even he wasn't sure about getting all the moving parts working smoothly. The saw made a racket too, which spooked the oxen and made them belligerent.

Clarissa was attempting to read to her students one day while the men were trying to get the saw started yet again. Louisa and Deer-in-Water were holding their hands over their ears. Red Corn was in class today too and she seemed completely bewildered by the noise of the raspy saw and bellowing cattle.

Suddenly in the midst of all the sawmill noise, Clarissa heard a shriek that she recognized as Sarah's. Had she seen another deer?

Then she heard a commotion from the boys' classroom. It seemed as if the whole mission was in an uproar.

The teacher set down her book. "What on earth is going on?"

Leah apparently thought she needed to find the answer to teacher's question for she jumped from her chair and went to the window. Pulling back the deer hide curtain, she looked out. With eyes as big as saucers she turned back to the class.

"Buffalo," she shrieked too. "I think it's buffalo."

Clarissa hurried to the window to look out also. Sure enough wandering among the corn stacks between the mission and the Trace was a herd of buffalo. The huge, shaggy beasts had never come this close to the mission before. There were so many tightly packed together that they had turned the landscape dark brown. Had the lows of their oxen drawn the animals here? Or was it a search for fodder among their cornfields?

The other girls crowded around her trying to look out. Clarissa could see that the boys had gathered at the door of their classroom. She didn't dare let her students do the same. She had heard too many tales from Mr. Bogey and Star-That-Travels about buffalo stampedes.

Leaning out, she spoke to Mr. Spaulding. "Should we let the men know?" she asked, with a nod of her head toward the restless herd.

He nodded, said something to the boys, and then strode across the compound toward the sawmill. Clarissa stepped away from the window and allowed the girls to move in close. She assumed that Deer-in-Water and Red Corn had seen buffalo before, but even they seemed fascinated with the large animals.

At the dining hall door, Sarah stood entranced by the

169

sight. She had read about buffalo and seen a drawing of one, but what she beheld now far exceeded what she had imagined of them. She wondered what it would be like to reach out and touch one. She moved toward the school building, wanting a closer look.

The other women were working behind the kitchen, doing Monday's wash. The men were still unaware of the herd's presence in the noisy sawmill. The boys were nearly beside themselves with excitement, except for Black Beaver, Mad Buffalo's oldest son. He stood with his arms crossed over his bare chest, looking as if the presence of a buffalo herd was an every day occurrence.

He said something in Osage. Jean Revoir interpreted for the other boys. "He says he has hunted buffalo many times."

"Can you show us how?" James Chapman asked eagerly. Jean translated the question.

Black Beaver looked at the buffalo for a long moment, eyes narrowed in thought. Then he gave a curt nod and motioned for the boys to follow him. Dropping to a crouch, he began a slow duck walk toward the herd. The other boys mimicked his motions.

Had Clarissa been standing close to the window she would have seen the boys in time to call them back. The girls observed the boys and exchanged surprised looks, but kept their mouths closed. Tattletales they were not.

Sarah was the only adult aware of the boys' action. She was not sure what they were planning to do, but she instinctively knew they could be in danger. She hitched up her bright purple skirt and ran toward them. It was the very thing she should not have done.

As the men emerged from the sawmill to check on the herd, they saw the seamstress flying down the trail toward the Trace. In the next moment, they caught sight of the boys, circling around the back of the herd. Their slow, stealthy actions probably would not alarm the massive beasts. Sarah, however, if not stopped, would likely set them in motion.

"I'll get Miss Clapp, you get the boys," George called to his brother. Will nodded and the two hurried across the mission compound. Will and George had hunted buffalo with the Osages and were familiar with their behavior.

Abraham headed for the barn where their horses had grown agitated from the scent of the herd. Telling Paul to stay with the oxen in the mill, Woodruff went for his gun in the blacksmith shed and the ministers, Marcus and John went to their cabins to do the same. Stephen hurried to his cabin also, stopping to alert the women and tell them to get indoors.

"Boys, you come back here," Sarah called as she ran.

They all turned to look at the seamstress. Black Beaver hurriedly flattened himself to the ground. The buffalo began to stir and paw the dirt.

"Miss Clapp," George called as he raced toward the seamstress. "Stand still!"

Sarah plowed to a stop so abruptly she nearly toppled forward. "The boys," she said, pointing in their direction. She was now only a few feet from the herd.

"Will's got them," George gasped as he reached Sarah. "Just don't move."

Keeping downwind of the massive beasts, Will reached the boys and led them away from the herd. Still hunkered low to the ground, the stonemason ushered them into the barn.

One large bull came toward Sarah and George, seeming more curious than furious. But Sarah caught sight of him out of the corner of her eye and gave a shriek before clamping her hands over her mouth.

The bull lowered his head and bellowed. George recognized this as a warning signal to the rest of the herd. Throwing Miss Clapp to the ground, he threw himself over her as the animals began to move. Slowly at first, but building speed, the buffalo tore across the prairie heading north. Because they were at the edge of the herd, only a few buffalo came close to where Sarah and George huddled face down on the ground. To Sarah it felt as if a mighty earthquake were happening.

The other missionaries all made it into one of the buildings and stood in horror at windows and doors as the massive brown tidal wave shook the prairie. They prayed fervently for the safety of George and Miss Clapp. The herd parted around the barn and flattened their springhouse, but otherwise did not damage mission buildings.

As soon as the thunder died away, George raised up. His white shirt was brown from the kicked up dirt still swirling around them.

"Are you alright, Miss Clapp," he asked.

"I think so," she replied, also sitting up. Her face was covered with dirt and her curls were full of straw. "You saved my life," she said in awe. Then she started to blubber. "I'm so sorry," she wailed. "I was just trying to help the boys."

Marcus and Stephen reached the couple first and helped them stand. George appeared to be limping slightly as everyone converged on the dining hall.

The boys certainly knew that they were going to be punished for their part in the afternoon's adventure. They sat quietly at one table, eyes studiously cast downward. Their sisters were throwing them, "glad it's you and not me looks," even though most had tears in their eyes. It had been a most frightening experience for all of them. Everyone was shaken and upset.

Rachel spoke for all the parents. "Don't you ever think about doing that again," she said with an angry quiver in her voice. "Do you hear me?"

The boys and Sarah all solemnly nodded. Black Beaver stared defiantly out the window.

Rev. Vaille more calmly spoke next. "We will have to find a suitable disciplinary action for your scholars, Mr. Spaulding," he said.

The teacher nodded. "This is a serious matter," he responded, clearly working to keep a quiver out of his own voice as he met the eye of his son Billy. "Your parents and I will discuss this, young men, and will let you know how you are to be punished."

The boys heaved sighs of dread. "For today," their teacher went on, "you will be confined to the classroom with no recess."

Quietly the students filed back to their classrooms with

John and Clarissa. When the parents of the Osage students came for them, they were told of the incident. The Osage parents were not nearly as shocked as the missionary parents. Buffalo stampedes were a familiar hazard of the prairie.

Supper was a quiet affair that evening and the missionaries held the children a little tighter when tucking them into bed that night. Seeing the fear in their parents' eyes was enough to help the children understand the seriousness of the situation. It was a lesson they would not soon forget.

In the bachelors' cabin that evening the Requa brothers and Marcus discussed the day's events.

"We are fortunate, indeed, that no one was hurt," Marcus noted.

"Yeah," George agreed with a grimace as he tried to remove his shirt. Clearly in pain, he was not able to shrug the garment off his shoulders.

"Brother, what is wrong with you?" Will asked as he crossed the room. Pulling back George's shirt he looked at his back. "Man, you are black and blue. Did those beasts run right over you?"

"A few," George conceded.

"Why didn't you say anything?" Marcus asked, joining Will in looking at the angry purple bruising all across George's back.

"Didn't want to upset anyone," George grunted.

"Anyone? You mean Miss Clapp," Will said, sounding disgusted. Marcus went for his medical kit and pulled out a bottle of liniment.

"Her too," George said. "It wasn't her fault. She was just trying to protect the boys."

"She nearly got you killed," Will harrumphed.

"Help him get his shirt off," Marcus interrupted. The two men helped George ease off the shirt. Marcus began to carefully feel along the mechanic's back.

"Couple of ribs feel soft, probably cracked," the doctor said. "You are fortunate it isn't worse. Could have punctured a lung."

George nodded, but said nothing. Clearly the pain he had

tried to hide all evening was now almost more than he could bear.

"Will, get to the kitchen and see if there's any coffee left. I'll add a little laudanum. And bring some bandage rolls," Marcus directed. "Need to wrap his chest to keep those ribs immobile."

Will nodded and cast a glance at his younger brother that was a mixture of annoyance and concern. Then he stepped out into the evening shadows and headed to the kitchen.

Marcus began to lightly rub the liniment over George's back.

"What you Requa brothers won't do for your women," the doctor mused as he worked.

"Miss Clapp is not my woman," George argued through gritted teeth.

Marcus paused and looked his missionary brother in the face. "You're the only one who thinks that," he laughed.

George closed his eyes, whether to block out the burn of the liniment or the truth, Marcus couldn't tell.

CHAPTER SIXTEEN

Union Mission
Fall, 1823

It took a couple of weeks for George to heal up from the buffalo stampede across his back. Honoring his wishes, Will and Marcus did not say anything about his injuries to the other missionaries. But Clarissa suspected he had been hurt given how slowly and carefully he moved during the days after the incident.

She and Eliza and Sarah were getting dressed in their cabin one day in late September just a week after the stampede. Suddenly, without any warning, Sarah began to cry.

"It's my fault," she wailed as she slumped down onto her bed.

"What's your fault?" Eliza asked.

"Mr. Requa was hurt trying to protect me," the seamstress said through her tears. "I was just trying to help, but I did more harm than good. Oh, why do I always jump into things without thinking?"

Clarissa sat beside Sarah and drew the girl close. It was so like the same pose she had taken with Eliza months ago. To play mother to women who were only four years younger than her made her suddenly feel old and matronly.

"No one blames you," Clarissa soothed. "We all know you were looking out for the boys. It's just as much my fault. I should have seen them and stopped them from ever approaching that herd."

Eliza put her hands on her hips and shook her head.

"Let's stop with assigning blame," she said, rolling her eyes. "The fault is with those young rapscallions who thought they could hunt buffalo with no weapons. What those boys were thinking is beyond me."

Sarah and Clarissa smiled at her words. Then Clarissa pushed Sarah to sit up straight. "Eliza's right," she said firmly. "You and I have both asked forgiveness of God and their parents. We need to forgive ourselves for our mistakes. Let's toss this into the 'sea of forgetfulness' just as God has done and put it behind us."

Clarissa made a motion with her hands as if gathering up a large bundle of laundry. Then she pretended to drop the bundle and said, "Splash. See, now it's gone."

Sarah laughed. "And no fishing allowed?" she asked.

"None," Clarissa agreed. "Let's shake on it." The two women gave each other an exaggerated handshake.

Sarah's smile faded. "But I haven't apologized to Mr. Requa," she said in a little voice. "I'm afraid to bring it up."

"I think Mr. George would just as soon you not mention it," Eliza offered. "It might ruin his attempt to appear impervious to harm."

"She's right," Clarissa said. "Our little Miss Eliza is proving to be quite a wise young woman." She threw the blonde a secret smile.

"Then pray for me, Eliza," Sarah said. "I could use some of that myself."

As the three walked to the dining hall for morning devotions and breakfast, they passed the schoolboys all carrying a load of firewood. Part of their punishment for the attempted buffalo hunt was helping Paul chop wood each morning before breakfast. The need for kindling was never ending, and the punishment stretched out before them for months to come.

The single women hid smiles as they watched the boys go about their duty. "No splashing for them for awhile," Sarah observed. The three suppressed giggles as they stepped into the dining hall.

A few days later Will and George hitched two of their horses to a mission wagon. They were on their way to Harmony Mission where Will would marry Susan Comstock. Following the doctor's advice, George was careful as he climbed onto the wagon seat.

The missionaries gathered around the wagon at the barn. In the wagon were the bedrolls of the men, their best clothes for the wedding and an ample supply of food packed by Amanda for the journey. The women had tucked in a few small wedding day gifts for Susan, regretful that none of them would be able to attend the ceremony.

George would stand up with Will during the wedding and Miss Woolley was to serve as Susan's maid of honor. The brothers bid a farewell to the missionaries and turned the wagon toward the road that would take them past Hopefield to Missouri.

They stopped briefly at Hopefield to make sure everything was ready at Will's cabin. Teresa assured them that she would keep the little house clean and would have a supply of firewood ready for Susan's arrival. She and Star-That-Travels were dressing out two huge buffalo that Star had shot, probably on the very day of the stampede.

After crossing the Neosho, they also paid a call upon La Saline. Here they also heard about the unusually close visit of buffalo. The herd had already moved into Texas most likely. Colonel Chouteau was away, but his wife Rosalee offered the brothers a fine meal of buffalo tongue which was her specialty.

The last few miles toward Harmony, Will seemed to be pressing the horses to make good time.

"You in a hurry or something, Brother?" George asked with a grin.

"You know I am," Will said, not even trying to pretend otherwise. "I promised Miss Comstock I'd be to Harmony by the seventh and I don't intend to be late."

"A man shouldn't be late for his wedding," George agreed.

They said nothing for a time as Will worked to maneuver

the wagon through some deep ruts in the road. "Too many wagons coming through here," he observed as they bounced over the cuts in the dirt track made by the metal-rimmed wheels of other wagons. George was forced to clasp his chest to protect his tender ribs.

"It's becoming the main road to Texas," he said. "Ought to start calling it the Texas Road."

"Wish it was smoother," Will said as they hit a particularly deep rut. "It's about to rattle my teeth out."

"Better slow down a bit, then," George teased. "I'm sure Miss Comstock doesn't want a toothless groom."

Will grunted at the remark, but did pull back on the reins just a bit. He kept the pace steady for the last hour of travel, pulling the wagon into the Harmony yard at lamp lighting time.

Two days later, on the Sabbath, Will stood nervously before Rev. Nathaniel Dodge, the director of the mission.

He continually smoothed down the cravat he had borrowed from Dr. Belcher and that George had tied for him. His own fingers were too clumsy to do the job. They waited for Susan and Harriett to arrive at the chapel.

Will was just pulling in another deep breath when the door opened and he almost lost that breath at the sight of beautiful Susan wearing a soft blue dress. Her blonde hair had sprigs of some flower in it and she was a wearing a smile that matched his own.

The two young women made their way to the front of the chapel and joined the brothers in standing before the minister. During the brief exchange of vows, Will and Susan had eyes only for each other. Harriett looked immensely pleased with herself while in the congregation Rev. Montgomery looked glum. When George glanced around the room while his brother and the bride shared a kiss, Mary Austin had the audacity to wink at him.

At Union Mission, the family was sitting at dinner a few days after the Requas had left for Missouri. They were discussing preparations for their annual trip to Three Forks for the Pumpkin Moon Rendezvous. Suddenly they heard the jangle of harness and creak of wagon wheels approaching the yard.

Thomas jumped up to look out. "Six covered wagons," he informed the group.

"Robbie woulda' see'd them wagons long before they got here," Paul said mournfully as they all rose to go greet their guests.

The wagons, pulled by oxen, circled up tight along the split rail fence that now separated the mission from the cornfields. It was a minor defense that the men had constructed in recent weeks. It wouldn't keep out stampeding buffalo, but they hoped it would keep adventurous boys inside.

With his long gait, Rev. Vaille as usual was the first to reach their visitors and he opened the gate to let them in.

Looking eager to climb down from their wagons, the travelers made their way inside. At the head of the group was John McKnight, the trader and explorer Clarissa remembered seeing at last year's Rendezvous. He wore the same large felt hat with feather, fancy gun and belt and fringed deer hide coat.

"Afternoon, folks," he said, as he removed his hat and made a deep bow. Striking a flamboyant posture, he paused as if giving everyone time to admire him. Mr. McKnight appeared to believe his own publicity for he and his exploits had often been written about in the *Arkansas Gazette*.

"John McKnight at your service," the man said. "I hope you don't mind our little group stopping in for a few moments. We're Texas bound and thought to find a respite from our journey at your bit of civilization here in the wilderness."

To Clarissa he sounded like a politician making a speech at an Independence Day picnic. She exchanged an amused look with Eliza and Amanda who were standing beside her.

"You're certainly welcome," Vaille said. "May we offer you some refreshment?"

"Indeed," McKnight said. The three women in the group

were eyeing their outhouse as if it were a thing of beauty. Rachel sidled up to one and whispered an invitation that they refresh themselves there first. The women all nodded gratefully.

Amanda, Phoebe and Martha went to the kitchen to pull together a quick meal of cornbread, ham and beans with some hot coffee. The travelers filed into the dining room and the children were dismissed for noon recess in the school yard. Clarissa was grateful when Mr. Spaulding told her he would watch the children during their play time. She was interested in hearing from McKnight and his pilgrim band.

"So you are settling in Texas, Mr. McKnight?" Chapman asked when all had been seated and served.

"Not myself, no," the trader said. "I met this group while visiting Governor Clark in St. Louis. They asked if I would act as a guide for them through the Indian Country down to the Austin Colony. Being quite familiar with this entire region, I was happy to oblige them."

Clarissa noticed that none of his fellow travelers shared their guide's verbosity. Most were quietly eating as if the simple fare was ambrosia. Recalling her own long journey to get to the Osage lands, she could understand their feelings.

One man, however, was not eating, she noticed. When his wife joined him at the table, he leaned over and whispered something to her, pointing toward Alexander Woodruff who sat in a chair near the kitchen. She nodded, her eyes growing wide. Throughout the meal, the two kept up a whispered conversation with many furtive glances sent toward Alexander.

As the group of travelers all stood to return to their wagons, the man lagged behind the others. Then he stopped and pointed a finger at their blacksmith.

"Say, aren't you from Port Chester, New York?" he asked.

Alexander's eyes took on a hooded look and his wife Martha froze in place at the door into the kitchen. The couple shared a look that seemed to hold a mixture of alarm and resignation.

"That's right," Alexander said as he slowly stood from his chair.

Sensing the tension between Woodruff and the visitor, everyone paused to watch their exchange.

"Yeah," the man nodded. "You killed a man there, didn't you? Killed him in cold blood and got away with it too." His tone was hard as he spat out the accusation.

Clarissa almost laughed at the absurdity of such a remark about their gentle blacksmith. But the look on everyone's face sobered her instantly.

"It was an accident," Alexander countered.

"That's not how I heard it," the accuser persisted. "My cousin was neighbor to the man. He said you beat him to death with your fists."

Clarissa expected the blacksmith to further defend himself or explain the circumstances surrounding the incident. Instead, he pushed back his chair and strode out the kitchen door without another word. Martha stood quietly, but the teacher could see tears in the woman's eyes.

"You let men like that in your mission?" the New York man asked, pointing his accusing finger now at Rev. Chapman.

"I'm sure there is a perfectly acceptable explanation," the minister said, but it was clear that the man's revelation had taken him by surprise.

"Bah," the man spat. "You can't explain away murder." Then he slapped his hat on his head, took his wife's arm rather roughly and left the hall to walk toward his wagon along with the other travelers. McKnight soon had the wagon train on its way south.

The silence in the dining hall was dreadful. No one seemed quite able to meet anyone else's eye. Was the accusation true or merely cruel gossip? Was there a perfectly acceptable explanation and if so, why hadn't the blacksmith offered it?

"Can you tell us about this, Mrs. Woodruff?" Rev. Vaille asked gently.

"He was acquitted of any wrongdoing," Martha said

quietly, but forcefully. "What was done that day was done in self-defense."

"But what happened?" Vaille pressed, concern clearly written upon his face.

Martha sat down rather shakily at the nearest table and everyone else took a seat as well. Clarissa knew she should go to her classroom, but she was afraid to even move. And to be honest, she wanted to hear what Martha would say.

"Alexander always had a young apprentice work with him," Martha began. "One day the boy was late getting to the shop. When he finally did arrive he was terribly upset. Seems his father had just arrived home after a night of drinking and the man was beating his wife because she didn't have breakfast on the table for him. The boy tried to stop his father and had suffered several blows himself. He begged Alexander to go home with him and try to stop his father. He feared he would kill his mother."

Clarissa felt her eyes fill with tears in sympathy for the poor woman's plight. It was an all too common occurrence, she knew.

"When they arrived at the boy's home, they could hear the woman's cries before they even stepped into the house." Martha paused to wipe her own eyes with the hem of her apron. "That *neighbor* was standing in his yard, but not lifting a finger to come to the woman's aid.

"My husband went inside and had to literally pull the man off his wife," Martha continued. "Then he turned on Alexander and began to beat him. Alex shoved him back and he tripped. He hit his head on the corner of the fireplace." Her voice lowered to nearly a whisper. "The man died the next day."

There were murmurs of sympathy around the room. To Clarissa's surprise it was Sarah who went to Martha's side and slipped an arm of support around her shoulders. The older woman patted the girl on the cheek. Then drawing a deep breath she continued the story.

"The neighbor called the constable," she said. "Alexander was arrested and stood trial. The neighbor

182

testified against him, but the boy and his mother offered their defense. He was acquitted of wrong doing.

"But the neighbor wouldn't let it rest. Seems he and the deceased man had been drinking cohorts. He told everyone that Alexander had beat the man to death. It got to where we couldn't even walk to church without fingers being pointed our way. And no one would bring any work to the shop. Even our two sons kept their distance and we couldn't blame them. They could ill afford to lose their livelihood too.

"So we decided to move away and when you spoke at our church, Rev. Vaille, we felt it was the Lord's way of leading us out here. We certainly never meant to cause any harm to the mission. I hope you believe that." She looked around the room with pleading in her eyes. "Forgive us if we did," she whispered.

"Unfortunately, this traveler is likely to spread his story," Rev. Vaille sighed while exchanging a look with Chapman. "I would hate for his lies to keep anyone from the mission or the work we are trying to do."

Martha nodded and dropped her head.

"We can leave if you want us to," Alexander offered. Everyone turned to see that the blacksmith had come back and was standing in the door. He entered the room and crossed it to sit besides his wife. "Sorry I left you to face this along, Lovie," he said. She reached for his hand and he took it as if grasping a life line.

"No need for doing anything hastily," Rev. Chapman said. "We'll pray about this and then decide how best to handle it."

Everyone nodded and stood to return to their daily work. But before anyone could do more than stand, Phoebe held up her hand and said, "Wait."

The missionaries seemed surprised by the commanding tone in the housemother's voice. They all paused and waited to hear what she had to say.

"I ain't much for making speeches," she said, throwing a smile at her husband. "But I feel I need to say something." She seemed to be asking permission of the ministers.

"Go ahead, Mrs. Redfield," Rev. Chapman said.

Looking around the room, Phoebe drew in a deep breath and unconsciously rubbed the swell of her belly where her baby grew. "Nearly every one of us came to this mission with something in our past," she began. "You all know about my past and you forgave me for it."

Clarissa recalled the moment two years ago when Phoebe had tearfully confessed to her mission sisters that she had been divorced. There were tears in her eyes again today.

"The Church ain't a place for perfect people," she said. "If it were, I wouldn't be in it and I daresay none of you would either."

Clarissa saw nods from many of her fellow missionaries. She certainly knew it was true about herself.

"The Church is a place of refuge, isn't it?" Phoebe went on. "A refuge for every one of us. We aren't a bunch of holy saints out here making some great sacrifice. We're every bit as needy as any lost soul we came to help. We can offer the Osages hope and forgiveness only because we know what it is to need it ourselves."

Tears were streaming down her face by now and her husband slipped an arm around her shoulders. Several others among them were wiping away tears as well. Clarissa felt as if she had heard one of the best sermons she would ever hear.

"If Mr. Woodruff needs to go then I guess we all just best go with him," Phoebe concluded. She threw a glance at the Woodruffs and Martha mouthed the words, "thank you."

Everyone smiled now. Clarissa imagined them packing up the mission, logs and all, and heading further west to the mountains Mr. Bogey was always talking about.

Chuckling, Rev. Chapman said, "Better watch out, Redfield. Your wife is proving to be as good at preaching as any of us."

"Didn't mean to preach at anyone," Phoebe flushed a bit.

"Your point was beautifully made though," Rachel Chapman spoke up.

"No one needs to leave the mission," Rev. Vaille added. "I don't believe any more prayer is required on this matter.

Should gossip develop in the neighborhood, we will address it honestly and," he smiled, "perhaps use it to teach the valuable lesson Mrs. Redfield has reminded us of."

"Amen," Chapman concluded and with that benediction, the missionaries filed out to their afternoon chores.

Two days later Phoebe and Martha worked in quiet companionship to bring a dark-haired daughter into the world.

"You have a beautiful little girl," Martha told Phoebe as she washed the baby, wrapped her in a blanket and then laid her at Phoebe's breast. "Do you have a name chosen for her?"

"Jane," Phoebe said. "That was my mother's name."

"A lovely name," Martha smiled as she pulled the baby's blanket a little tighter around her. "For a lovely young miss with a lovely mother."

Phoebe shook her head. "I'm as plain as they come," she protested. "We'll hope this one gets her father's looks."

"You are lovely where it matters most," Martha returned. "On the inside. Don't ever forget that for I know that I never will."

CHAPTER SEVENTEEN

Union Mission
Winter, 1823

The Requas returned to Union just before Rendezvous
and the missionaries all traveled up to Hopefield to help Will
and Susan get moved into their cabin. Everyone had
contributed handcrafted items to help furnish the little home.
One of their wagons contained sawn pine lumber for a floor
for the log home. The men had finally gotten their sawmill in
good working order and were gradually placing floors in all
their buildings.

After Rev. Chapman prayed a house blessing over the
cabin, Susan invited everyone to crowd inside for the dinner
Amanda and Sarah had packed for the occasion. The women
all admired the design of the cabin with a beautiful stone front
stoop, a flowerbox at the window with its small glass panes,
and the two doors. The back door stepped out to the large
garden George had plowed over the summer. Amanda had
supplied seed potatoes for a first crop that would keep in their
root cellar nearby. Will had done his best to give his happy
bride the house she had designed.

They all took a break to travel again to Three Forks for
the Rendezvous at the end of October.

An unusually early snow in mid-November gave them
concern about facing a hard winter. Star-That-Travels assured
them that he could not forecast the weather, but according to
him the persimmon seeds portended a winter with much
snow.

Soon after that first snowfall the whole neighborhood was abuzz with news that caused everyone concern. Word had reached Captain Pryor that Mad Buffalo had been involved in a skirmish down along the Red River. He shared what information he had on the incident when he stopped by the mission on his way to his cabin near Hopefield.

"Mad Buffalo and a small hunting party were chasing an elk herd down in Miller County," Pryor told the group as they sat in the dining hall after an early supper one evening. "Bird was one of the warriors with him. Somewhere near the juncture of the Red River and the Kiamichi, he and his men ran across a group of hunters from Arkansas. Shots were fired and one of the Americans was killed."

"Who fired first," George asked. "That's always the question, isn't it?"

"Yes," Pryor agreed, "and as always, the answer isn't clear. Of course, for the folks in Little Rock, it doesn't matter who fired first. The Osages will always be to blame as far as they are concerned." Pryor's tone was bitter. He was related by marriage to Mad Buffalo and Chief Claremont. He usually took their side in a conflict.

"I thought the Osages had a peace treaty with the United States," Rev. Vaille said. "Why would Mad Buffalo violate the treaty?"

"He says he thought the men were Mexicans," Pryor explained. "They were coming up from the south across the Red."

"Have you heard what Colonel Arbuckle plans to do about this latest incident?" Chapman asked.

"He'll be visiting Claremont's Town shortly," Pryor answered. "Expect a visit from him here at Union Mission in the next few weeks. From what I'm hearing, the top brass in Washington City have made a decision about more western forts. Arbuckle may finally get to set something up around here."

"That will be good news," Vaille said. "At least this incident didn't involve the Cherokees. Hopefully we won't have to fear any reprisals for it."

"Don't let your guard down," Pryor advised. "Folks tend to take the law into their own hands out this far from the authorities. And they have few qualms about attacking the Indians."

The missionaries were sober as they walked with Pryor out to his horse at the corral. "Sorry to bring such news," the trader apologized as he mounted the high spirited mustang. "You folks might be asking the good Lord to keep things calm around here. Every time something like this happens it gets things stirred up."

"We certainly will," Rev. Chapman said. "And we'll share your warning with our folks at Hopefield."

Pryor nodded and then set out for his home where he would settle in for the winter. Traffic and trade would slow now that the cold was setting in. The missionaries returned to the warmth of the cheery fire in the dining hall for their evening devotions. Outside the November gloaming made the cold landscape seem fearful and forbidding.

As Pryor predicted, Colonel Arbuckle with the handsome Lieutenant Summers and the fort sutler, Colonel John Nicks, paid a call at the mission two weeks later. Since it was a Saturday, with no classes in session, Clarissa and John Spaulding joined the missionaries in visiting with the military contingent.

"Captain Pryor told us this latest incident with Mad Buffalo has resulted in decisions about a new fort," Chapman said as the men all sat down for coffee.

"We still don't have official orders," Colonel Arbuckle grunted as he took his seat and accepted the cup of coffee Amanda offered him. "But the Commissary General, George Gibson, has put out a request for bids on supply contracts for two forts – one on the Arkansas and one on the Red."

"I've already submitted a bid to service the fort here on the Arkansas," Nicks added. "I should hear soon whether I received the contract, but I expect I shall."

"Gibson seems to be the only general in Washington City who can make a decision," Arbuckle added. "If I can, I'm going to name the fort after him. I'm sure not going to name it for Scott, Gaines or Jackson."

There was a ripple of laughter among the group gathered in the dining hall. Colonel Arbuckle's frustration with the generals he reported to was well known.

Nicks went on, "I'm confident enough that I'll get the contract that I've joined Colonel Arbuckle on this trip to scout out a location for my store."

"So you'll be building down at Three Forks?" George asked. "On the Verdigris River?"

"Not enough room for a fort on the Verdigris," Arbuckle spoke up. "It's lined with fur outfits from its mouth to its falls. We've decided to build on the Neosho. The fort will be just across the river from Big Tracks' village."

"When will you start construction?" John asked.

"Early next spring," Arbuckle replied. "We'll be all winter getting the materials together for it."

During this exchange, Lieutenant Summers had tried to engage Eliza in conversation. He had managed to get a seat beside her at the next table.

"It has turned rather cold for this time of year," he began, keeping his voice low so as not to interrupt the colonel.

"Yes," Eliza agreed but said nothing more. Ignoring her finishing school training, she made no effort to keep the conversation going.

Clarissa was sitting close enough to hear and gave Eliza a little frown. Such a taciturn response bordered on rudeness and wasn't like Eliza at all. She usually never missed an opportunity to flirt with handsome soldiers.

"I suppose it might bring us snow for Christmas," the young man tried again. "I certainly do miss that down here . . . having snow, I mean."

Seeing Clarissa watching her, Eliza offered a more congenial reply. "Yes, the children here are always hoping for snow. I don't think our Osage students can understand that sentiment though." She smiled at the lieutenant and he looked pleased.

Clarissa didn't want to further eavesdrop on the two

young people so she turned to Phoebe who was sitting next to her and cooed some nonsense to baby Jane who looked up at her with light blue eyes. Shortly Charles and Eliza stood and walked to the dining room door where he helped her with her cloak. They stepped out into the afternoon sunshine.

Clarissa didn't try too hard to hide her smile until she caught the eye of Dr. Palmer. Like all the missionaries, he had watched the officer and Eliza step outside for an apparent walk around the mission.

Marcus also smiled and gave the schoolteacher a little nod as if in approval. It was as if they shared a secret and it made Clarissa feel warm inside. She turned back to the baby to hide the blush rising to her cheeks. Marcus gave his attention to his coffee cup.

Of everyone else in the room, only Eliza's sister was not smiling.

Later that evening the three single women were preparing for bed by the soft glow of the fireplace. Sarah hastily pulled her night dress over her head with a shiver in the cold. Then she picked up her hair brush and tried to work it through the snarl of her tight brown curls. The action created little snaps and sparks in the dry winter air.

"So is that handsome lieutenant paying you court?" she asked Eliza. Never one to be subtle, the seamstress looked ready to tease her cabin mate.

"No," Eliza responded with diffidence as she too started the hair brushing ritual. "He asked if he might after the new fort is built nearby, but I didn't want to encourage him."

"Whyever not?" Sarah asked in surprise.

"I'm not interested in life at a frontier fort," Eliza explained with a sigh. "I want to go back to New England."

"Oh," Sarah said, looking somewhat confused. She found life on the frontier an adventure and while she missed her family, she had no desire to return to the life of poverty and hard work she had known.

Clarissa felt Eliza was making a mistake to discourage the young officer's interest but she didn't want to push the issue too forcefully in front of Sarah. She did offer one observation through. "Lieutenant Summers won't be at the new fort forever, I'm sure. His tour of duty on the frontier will end and he'll be given another assignment. He might very well ask for a New England station. You said he was from Boston, didn't you?"

"Yeah," Sarah chimed in before Eliza could answer. "I read in the *Gazette* that every Military Academy graduate has to do a tour of duty on the frontier. But it's usually for only four years."

"Which means the lieutenant has two more years out here," Eliza countered somewhat stubbornly as she laid down her hair brush and slipped under the quilts on her bed. "Besides, Alice doesn't approve."

This Clarissa could not understand. After all, Alice had chosen to marry a school teacher which was not considered one of the "smart" professions either.

"What does Alice object to?" she asked.

"Yeah," Sarah would not miss a chance to speak. "He's quite handsome, evidently educated and seemed very well mannered. My mother would heartily approve of him."

"Alice thinks he must not have had much opportunity for pursuing a profession. Why else would he have joined the military?"

"That doesn't seem fair," Clarissa countered and then threw Sarah a look when she opened her mouth to interject another opinion. Sarah shut her mouth contritely and also slipped under her bedcovers.

"When has anything in my life ever been fair?" Eliza responded. Then she closed her eyes and settled on her pillow in a clear indication that the conversation was over for her.

Clarissa quietly continued her hair brushing and then scooted little Thea over so she could slip into bed beside her. Like Thea, Eliza had lost her mother at a young age. The teacher could well understand why life did indeed seem very unfair to the young woman. She said a prayer for all of her girls – cabin mates, students and her own sleeping child before she drifted off to sleep herself.

The following morning at Hopefield, Susan bent over her fireplace and flipped the thick strips of bacon she was cooking for Will's breakfast. Her husband was out milking their cow and would be in soon from the cold.

When Will stepped into the snug little cabin, he carried not only the pail of frothy milk but also a few more sticks of firewood. They would need to keep the wood box filled for the clouds suggested another snowfall might occur today.

Will set down the milk pail and bent down to give his bride a kiss.

"Ooh, you're cold as an icicle," Susan laughed pulling back as her husband tried to rub his cheek against hers.

"Gonna snow," Will predicted as he stood and unwound the scarf around his neck and then shrugged out of his coat and hung it on a peg by the door.

"Oh, dear," Susan sighed. "I've been putting off running to the outhouse hoping it would warm up some. I guess I'd better go now. Will you watch the bacon for me?"

"Sure," Will agreed, taking her place in front of the hearth. "Wear my coat," he suggested.

Susan wrapped his scarf over her hair and pulled on Will's bulky coat which swallowed the tall but willowy young woman whole. Will smiled at the sight of her.

Susan opened the door to step outside but stopped on the threshold.

"Will," she said and there was something in her voice that caused him to look up quickly.

"What is it?" he asked.

"You need to come here," Susan said, her high treble voice quaking slightly.

Will hurried to remove the frying pan from the fireplace grate and set it on the hearthstones. Then he rose and joined his wife at the door.

Outside about a dozen Osage ponies and riders waited in silence and perfect stillness. Four mounted warriors wore their colorful trade blankets and full leather leggings. Behind them, also mounted, were several women and children swathed in their blanket coats. As if frozen in place, they might have been a scene from an artist's newspaper illustration.

"I never even heard them," Will whispered to his wife. Normally visitors on the frontier would always call to a house when approaching it so as not to cause alarm or get shot by mistake. But the Osages practiced a stealth that made them silent masters of the land.

Will spoke a welcome to them in Osage. At his greeting, the oldest of the men moved his mustang forward and returned the greeting. From his nearby cabin, Star-That-Travels opened the door and stepped out. Striding across the clearing, he also greeted his fellow warriors.

After speaking with the visitors for a time, Star turned to Will and Susan. "This is Monepasha, his two sons and brother," he explained. "They want to join us here at Hopefield and learn field making."

"Why didn't they call to the house?" Will questioned. "How long have they been out here?"

"Not long," Star assured him. "They knew from Harmony Mission that you were newly married. They did not wish to disturb you."

Susan blushed furiously and all the Osage men grinned.

"Well, invite them in," she said quickly to cover her embarrassment. "We were just about to eat breakfast. You and Teresa come too."

Star nodded and then motioned toward his cabin where Teresa stood in the door. The Requa cabin was soon filled with their Osage guests who sat in a circle on the floor. While Will and Star conversed with the men, Teresa helped Susan cook more bacon and grits.

The Osages tentatively sampled the unfamiliar foods while looking around curiously at a lodge with a wooden floor.

"Monepasha is second chief to Pawhuska," Star-That-Travels translated for the older man who acted as spokesman for the group. "He learned about this place from Harmony. He says he is ready to try the white ways. The People are growing hungry as the game is less abundant in Missouri."

Susan whispered to Teresa where they sat outside the circle near the fireplace. "What does Monepasha mean in English?" she asked.

Teresa thought for a moment as if trying to work out the translation in her mind. "It means 'he-who-is-not-afraid-of-the-gopher,'" she said.

"Oh," Susan responded. "I guess we'll just call him Monepasha. The English would be quite a mouthful, wouldn't it?"

Teresa smiled. "Monepasha is known for his fearlessness," she explained. "He does not care that many of the People will not agree with his decision to come here."

"Then he has your courage," Susan responded.

Teresa shrugged at the compliment. "It is not courage to want better for your children," she said simply.

"Yes, it is," Susan replied.

By the end of the day the women of the four Osage families had erected their round lodges several yards upstream from Teresa's cabin. Will stood at their window watching as the glow of fires could faintly be seen from the lodges.

"What an answer to our prayers," he said, showing his excitement. "I wasn't sure we would have any Osages besides Star and Teresa here for the coming planting season."

"You will still have to convince the men that farming is a worthy occupation for a warrior," Susan reminded him as she set out cornbread and stew for supper.

"Yes," Will agreed, turning back from the window to sit down at their little table. "I'm hoping Star will be able to help with that."

"I'm not sure Star is convinced that he wants to farm," Susan said. "He always refers to the planting as Teresa's work."

"I know," Will said as the two of them took hands to offer a blessing over their supper. "But I am hopeful."

CHAPTER EIGHTEEN

Hopefield Farm
January, 1824

Despite a light snowfall every week, the missionaries worked to harvest lumber for additional cabins at Hopefield. The two sons of Monepasha were at first reluctant to help with the work, believing manual labor was beneath a warrior, but a few sharp words from their father brought them in line. Will and Alexander showed the men how to fell the trees with axes borrowed from Union Mission.

"Good thing we have plenty of tools at Union," Will observed to George and Abraham Redfield as they paused from cutting limbs from several downed pine trees. The breath of the men was visible in the crisp morning air and a light snow crunched beneath the pine branches. The fragrance of the cut logs was reminiscent of the Christmas decorations that had adorned the dining hall and school at Union.

The Hopefield families had all traveled down to Union last week for the Christmas service and children's program and for the feast that followed it. With the addition of seventeen people from Hopefield, the dining hall was nearly bursting at the seams.

The school would have six more children in class and many of them were boarding with the missionaries through the snowy winter months. Phoebe and Abraham had moved out of their cabin and acted as house parents in the dormitory above the classrooms.

When Bird had attended the church service to see his children perform in their Christmas program, he had inquired about also building a cabin at Hopefield. In a matter of just a few weeks, the new farm project had grown into a small village and Will and Susan were quite pleased with the prospect of developing a true working farm in the spring. They had sent word with a passing freighter to Harmony Mission to ask Rev. Montgomery to join them at Hopefield as soon as possible.

They would stack the logs taken from the *spavinah* and let them cure through the cold months of January and February. But by early spring they hoped to have several new cabins built and could then start the arduous task of breaking up the heavy prairie soil for planting corn.

They were already holding church services each Sunday. Either Rev. Vaille or Rev. Chapman would ride up from Union to deliver a sermon. So far only Star, Teresa and her baby were in attendance. Monepasha was respectful of the church, but neither he nor his family had come to the little gatherings held at Will and Susan's home.

At Union Mission the family was lingering in the warm dining room before beginning their chores on this winter morning. With Abraham, George and Alexander working in the *spavinah*, there was plenty of work to be divided among them. Stephen had even mentioned at breakfast that they needed to take on another apprentice or hire a man to help with the farm work come spring.

"We'll have to inquire in Three Forks the next time some of us are down there," Rev. Chapman agreed as he held a mug of coffee with both hands as if to warm them. "Or perhaps Mr. Bogey will stop in soon and we can ask him. He knows the neighborhood as well as anyone and would certainly know if someone is looking for work."

"Can we afford to hire a laborer?" Rev. Vaille asked the mission director quietly as the women worked to clear the dishes and the teachers encouraged their students to don their winter wraps and walk to the school house.

"We should," Chapman said. "It's Fuller's belief that

we'll be able to sell surplus corn to the new fort. That will provide income we haven't had before."

"Colonel Nicks asked me about supplying corn when he was here with Colonel Arbuckle," Stephen chimed in. "If we have the same yield we enjoyed last year, we should be able to pay the wages of one or two men. I would propose that we offer a position to Paul. He's proven to be a good worker."

"Well, if you think we can generate the income, I am certainly for it," Vaille nodded. "We're trying to sustain two mission sites now with Hopefield getting started. Hopefully our grist mill and saw mill will provide income as well."

Chapman laughed ruefully. "We haven't sawn a single plank for anyone but ourselves so far. But who knows what the future will hold. The new fort may bring new people to the area. Some might want plank homes instead of log cabins."

"Nicks will for certain," Stephen said as the men stood to get into their own coats and head out. "He told me he'll be bringing a new bride with him when he gets settled near the fort. He wants something nice for her and I think he has the money to do it."

"Yes, from what Bogey says, he's well off, having a mercantile in Fort Smith, government supply contracts for two forts and serving in the territorial legislature. He's even planning to get a postal contract as well."

"He's ambitious, for sure," Chapman said. "My mother-in-law would approve of him." There was a touch of bitterness in his voice.

"Weren't you expecting a visit from Mrs. Chapman's mother?" Rev. Vaille asked as all three men walked toward the barn.

"Yes," the other minister confirmed. "We had expected her for Christmas. I'm sure that was when she intended to arrive. But travel is so unpredictable, we are getting concerned."

"We can make it a matter of prayer in the evening devotions, if you wish," Vaille said. "You certainly want her to arrive soon."

"Certainly," Rev. Chapman echoed, but there was no certainty in his tone.

Two days later, a wagon pulled off the trail they now referred to as "the Texas Road." Slowly it made its way toward the mission in the growing dusk of late afternoon. Pulled by two mules, the wagon was a large freight hauler, but today its cargo was four people, plus a dark bearded driver. The rattle of the wagon's wheels over the frozen, rutted trail alerted the missionaries of the approaching visitors.

Curious, they made their way from varying locations in the compound, setting aside chores to greet their guests. As everyone converged at the corral, Clarissa heard Rachel Chapman gasp. "Mother!" she whispered, sounding almost shocked. "You really came."

The driver halted his mule team and set the brake then agilely jumped from the bench and made his way to the back of the wagon. Lowering the tail gate he set down a step stool and helped his passengers exit the wagon bed.

The first to descend was the woman Clarissa assumed to be Rachel's mother. Dressed in a dark wool traveling suit with a fur muff and high brimmed bonnet, the woman appeared to be in her mid-fifties and was quite attractive with the same pale blonde hair as her daughter. Rachel gave her mother a gingerly hug as if the woman would not approve of public displays of affection.

"It's so good to have you here, Mother," she said, rather breathlessly.

Margret Smith's smile seemed strained, "Thank you, dear," she responded.

Following her from the wagon was a young woman with dark curls, wearing a blue coat trimmed in black with black kid gloves. She held the hand of a tall man wearing a beaver hat and great coat.

"Have you met Rev. and Mrs. Washburn?" Mrs. Smith asked. "They accompanied me from Connecticut."

"We are pleased to have you here," Rev. Chapman stepped forward to shake hands with the fellow minister.

Cephas and Abigail Washburn led Dwight Mission near
Dardanelle.

The last to alight from the freighter was the priest from
Three Forks, Pierre Menard. He was dressed in his usual
fringed buckskin coat, leather britches and moccasins. He
carried a large basket covered with a light blanket.

"*Gracias*, Jose," Father Menard said to the freighter.
"Appreciate you driving all of us out here."

"My pleasure, *Padre*," the Mexican driver responded.
Then he helped Stephen to unload a trunk and two leather
valises before he closed up the wagon bed and sprang back up
to the bench seat. "Send word for a ride back to Three
Forks," he told the priest as he doffed his hat. "I am staying
there until it warms up some."

"I'll want a ride back tomorrow," the priest told him.

"Why don't you just spend the night as well, Jose?" Rev.
Chapman offered. "Plenty of folks bed down in our barn.
You're welcome to also."

Jose grinned. "And enjoy Mrs. Fuller's cooking?" he
asked eagerly.

Everyone laughed at the man's hopeful expression. "I'll
dish up something special for you, Mr. Ramirez," Amanda
offered.

Mrs. Smith pursed her lips at the exchange. Leaning in
close to Rachel's ear she said, "I realize this is a mission,
dear," she said. "But really . . . you allow the hired help to sit
at table with you?"

Rachel drew in a calming breath and then slipped her arm
through her mother's. "Yes, Mother, this is a mission." Then
in a louder voice she added, "Please let's all get inside out of
the cold. There is hot coffee on the hearth."

Everyone made their way to the dining hall. Cloaks were
removed and most everyone took seats while introductions
were made all around. Amanda, Sarah and Martha hurried to
the kitchen to gather up coffee mugs and set out biscuits and
cheese. The aroma of a supper of venison stew filled the
dining hall.

The children had become aware of the arrival of guests

and came from the barn where they had been playing in its warmth of oxen, horses and hay. When the Chapman children saw their grandmother they hurried across the dining room to greet her.

A look that could only be fear passed briefly over the older woman's face as she saw the Indian children who gathered in the dining hall along with the children of the mission family.

"Grandmother, I'm so happy to see you!" Leah Chapman squealed and rushed to throw her arms around the woman's neck. Mrs. Smith seemed rather surprised at the display, but patted the girl's back before thrusting her away. "I am too, dear," she said, "but you smell like a barn."

"That's because we've been playing in the barn," Leah explained with a child's matter-of-fact innocence. She clearly didn't know how completely unacceptable such behavior would be to her grandmother. Rachel blanched at her daughter's words.

The older Chapman children stood politely and waited for their grandmother to acknowledge them. "Oh, children," she said, "how you have all grown." Thomas and James gave stiff little bows and Abigail made a pretty curtsy.

Meanwhile Father Menard had set the large basket he carried on one of the dining tables. Curious, Marie Lombard asked, "What have you brought, Father?"

"Is it a Christmas gift?" her cousin Louisa added.

"Well, you might say that," the priest said with a glance at the adults all watching him with the same curiosity. The Washburns were smiling as if they knew the priest's secret. "In fact, it's very much like the first Christmas gift. Do you know what that was?"

"Gold, frankincense and myrrh," Richard Vaille stated confidently. It was his line from the program the children had performed at Christmas.

"That is a good answer, young man," the priest said as smile wrinkles lined his weathered face. "But I am thinking of the gift given even before the magi arrived."

The children silently pondered the riddle. Finally a look

of understanding crossed Lena Bradley's face. "Was it the baby Jesus?"

Before Father Menard could answer the blanket over the basket moved. "Ooh," the children said in unison and each took a step closer to the mysterious gift.

"Smart girl," Menard nodded. Again the blanket moved and a little mewling sound came from underneath its folds.

"Is it baby kittens?"

"Or puppies?" the children clamored and inched closer still.

The priest pulled back the blanket to reveal two Osage babies nestled inside. They looked to be about two months old.

"It's baby People," Deer-in-Water exclaimed.

Clarissa smiled at the normally shy little girl's response to seeing the two Osage children.

"Yes, and they're sure to be mighty hungry after the long trip out," Menard said regretfully. "I brought them out to you because their mother just passed yesterday and their father brought them to me. There's no one at Three Forks who will care for them."

"No one from Big Track's village?" Rachel asked in dismay.

"It's because they're twins," the priest explained. "Some folks think they're bad luck and their mother's death seems proof of that to their minds."

"Oh, the poor dears," Phoebe said as the two babies began to fuss. Handing her own daughter to Clarissa, she rose and went to pick up one from the basket. "I can certainly help with feeding them."

"I was for certain hoping you folks here would see to the two of them," Father Menard confessed. "Mrs. Washburn assisted with changing nappies or I would have been in great trouble just trying to get them to you."

"What are their names?" Sarah asked as she cooed to the other baby.

"Don't yet have names," Menard replied. "Their mother was sick from the time of their birth, I understand."

"Boys or girls?" Sarah asked.

"One of each."

"Well, the boy should be Moses, don't you think?" she looked around the room. "Since he came to us in a basket."

"And the girl can be Miriam, his sister," Phoebe added.

Everyone seemed to agree with the name choices for there were nods all around.

Sarah lifted the other baby who the priest said was the girl. "Well, I can't nurse her," she said, "but I can take her to raise. I helped my ma with my younger sisters so babies aren't a worry to me."

Mrs. Smith looked aghast. Again she spoke her concerns softly to her daughter. "Rearing an Indian? What can be she thinking? They could have all manner of disease. I was concerned just in riding in the same wagon with them."

Rachel gave her mother a baleful look and then exchanged an entirely different one with her husband.

He nodded and then cleared his throat. "Mrs. Chapman and I will be happy to take charge of the little boy." He pointedly did not look at his mother-in-law. "Dr. Palmer, perhaps you can check the babies over and see if they have any particular needs."

Marcus smiled and nodded. "I'd be glad to," he said. "But I think their first need is to be fed."

"I can help with that," Alice Spaulding said. To Eliza she added, "Watch Billy and Allie for me." Eliza nodded.

The two young mothers donned their coats and stepped outside to carry the babies to their cabins.

"Well, at least you have a wet nurse for her," Mrs. Smith harrumphed. But she still looked none too pleased.

"Is the baby ours, Mother," Leah asked, sliding into the chair next to her mother.

"Yes, dear," Rachel answered. "At least for now."

"Oh, good," the compassionate girl said. Then she inched closer to her mother and whispered, "Why does grandmother look as if she ate a green persimmon?"

Rachel rolled her lips to stifle a smile. Then she put her finger to her mouth to shush her forthright daughter.

"Grandmother is very tired from the journey," was all the explanation she offered.

Leah nodded sagely. "It's a long way from Connecticut," she observed.

"In more ways than you know, dear," her mother softly agreed.

The Washburns were offered the Redfields' former cabin to spend a week visiting at Union before Jose returned to transport them back to Three Forks. Mrs. Smith shared a bed with Rachel for the week while Rev. Chapman slept in the bachelors' cabin where George and Marcus drolly sympathized with the minister.

When Cephas and Abigail had left, Mrs. Smith was then moved to the vacant cabin where she planned to stay until spring.

After the children were put to bed one evening, Rachel sat with her mother in the glow of the fireplace and a single candle, sipping on the hot chamomile tea Mrs. Smith had brought with her.

"Why have you come, Mother?" Rachel finally said after a few moments of small talk. "I know you didn't want to experience prairie life."

"Hardly," her mother said, throwing a look around the little log cabin. "Although I am glad I have been able to see for myself exactly what the living conditions are in this desolate place to which you have dragged my grandchildren."

"This is our home now, Mother," Rachel frowned. "You knew when we left Connecticut that we would face a primitive beginning. But we are building a life here and the children are quite happy."

"Are they really?" the older woman asked with incredulity in her voice. "You have deprived them of all the finer things of life. I suppose they are too young to realize it, but at some point in time they will come to resent it."

"Not if I teach them what is truly important," Rachel countered stubbornly.

"And what is that, dear?" Mrs. Smith responded with an

equally stubborn set to her jaw. "To wear hand-me-downs, ruin their hands with chores, risk death from disease? Don't think I don't know about Leah being sick."

Rachel looked startled, then sighed with resignation. "I suppose Leah told you."

"No, it was James," her mother said. "He told me he prayed and God healed her. You are filling their heads with religious nonsense."

"How can you say that, Mother?" Rachel asked. "My own grandfather was one of New England's most prominent ministers. This is their heritage."

"Your grandfather built a great church, provided well for his children, saw his son pursue the law and rise to equal prominence. Don't you want something better for your own children?"

Rachel looked hurt at her mother's implied accusation. "I certainly want good things for my children."

"Then let me take them back with me to Connecticut," Mrs. Smith proposed. "They should be attending better schools that will prepare them for successful lives."

"They are receiving a very good education here and as you have said they are too young to be separated from their parents," Rachel responded.

"Mr. Spaulding and Miss Johnson are fine teachers," she went on. "When the children are older and ready for university, we will certainly see to it that they have the opportunity to attend."

"Thomas should already be at a preparatory school if he expects to read for the law," Mrs. Smith argued.

"He is only twelve; he has one more year of common education."

"Common, no doubt, is the appropriate word."

Rachel's face turned a bright red. "Thomas has never indicated that he has any interest in pursuing a law career . . . or a political one," she added pointedly. "I reserve for him the right to choose his own path in life."

"What a foolish notion," Mrs. Smith said, setting down her teacup with a decidedly uncultured rattle. "I'll not have my grandson choosing to be a farmer." She said the word with as much disdain as the Osage warriors did.

"There is nothing wrong with feeding people," Rachel said, though without true conviction. "He could choose a far worse profession."

"Oh, yes," Mrs. Smith made her last point with anger. "He could be a missionary."

Rachel stood and without another word walked out of the cabin, leaving her mother to finish her tea alone.

CHAPTER NINETEEN

Union Mission
February, 1824

Clarissa walked with her students from the school building to the dining hall one afternoon in early February. They had enjoyed several mild days and snow only lingered ,now in the shadows of the buildings. She shared her students' hopes that spring would soon arrive. Already the daffodil bulbs that Amanda had planted were poking their thin green leaves through the moist soil in front of her cabin. The cook had been delighted to find the bulbs at Chouteau's trading post last fall during Rendezvous.

Clarissa felt something akin to envy as she passed the Fullers' cabin. Though Amanda was not as artistic as Susan Requa, she did have a gift for growing things. Besides the daffodils, she was also nursing along five little apple tree seedlings now sitting in sorghum buckets on the front stoop. It created such a homey feel that Clarissa briefly wondered if she would ever know a home to call her own. She didn't mind sharing a cabin with Eliza and Sarah, not really. But would she ever be mistress of her own home?

She shook off the thought and settled her girls in the dining room for afternoon "tea," as Leah had suddenly begun to call their after school meal. Actually they would enjoy some cornbread crumbled into hot broth.

Clarissa noted that Mrs. Smith had vacated the dining room where she normally spent the day being waited on by Rachel and some of the other women. Mrs. Smith either didn't like the rambunctious students or she didn't want to sit with the Indian children. She would take to her cabin for a nap when school was dismissed.

The missionaries had tried to be considerate of Mrs. Smith's sensibilities, but Clarissa knew it was hard sometimes for all of them to hold their tongue around the woman. Rachel looked frazzled as she tried to meet her mother's demands, which was totally uncharacteristic of her.

The teacher stepped into the kitchen to see if she was needed for supper preparations. To accommodate Rachel's mother, they now served the students first and then sent them to the dorm rooms where Phoebe and Abraham would assist with any school work they needed to complete.

Then the adults would eat and spend an evening of quiet conversation and the never-ending hand chores before devotions and bedtime. Amanda had rolled her eyes when the arrangement had first been proposed, but Clarissa found that the moments away from the children were a welcome respite.

In the kitchen, Sarah was trying to soothe Miriam who Dr. Palmer had diagnosed with colic. Martha and Amanda were offering suggestions on dealing with the malady.

"I think we have supper under control," Amanda stated when Clarissa checked in.

"Then I think I'll go get Thea," Clarissa said. "I'm sure Phoebe could use a break."

"Phoebe loves them babies, every single one," Sarah replied over her baby's unhappy mews. "She doesn't see them as any trouble."

"I know," Clarissa smiled. "But I also know even the most loving mother or nanny needs some help now and then."

She exited the kitchen and skirted around the clothesline where dozens of diapers flapped in the light breeze. With six little ones at the mission, diapers were laundered every day now. The women had requested an indoor laundry and so Abraham and George had returned from the Hopefield log harvest to saw some of the logs into lumber for the new building.

In fact George and Stephen Fuller had driven down to Three Forks early this morning to pick up a keg of nails from

Mr. Bogey. They would spend the night at the trade community and return tomorrow.

The two men had just exited Bogey's trading post when a commotion erupted up the trail near Hugh Love's post. The trader, in reality, ran a saloon where most of the rivermen who worked on the keelboats paid a visit whenever they were anchored at the little community.

The two missionary brothers stood at their wagon and watched a drunken brawl as it sprawled out from the post and filled the muddy trail that passed for a street. At least a half dozen men were engaged in a staggering, stumbling match of fisticuffs that might have been amusing were it not so serious.

There was no law enforcement west of Fort Smith for peaceful citizens to call upon, so everyone who didn't want to be embroiled in the melee simply kept their distance.

Joseph Bogey stepped out onto the front porch of his establishment and joined others along the street in watching the spectacle. "Hugh ought to know better than to start serving this early in the day," he groused to the men.

"Should we try to intervene?" Stephen asked, though he did not look eager to wade into the fight.

"You're too wise for that," Bogey smiled. "And I'm too old for that."

"Looks a little one-sided," a voice called to them from Nathanial Pryor's post which sat between Bogey's and the Love saloon.

The men turned to see the Fort Smith sutler, John Nicks, making his way toward them.

"Colonel Nicks," Stephen greeted the man. "What brings you to Three Forks?"

"I'm working on my cabin across the river," he replied, gesturing east toward the Neosho. "Been cutting logs for the last few days. I'll build downstream a bit from where Arbuckle plans to put the cantonment."

"The cantonment?" Stephen asked.

"Yes, Cantonment Gibson. Arbuckle has gotten approval for that name." The man smiled at the shared secret. "A cantonment is smaller and less permanent than a fort. Mostly tents for housing the men. He wants to get something up fast before the generals change their mind."

"When will the work begin?" George asked.

"Actual construction will commence sometime in April, most likely. A corps will arrive soon to start felling logs for the palisade."

"Finally have some decent weather for it," George observed. "We've been cutting in the snow."

"Yes, and I'm glad I ran into you here," the colonel said. "I'd like to get my logs sawn. Would I be able to haul them up to the mission next week?"

"Come ahead," Stephen agreed. "We're hoping folks in the area will start using the sawmill."

"Very good," Nicks said. Then he started to pat at his pockets. "Just remembered," he explained as he withdrew an envelope from his coat. "I have a letter for Miss Cleaver from Lieutenant Summers." He held it up with a grin. "You can see that she gets it?"

"Certainly," Stephen said and took the letter to tuck into his own coat pocket.

"Seems the young man is quite smitten with your Miss Cleaver," the colonel winked. "And who could blame him. She's quite a beauty. I might have taken an interest myself were it not for Sarah."

"Sarah?" George asked rather sharply.

"Yes," Nicks replied. "My fiancée, Sarah Perkins. We're to be wed at the end of the month. That's why I'm in such a tear to get this cabin completed."

Stephen gave the mission mechanic a sly look, causing George to flush slightly.

"I think you're right about that fight, colonel," George changed the subject. "Two against one isn't fair."

The men all turned their attention again to the brawl that had continued while they visited. Most of the men involved had dropped out but two men were still pounding away at one other man. He looked about to collapse, but one of the rivermen was holding him up so his companion could continue the pounding.

"Well, we can't let them kill the man," Bogey said. He reached inside his building and pulled down a musket that he kept hanging over the door.

"If you gentlemen will join me," he said.

All four of the men started up the trail. The men involved in the fight seemed oblivious to their approach, but the street began to clear of everyone else.

When Bogey was within a few yards of the fighters, he cocked his flintlock. The sound caught the men's attention and made them hesitate for a moment. Their victim collapsed to the ground in a heap, his face bloodied and bruised.

"Does your captain know you're wasting your pay on rotgut and pounding one of his men into a pulp?" Bogey asked in a voice that commanded attention.

"It's no' of your business," slurred one of the men who stood upright with only the most concentrated effort.

"But I do a good bit of business with your captain," Bogey continued. "And I'd hate to have to take my money elsewhere if he can't control his men. Would he want you losing him business?"

Bogey's words seemed to slowly penetrate the fog of their drunkenness. One picked up his cap and slapped it back on his greasy hair and the other gave a final half-hearted kick at the downed man. Then both stumbled down the path back to their keelboat.

Stephen squatted down beside the man who lay in the mud. "Can you sit up?" he asked, holding out a hand of assistance.

"Lea' me alone," the man muttered. He tried to raise up on his own, but quickly flopped back onto the sloppy street.

Stephen kept his hand extended and just waited. Finally, with a grunt, the man reached for him and allowed the farmer to help him to a seated position. He appeared to be an older man with plenty of gray in his full beard. He had two teeth missing, but with so much blood on his face it was hard to tell if he lost them in this fight or perhaps in a previous one.

"What's your name?" Colonel Nicks asked from where he stood over the man.

"Howard," he replied with a cough that brought blood. "Richard Howard."

"Mr. Howard, you need a doctor," Stephen said. "We'll take you up to Union Mission."

"Don' wan' a doctor," Howell argued. "Jus' need a drink."

"Another drink is the last thing you need," Bogey responded in disgust.

"You can sleep in our wagon tonight and we'll take you up to our doctor in the morning," George proposed. "You'll need your face stitched and probably need your ribs wrapped. Palmer is good at both." The mechanic smiled ruefully at Stephen. Both men had required the doctor's skilled care in the past.

"Can't," the riverman shook his head. "My boat leaves in the mornin'."

"But you won't be on it," a voice boomed from behind them. They all turned to see the keelboat's captain approaching. Alerted by his returning men, he had come to round up his crew.

"You're fired, Howard," the captain announced. "I'm tired of your fights and your drinking."

The older man dropped his head into muddy, bloody hands. "But, captain," he almost sobbed. "I need this job. I'll stop my drinking; I promise."

"I've heard it before, Howard," the captain shook his head. "Have your new friends collect your gear and your pay before nightfall or the other crew members will divide it among themselves." Then he continued on to the Love post and within a minute had the rest of his crew heading back down river to where his boat was moored.

Howard began to cry in earnest now, a slight heave of his shoulders announcing his despair. Exchanging a look of annoyance mixed with pity, George and Nicks reached down and as gently as possible hauled the man upward. Then they helped him slowly walk back to the mission wagon where it took both of them and Stephen to get him into it.

"I'll get his things," Bogey volunteered. "Pull your

wagon round back and he can sleep it off there." Stephen
nodded.

"You'll leave at dawn tomorrow?" Nicks asked.

"Yes, at first light," George replied.

"Then I'll meet you here with a skiff loaded with logs
and follow you up to Union," the colonel said. "See you in
the morning." He sketched a salute and then headed to his
camp on French Point.

At daybreak the next morning, Nicks arrived at Bogey's
post where George and Stephen had camped, keeping an eye
on the injured riverman who slept fitfully in their wagon. As
soon as they doused their fire, the men began the journey
north along the Texas Road. They kept a slow pace for the
sake of the mules hauling Nicks' logs and for Mr. Howard
who held his ribs and moaned in pain as the wagon bumped
over the road's deep ruts.

When they arrived at Union night was falling, but the
missionaries were mostly still gathered in the dining hall.
Marcus and Alexander helped to get Howard into the men's
quarters and the doctor immediately began his examination of
the injured man. The smell of whiskey permeated his clothes.

"What caused all this?" he asked, looking up at George
who held a lamp for him.

"Whiskey," George responded.

Marcus smiled grimly and shook his head.

"And a couple of roustabouts half his age," the mechanic
continued.

"From the amount of blood he's coughing, I'd say he's
had a rib puncture his lung. I'll need to operate."

"What do we need to get you?" asked Rev. Chapman
who stood at the end of the bed.

"Hot water and lots of cloths, more lamps, soap and
towels," Marcus continued his list as he went through his own
medical kit, pulling out the instruments he would use.

"And ask Mrs. Woodruff if she can assist," he added.
Then he hesitated a long moment. "And Miss Johnson, too, if
she's willing."

Now it was George who smiled as he left to take care of the doctor's requests. Within just a few moments the others had sprung into action and were gathering the supplies he needed. Amanda started a broth simmering and steeped some willow bark tea.

Clarissa helped Martha carry the supplies to the men's cabin. She felt the same queasiness in her stomach that she felt every time she was called upon to assist with a surgery or injury. But she was determined to be a help to the doctor.

She set the basin of hot water, soap and several towels on the table next to the gleaming surgical instruments the doctor had laid out. Marcus removed his coat and rolled up his shirtsleeves and then plunged his hands into the basin. He exchanged a look with the schoolteacher, giving her a smile of thanks and encouragement.

The room suddenly felt much warmer to Clarissa and her heart pounded. *Please don't let me faint*, she inwardly prayed.

Martha and Clarissa had scrubbed their hands thoroughly in the kitchen so as soon as Dr. Palmer dried his hands, they all gathered at the bed to begin the surgery. Chapman and George held lamps close while Alexander held the legs of the now sedated man.

Though this surgery took far less time than it had taken to suture Stephen's wounds from the panther attack, it seemed much longer to Clarissa. She could not watch the doctor actually cut into the man's chest. She kept her focus on the instruments that she was asked to hand to the doctor and kept up a litany of prayer in her head.

When Marcus asked her to thread the catgut suturing into the curved needle to close the incision, her hands trembled. *Sarah should have done this*, she thought. But she wouldn't have wanted Sarah standing close to the doctor's shoulder, feeling the warmth of his hand when he took the needle, receiving another smile of thanks.

Finally the doctor snipped the last suture and rocked back on his heels beside the cot. He rolled his shoulders to release the tension that always built in his neck when operating.

"We've done all we can," he said quietly. "I thank you all for your assistance."

"Will he survive this?" Chapman asked.

"From the jaundice, I'd say he's ruined his health with drink," Marcus said slowly. "We'll have to watch for infection and pneumonia. The odds are not in his favor."

"We will pray," the minister said.

Marcus nodded, but seemed distracted. His shoulders now drooped and Clarissa recognized the brooding, introspection that always took over the doctor's thoughts when a patient's life hung in the balance. She wanted to reach out and squeeze a shoulder as he continued to kneel by Mr. Howard's bed. But her fingers were bloody and the others stood around them in the lamplight quietly praying for the man. All she could do was stand with them, wishing she could do so much more.

The following morning, the missionaries were relieved to find that Mr. Howard had lived through the night. His recovery would he slow, and Marcus did not seem hopeful when Clarissa asked about the riverman at breakfast the next morning.

"If he does indeed recover from these injuries," Marcus said quietly over a final mug of coffee, "his greatest obstacle to health will be in overcoming his desire to drink. I know that alone can kill a man."

Clarissa nodded but didn't know what to say. Coming from a family that eschewed strong drink, she had little experience with the matter.

"I know that for a fact," Sarah said from where she sat at the other end of the table. Most everyone else was already up and on to chores, but Sarah lingered over the last bit of her hot drink.

Both Marcus and Clarissa turned to the young seamstress. "My father," she said simply to their unspoken question.

"I'm sorry," Marcus said with sympathy and Clarissa reached over and squeezed her hand.

"It was a long time ago," Sarah said with a shrug. "I don't even remember him well anymore. Just remember Mama pleading with him to stop. But he never could."

"Yes, it can grip a man to death," Marcus observed. Clarissa cast about in her mind for a comment but could think of nothing. The silence was interrupted by George entering the dining hall.

As he stepped through the door, he brought with him a cold draft of air and the woodsy scent that Clarissa always associated with winter . . . and with George. He walked over to the table while stuffing his cap into a pocket.

"Miss Clapp," he said when he arrived at their table. "I was down to the river this morning and spotted a doe with twin fawns. I thought you might like to see them. They're newborn so she won't be moving them for awhile."

"Ooh," Sarah nearly squealed as she set down her cup with a thunk. "I would love to see them, Mr. Requa. You know I love prairie wildlife." Then her face went red as if remembering what her interest in wildlife had once cost George. "I'll just take my cup to the kitchen and get my coat." She stood and with a whirl of her skirts, she was off to the kitchen her words trailing behind her.

Clarissa hid her smile in her own coffee cup but peeked over the rim to see that Marcus was doing the same. They shared a conspiratorial look.

In a flash, Sarah was back, wearing her coat and tying her black winter bonnet. "Oh, Mr. Requa, I'm so excited," she exclaimed as she took the arm he offered. "I've never seen a baby deer up close before though I've seen several does from a distance coming through the cane near the river." She and the mechanic made their way to the door, Sarah chattering away.

Finally George stopped and said, "Miss Clapp."

"Yes, Mr. Requa."

"We'll need to be quiet so as not to frighten them."

Sarah smiled, revealing her dimples. "Believe it or not, Mr. Requa, I can be quiet when I need to be."

George laughed. "This is a time when you need to be."

Sarah pressed her lips together but a giggle escaped. "Yes, sir," she whispered as the two of them stepped out into the cold.

"They're right for each other," Marcus said to Clarissa.

"Yes," Clarissa said, feeling a little breathless that she was now alone in the dining hall with the doctor. She couldn't recall that ever happening.

"Wouldn't be surprised if they marry soon."

"You're probably right." Clarissa said. "It wouldn't be a surprise at all."

Marcus stared into his coffee cup and then drew a deep breath. "Is marriage something you have decided against for yourself, Miss Johnson?"

Heart pounding, Clarissa knew she had to be honest. "No," she nearly whispered. "I am open to marriage."

"Then perhaps . . ."

Eliza stepped into the dining hall from the kitchen just then, carrying a dishcloth to wipe down the tables.

"Oh, I thought you had gone to class, Miss Clarissa," she said in surprise.

"I guess I should," Clarissa said, glancing up at the mantle clock. She sent a look of regret to the doctor.

"And I should check on our patient," Marcus said. He stood and walked around the table to pull out Clarissa's chair for her.

When she stood she was just inches from the doctor who did not step back from her chair. While Eliza worked nearby, he said quietly, "Perhaps we could take a walk some day after classes are dismissed?"

"I would like that," Clarissa agreed.

Marcus smiled. "Then good day to you, Miss Johnson," he said with a slight bow.

"Good day," she replied though she could scarcely get the words out. She watched him walk to the door and take his hat from a peg before stepping outside.

"Well, finally," Eliza said under her breath as she scrubbed at a dried bit of jam on the table.

"What?" Clarissa asked, as if coming out of a daze.

Eliza simply smiled sweetly and said, "Good day to you, Miss Johnson."

Clarissa blushed and reached for the wool shawl on the back of her chair.

"Your time is coming, Eliza," she said with a smile and then walked to the door herself.

As she opened it, Stephen Fuller stepped inside in a rush.

"Excuse me, Miss Johnson," he said, looking surprised to find her standing right there. Then seeing Eliza, he hurried over to her.

"Miss Cleaver, I owe you an apology," he stated as he pulled a rather crumpled envelope out of his pocket. "Colonel Nicks gave me a letter for you from Lieutenant Summers and I forgot to give it to you yesterday." He held it out to the young woman.

Eliza looked at the letter as if it were a snake coiled to strike and made no effort to take it.

"Eliza," Clarissa said in her teacher voice.

The girl glanced at the teacher and then reached for the envelope. Without looking at it, she stuffed it into her apron pocket. "Thank you, Mr. Fuller," she said.

Looking relieved to be free of this responsibility, the farmer nodded and then went to the kitchen where his wife was already hard at work on preparations for the noontime meal.

Eliza went back to her work as if nothing had disturbed it. Clarissa just shook her head and stepped outside into the mild morning air. As she walked to the schoolhouse she passed Colonel Nicks who doffed his hat in greeting.

"Spring . . . or something like it . . . seems to be in the air, Miss Johnson," he said.

"Yes, Colonel," Clarissa agreed. "Definitely something like it." She watched for a moment as he walked on toward the sawmill. "And who knows what beautiful things might grow" she added quietly to herself and continued on to her waiting class.

217

CHAPTER TWENTY

Union Mission
Early March, 1824

When Clarissa carried Thea into her cabin after supper that evening, she found Eliza alone. The young blonde had quickly stuffed the lieutenant's letter under her pillow when Clarissa arrived.

"Where's Sarah?" the teacher asked.

"She went for a walk with Mr. Requa."

For a time Clarissa said nothing more as she prepared Thea for bed. The little girl was almost asleep already so her mother quickly got her into her night dress, re-braided her hair and tucked her into their bed with a kiss.

Then she turned to Eliza. "You can tell me it's none of my business and I'll respect that," she began, keeping her voice low. "But I hope you will at least pay the lieutenant the courtesy of a response to that letter."

Eliza sighed and pulled the crumpled missive back out into the lamplight. "He says he'll be assigned to the corps that will build Cantonment Gibson. He expects to arrive next month and wants to pay a call."

Clarissa crossed the small room to sit beside Eliza on her bed. "And what do you want?" she asked quietly.

"I don't know?" Eliza said. "I don't want to make a mistake."

"Allowing a gentleman to call on you is not a commitment to marriage," Clarissa advised. "It's an opportunity to get to know him better. It may not be my place to say this, but I think you should give the young man a chance. He won't be a frontier soldier forever."

"I suppose," Eliza said, looking down at the letter. "But I've been doing a lot of soul searching since the Beans." Her face flushed. "I don't want to use some man just to get back home. How would I ever know if I wasn't just using Lieutenant Summers?"

"Oh, you will know," Clarissa smiled. "If there comes a day when you will follow that lieutenant anywhere he plans to go, you will not be using him."

"Then you think I should ask him to visit Union?"

"Yes, I do," Clarissa affirmed. "And with your beauty and Amanda's cooking, I think we'll see him for supper quite often."

Eliza smiled. "Perhaps he is just using me to get a home cooked meal."

Clarissa laughed, but then quickly sobered. "I seriously doubt that, little sister." She gave the girl a hug. "Just be honest with yourself and with him and I think everything will work out as it should."

Eliza pulled back from the hug and looked closely at the teacher. "Like it finally has for you and Dr. Palmer?"

Now it was Clarissa's turn to feel heat rising to her face and she lowered her eyes and pretended to brush some unseen dust from her skirt. Finally able to speak without betraying her emotions, she almost whispered, "Yes. At least I think perhaps it is. In my own way I may be just as uncertain as you are, Eliza."

"But why?" the younger woman asked. "He's always been fond of you. I know. I tried very hard to win his affections, all to no avail."

"Do you think so?" Clarissa countered. "I suppose I hesitate because I thought a man loved me once before. He said he did. But he was quick to leave me when someone else came along. Someone more beautiful and with more money."

Clarissa was surprised that she could still feel the bitterness of her broken engagement even now so many years later.

"That will hardly be a concern with Dr. Palmer," Eliza responded. "If money were what interested him he wouldn't be serving here on the prairie. And at the risk of sounding vain, he isn't one easily turned by another pretty face either."

"No," Clarissa said, her eyes filling with tears. "He is as giving and caring a person as I have ever met. I don't doubt his character; it's my own worthiness I doubt. It fills me with fear. I don't know if I could endure rejection a second time."

"He has patiently waited for you," Eliza said. "He has planted many little seeds of concern and kindness, hoping one might find its way into your heart. I can't imagine him changing his mind after these three years of waiting."

"My, Eliza, you sound like a poet," Clarissa smiled. "I suppose my heart has been like a fallow field, broken up but yielding nothing. And now hope has sprung up at last and I'm afraid of being disappointed."

"Then I'll give the same advice that you gave me," Eliza concluded. "Give the young man a chance."

Clarissa gave Eliza a look that she usually reserved for a wayward student. But instead of having its usual effect, it caused Eliza to lapse into bubbling laughter. The two were trying to keep their laughter quiet when Sarah entered the door.

She hung up her coat and bonnet at the door and came over to Eliza's bed where her two roommates sat. With no apology, she wiggled into the space between them and slipped an arm around each.

"What are we laughing about?" she whispered with a smile on her own happy face.

"Young men," Eliza could barely stammer her answer around her giggles.

"Well," Sarah said with a wink," then let me join you for I have just secured a young man of my own."

"Does that mean . . ." Eliza began sitting up straight.

Sarah nodded and her curls bobbed up and down. "He asked me for my hand tonight."

"Sarah, congratulations!" Clarissa exclaimed giving the seamstress a hug. Then she took on an exaggerated look of concern. "Does George know what he is getting himself into?"

"No," Sarah said, going along with the joke. "And don't either of you tell him."

Then all three young women collapsed on the bed in a mix of joyful tears and laughter.

Clarissa had been only vaguely aware of how hard Dr. Palmer worked at the mission. Besides spending several hours a day attending to the injured riverman, it seemed that the doctor was often called upon to tend to an injury or visit someone in the neighborhood who had taken ill. And since the neighborhood covered La Saline, Hopefield, Claremont's Town, Three Forks and the La Cascade area, travel often took him away for two or three days at a time.

Despite her determination to exercise the same patience Eliza attributed to the doctor, Clarissa found herself discouraged when the promised walk had not occurred after a busy week at the mission.

Mr. Howard was proving to be a cantankerous patient. He railed against his confinement and showered curses upon the doctor for not giving him more than a few drops of whiskey to manage his pain. While the cuts upon his hands and face were healing, his ribs were still fragile for he would not remain quietly in bed as Marcus advised.

"The man's as mean as a snake," Amanda said under her breath as she returned to the kitchen one morning after taking breakfast to the convalescent. "I don't know how Dr. Palmer puts up with his ugliness."

"Our good doctor is a saint," Rachel observed. "He never loses patience with mother and her 'vapors' either."

Amanda smiled and threw a wink Clarissa's way where she tried to help Thea finish her scrambled eggs at the kitchen work table. Thea wanted to feed herself and would not suffer assistance even though most of her food ended up in her hair or down the front of her pinafore.

"Our good doctor will make someone a fine husband," the red-haired cook observed playfully.

Clarissa knew her face was suddenly very red but she did not want to respond to Amanda's gentle teasing. There was still too much doubt in her heart to even pretend that she was considering marriage to the good doctor.

Her silence, however, seemed only to confirm Amanda's hint and the cook sent a conspiratorial smile to Rachel and Phoebe who worked alongside her getting breakfast ready for the children.

Clarissa felt so discouraged that she ate with the children and then walked with her girls to class rather than eat with the adults. There seemed no point in lingering in the dining hall, hoping the doctor might be present. Often he chose to help Mr. Howard with his breakfast and did not leave his cabin until mid morning.

It was late afternoon that day when visitors arrived from Three Forks. Colonel Nicks brought his bride to introduce her to the missionaries. They had been married in Fort Smith and were now settled in the plank cabin he had built for her.

"I expect the first corpsmen to arrive in about two weeks to start the log harvest for the cantonment," Nicks told the missionaries during supper. "I plan to hire some to help me dig a well while off duty. I promised Mrs. Nicks I'd give her a well right near the door. There's no spring nearby and I don't want her to haul water from the river when I am away."

"You'll have some distance to travel for the legislative session, Colonel," Rev. Chapman observed. "I'm surprised you chose to live so far west."

"Well, we'll retain a room at a boarding house in Fort Smith," the colonel said while he carved into the buffalo steak on his enamel plate. "And, of course, I have rooms in Little Rock. But I want to keep abreast of the happenings out here. Few of my colleagues in the state house really understand the conditions that you all face."

"Will you travel to Little Rock with the colonel, Mrs. Nicks?" Rachel asked, hoping to draw the young woman into the conversation.

"Sometimes I will," Sarah Nicks responded. "But I grew up in my cousin's home in Arkansas so I'm comfortable on the frontier. And you can ask the colonel if I know my way around firearms." She smiled over her coffee mug at her husband.

"A stranger would not wish to encounter my wife in the dark."

"Besides, I'll be within shouting distance of several hundred soldiers once Gibson is fully staffed," the woman went on. "And we plan to do a brisk business in trade goods, so I'll rarely be alone. All of you are always welcome at our home as well."

"Upon Colonel Arbuckle's advice, I've taken a partner named John Rogers who is married to a Cherokee woman. He'll be moving into the neighborhood soon, with his wife and children. We expect Cantonment Gibson to give birth to a real town very soon." Colonel Nicks had the satisfied look of a man who finally had all his plans falling into place.

Before everyone retired for the night, Eliza slipped away to her cabin and then returned to the dining room where everyone still stood visiting. Trying to appear casual about it, she handed an envelope to Mrs. Nicks. Quietly she said, "Would you be able to post this at Three Forks?" she asked.

The sutler's wife looked at the name and address. "I can certainly post it for you," she said. "But I believe Lieutenant Summers will be here shortly. I wouldn't want it to cross paths with him between here and Fort Smith. Shall I just give it to him instead? I'm sure he will call upon us as soon as he arrives. He and John are quite good friends."

"Oh, yes, that would be fine. Thank you, Mrs. Nicks." Eliza seemed relieved to have taken this action.

"Call me Sallie," Mrs. Nicks said. "Everyone does, though my given name is Sarah. The colonel teases me about being Russian royalty, but I'm really just plain Sallie."

Eliza glanced at Mrs. Chapman and her mother who stood nearby. Then raising her chin as if in defiance of propriety, she said, "Alright, Sallie. Thank you."

Sallie went on to say, "I do hope you and the other

women will call upon me whenever you can. I shall not be alone with the military nearby, but I may get lonely for female companionship. Only a few of the soldiers are married and I don't know if any of those wives will choose to join their husbands out here."

"We don't get down to Three Forks often," Eliza said regretfully. "But we will certainly pay a call to you whenever we can."

"Then I shall look forward to that." Sallie squeezed Eliza's hand and then slipped the envelope into her pocket. She gave Eliza a knowing nod and joined her husband at the door. They had been offered quarters in the Fullers' cabin and so everyone departed the dining hall for the night.

The following day just as the Nicks were preparing to leave, a rider reached the mission. It was Monday, one of the slaves at La Saline. He asked that Dr. Palmer come assist a young Indian lad who had fallen off his horse during a race. Colonel Chouteau maintained a rough race track at his home and the races were popular with the Osages.

Clarissa sighed as she watched the doctor rush to get his medical kit while Mr. Redfield saddled a horse for him. Within just a few minutes Marcus was accompanying Monday back north and would likely be gone for a day or maybe two.

Clarissa felt tears sting her eyes and scolded herself for her selfishness. Of course Dr. Palmer would go when called upon. This was his duty and his ministry.

But realizing this made the teacher face a sobering reality. The life of a doctor's wife was one of always seeing your husband off to tend to someone who was injured or sick. If she felt this way with no claim upon the man, how would she feel if they ever did reach an understanding?

Her heart and mind were warring with each other today. It made her feel tired and it was still early in the day.

Rachel's mother stood nearby among the group that had gathered to bid farewell to the Nicks and now to Dr. Palmer. She gave the young woman a discerning look.

"My dear," she said quietly, "if you want something, sometimes you have to go after it."

Then she turned and accompanied Rachel back to the dining hall, leaving Clarissa looking at her in astonishment. Such advice from the very proper Mrs. Smith seemed completely out of character.

Go after it, Clarissa thought as she walked toward the schoolhouse. *How am I supposed to do that?* She had a mental picture of herself mounting a horse and chasing the doctor up the road. The image made her smile because that was how ridiculous it would be for her to go after a man like Dr. Palmer.

At Amanda's request, Clarissa helped to carry supper to Mr. Howard and George in the men's cabin. The doctor was still away so the duty of helping the injured man with supper fell to the mechanic. George did not share the doctor's patience, however.

Mr. Howard's hands shook so badly he could hardly hold the spoon to eat the potato soup Amanda had prepared for him. Marcus had asked her to offer only soft foods to the man, but he wasn't happy with it.

"Bah! More lady food," the man groused when she set the bowl on the half keg that served as a table beside his bed. "A man wants some meat, not this mincy lady food."

He roughly pushed the bowl away from him.

Amanda visibly worked at keeping her tongue.

Clarissa set his willow bark tea on the table and backed away quickly.

"And that tea," Howard gestured with his shaking hand. "Trying to kill me with that bitter stuff. Just give me some whiskey. That's all I need."

"It's the last thing you need," George said tightly. "Just eat your soup. Or do you need me to feed it to you."

Howard looked at George through slitted eyes. "I need no help from you . . . from any of you." Then he glared at the two women. "What are you standing there for? You brought this garbage so now you can just leave."

"Gladly," Amanda said, her anger at the insult visible on her face. She gave George a look of sympathy and then she and Clarissa stepped out of the cabin, relieved to be done with the distasteful duty.

George kept his distance from the surly riverman and sat quietly at the little table in the cabin, enjoying the stew and cornbread the women had delivered.

Mr. Howard eyed him resentfully for several minutes but when it became apparent that George did not plan to assist him, he began to slowly eat his own soup. Much of it missed his mouth for no matter how hard he concentrated he could not still the shakiness of his hand.

When he had eaten his fill, he roughly pushed the bowl away again and settled onto his bed, turning his back on George to face the wall. Soon his snores told the mechanic that he was asleep.

George took his dishes and stacked them with his own and carried them to the kitchen where the women were washing up. Then he found Sarah in the dining hall.

"I'm afraid we won't be able to take a walk this evening," he apologized. "Dr. Palmer asked me to stay close to our cabin and keep an eye on Mr. Howard. He suspects he has tried to help himself to the medicinal whiskey the doctor keeps in his trunk."

Sarah nodded in understanding. "Another time then, George," she smiled.

"Yes," he said, taking her hand briefly and giving it a slight squeeze. "Then I'll bid you good evening."

"Good evening, George." Sarah watched him exit the dining hall then resumed her chair to help Martha untangle a skein of yarn for the socks she was knitting.

Mr. Howard was sleeping soundly when George returned to the cabin. Rather than light a lamp and disturb the man, George simply sat outside the door for a time, watching a bright full Redbud Moon slip up from the horizon. Then he too turned in for the night.

George was roused from sleep some time later. He looked around to see what had disturbed him. As the doctor had suspected, Mr. Howard had lifted the lid on the trunk that sat next to the doctor's bed.

"What do you think you're doing?" George asked, his voice raspy from sleep. He sat up and swung his legs over the side of his bed.

"None of your business," Howard groused, but he stood quickly and thrust his hands behind his back. "Couldn't sleep is all and I was just stretching my legs. Go on back to sleep." The man sidled towards his own bunk.

With the quickness of a cat, George crossed the room and pulled Howard's arm from behind his back. He held a half-full bottle of alcohol.

"You don't want this, Howard," George said. "You know the doc says this will kill you."

"I'm dying without it," the older man nearly whimpered, putting a pathetic look on his face.

George hesitated, but then proceeded to try to take the bottle out of the older man's hand. "I'm just following the doctor's orders," he said.

But the riverman would not release the bottle. With a ferocity born of desperation, he gripped it tightly. With his other hand he gripped George at the throat, his fingers digging deeply into the mechanic's neck.

George's face went red and his eyes widened in surprise. He tried to wrest the man's hand away, but Howard only gripped him more tightly. They grappled against each other for a time like two wrestlers, each unwilling to release their hold.

Finally George let go of the hand at his throat, and tapped the man on his tender ribs. The action forced Howard to release George's throat as he instinctively wrapped his arm across his chest. George then tried to twist the bottle from the man's other hand.

The bottle dropped to the plank floor and broke into several pieces. Its contents splattered across the floor.

"No," Howard moaned and then dropped to his knees. With little regard for the slivered glass, he picked up a piece of the bottle and tried to drink what whiskey remained.

George shook his head in disbelief. Then he kicked at the shards, scattering them and the whiskey across the floor. Even that did not deter the riverman. He began to lap at the floor, unmindful that he cut his tongue and his own blood now mingled with the spirits.

George bent over with his hands at his knees as if gut struck by the man's awful desperation. He bent further and tried to pull the man up, careful not to grasp him too tightly lest he re-injure his ribs.

Howard waved away George's efforts. "Just let me die," he moaned. "Just leave me here to die."

Though strong enough to forcibly lift the emaciated man, George ceased to pull at him. Finally he shook his head and left the man in a heap on the floor. Quickly pulling on his britches and throwing on a coat, he stepped over the man and opened the cabin door. He walked down to the Woodruffs' cabin and tapped lightly on their door.

It took a few moments, but Alexander finally opened it, still pulling up the suspenders of his pants.

Surprise, then concern, registered on his face. "What is it, George?"

"I need help with Mr. Howard," George explained quietly. "He's out of bed and on the floor. I can't lift him alone."

Martha peeked around her husband's shoulder, her night cap slightly askew over her hair. "We thought one of the babies was sick," she said. "Is there anything I can do?"

"I would hate for you to see this, ma'am," George responded. "He's a mess."

"I've seen the inside of that man," Martha reminded the mechanic. "Nothing's going to shock me."

George nodded. "Then could you ask Rev. Vaille to join you, and both of you come. The man's in need of a miracle."

"I will," Martha agreed. "You go on and get him into bed and we'll come shortly."

Alexander lifted his coat from a peg by the door and followed George back to the men's cabin.

They found Howard on the floor, lying so still he looked

unconscious. But he stirred and tried to fight them off as they grasped him beneath the arms and walked him back to his bunk. He collapsed on the bed and immediately curled into a tight ball. Dried blood marred his chin.

George carefully picked up the glass shards and placed them on the table. Moments later, the pastor arrived followed by Martha who had pulled a cape over her night dress. George briefly explained what had happened.

Rev. Vaille pulled up a chair close to the man's bed. He held his small Bible between his hands.

Alexander pulled another chair out from the table for Martha to sit in, then he stood behind her with his hands resting lightly on her shoulders. Both bowed their heads in prayer.

George stirred embers in the fireplace and added another piece of kindling to bring light and warmth into the room. Then he sat on his own bunk.

"Mr. Howard," Rev. Vaille began quietly. "We are not trying to harm you. We are only trying to help you."

The man was silent for a long moment. Then he shook his head. "Nothing can help me. I am hopeless."

"No one is hopeless who calls out to God."

"God don't care about me," Howard said. "He gave up on me a long time ago, just like everyone else."

"God would pursue you to the end of the earth to see you set free," Rev. Vaille said.

"I've tried to get free," the riverman said. "Can't count the number of times I tried. I always fail. I'll die in my vomit like the dog that I am."

Perhaps you have failed because you tried in your own strength," the pastor explained. "Some things are so hard we cannot succeed without God's help. Have you ever called out to him? Surrendered your life to him?"

The room was silent for another long moment, the only sound being the crackle of the fire. Its light glinted on the tears quietly coursing down Martha's face.

"God wouldn't want me," Howard finally said. "You can't tell me God wants anything to do with me."

"No?" Vaille asked. "He made sure two missionaries saw you drop to a muddy street in a scrappy little town on the edge of civilization at that moment in time when you were finally going to reach bottom. You're not here by accident, Mr. Howard."

The older man finally looked up at the minister. He swallowed visibly as if tasting a new kind of spirit, one he had never consumed before.

"He did?"

"Yes," Vaille confirmed. "God's eyes run to and fro over the whole earth to show himself strong to those who need him. He waits with an eternal hope for us to reach out to him."

"He does?" Howard asked, then shook his head. "That's too simple; too easy."

"Incredibly simple," the minister said. "But not easy; it's incredibly hard. That's why we must have God to help us do it. But it is incredibly life changing also. Do you want to be free, Mr. Howard?"

Another long moment of quiet then the older man gave a gut wrenching sob and grabbed at his stomach as if something terrible were happening inside him. "Yes," he gasped. "I want to be free. Help me, God, I do."

Martha was crying quite freely now and her husband gripped her shoulders as if to keep his own tears in check. George swiped at his eyes as well.

Great heaving sobs shook Mr. Howard's bed as if the man emptied himself of all the failure, heartache and pain of the past. He cried for several minutes to the place of exhaustion.

"Now, you've emptied out the bad, Mr. Howard. It's time to ask God in. You can fill that empty place with him."

The man nodded. "Come, God, please come," he prayed. His words were quiet but sure. New tears flowed now, but they were clearly different. These were tears of joy and hope. The man smiled for the first time since coming to the mission.

CHAPTER TWENTY-ONE

Union Mission
Spring, 1824

The missionaries had been buoyed by the news of Mr. Howard's miracle. Dr. Palmer had been quite surprised to be greeted with a hug by the riverman after returning from La Saline. The change in the older man was remarkable. While his injuries still required time to heal and the tremor in his hands remained, his attitude and outlook was completely changed.

A few weeks later, on the Sunday George and Sarah and chosen for their wedding day, the man sat on the front row of chairs in the chapel. He had credited George with saving his life when he had given witness to his conversion and been baptized. Now his face beamed with happiness as the wedding ceremony took place.

Sarah had sewn a new poplin traveling outfit in a pretty pink that complemented her dark hair. Eliza and Clarissa had pooled their money and sent it to Sallie Nicks to help with the purchase of a new hat for their sister. George wore a borrowed suit from Rev. Chapman for the occasion. His brother Will stood with him and Clarissa had been honored when Sarah asked her to be her second.

Marcus sat next to his patient as Rev. Vaille read the marriage vows. His eyes were not upon the pretty bride though. His gaze never left Clarissa's face. She glanced back at him once and he saw her cheeks grow pink when her eyes met his.

In the time since he had first asked her about her thoughts on marriage, they had managed only two evening walks. Sometimes the doctor wanted to put out a "closed" sign but loyalty to his oath would not allow him to do so. He was frankly surprised that Clarissa hadn't lost all interest in pursuing a relationship with a doctor who rarely had time to call his own.

Applause from the audience brought Marcus out of his reverie. Rev. Vaille had introduced the newest Mr. and Mrs. Requa and they were now receiving congratulations from their fellow missionaries. Mr. Howard had been among the first to jump up and shake George's hand.

Clarissa stepped out of the crush of people who were gathering around the newlyweds. She bumped into a rock solid mass and turned to find Dr. Palmer behind her. She had not realized he had skirted the crowd to reach her.

"Doctor," she said in surprise. She felt the same pulse quickening sensation whenever she was close to the man.

"Miss Clarissa," he greeted her. Then nodded toward Sarah and George he said, "They look very happy."

"Yes," Clarissa agreed with a smile. "Sarah has driven Eliza and me mad with her raptures over her Mr. Requa and all the plans they have for their new life together and their ready-made family."

"It was quite charitable of Mrs. Smith to give up the extra cabin so they could live there," Marcus observed.

"Yes," Clarissa nodded, glancing over to the older woman whose feathered hat towered above her head. "Poor Rev. Chapman shall be put out of his home for the next month or so."

Then she looked back at Marcus. "But perhaps that was uncharitable of me to say," she murmured, embarrassed that she had spoken the thought out loud.

"I doubt he will mind so much," Marcus winked. "Besides with him in the men's cabin, it will give me a chance to keep a better eye on his health. He has had a persistent 'cough the entire winter."

"I've noticed that," Clarissa said, as the little

congregation began to make their way out of the schoolhouse. "And the children too, all seemed to have passed a cold around this year."

"Fortunately we've had little fever," the doctor said as he walked beside Clarissa with a hand gently placed upon her back. It gave her a wonderful sense of belonging.

"Yes, but . . ." the teacher hesitated.

"What is it?" Marcus asked.

"It's just that I was reminded that Thea felt a little warm this morning and seemed flushed."

"Perhaps another tooth is coming in," Marcus said as he held the door of the dining hall open for her. Their conversation blended in with the many being held among the group of worshipers. "I can look at her after dinner."

"Oh, no, it can wait," Clarissa said, shaking her head. "It's the Sabbath; you shouldn't have to work today."

"Caring for the sick is work allowed on the Sabbath," Marcus reminded her.

"Still, I'm sure you're right about the tooth," Clarissa returned. "Judging from the amount of drool I'm always wiping off her chin." The two shared a laugh as the little girl in question came running toward them after Phoebe let go of her hand.

Marcus reached down to pick her up and she went to him willingly. The doctor was almost as much a favorite among the children as Phoebe was.

He tickled Thea under her chin, trying to get her to laugh and open her mouth wide enough for him to take a look at her gums. Watching this man interact with her daughter reminded Clarissa of something her mother had once advised. See how a child reacts to the man you have an interest in. It will tell you something of his character.

As Thea threw her little arms around the doctor's neck, her black eyes sparkling, it confirmed what Clarissa knew. This man's character was sterling. She felt her heart swell as if he had suddenly stepped inside it. In this most unromantic of moments, she knew she had found someone to love. If only she could trust him to love her.

"Can you help with the cake, Miss Johnson?" Amanda interrupted her reverie.

"Oh, certainly, Amanda," Clarissa said, blushing slightly for she knew the perceptive cook would have observed the little "family" moment she had shared with the doctor.

She turned to him but before she could apologize he said, "Thea and I will find a seat and be out of the way of the bridal festivities."

"Thank you, Doctor."

Clarissa set down her little nosegay of early wildflowers on the decorated table where the cake would be placed and made her way to the kitchen to assist the other ladies in setting out the meal and beautiful cake Amanda had prepared.

She shared a hug with Susan Requa who was starting to show her impending motherhood and greeted Teresa Revoir, both of whom were helping in the kitchen. Quickly the food was dished up and set out and everyone took their seats and bowed their heads for the blessing.

Because she was in the wedding party, Clarissa sat at a different table from Marcus and Thea, but she didn't mind. It gave her another opportunity to watch them together. It seemed that love was blossoming between them too and it filled her heart with thankfulness and her eyes with happy tears.

After dinner, the newlyweds changed into their traveling clothes and walked toward the mission wagon for their honeymoon trip. Because it was still rather cool they planned to travel south to Fort Smith rather than go north to Harmony Mission. Fort Smith was growing into a regular town and would offer comfortable accommodations for their short stay.

Sarah pulled Clarissa and Eliza into a hug before George helped her into the wagon. "You two are next," she whispered so only they could hear. Eliza and Clarissa smiled, but both held a bit of skepticism in their eyes.

"Best wishes, Sarah," was Clarissa's only reply. She joined the others of the group in waving goodbye as George turned the horses and set them on a steady clip clop toward the Texas Road.

They were all turning back to the dining hall when Mr. Howard pulled a big red bandana handkerchief out of his pocket and blew his nose loudly.

"That young man's like a son to me," he said to explain his emotion. Everyone smiled and Stephen slipped an arm around the older man's shoulders. "Well, while Requa is away, I could use some help with the plowing. I understand you have some farming experience."

Clarissa could tell that Stephen was trying to make the man feel he was a part of the mission family.

"Yes," Howard nodded and he put the handkerchief away. "Grew up on a farm in Tennessee. I've walked behind a yoke of oxen many a spring."

"Then you're hired, Mr. Howard," Chapman said. "If you feel you're up to some hard work."

"Hard work is exactly what I need," the man replied. "And thanks to the doc I'm healed up and ready to start over."

Clarissa glanced over the fields already partially turned for planting. Oh what hope she felt for a good harvest this year.

A few days later the Union fields had all received the first turn of the soil with Paul and Howard working with Stephen. The farm director then left two yoke of oxen for these men to continue the cross plowing. Then he and Will Requa drove the four remaining oxen with a wagon filled with the plow equipment up to Hopefield to start the plowing there. After an afternoon of walking out the area, the two missionaries determined where they planned to create four fields of about five acres each.

Besides the Requas, there were six Osage families at Hopefield. Stephen planned for two families to share each field, thus transitioning from their tradition of communal gardening to eventual homesteading as individual families. Convincing the warriors to push a plow, however, would likely be the hardest task for Stephen and Will.

Sitting down to breakfast the next morning, Stephen and the Requas discussed their plans. "I think I've convinced

Star-That-Travels to try plowing," Will said as he cut into a plate of Susan's flapjacks. "But Monepasha and his sons just shake their heads when I discuss farming with them. They have no experience with a team of plodding oxen and see it as too sedate an effort for a warrior. If they could dash across the fields on a prancing mustang, they might be all for it."

"You should tell them to train their mustangs to plow," Susan suggested as she stood to get the coffee pot and warm each mug. "Isn't training the horses the work of a warrior?"

"Well, yes," Will agreed. "But they don't think their mustangs would be any good at plowing."

"Then that is the challenge," Stephen mused. "We both know horses can be good farm animals, especially for working smaller fields. Perhaps if we challenge the warriors to prove their prowess at training horses, we could get them and their mustangs into the field."

Will pondered the idea for a moment. "I'll talk to Star about it," he finally said. "That may interest the men. They are expert horsemen and take pride in their animals. Watching them together in a buffalo hunt is an amazing thing to see. It's like man and rider are one."

Stephen downed the last of his coffee. "Well, we have to get the fields ready right now which means using our oxen. I'll start hitching them up."

Star-That-Travels joined the two men at the barn and watched closely as Stephen settled the yoke over the shoulders of the oxen and ran the traces back to the plow. The Osage seemed torn between wanting to learn the craft of plowing and wanting to join his fellow warriors who all sat in the early morning sunlight outside their log lodges.

Their elder, Monepasha, watched with interest as Will and Stephen began the plowing, yet he did not leave the fire for a closer look. After observing the two farmers for a while, Star asked to give the plow a try.

Stephen helped him loop the leather lines over his shoulder and back down to his hand on the plow. Then he gave the hup to start the animals. The jerk of the plow took Star by surprise and it was almost pulled out of his hands.

He looked at Stephen with a sheepish grin. "They are strong."

"Very strong," Stephen agreed as he walked beside the warrior. "But they are docile, slow. They never get in a rush so they never tire themselves out."

Star nodded and concentrated on keeping the plowshare dug into the burned-off land. By the time they had traversed the field once he had settled into the slow pace of the oxen. The row was not uniform, but good for a first effort. The leather lines chafed at his bare shoulder, however, so Stephen insisted on relieving him after only a few passes over the field. Star seemed ready to relinquish the plow and return to the work he was better acquainted with. He went to sit in the shade of Teresa's cabin and took up the flint he was knapping for arrow points.

Susan and Teresa worked together hanging out their laundry, glancing up occasionally to watch the men and their animals slowly turn the rich silt-laden earth.

"Planting will be more . . . better," Teresa observed in her uncertain English.

"Do you have plenty of seed corn?" Susan asked.

Teresa eyed the fields and then shook her head. "Not for that much earth. We do not ever plant so much earth. We could not eat so much corn."

"Union has plenty of seed they will share. And you can have your crop ground there," Susan told her. "It will keep in barrels and if the barrels are tight enough you hardly have to sift out any bugs."

Teresa nodded at this information.

"Besides, Will believes you'll produce enough to be able to sell the extra to the new fort. You'll have money . . . or trade goods from Colonel Nicks."

"We have little use for money," Teresa said, "but we trade the Mexicans for their silver pieces sometimes in exchange for our horses."

"Yes," Susan said. "It will be like that. Then you trade the silver with Mr. Bogey or Mr. Chouteau for something they have in their store."

"Trade is not all that money is good for," Teresa said. Then she pulled out a necklace from beneath the blanket she wore against the morning chill. To a rawhide lace she had sewn bright beads, polished stones, dyed feathers and two pierced pieces of silver coin.

Susan drew in a pleased breath. An artist herself, she clearly appreciated the beautiful handiwork. "That is lovely, Teresa. Do you ever trade the jewelry you make?"

Teresa shrugged. "Sometimes. Buffalo Woman gave me a clay bowl she made for a necklace I made."

"You should make more for trade," Susan advised.

Their conversation was interrupted when the husband of Buffalo Woman rode into the circle of cabins that made up their little community. With him was Bird, the father of two students at Union Mission School. He had yet to build his cabin at Hopefield. The visitors dismounted their mustangs to stand near Monepasha. For a time they watched as Star again took over the plowing. Mad Buffalo said something to the older man. Some of the younger men laughed, but Monepasha did not.

"What did he say?" Susan asked Teresa.

"He called *Wah-She-Hah* a field-maker," Teresa explained. "It is meant as an insult. It is like calling him a woman."

Susan squinted her eyes in anger at the Osage leader as he continued to joke with his fellow warriors. Then she glanced at her own husband happily plowing a second row behind Star. "I can think of worse things to be called," was all she said.

Teresa smiled. "So can I," she added and the two women laughed quietly at their shared humor.

Mad Buffalo and Bird joined the warriors sitting cross legged in a semi-circle near a communal fire while their wives worked at family chores around them. The men passed the pipe for a time, the smoke from their tobacco curling upward in the still morning air.

"Does Bird live at Claremont's Town?" Susan asked Teresa in a low voice.

"No, he keeps his lodge on a creek toward the sunset," Teresa explained. "His wife died but he has not taken another. Most warriors do not remain without a wife, but Bird walks his own path. That is why he does not live at Claremont's. We call the creek Bird's Creek because he runs beaver traps along it."

The smell of the tobacco smoke began to make Susan cough, so she hung her last towel and told Teresa she was going inside to start dinner. When she looked out some time later, Mad Buffalo and Bird were gone.

"I'm afraid Mad Buffalo will be a discouragement to the men here," Will said when Susan told about the warrior's visit over the noon meal. "No man wants to be ridiculed by his peers."

"It takes a courageous man to go against them," Stephen agreed as he sopped his biscuit in a bit of ham gravy. "Star-That-Travels has his faith to aid him, but the other men don't . . . yet. No wonder there is such reluctance to make a change."

The three were finishing up second helpings of the fried ham and potatoes when they heard the jangle of harness and creak of a wagon arriving at the farm.

"Today seems to be the day for visitors," Will remarked as they all stood from the table and made their way outside.

"Who is it?" Stephen asked as they waited on the front stoop for the wagon to approach.

"Looks like Rev. Montgomery from Harmony," Will said. "He has his little girl with him." Mary Montgomery, now four years old, could be seen standing in the bed of the wagon behind her father's shoulder. A woman also sat in the wagon bed, her back to them.

"Odd that he would have a woman traveling alone with him," Susan commented. A four-year-old child would hardly be an appropriate chaperone for her widowed father and whoever this woman was.

As the wagon reached the cabin, the woman in question turned and they could see her face.

"Harriett!" Susan gasped. "Harriett Woolley, is that

you?" She hurried to greet her friend.

Montgomery halted the wagon and jumped down from the high seat. He lifted Mary out of the bed, then walked around to the back to assist Harriett from the wagon.

Mary ran to Susan and threw her arms around her skirt. "Mith Comthock," she lisped around a missing front tooth.

"Oh, Mary," Susan said, lifting up the little girl. "What happened to your tooth?"

"She knocked it out because she wouldn't sit still back here," Harriett explained as she stepped onto the ground and shook out her wrinkled skirts. "That's why I joined her back here for the last day of travel."

"It was awfully good of you to accompany Rev. Montgomery and care for his daughter," Will observed though there was a question in his voice about the propriety of such an arrangement.

Montgomery smiled. "Harriett is not here as a housemother," he said. "She has done me the honor of becoming my wife."

"Harriett," Susan gasped a second time. She set down the little girl and reached out to her friend, "Congratulations!"

As the two women shared a hug, Susan whispered so only Harriett could hear, "How did this happen?"

"I'll tell you later," was all Harriett would say.

"I suppose you are hungry and ready for something to eat," Susan then said to the newlyweds.

"We are," Montgomery replied while shaking hands of congratulations from Will and Stephen. "I hope it's not an inconvenience to have us here."

"Certainly not," Susan replied and waved them all into the cabin. She could see curious looks from their Osage neighbors.

They all stepped inside and Susan set the skillet with the ham and potatoes back over the fire to warm them. She poured some warm water from a kettle into the wash basin for her guests to freshen up.

"I had hoped we would arrive before the spring planting," Montgomery said after everyone had been seated. "I didn't miss it, did I?"

"You're in time to help us finish the plowing," Stephen replied as he sipped his coffee.

"Good," Montgomery said. "I want to pull my weight here. If you'll show us a good location for our cabin, Harriett and I will get a camp set up around our wagon there."

"Nonsense," Susan countered. "You can sleep in our loft until you get a cabin built. You won't mind bunking in the barn tonight, will you, Mr. Fuller?"

"Not at all," Stephen replied. "After a day of plowing, I can sleep anywhere."

Conversation during the meal centered on the journey from Harmony and conditions at the Missouri mission. When the Montgomerys had eaten their fill, the men rose and donned coats and hats to go back to the field work.

Harriett used a cloth to wipe Mary's face and hands and then put the little girl on the Requas' bed for a nap.

"I can tell you are dying of curiosity," she said when she joined Susan in washing the dinner dishes.

"I had no idea you and Rev. Montgomery had formed an attachment," Susan said, handing her friend an enamel plate to dry. Her eyes sparkled with interest in hearing the story of their courtship and marriage.

"Well, let's say we reached an agreement," Harriett replied.

"What do you mean?"

"He came to me a month ago," Harriett said while wiping the dish slowly. "Asked me if I would be interested in taking Mary."

"Taking her?" Susan brow wrinkled. "You mean adopting her?"

"Yes," Harriett responded, the tightness of her lips telling of her dislike of the proposition. "He wanted to be here, but didn't want to bring Mary without someone to care for her. He thought she would be better off with a mother alone than a father alone."

"Most men do," Susan mused, "especially with girls. That's why Bird truly walks his own path."

"Bird?" Harriett asked.

Susan waved a hand. "I'll tell you about him later," she said. "I want to hear about you and Montgomery."

"Well, as you say," Harriett continued, "most men seem uncomfortable in trying to raise children alone. They leave them with a friend or relative, vowing to return for them someday after they take a wife, or settle in a new place, or finish some business or make their fortune . . . or some other such excuse for not taking responsibility. I suppose many of them mean well, but all too often they never return for the child. And it is devastating for that child."

"You sound as if you know that firsthand," Susan said.

"My father promised my aunt he would be back within a few months," Harriett shook her head, her voice tinged with bitterness. "That was the last we saw of him. I was young, like Mary, but I never forgot that my father had abandoned me."

"I'm sorry, Harriett."

"Well, it made me quite upset when Montgomery approached me about Mary," Harriett went on. "I told him in no uncertain terms that I would not help him abandon his child. I could tell it upset him to be accused of such a thing, but I knew that would be how Mary would see it. I told him serving the Lord began at home and if he couldn't care for his own child, how could he represent our Father and claim that he cared for us as his children?"

"What did he say to that?"

"Nothing, for a few days," Harriett said, taking another dish to dry. "But I could tell he was pondering it, praying about it."

"So he asked you to marry him."

"Hardly," Harriett replied with a roll of her eyes. "He convinced Dr. and Mrs. Belcher to care for his daughter. He was determined to come to Hopefield and fully believed that he would be back for Mary soon. I suppose he thought he might find a wife at Union."

"But . . ." Susan looked puzzled. "He married you."

"I just couldn't let him leave Mary," Harriett confessed.

"So I proposed to him . . ."

"You asked him to marry you?" Susan interrupted in delight.

"I offered to marry him so that I could care for his little girl and he could come to Hopefield as he was so desperate to do. We all would come to Hopefield and Mary would never have to know the devastation of abandonment."

"And he agreed to it?" Susan concluded.

"I gave him my famous 'obey me or else' look," Harriett smiled. "He could not refuse."

"Harriett," Susan hugged her friend, mindless of her soapy, wet hands. "How good you are to sacrifice your own chance at happiness for the sake of a little girl."

"Oh, please," Harriett pulled back from the hug into her ramrod straight posture. "I am hardly a saint; don't make me out to be one."

"But still, Harriett," Susan countered. "To marry without love . . . it is a sacrifice."

"Love grows," Harriett shrugged and she looked down at her hands as she carefully folded her dish towel. Her voice took on a soft tone, almost a whisper to herself. "And who is to say that I didn't love him when I suggested we marry."

"Harriett," Susan exclaimed yet again at this revelation. "I never knew. You certainly hid it well."

"Everyone thought of me as the stern old maid," her friend said. "I couldn't ruin my own reputation, could I?"

"Well, you've ruined it now," Susan laughed.

"Yes, I guess I have," Harriett agreed.

CHAPTER TWENTY-TWO

Cantonment Gibson
April, 1824

"Our corn is finally planted," Will Requa told the Gibson
,sutler John Nicks a few weeks later. He and Montgomery had
traveled to Three Forks for supplies for Hopefield and had
crossed the Neosho to visit the sutler in his new home.

"We couldn't induce any of the warriors to help with the
planting, but the women did a fine job of putting in the seed,"
Montgomery said as the men sipped coffee at the Nicks' table.
"Union dismissed classes for a couple of days so the older
children could help with their planting. Fuller has nearly 50
acres in corn and about ten of potatoes and ten of oats.
They're fencing pastureland too with so many horses and
oxen now."

"Mr. Fuller seems to be a capable farmer," Nicks
observed. "I'm as hopeful as you are that your fields will
have a good yield. I'll want every bushel beyond what you
need for yourselves. Feeding the army is a massive job."

"Have they arrived yet?" Will asked.

"Three companies marched in from Fort Smith a few
days ago," Nicks answered. "They're already hard at work.
Did you go by the site for the cantonment?"

"No, we came straight here from Mr. Bogey's post."

"Would you care to walk up there and see what progress
they're making?" the sutler asked. "I try to visit every day."

"Certainly," Will agreed and the minister nodded. "The
folks at Union will be interested in the progress. We've all

wanted a military presence close by since we arrived three years ago."

The men stood and took up their hats. Nicks paused at the back door and called out to his wife who was planting cold crops in her garden.

"Sallie, we're going to walk up to the cantonment."

She looked up from her work and gave a wave. "Come back by before you leave, if you would," she said to their visitors. "I'll have something for you."

"Yes, ma'am," Will nodded and doffed his hat to her.

The men followed the river northward for about a mile to the site of the military camp. Colonel Arbuckle had wasted no time in getting his troops to work digging the trench for the large log palisade that would make up the exterior walls. At each corner two-story guard posts were already under construction.

"It looks as if they are expecting an attack," Montgomery noted as they approached.

"I don't think Arbuckle truly anticipates such a thing," Nicks said. "But Mad Buffalo did attempt one on Fort Smith when it was first built."

"I had never heard that," Will expressed his surprise.

"Major Bradford brought out a few cannon and pointed them across the river at the Osage camp. Mad Buffalo saw the wisdom of not crossing the river and the warriors slipped away in the night." Nicks explained. "At least that's how I heard it told."

"Mad Buffalo seems to be keeping a close eye on Hopefield," the minister said. "I haven't decided if that is a good thing or something to be concerned about."

"If he's openly checking on you, it's probably good," Nicks observed. "If he was planning something against the mission, you likely wouldn't see him or even know he was close by."

"You are right," Will agreed, then he pointed across the Neosho where a group of warriors from Big Tracks' Town stood watching the construction. "Everyone in the neighborhood seems interested in the new cantonment."

"It will be an agent for change for this region," Nicks predicted. "The first of many from what I am hearing in Little Rock."

By this time the men had reached the center of the palisade where Colonel Arbuckle consulted with his three junior officers. One of the men held an unrolled parchment with apparent plans for the military structure.

"You have made good progress since yesterday, Colonel," Nicks greeted the commanding officer.

Arbuckle looked up from the plans and then nodded to the visitors. "My men are as anxious to get it completed as I am. A miserable rain shower like last week's makes our temporary quarters soggy and unpleasant. Once the palisade is complete, we can start on enlisted quarters."

Nicks proceeded to make introductions among the men. Besides Lieutenant Summers, another officer stood with the colonel. "This is Captain Pierce Butler," Nicks said of the man holding the building plans. "He's the engineer leading the construction."

Butler nodded to the two missionaries as Nicks introduced them.

"You know, Colonel, that you and your officers are welcome to bunk at our home while your permanent quarters are being built," Nicks offered. "Sallie welcomes guests. She's always been known for her entertainments."

"I thank you," Arbuckle said. "Our tents are fine unless we get another frog-strangler. Then we might take you up on your offer."

Turning to his aide he said, "Summers, show our visitors around. Butler and I need to discuss these plans further."

"Certainly, sir," Summers saluted. Then with a gesture, he led Nicks and the missionaries around the palisade walls sitting about 500 yards from the river's bank.

"You're close to the river," Montgomery noted after they had inspected the structure. "Aren't you concerned about flooding?"

Summers shrugged. "I think that is what Arbuckle and Butler are discussing. We must be within sight of the water to be aware of potential attacks. But we also need to be on high enough ground to avoid a flood. The final location of the riverfront elevation is still being debated."

"When do you expect to have the cantonment completed?" Nicks asked.

"Another two to three weeks, depending on the weather."

"I will hold you to that," the sutler smiled. "Sallie plans a soiree to welcome the new post surgeon in a fortnight or so. He will be here by then, won't he?"

"Should be," Summers replied as the men began to walk back toward the sutler's post. "Dr. Baylor is already at Fort Smith. But he has his wife with him; children, too, I think. He didn't want to come out here before there was adequate shelter."

"Well, send word to the Baylors that Sallie will host them so they can come at any time," Nicks generously offered. "She's looking forward to having other women here."

"We send a dispatch over every Thursday," Summers said. "I'll send your invitation along tomorrow."

The men parted with the officer then and continued on to the Nicks' home. Sallie had finished her gardening and was watching for their return while churning butter on the front porch.

"Good, you remembered to stop by," she said as the men climbed the porch steps.

"Yes, ma'am," Will said.

"I have an invitation to all of you at Union and Hopefield," the woman said as she reached for two envelopes sitting on the window sill. "I'm having a welcome party for the officers and their families in three weeks. It will be after planting and well before the harvest so I hope you all will plan to attend."

"Thank you for the invitation," Montgomery said as he reached for the envelopes. "I'm sure everyone will look forward to it as a welcome diversion from the work at the mission."

Indeed the invitation to Sallie's party brought excitement

to the missions. Susan would not be able to attend due to her
pregnancy. The same was true for Asie Vaille. Asie actually
cried that she would not get to attend. She was always
emotional when expecting a child but she seemed particularly
morose at the thought of missing the social gathering.

Rachel's mother seemed to regard the event with disdain.
Leah had clapped her hands in excitement at the news and
innocently asked, "Isn't it wonderful, Grandmother? I wish I
could go."

"Hardly," Mrs. Smith sniffed. "Gathering at a log fort
out of doors? Everyone will be eaten to death with these
infernal mosquitoes in the company of uncouth soldiers."

Leah looked surprised at her grandmother's vehemence.
"I expect some of the soldier are cute," she replied, causing
stifled laughter from the women who overhead the exchange
in the dining hall. Even Mrs. Smith could barely suppress a
smile.

"Don't you want to go, Grandmother?" Leah then asked.

"I'll be leaving before then, dear, and won't be subjected
to the possibility."

Leah got a sad look on her face. "We will miss you,
Grandmother."

Mrs. Smith patted her granddaughter on her shoulder. "I
hope you won't have to miss me, dear."

The older woman sent a look toward Rachel who said
nothing but met her mother's gaze with a look of defiance.

Because children were not invited to Mrs. Nicks'
reception, the teachers asked for permission to have an end-
of-school party for the students. The final exams would be
given just before the big event and Clarissa hoped the
distraction of planning for the party would not affect her
students' grades.

"Girls," she admonished them just before she dismissed
class one day in early May. "Don't forget we'll have our
spelling and composition tests soon. Spend your evenings
studying, not worrying about what hair ribbon you're going to
wear to the party."

Tassie Bradley rolled her eyes.

Instead of saying anything more about the event she dismissed her students but asked thirteen-year-old Tassie to help her with classroom cleanup. She usually asked one of the girls for help at the end of each week.

The two worked quietly to clean the blackboard, pick up stray chalk, and straighten books and the stack of slates.

"You'll be graduating in a few days, Tassie," her teacher said. "How do you feel about that?"

"Kinda' happy and sad both, I guess," Tassie said. "Won't get to stay up here no more."

Clarissa smiled, knowing that it wasn't school alone that made Tassie want to be at Union Mission.

"You'll miss Paul, won't you?"

Tassie nodded shyly. "We's planning on gettin' married."

Clarissa raised her eyebrows in surprise. "Not for a while, Tassie. You're too young to be thinking of marriage."

"Got no reason to wait," the young woman said. "I know how to keep a house 'cause Mama taught me. I can cook real good too, just like her."

"Does your mother know your plans?"

"She knows."

"Does she approve?"

"She wants us to wait 'til I'm fifteen," Tassie said. "I think she thinks we'll change our minds. But we won't. Now that Paul has a job here, we just need to build us a house. I'm thinking to ask Mrs. Chapman if I can get a job here too. I could help Mrs. Fuller in the kitchen or Mrs. Requa with the sewing and laundry."

"Just don't rush into marriage, Tassie," her teacher advised. "Enjoy being young a little while longer before you take on the responsibility of a family."

Clarissa wanted to encourage Tassie to pursue more education for she was a bright girl who had excelled in her studies during the one year spent at Union. But she knew that would be unrealistic. The closest finishing school was in Little Rock and she doubted the Bradleys could afford to send

Tassie there. She doubted, too, that Negro students were accepted.

"Can I go now?" Tassie asked, clearly not interested in her teacher's advice.

"Yes, thank you, Tassie," Clarissa said. She watched her student through the open classroom window as she walked to the dining hall, keeping her head up just as she had practiced while balancing a book on her head.

The Washburns, directors of Dwight Mission, arrived the following week in time to participate in the closing exercises for the school year. They would accompany Mrs. Smith to Little Rock for her return journey home. From there the Crittendons, Arkansas' former territorial governor and his wife, would accompany Rachel's mother to Pittsburg. She had made the arrangements on her journey out to Union Mission. Robert Crittendon was an old law school friend of her husband.

As she pulled on her gloves the morning before her departure, the older woman tried one last time to convince Rachel to allow her to take the children back to Connecticut with her.

"I know I will never convince you to return home where you belong," the woman said, "but you ought to care enough about the future of your children to allow them to come with me."

"I could not care more for my children's future, Mother," Rachel said, keeping her composure. "I simply have a different desire for that future. My children will experience more out here that will prepare them for a life of service, compassion and acceptance of others. These are lessons not taught at finishing schools and preparatory academies."

Margret Smith looked out the open cabin door to the children playing in the school yard. Their laughter could be heard as they romped with the Osage students, excited that this was the last day of school. The party would take place this afternoon. It was enough to make this a glorious day for the students.

Beyond them the fields of corn waved in the breeze and early morning sunshine. The oat field was such a bright green it almost hurt the eyes to look at it.

"Well, they seem happy," Mrs. Smith allowed with a begrudging tone. "I can only hope they will not suffer any more from the dreadful diseases you have out here."

"Life is uncertain everywhere, Mother," Rachel returned as the two women stepped out of the cabin and made their way toward the classroom. "I will pray for your safe return home."

"You'll be glad to be rid of me, you mean," Mrs. Smith murmured softly. Rachel gave no indication that she had heard the remark.

Some parents were in attendance for the closing school exercises. Bird came for Bearpaw and Deer-in-Water. The Chouteaus were present as were Teresa and Star-That-Travels. Mrs. Bradley had caught a ride with the Washburns in Mr. Ramirez' freight wagon and she had brought along a shoofly pie for the party.

John rang the school bell to call everyone into the boys' classroom.

As everyone settled into place, Clarissa took a seat at the back but on the center aisle where her students could see her while they recited their memorized pieces. Knowing she would be there to prompt them seemed to have settled their nerves this morning.

Marcus slipped into the seat beside her with Thea in his arms. Clarissa turned to give him a somewhat tremulous smile. Her students might not be nervous, but she was on their behalf.

"Are you alright, Miss Johnson?" the doctor asked with concern in his eyes.

"Just nervous for my students," she whispered while trying to pull Thea's braid out of the little girl's mouth. "I want them to do well and make their parents proud."

"They'll be fine, I'm sure," Marcus said. "No one expects perfection. The little mistakes just add to the charm of the program."

"You're right, of course," Clarissa said in admiration of the man beside her. "You always are."

"Hardly," he flushed. "I make more than my fair share of mistakes."

"It's a shame we adults aren't as quick to forgive each other's mistakes as we are the children's," Clarissa mused as Rev. Chapman began the program.

"The world would be a far better place if we did, wouldn't it," Marcus observed as everyone stood for prayer.

The program was quite charming with few of the children delivering their recitations without a mistake or two. But as Marcus predicted, the little flubs only brought gentle smiles or sympathetic chuckles from the adults.

After the children had completed their recitations and singing, Rev. Vaille dismissed everyone to the dining hall for a light noontime meal. It was followed by the end-of-school party with games and little gifts for each of the students.

Everyone was enjoying a slice of strawberry shortcake after the children had opened their presents. Clarissa noticed that Mrs. Smith had discreetly added a small gift of her own for each of her grandchildren. She sat by Thomas and appeared to be in a very serious conversation with the twelve-year-old.

"Have you thought some more about what we discussed regarding your schooling?" Mrs. Smith asked in a low voice. She glanced across the room where Thomas' parents stood talking together.

"You mean about going back with you to Connecticut?" Thomas asked, pausing only slightly in devouring his cake.

"Yes," his grandmother said. "You know I believe that you need to get into a good school if you are going to have a successful career."

"I don't think Mother and Papa want me to go," Thomas said.

"I certainly don't wish you to disobey your parents, Thomas," the woman said. "But I also believe they want what is best for you and if you were to ask them for permission to return home with me, they would say yes."

Thomas turned to look at his parents. Rachel saw her son's inquisitive look. She frowned slightly and said to her husband, "Mother knows I don't want her to take Thomas back with her. Why does she persist in this?"

"She's used to having her own way," Chapman replied. "Even with your father." He hesitated a long moment. "Would you hate me if I spoke with her?"

"No, of course not," Rachel said, seeming surprised. "Don't you know that by now?"

"I never wanted to come between you and your parents," he said. "I have always felt I was walking a very fine line between you and your mother."

"You needn't have," Rachel said. "I never wanted Mother's control over me. You rescued me from what would have been a stifling life of teas and dress fittings."

Chapman smiled. "I'm glad I could be of service," he said dryly. Then looking toward Mrs. Smith, he added, "Say a prayer for me that I don't lose my temper."

The minister crossed the room and stopped at his mother-in-law's elbow. "Would you step outside with me, Mother?" he asked quietly.

She glanced up at him, a wary look on her attractive face. "Am I being called out, Mr. Burr?"

Chapman smiled at her reference to the famous Burr-Hamilton duel that had shocked the nation twenty years before. "Perhaps you are, Mr. Hamilton," he replied, going along with the attempt at humor.

"Oh, dear," the woman sighed. "Things did not work out well for Mr. Hamilton."

"I promise no shots will be fired," Chapman said, but offered his hand to the woman to help her rise from the table. The two exited the dining hall. Rachel didn't seem to even realize her hands were clasped tightly in a gesture of desperate prayer as she watched them go.

The minister allowed Mrs. Smith to take his arm as they walked along the path toward the school. They both were silent for a moment, then Chapman began.

"I want you to know that I appreciate your concern for

the children. Your visit has meant a great deal to them and to Rachel."

"But my purpose in coming shall be thwarted nonetheless."

"I am afraid so," Chapman said. "Please understand that Rachel and I want and fully intend to give our children a good education. But they are young still and need to remain with their mother."

"Thomas is only a year away from completing his primary education. He is quite a mature young man and would thrive at a good preparatory school."

"Yes, he will," Chapman agreed. "In another year. In the meantime, we are giving him experiences that his classmates will have only read about in books."

Margret stopped and let her eyes wander over the fields and pasture land of the mission. Her face took on a thoughtful look. "I would not have believed my daughter would enjoy life on the frontier. But I cannot deny that she and the children seem to be happy, if not entirely healthy." She paused and then turned to look the minister in the eye. "I never hated you," she said. "I know you probably don't believe that. I just wanted the best for my daughter."

"And you never believed I was that."

"I see now that I was wrong," Margret conceded with a slight bow of her head.

Chapman looked astonished, but he left the comment alone.

"I hope that our current decision will not keep Thomas from being welcome to spend his summers and holidays with you when we send him back east next year."

"You all will always be welcome," the woman said. The two turned to walk back to the dining hall.

"Thank you," Chapman said when they reached the door and stepped inside. Rachel closed her eyes briefly in gratitude and then sank into a chair as if suddenly weak in the knees.

Later that evening the Chapman children said goodbye to their grandmother who would be leaving at first light the following morning.

"Come and see me," she said as each one gave her a kiss and a special handmade gift they had worked on for weeks.

"You aren't angry at me, are you, Grandmother?" Thomas asked when he said his goodbye.

"Of, course not, young man," the woman said somewhat brusquely to hide her emotion. "I'll expect to see you before classes begin next year."

In the morning, when Rachel parted with her mother their hug was genuinely filled with affection.

"I'm glad you came, Mother," Rachel said before Mrs. Smith boarded the wagon. "You see now that you do not have to worry about us out here."

"A mother always worries," Margret returned. "At least now I can envision what I'm worrying about." She smiled and then let Chapman help her step up into the freight wagon and take a seat by Mrs. Washburn. She waved as Mr. Ramirez hupped his mules and they set out for Three Forks.

Rachel slipped her hand into that of her husband's and with a sigh of either contentment or relief they walked back to their cabin.

CHAPTER TWENTY-THREE

Cantonment Gibson
May, 1824

The following week, Clarissa joined several of her fellow missionaries in climbing into their wagon for the trip to Cantonment Gibson for Mrs. Nicks' party. She followed Eliza into the wagon bed in which Stephen had placed two bench seats. As she stepped up on the mounting block, Dr. Palmer was quickly at her side, offering a hand to help her aboard.

"May I sit beside you, Miss Johnson?" he quietly asked.

Standing on the block made Clarissa almost at eye level with the tall doctor. She smiled at him. "Certainly," was all she had breath to say.

Marcus followed her into the wagon and since there were several others also waiting to enter they had to sit very close together. Next came Mrs. Chapman, helped up by her husband. Sitting across the wagon were Sarah and George, William and Harriett and Martha and Alexander. Stephen and Amanda would ride on the wagon's buckboard. A yoke of oxen stood patiently as the missionaries boarded the wagon.

Star-That-Travels and Teresa were joining them as well, but they chose to ride their mustangs. Wagon travel was too uncomfortable for them, they explained. Clarissa watched Teresa swiftly mount her horse and wondered how riding astride without a saddle or stirrups would be more comfortable than the wagon. She exchanged a look with Harriett that told her the housemother was thinking the very same thing.

"She makes it look easy," the woman observed. "I would land on my head."

Eliza and Sarah stifled giggles at the remark but were silenced immediately by the jolt of the wagon as the oxen moved out. Though the pace of the work animals was slow, the rutted road did make travel very bumpy.

"Perhaps we should have all ridden horses," George laughed after an especially hard bump.

"Hey, I'm doing the best I can," Stephen threw over his shoulder with a laugh as well. "Mr. Austin needs to stop offering land in Texas. Then maybe we would get our smooth road back."

Despite the teeth-rattling ride, the missionaries remained in a happy mood as they traveled south toward Three Forks. For the women, having only ventured down to the trade community for the fall rendezvous, it was a welcome chance to cross the prairie when it was abloom with wildflowers.

They made a stop at Flat Rock Creek where several clumps of scrubby cottonwoods offered privacy for an outhouse break. Amanda had packed ham sandwiches made with her wonderful sourdough bread, and chewy molasses cookies. After cleanup in the cold, clear creek, they continued on.

The group arrived in mid afternoon and parked their wagon at Mr. Bogey's post. They took about an hour to shop at the Chouteau Trading Post before taking the ferry across the Neosho to Cantonment Gibson. Operated by soldiers, the ferry landed just below the new fort.

It was the first time for all but a few of them to see the log structure now that it was completed. It looked as if Sallie Nicks had taken over the garrison for her gathering. Logs spanning barrels made rough tables where an array of food was already being set out. Near the center of the square palisade a pit had been dug and a spit was being turned slowly over the open fire. The smell of cooking beef mingled with the smoke of the pecan wood.

Everywhere soldiers in their blue wool uniforms bustled about doing Sallie's bidding. Lanterns were lit around the compound and drew the missionaries up from the riverbank like moths drawn to the flame. Red, white and blue bunting and ribbons served as colorful decorations. Sallie did indeed know how to throw a party.

Their hostess hurried over to greet them when she saw the group from the mission arrive. Extending both hands to Rachel, she smiled her welcome.

"I'm so glad ya'll could join us this evening," she gushed in her Arkansas drawl. "We have just a wonderful gathering from all over the neighborhood."

"Thank you, Mrs. Nicks," Rachel replied. "It does look as if you have managed to secure guests from all of Lovely's Purchase."

Clarissa glanced around the stockade and saw that besides the many soldiers present, there were several of the traders from Three Forks, Osages from Big Tracks town, including the chief himself, and even some Cherokees who stood visiting with Colonel Nicks.

"Now call me Sallie," their hostess reminded them. "We hardly need to be so formal in this frontier setting, now do we."

Clarissa watched Mrs. Chapman closely. Her face said that she didn't quite agree with this sentiment, but she smiled graciously and said, "As you wish, Sallie. We are very grateful for the invitation to see the fort completed. We have long wanted a military presence nearby."

Sallie glanced around the stockade, keeping an eye on things even as she conversed with her guests.

I think you'll find that there will be a new community growing around the cantonment," she said. "That is certainly what happened at Fort Smith."

Then with a wave of her hand Sallie invited the mission visitors to help themselves to some cider being served at one of the makeshift tables.

"Oh, Tassie's here," Clarissa said when she saw that it was her former student serving the cider.

"Yes," the hostess said, looking pleased. "As soon as I arrived here, I heard nothing but praise of Mrs. Bradley's cooking. So naturally I hired her and her daughters to help me get ready for this evening. They have been a godsend."

"Tassie will be glad to earn some money for her wedding," Clarissa observed.

"Yes, she told me about her beau," Sallie smiled. "I think I'm going to hire her full time. She can help in the store and will be good company for me when Colonel Nicks is off to Little Rock."

"Will you have a true mercantile?" Sarah Requa asked.

"My yes," Sallie said. "John and his new partner have plans to build the biggest emporium west of Fort Smith."

"Will there be a need for such an enterprise?" Rev. Montgomery asked.

"You wait and see," Sallie replied. "Folks flock around military posts."

The sutler's wife cast another look around the stockade while the Fullers and Woodruffs made their way over to the refreshment table. "Let me introduce you to John's partner." She waved a family of four over to her from where they had been visiting with Lieutenant Summers. When the young lieutenant saw that the missionaries had arrived, he trailed behind them to stand beside Sallie.

"Mr. and Mrs. Rogers, I'd like you to get to know the folks from Union Mission," she said. Then to the mission group she introduced the family. "This is John and Nancy, their daughter Tsiana and their son Clem."

John Rogers had reddish brown hair and a full beard. Mrs. Rogers looked to be Cherokee and wore a traditional tiered calico dress adorned with ribbons and beads. Her daughter was a pretty girl of about fifteen and she was tall like her father. Her dark braids had just a hint of red in them, reflecting her heritage from both parents. Clarissa remembered that Colonel Nicks had said John Rogers was Scottish. Tsiana's brother appeared to be about thirteen and looked rather bored with Sallie's party. He was dressed like a trader rather than wearing traditional Cherokee clothing.

Rev. Chapman made introductions of all the missionaries still nearby and included Teresa and Star-That-Travels. The two Indian women appraised each other rather coolly, it seemed to Clarissa. She wondered if Mrs. Nicks had been made aware of the long-running feud between the two tribes.

The brief moment of tension was broken by Lieutenant Summers who had managed to move around the group to stand before Eliza. The buttons on his blue uniform had been polished so that they winked in the lamplight and his brown hair was slicked back with a musky pomander. "It is good to see you, Miss Cleaver," Charles said with a slight bow.

Eliza cast a sideways look at Clarissa and then gave the young officer a bright smile. "And you as well, Lieutenant," she responded.

"Might I assist you in getting something to drink?" he offered.

"That would be kind of you," Eliza agreed and then took the arm that he offered her. They walked across the compound with Sarah and George following behind them.

The Chapmans and the Rogers family were moving away to seating at one side of the stockade, upwind of the smoke from the barbecue pit. Clarissa thought it looked like Mrs. Chapman wanted to separate Mrs. Rogers from Teresa and Star-That-Travels.

The teacher felt thirsty herself and was just about to suggest to Marcus that they also get some cider. But before she could Sallie spoke to him.

"Oh, Dr. Palmer," she said, as if something had just occurred to her.

"Yes, Mrs. Nicks?" the doctor asked.

"It's Sallie, remember," she admonished playfully.

"Yes, Sallie," Marcus returned her smile.

"I wanted to be sure and introduce you to our other newcomers," the hostess looked around the compound again. "Dr. Baylor is around here somewhere. He's to serve as the post surgeon and he was quite interested to learn that there was another doctor in the area."

Sallie snagged a young private walking by. From his boyish face, Clarissa thought him no older than sixteen.

"Private, can you assist me?" Sallie asked him.

"Yes, ma'am," he said.

"Find Dr. Baylor and ask him and his family to join us, will you, dear?"

The boy's face went red at her endearment, but he seemed to like it as well. "I will, ma'am," he grinned. Then he hurried off to do her bidding.

While they waited for the Baylors to arrive, Harriett asked Teresa if she knew the other Osages at the gathering.

"Yes, the large man is Big Tracks, our chief," she said.

"With him is Running Horse, the second chief and Black Dog, our medicine man," Star-That-Travels added.

"A medicine man?" Sallie asked. "Perhaps Dr. Baylor would like to meet him as well."

"He should," Marcus agreed. "I have consulted with Black Dog and he's very knowledgeable about natural prairie remedies."

"I'll see to the introductions then," their hostess said.

Shortly Dr. Baylor approached them along with two attractive women. Sallie introduced Dr. John Baylor, his wife Sophie and his daughter Elizabeth. Both of the women were dressed quite fashionably and the daughter, about twenty years in age, wore her dark hair parted in the middle and then gathered in ringlets over both ears. It was a becoming style on her and she made Clarissa feel rather frumpy.

The feeling changed abruptly to something akin to jealousy, or maybe it was fear, when Elizabeth Baylor placed a hand on the arm of Dr. Palmer. "Oh, another doctor in the area," she said with excitement as if she had just been handed a gift.

"Father and I were just saying we hoped there was someone out here who would know about local ailments and how to treat them," the young woman went on to say.

"My daughter often acts as my medical assistant," Dr. Baylor explained. "I think were she not a woman she would be a doctor herself."

Clarissa saw Harriett purse her lips as if she were biting her tongue at the remark.

"Have you treated this dreadful fever we've heard about

from Dr. Russell at Fort Smith?" Elizabeth asked. Her hand remained on Dr. Palmer's arm. Clarissa thought the gesture was very forward of the young woman.

"Unfortunately, I have," Marcus replied. "And like Dr. Russell, I have found it difficult to treat."

"Perhaps we could discuss it," Elizabeth proposed. "Over a cup of cider?" She smiled a bright coquettish smile and Clarissa thought she was going to be ill.

"Yes," Marcus agreed. "Why don't we all get some cider? I was just about to propose that to Miss Johnson." He turned and gave Clarissa a smile and she thought she saw just a very slight wink.

Then he offered Clarissa his arm and she slipped her hand into the crook of his elbow. It took all her will not to throw a triumphant look toward Dr. Baylor's daughter who had removed her hand and now wore a pout on her pretty face.

They made their way to the table where Tassie served the tangy beverage. Mrs. Baylor drew Elizabeth close to her side and said in a low voice. "Don't pout, dear," she advised. "It is not becoming. Look around you. There is no lack of men here for you to conquer."

Elizabeth did as her mother said, casting a look around the stockade. "Yes, mother," she smiled.

Sallie Nicks excused herself from the Montgomerys, Teresa and Star-That-Travels after urging them to avail themselves of the refreshments. "We'll be serving the meal soon," she said.

Then she made her way across the compound to where her husband stood with their Cherokee visitors.

As Sallie left, Rosalee Chouteau hurried over and slipped her arm across Teresa's shoulders. "I am sorry, Teresa," the Osage woman said quietly. "I did not know he was to be here. I would have warned you if I had known."

"Who?" Teresa asked. "Who is here?"

"You do not know who that is?" Rosalee asked with a nod toward the four Cherokee men.

"The man in the brown turban is the chief, John Jolly, isn't it?" Montgomery asked.

"Yes," Rosalee replied, her face grim. "He is brother to Nancy Rogers," she explained. "The man next to him is George Guess. He is a great man among the Cherokees though he is not a warrior. They call him Sequoyah."

"And the man in the beaver hat?" Harriett asked.

Rosalee's eyes hardened and seemed filled with hatred as she looked at the man whose back was turned to them. "He is Walter Webber."

Teresa gasped and covered her mouth with a look of horror on her face. Walter Webber was widely believed to be responsible for the murder of Teresa's first husband, Joseph Revoir. Joseph had been Colonel Chouteau's trade partner.

"Why is he here?" Teresa whispered. Star-That-Travels reached for his wife's hand and she clasped it tightly.

"They came to visit Nancy," Rosalee replied. "She invited them to Mrs. Nicks' party."

Though the Montgomerys had been at Harmony Mission at the time that Joseph Revoir was killed, they had heard about the incident. The feud between Webber and Mad Buffalo had sparked the confrontation at La Saline. When Revoir had refused to reveal Mad Buffalo's whereabouts, someone in the Cherokee party had fired the shot that killed him. Most believed the fatal shot had come from Webber's gun.

Walter Webber had never denied the Cherokees' involvement in the matter, but he claimed it was self defense. He also claimed his rights under the law of the avenger. Officials at Fort Smith had been reluctant to interfere and no one had been arrested for the murder.

Rosalee narrowed her eyes and spoke to Star-That-Travels. "Joseph's death has never been avenged." She seemed to be challenging the warrior to take some sort of action.

Star looked around the cantonment. Soldiers were everywhere and any confrontation here would be pointless. Calling someone out to a duel was not the way of the avenger.

Harriett moved in front of Teresa as if to shield her from the man.

"If you want to leave, we'll go with you back to our camp," she offered in a quiet but clipped tone.

Teresa looked up at her husband as if seeking his guidance. He took a long moment to stare at the back of Walter Webber. His face was hard and his jaw was tight. His lips moved in a quiet prayer and gradually the anger left his demeanor. He looked Teresa in the eye.

"A warrior does not run . . . or hide," he said. Then reaching for Teresa's other hand he added, "And a Christian does not hate or seek revenge." It was clearly hard to say these words, but he had made his choice.

Teresa nodded and there were tears in her eyes.

Rosalee stepped back, her disgust obvious. "It is good then that Mad Buffalo does not share your faith," she spat. "He will avenge Joseph, if you will not." Then she walked away to join her husband.

Montgomery clasped Star's hard-muscled shoulder. "I know that was hard," he said with admiration in his voice. "And I respect you for it."

Star nodded, his aquiline features seeming noble for having gone through the struggle of conscience.

"Webber will hear of this," the minister predicted. "And it will change him."

"It better," Harriett said. She sent one of her famous looks toward the Cherokee leader. As if becoming aware that he was the subject of discussion, he turned to look their way. Instead of lifting his chin in the haughty anger the missionaries had witnessed at Dardanelle, the man lowered his eyes as if saddened and ashamed.

CHAPTER TWENTY-FOUR

Union Mission
Summer, 1824

Sallie's party was the talk around Union Mission for days afterwards. Despite the tension that lingered through the evening, the presence of the military had kept things civil. The Osages sat on the grass on one side of the camp to enjoy the meal of barbecued beef, potatoes, baked beans, roasted green corn and pan after pan of Mrs. Bradley's fruit cobbler. The Cherokee guests kept to the other side of the stockade, visiting with the Rogers family.

The missionaries had felt relief as they said their thanks and goodbyes to the Nickses and a few of the post's officers.

"I just realized," Amanda said one morning during breakfast in the dining hall. "Colonel Arbuckle was not present the other evening. Neither was Lieutenant Bonneville."

"I heard Arbuckle and a corps of engineers were down at Red River laying out a new cantonment there," George told her. "Bonneville has been called back east."

"Did you hear what he's going to name this fort?" Stephen asked.

"Cantonment Towson, according to Colonel Nicks," George responded. Always the curious one among the missionaries, George was never afraid to ask questions.

"And who is Towson?" Marcus asked.

"Postmaster General," George grinned. "Arbuckle is having his revenge on the commanding officers in Washington."

The others grinned at the mechanic's observation. He went on to say, "And the lieutenant is acting as an aide to the Marquis de Lafayette who's touring the country." He sounded impressed with the plum assignment.

"I wonder how Teresa is doing?" Rachel then asked. "I know the event was quite unsettling for her. She was totally silent on the trip back up here."

Her question sobered the missionary family. It was heartbreaking to see how upset their Osage friend had been by the ordeal of having to spend the evening in the presence of the likely killer of her husband.

"She's a stronger woman than I am," Sarah observed. Clarissa had to hide a smile. Her friend would indeed have found it difficult to be as silent as Teresa.

When George had explained the situation to his wife on the journey home, she had nearly exploded with anger. Only the shushing of the others had kept her from offering her opinion to Teresa and Star. Had she known about the La Saline incident while they had been at Gibson, she might have offered her opinion to Walter Webber as well.

"Howard and I are planning to head up to Hopefield today," Stephen said with a nod to their hired man. "They had their corn planted earlier than us because their fields are smaller. They will be ready to start their harvest soon. I'll speak with Will and Susan about Teresa . . . see how she's faring."

"Thank you, Mr. Fuller," Chapman said. "We would appreciate that. I would imagine that Star-That-Travels will face pressure from Monepasha's group to follow their law about avenging a death. This matter with the Cherokees will be almost as difficult for him as for his wife."

"It certainly is a matter for our continued prayer," Rev. Vaille said. His words were a signal for them all to stand for the morning prayer and then all parted the dining hall to begin their daily chores.

At Hopefield, Susan, Harriett, Teresa and her daughter Louisa had spent the morning picking green beans and now sat on straight-backed cane chairs in the shade of the Requa cabin, snapping the beans for canning.

Harriett had told Susan about what had transpired at Cantonment Gibson. Both women tried to be considerate of the Osage woman's feelings in the following days. Seeing Walter Webber had opened an old wound and they could tell that she was mourning Joseph's death all over again.

Star, along with Bird, had been gone for a few days, tracking a black bear they had sighted down by the river. Star had taken Jean with him, leaving Louisa to solicitously follow her mother around and offer what comfort she could.

The women sat in companionable silence for a time, the only sound, the snap of the beans and the backdrop noises of birdsong and the rustle of cornstalks in a gentle wind. A family of purple martins darted around the dried gourd birdhouses Teresa had made. She had hung them on the lower branches of the only tree in their little community.

Montgomery walked with Monepasha along the edge of the cornfields, occasionally pulling back a husk to check the ripeness of their crop. It was the closest Monepasha had been to the fields, and he seemed pleased with what looked to be a bountiful yield. If no hail or windstorms came, their harvest would be more than enough for the community and the excess could be sold.

Behind the Requa cabin, Will worked to sharpen several knives on a whetstone. The steady rasp of the blades provided a counterpoint rhythm to the turtle shell rattle Teresa's baby shook with gusto.

The little boy had quickly earned the name Turtle because of his love for the rattle. He sat happily in the grass at Teresa's feet, occasionally throwing the shell so Louisa would have to jump up and retrieve it. The scene would have seemed a completely happy one were it not for the stoic sadness on the Osage woman's face.

"I hope my baby is as happy and healthy as yours, Teresa," Susan said as she paused from her chore to rub her back. Susan's baby was due very soon.

Teresa didn't respond for a moment as if her mind was

returning from somewhere far away. She glanced down at Turtle and her eyes softened, but she did not smile. "Yes," was all she said.

Susan and Harriett shared a concerned look. Their friend seemed to slip further and further into despondency.

"I have to admit, I'm a little frightened about giving birth," Susan confessed to the women. She kept her voice low so her husband wouldn't hear. "I hope you both will be there to help me."

Teresa finally looked at Susan. "You will be fine," she assured the blonde woman. "You are young and strong."

"I'm sure she will," Harriett agreed, smiling at Susan but giving her a look that seemed to say, "follow my lead."

Then she turned to Teresa and in her usual forthright manner she stated, "But you have learned through grief that being young and strong is not always a guaranty in this hard life."

Teresa lowered her eyes, "No it is not," she said, her voice husky with emotion. "Do you think me wrong to feel such anger about it? Do I fail as a Christian?"

"No," Susan and Harriett both responded quickly.

"I would be astonished if you didn't feel anger," Harriett added. "Your feelings are natural and I know that God understands them. But we are responsible for what we do with our anger. It cannot be an excuse for another wrong."

"My clan despises me . . . *Wah-She-Hah* and me . . . because we have not followed the avenger law." She sighed. "This God-path is hard to walk."

"Yes, I know it is," Harriett agreed. "And I would not suggest otherwise to you. But I believe, because I have witnessed it myself, that God can bring good even from something evil."

"I always think of that scripture about how a seed must be planted into the dark earth before it can produce fruit," Susan said in her child-like voice. "It's like there has to be death before there can be life."

Teresa lifted her eyes to look at their fields. The green cornstalks stood tall and the silk tassels were browning in the summer heat. Those fields did indeed represent hope for a new life for the *Wahzhazhe* on the changing prairie.

"But what good can come of Joseph's death?" she asked softly, almost as a prayer.

Both Susan and Harriett were silent for a moment as if searching for the right words. "It is hard sometimes to know," Harriett finally said. "It can take a very long time to see any kind of good come.

"But this I believe, Teresa. Your people may say they despise you, but they are watching you and they are seeing great strength in you. Your witness to them is greater than that of any of us from New England. You are planting seeds, Teresa. And the harvest will be seen for generations to come."

Teresa kept her eyes on the green fields and gradually her face softened. For the first time since Joseph's death, she cried.

In the next few days the harvest began at Hopefield. All the women in Monepasha's clan joined Will, Montgomery, Stephen and Mr. Howard in filling bushel baskets with the ripened ears of corn. Teresa and Harriett helped as well by husking mounds of the ears while keeping a close watch on Susan.

After Susan endured a long labor, the Requas welcomed a daughter into the world. They named her Susan with the plan to call her Susie.

Within the week another baby joined the mission family at Union. Asie Vaille gave birth to her fifth child named Charlotte. The women gathered in the Vaille cabin and passed the sweet baby around the day after her arrival. Clarissa noticed that her brother Joseph seemed jealous of all the attention the baby was receiving. It seemed a little odd since there were so many babies at Union almost every one of the women had one in her lap. But Joseph had already sensed that Charlotte's arrival would change his position in the family.

While the ladies offered little hand-made gifts to Asie,

Clarissa leaned over from her chair to pull the two and a half year old close. "It's good that your mama has a new baby to care for," she said. "Because you are becoming such a big boy, you're not a baby anymore."

Her words seem to help for Joey pulled himself up and said, "I go fishing with Billy."

Clarissa smiled. "Yes, with Billy and the other boys. You know you can't go fishing by yourself."

The mission parents had a strict rule that the children must always be accompanied by an adult when going down to the river. Often Paul was the adult the boys asked to supervise their fishing or crawdad expeditions. Paul had grown up on the Mississippi River and knew how to find good fishing holes. The missionaries had long remarked that all the boys should learn to swim, but with their never-ending chores, swimming lessons were always being put off. Even most of the adults could not swim.

Joseph seemed satisfied for the moment with his status as a big boy and wiggled out of Clarissa's arms to join Thea in play near the cold fireplace. The stone hearth was a good place to roll a ball of twine back and forth.

"Our harvest will be startin' soon accordin' to Stephen," Amanda was telling the ladies. "We'll be up to our ears in ears in just a few days."

"Oh, Amanda, that's such a corny joke," Sarah quickly returned.

The women all laughed. It was good to have a moment for fellowship and fun. Most days offered little but hard work on this prairie outpost.

"Is he expecting a good harvest?" Alice asked.

"He says it should be, though the west field has felt the effect of the wind we had this spring. It dried that field out more than the others," Amanda said.

"Can't wait for some fresh ears of roasted corn," Martha said. "Such a welcome summer meal."

"Especially the way you cook it, Amanda," Sarah complimented the cook.

"Well, now that we are all looking forward to the first of

the harvest, I suppose it is time for us to get back to work," Rachel pronounced.

Reluctantly the women took their leave of the quiet mother, gathered up their own small children and each went her way to appointed tasks awaiting them.

A few days later, the women were gathered again, this time in the kitchen. The men and older boys were in the fields, pulling the ears of corn and tossing them into bushel baskets.

The women were husking the corn, cleaning and blanching it and then preparing it for canning or making hominy. Martha was cutting the dark golden kernels from the cob, spatters of the corn sprinkling her apron. Suddenly her knife slipped and bit deeply into her palm. Immediately blood began to flow and she hurried to the wash basin to plunge the injured hand into the tepid water.

All the women stopped their work to see if the midwife needed assistance.

Amanda hurried over to the wash stand to see that the blood still flowed freely.

Oh, Martha," she breathed, "that looks bad."

Rachel quickly emptied her lap of corn and walked to the kitchen door. Outside the older girls were stuffing husks and cleaned cobs into burlap sacks.

"Abigail," she said to her oldest daughter. "Run to the field and find Dr. Palmer. Ask him to come to the kitchen and bring his medical kit."

"Is something wrong, Mother?" the girl asked.

"All will be fine," Rachel replied. "Just hurry and do as I ask."

The girl nodded and raced to the cornfield. "Just a little accident, girls," Rachel tried to reassure them and ease the worry that filled their faces.

In the kitchen Amanda and Sarah were working to press bandages against Martha's hand to staunch the flow of blood.

"Now don't fuss girls," Martha protested. "I've had worse than this happen." But her face was growing a bit pale and her hands shook. It was clear the older woman was in pain.

It seemed to take forever for the doctor to arrive. When he finally stepped into the kitchen, he looked around quickly not knowing what the situation was that needed his attention. Despite himself his eyes lingered for a moment longer than necessary on Clarissa's face. He felt relief that it was not she who needed medical help. They exchanged a smile and only Amanda's voice pulled his gaze away from her.

"Martha has cut her hand," she explained.

"Mrs. Woodruff," Marcus said as he crossed the kitchen and accepted the hand she offered him. "I thought you knew better than that."

The doctor and his patient shared a smile of their own. They had worked together often over the injured and ill and had developed a close friendship.

"You'd think so, wouldn't you," Martha laughed and immediately relaxed. The doctor had a way of putting his patients at ease with his gentle humor.

After quickly washing up, Marcus removed the pressure bandage and the flow of blood began again. He probed the cut with care and his concern showed on his face.

"The cut is to the bone," he finally said. "I think a few stitches are in order. Let's go into the dining hall."

Sarah and Rachel quickly prepared a clean place for the doctor to work while he washed his hands more thoroughly. Thea had been playing in the room with the twins Moses and Miriam. Clarissa took her daughter's hand and led her into the kitchen to be out of the way. The babies being watched by Phoebe and Asie were all settled on the other side of the room.

Clarissa wanted to offer her assistance to Marcus, but Thea was frightened by the hushed and hurried atmosphere and clung to her mama's hand. Tears filled her eyes. Clarissa sat down and lifted the girl onto her lap and hugged her close.

Marcus and Martha sat at the cleanly scrubbed table with a fresh towel placed over it.

"Bring me a cup, Mrs. Fuller," the doctor directed.

Amanda returned with it and Marcus poured a small amount of whiskey into it.

"Now, Mrs. Woodruff, I know you're a temperance woman, but this is strictly medicinal and you need to drink it all down."

Martha took the enamelware cup and slowly swallowed its contents. She made a face and shuddered as the burning liquid passed her throat. "Every time I have to drink that awful stuff I'm reminded why I'm a temperance woman."

Marcus smiled and worked to clean and sterilize the wound, giving the medicinal liquor time to take effect. He set out his instruments carefully. When he felt the motherly woman was ready, he quickly took three stitches and tied each one off. He was done in less than a minute.

"You're getting too good at that," Martha observed. She sat quietly while the doctor wrapped her hand with fresh bandages.

"People need to stop getting hurt around here," Marcus replied. "I get too much practice."

He carefully tied the bandage at the top of her hand. "Now I would suggest you drink some willow tea and then lie down for a bit."

"Posh. I'm fine," Martha protested, but her words sounded weak. "There's too much work this morning and I still have one good hand."

"The work will get done," Rachel stated, placing a hand on Martha's shoulder. "You need to follow doctor's orders and give your body time to heal. You know that is the advice you would give us."

"I'll help you to your cabin," Sarah offered, "and Amanda will have your tea in just a bit."

The cook was already steeping the willow bark she kept on hand.

As Marcus began to clean the surgical area, Thea cupped her hand over her mother's ear and whispered loudly, "I go potty."

Amanda laughed and threw a look at the teacher. They smiled at the childish indiscretion.

"Well, aren't you a big girl," Clarissa said. "Let's go then."

They made their way to their cabin as Sarah walked with Martha to the Woodruff cabin next door. After Thea had taken a very long time on the chamber pot, Clarissa washed her little hands at the wash basin and then tried to hurry her back to the dining hall. They passed Dr. Palmer who was taking his medical kit to his cabin before returning to the fields. Clarissa and Marcus stopped to speak briefly and Thea took the moment to start picking little white wildflowers growing beside the path.

"Oh, Thea, you're getting your dress dirty," Clarissa scolded.

The girl held up a fistful of flowers. "Yours, Mama," she offered.

"You can't remain angry after that," Marcus laughed.

"I can't stay angry with her about anything," Clarissa sighed. "Come along, little miss. Aunt Phoebe needs you for something, I'm sure."

"Bebe," Thea said and suddenly she was in a hurry to get back to the housemother. Marcus laughed once again and then reached out to give Clarissa's hand a little squeeze before they parted.

He continued on to the cabins and Clarissa opened the dining room door to let Thea in. She was about to walk into the kitchen when she decided to visit the outhouse herself before settling into more harvest chores.

As she crossed the compound, James Chapman came running through the cane that grew vigorously at the eastern edge of the mission. Spotting the teacher, he began to call to her. "Teacher, Teacher," he said as he continued to pump his legs in a desperate sprint. His pant legs were wet and his face was flushed. The clear sound of fear in his voice stopped Clarissa in the path.

"What is wrong, James?" she asked, turning to catch the ten-year-old as he hurled himself at her.

"It's Billy," James gasped breathlessly. "He fell in the river."

"The river?" Clarissa repeated in shock. "What was he doing there? Can't Paul get to him?"

"Paul didn't come with us," James said, his words giving way to tears. "He said he had to work the fields. So me and Billy and Joey went."

"James, you know you're not supposed . . ." Clarissa stopped herself. Now was not the time to scold. Billy couldn't swim and who knows what might happen to Joey left alone at the river.

She drew a deep breath to steady herself. "Where is Billy?"

"By the big rock where we picnicked last week," James said. "We didn't mean to get close to the water, honest."

Clarissa knew exactly where the large outcropping of sandstone was located. It was a favorite spot among the missionaries for an outing.

She knelt to be at eye-level with the frightened boy. "James, listen to me. Go get Dr. Palmer. He's in his cabin. Tell him I've gone down to the river and he needs to come as quickly as possible. Then go get your papa. Can you do that?"

"Yes, miss," James said already running to the doctor's cabin at the far end of the compound.

Clarissa considered telling someone about the situation herself, but knew she had no time to do so. Hitching up her skirts, she began to run, praying all the while.

They kept a path cut through the river cane and Clarissa hurled herself down it so fast she almost lost her footing a few times. She reached the sandstone rock to find Joey sitting on it, crying.

She knelt beside the boy. "Shush, Joey," she said. "Tell me where Billy is."

All he could do was point. Clarissa followed the direction of his grubby finger and briefly saw Billy's head bob above the water. He was thrashing about, clearly too agitated to keep himself afloat.

Clarissa thrust off her slippers, grateful she wasn't wearing her lace-up boots. Then she threw her legs over the rock ledge and eased into the water, hoping it was shallow enough that she could walk out to the frightened boy.

Her skirt and petticoats began to float around her as she felt her way across the rocky river bed. The rocks had been worn smooth by the water; otherwise she might have cut her feet. But the stones were slippery and she had to move cautiously as the current increased in the deeper water. She called to Billy.

"I'm coming, Billy," she said. "I'll get you. Stop fighting and try to float."

Billy seemed not to hear.

Just before she reached him, Clarissa felt the bottom of the river drop beneath her feet. It happened so suddenly, she slipped under the water and had to thrust herself up to the surface. She was not an expert swimmer but could paddle adequately. She reminded herself to stay calm and edged closer to the boy.

"Billy, be still," she said as she reached him. "I have you now."

In desperate relief Billy threw his arms around the teacher's neck. His sudden weight pushed her under and for a moment she fought to get both of them above the water.

A flash of fear filled her mind and it was as if she were back in the Mississippi River where she had almost drowned on the voyage out to Arkansas Territory. If Dr. Palmer hadn't saved her four years ago, she would have been lost.

"Please, God, please, God," she began to pray just as she had on that fateful night near Wolf Island. With Billy's weight and the tug of her soaked skirts, she felt herself being pulled under.

She slipped beneath the surface again and thought she heard her name being called. Pushing herself and Billy up once more, she gasped for air.

Dr. Palmer was rushing down the path with even great speed than hers. He was calling her name, desperation in his voice. "Clarissa!"

"Here," she managed to call.

Without even taking the time to remove his boots, the

doctor rushed past Joey to the end of the rock ledge and with a great leap plunged feet first into the water.

The splash of it rocked Clarissa and Billy but before they could even react, the doctor had reached them. "Hand him to me," he instructed the teacher. "The others are right behind me."

Clarissa thrust Billy into his arms. The doctor was tall enough to walk back to the shore where Rev. Vaille and John Spaulding now appeared. The minister scooped up Joey off the rock and John reached to take his son from the doctor.

"Get them to their mothers," Palmer gasped. Then he turned back toward Clarissa who was paddling awkwardly toward the shore. He strode forcefully through the water as if he would part it by sheer will.

He reached for her, slipping his arm around her waist and pulling her firmly to his side. He helped her step back up on the sandstone ledge. Then drawing her into his arms in a full embrace they stood for a moment in grateful, dripping silence.

"I was scared to death," Marcus finally murmured against her temple. "Don't ever do that to me again."

"It felt like Wolf Island," Clarissa said. "But I knew you would come for me."

Marcus pushed away a little so he could look at her face. He cupped his hands behind her neck. "I'm not letting you out of my sight ever again," he declared fervently.

"That would hardly be proper, sir," Clarissa smiled with lowered eyes.

"It would be if we were married," he replied and her eyes flew up to meet his. "I love you, Clarissa. Say you'll marry me. I have wanted to ask you that since Wolf Island."

Clarissa smiled, her happiness written on her face. "Then what took you so . . ." Before she could finish, his lips captured hers in a gentle kiss.

And to him she smelled like fish and mud and roses.

CHAPTER TWENTY-FIVE

Union Mission
Late Summer, 1824

"Palmer!" the voice of Rev. Chapman reached Marcus and Clarissa as they stood trembling on the sandstone rock. Others from the mission were hurrying through the cane. Instinctively they stepped back from one another and Clarissa tried to slip her feet into her shoes. Marcus grasped her elbow to steady her.

"Miss Johnson," Chapman called again. "Are you alright?"

"We're both fine," Marcus assured them as the minister along with Stephen and Paul came into view. "Just very wet."

"Is Billy alright?" Clarissa asked.

"He seems to be," Chapman said. "He's mostly frightened . . . and chastened. But I believe Mrs. Spaulding will want you to check on him, doctor."

"Certainly," Marcus agreed. He helped Clarissa start up the path toward the mission. "As soon as we've had a chance to dry off a bit." He smiled at his understatement.

"You dove in yourself, Miss Johnson?" Paul asked.

"More like tiptoed in, Paul," Clarissa replied, feeling self-conscious about her sodden appearance. "Fortunately the river is rather low right now."

"I's real sorry I wasn't with them boys," Paul said, shaking his head.

"Don't blame yourself," Stephen told him. "The boys broke the rules. They know they are not to visit the river without an adult."

"Let's just be grateful to God that they are safe," Chapman said. They finished the trek to the mission yard in thoughtful silence.

As they all came around the corner of the cabins, Clarissa and Marcus were met by the rest of the family as conquering heroes. Alice Spaulding quickly handed Billy to his father and embraced the teacher.

"Thank you," she whispered tearfully into Clarissa's ear. "And thanks to God it was you that James told. You were exactly the person who could save Billy."

"I was glad I could help," Clarissa said. "But I would have been in trouble myself had not Dr. Palmer come when he did."

Alice then turned to the doctor. "It may not be proper," she said, opening her arms, "but I must show you my gratitude as well." Marcus bent down to receive her hug.

"The credit goes to Clari . . . Miss Johnson," he said. He looked over Alice's shoulder to the teacher and Clarissa saw the same look of admiration in his eyes that she had seen after Wolf Island. Warmth flowed through her as they shared a smile.

Later in her cabin, Clarissa slipped out of her wet clothing and donned dry ones. She was toweling her hair when Eliza knocked briefly and then stepped inside. She also embraced the teacher in a hug of gratitude.

"We were frightened to death when we finally understood what James was crying about," she said. "Alice would have run down to the river herself if she hadn't been nursing Allie."

"I was quite frightened myself," Clarissa said, but her voice seemed distant.

Eliza pulled back to look her friend in the eye.

"You don't look frightened," she said. "You look suspiciously happy." There was a speculative gleam in the younger woman's eyes.

Clarissa smiled broadly, "That's because Dr. Palmer asked me to marry him."

"Today?" Eliza asked. "Down at the river?"

Clarissa nodded.

Eliza clapped her hands. "And what did you say?"

The teacher was thoughtful for a moment, suddenly realizing she had not given the man an answer.

"I asked him what took him so long?" she laughed.

Eliza joined in the laughter but then sobered. "You had better give him an answer," she said, trying to sound stern, "lest someone else catch his eye."

The pretty doctor's daughter Elisabeth Baylor came to Clarissa's mind and she felt a moment of fear. Then she remembered that even that dark-haired beauty had not been able to tempt her patient, faithful man.

But Clarissa wasn't going to tempt fate. "I'll give him my answer as soon as I can!"

It was not until the evening meal that Clarissa even saw Marcus again that day. The men ate their ham sandwiches at noon out in the cornfields. The women worked in the kitchen putting up jars and jars of canned corn. As punishment for the river incident, James, Billy and Joseph had to stay in the kitchen as well. The older two boys were put to work sweeping up the corn silks and spattered corn that quickly covered the plank floor.

At supper Marcus slipped into a chair beside Clarissa. Thea was sitting quietly in her mother's lap, gumming a biscuit, but she immediately clambered into the doctor's lap. She grinned up at Clarissa and her happiness seemed to reflect her mother's.

As the dishes were passed along the table following grace, Clarissa couldn't help but notice that all the women seemed to be smiling her way. Had Eliza already shared her news? It made her extremely conscious of the fact that she had not yet given Marcus her answer.

They conversed quietly with others around the table for a time and all the while Clarissa debated in her mind. Should she say something now or wait and hope they would have a private moment after the meal?

Alice had already requested that the doctor check on

Billy after supper for he seemed to be developing a cough. Marcus assured her he would just after he had visited Martha to see how her hand looked. The evening would probably be spent with patients for Marcus never rushed through an exam.

Finally Clarissa decided to go against her rather timid nature and do something very bold – at least bold for her. Leaning close toward Marcus so that their shoulders touched she said quietly above Thea's tousled hair, "Yes."

Marcus raised a puzzled eyebrow as he looked at Clarissa. She said nothing more, hoping she wouldn't have to with so many people around them. She looked him squarely in the eye, praying he would understand her meaning.

At last he smiled too. "Thank you," he replied. Then with something of a sigh, he added quietly, "My time seems to be claimed this evening. Could we take a walk together in the morning?"

"Yes," was all Clarissa said. The look of love they shared said all else that was needed.

The following day as work continued on the corn harvest, Clarissa could tell that her mission sisters were curious about her new understanding with their doctor. But they seemed reluctant to question her about it. Finally Amanda could stand it no longer.

"Well, do you have some news for us or not, Miss Johnson?" she questioned with her hands on her hips in a pose of exasperation.

Clarissa laughed and threw a glance at Eliza who was trying to look innocent.

"Dr. Palmer and I have set a marriage date of August 24," she said. "My mother would be scandalized by such a short engagement, but we wanted to be married before school starts in September."

The other women were quick to put aside their work and gather around the school teacher and offer hugs with their congratulations. Soon the kitchen where they worked was filled with their plans for the wedding.

Clarissa was so grateful for her mission sisters. At a time

like this, she missed her mother and own two sisters very much. Her only regret for this happy occasion was that her family would not be able to attend the wedding.

The days seemed to speed by in the next few weeks. The corn harvest was completed and canning vegetables from the garden followed. The men used the time to make needed repairs and adjustments to the grist mill. Once the corn was dried they would begin the process of grinding it into meal.

Some days later at Hopefield, Will, Montgomery and Star-That-Travels stood admiring the 15 barrels of cornmeal they had just loaded into a wagon. They would take the grain to Cantonment Gibson tomorrow in hopes that Colonel Nicks would purchase it. Additional meal as well as dried cobs filled the Requas' barn, stored for use by the entire Hopefield community.

Monepasha, the Osage elder, joined them.

"*Wah-Kon-Tah* has given us much today," he said, speaking in his native tongue. His voice was graveled from smoking and age.

Star translated his words for Rev. Montgomery. "We have never harvested this much corn . . . beans and squash, too," Monepasha added.

"God has certainly blessed us with a good harvest this summer," the minister agreed.

Their conversation was interrupted with the arrival of a rider coming at a steady lope across the prairie from the Texas Road. As he neared, Montgomery recognized that it was Daniel Austin from Harmony Mission.

"Brother Daniel," he greeted the man when he slowed his horse to a walk at the Requas' barn. "What brings you to Hopefield?"

"Nothing good, I'm afraid," the Harmony millwright said as he stiffly dismounted. He face was grim.

"What is it?" Will asked.

"Smallpox has broken out in Pawhuska's town," Austin explained while handing his horse's reins to Star's offered hand. "It's spread to Pappinville as well. People are in a panic. The townsfolk blame the Osages for it and the Osages blame the white man for it. Dr. Belcher has gone to Pawhuska's and is trying to keep his town quarantined. But before he left he asked me to come down and request that Dr. Palmer work in Pappinville. They don't have a doctor."

"What about Harmony?" Montgomery asked. "Has anyone been affected there?"

"Just one case," the millwright said. "We isolated the little girl and hope that will keep the other children from contracting it. But Dr. Belcher would only allow me to leave Harmony in case someone else might have been exposed. I survived a mild case of it years ago so he believes me to be immune."

"Come to the house and let Harriett fix you something to eat, Brother," Montgomery invited. "You look done in."

"I've changed horses twice to get here as quick as I could," Austin agreed. "But I can't stay here long; I need to get on down to Union."

The two men walked quickly to the Montgomery cabin. Harriett looked happy to see their brother from Harmony until her husband quickly explained the reason for the man's visit.

"Do they need additional workers?" she asked while she scrambled eggs and boiled a fresh pot of coffee.

"I'm sure Dr. Belcher does," Austin replied as he sat down at the table. "Black Dog is there, but I don't doubt that more nurses are needed."

"We could go, couldn't we?" Harriett asked Montgomery. "Susan would be glad to watch Mary while we're gone. Mary loves being over at their cabin."

"If you are willing," the minister agreed, "I certainly am."

"We can put together a wagon of supplies," Harriett said, her mind clearly working out a plan for the efficient packing of those supplies. "Maybe Mrs. Woodruff from Union would be able to go as well."

"We don't want too heavy a wagon load," her husband cautioned her. "Speed will be important and too many riders could slow us down."

"Oh, yes," she agreed. She set a plateful of eggs and cold cornbread on the table and poured coffee for the men. But rather than join them, she went immediately to a trunk at the end of their bed and began to look through it for items that might be useful for the mission.

While Mr. Austin ate, they discussed their plans. When they stepped outside again, they found Star waiting patiently with a fresh mount for Daniel.

"I will go too," was all the warrior said. As Austin mounted the mustang, Star leapt onto his own rangy pony. Then the two men started out at a quick trot to cover the five miles to Union. The Montgomerys walked over to the Requas' cabin to explain their plan to accompany Daniel and Dr. Palmer back to Missouri.

At Union, Amanda insisted on serving the visitors her honeyed peach pie while the men paused from their work to hear Mr. Austin's report from Harmony. "Hate to take you away from your work here, doctor," he said, "but the need is great and Dr. Belcher is truly overwhelmed with it all."

Marcus hesitated before replying. It was the first time Clarissa had ever seen him show reluctance to assist someone in need and she knew why. Their wedding date was less than two weeks away now. It would obviously have to be postponed. She felt a sinking in the pit of her stomach and a nagging little voice in her head told her she would never be married.

The doctor looked her way and she silently shushed her fear and gave him a nod.

"I will certainly offer Dr. Belcher my assistance," he said. "We'll need to get some supplies together."

"The Montgomerys plan to go as well and thought to borrow a wagon from Union," Austin told them. "They thought Mrs. Woodruff might also be able to go."

Martha nodded her head and seemed ready to agree when her husband said, "Best not, Lovie. Your hand's still not healed completely."

The midwife looked down at her hand, still encased in a

bandage. She had often decried the fact that it seemed to be healing so slowly, hampering her ability to help with the canning. "I suppose I wouldn't be as much help as I'd like to be," she said regretfully.

"You don't want to overtax your hand, Mrs. Woodruff," Marcus agreed.

Who else could go, Clarissa wondered. Most of the women at Union had babies to care for and she had classes beginning in less than a month. Eliza was free, but she had never been inclined to help with nursing duties.

As the meeting came to an end and everyone returned to their work, Marcus sought Clarissa out as she walked to the school where she had been getting lesson plans prepared.

"Clarissa, I am so sorry," he said as he took her hand and walked with her. "I won't go if you don't want me to."

"You have to go," Clarissa responded with a sigh. "I knew when I agreed to marry you that I would share you with those in need. We'll just put the wedding off until you return."

Marcus ran his free hand through his hair in frustration. "We could push the wedding up," he said hopefully as they reached the schoolhouse and stepped into Clarissa's classroom.

"You'll need to leave at first light in the morning," Clarissa argued, wishing she didn't have to be practical. "And I don't want to begin our marriage with you gone."

"I'm sorry," he said again and pulled her into an embrace. He seemed almost more disappointed than she felt.

"You waited on me for a very long time," Clarissa murmured against his shoulder. "Now it is my turn to wait on you. I will try to be as strong and patient as you are."

"I feel neither strong nor patient at this moment," Marcus said.

They stood in their quiet embrace for a moment longer and Clarissa felt tears gathering. To keep them at bay she pushed back from the man she loved and took on her schoolteacher's voice.

"You'd best get ready to go," she said. "Martha and

Amanda will have gathered up the supplies you need by now."

He nodded, but didn't move for a moment. Then with a kiss he left the classroom.

Clarissa stood still, hugging herself as if to retain the feel of him, the smell of him. She had to fight the urge to run after Marcus and tell him she had changed her mind. She didn't want to share him with the faceless people of Pappinville, Missouri.

"If you want something, sometimes you have to go after it." The long ago advice of Rachel's mother came unbidden to Clarissa's mind. It had seemed a ludicrous idea when Mrs. Smith had offered it. Now it seemed to shout so loudly to her that she almost looked around, expecting someone to be standing in the classroom with her.

"Go," a nudging voice spoke inside her. Was it her heart or her head? Or perhaps her spirit? Where ever it arose from, there was an urgency in it that could not be denied.

"Should I go, God?" she prayed in a whisper.

"Go."

Clarissa took a deep breath as if to draw courage into herself. She grasped the door handle and opened it forcefully, then made her way to her cabin. Her mind was whirling with items she should pack.

When she reached the cabin, she found Eliza taking her recommended afternoon rest. The young woman looked up at her when Clarissa stepped inside.

"Eliza, I'm going to Missouri with Dr. Palmer," she announced as she pulled her carpetbag from beneath her bed. "Can you keep Thea while I'm gone?"

Eliza sat up, looking puzzled. "You aren't going near the smallpox, are you?"

"I'll go wherever Marcus is," she replied, unaware that she had slipped and violated propriety in calling him by his given name.

Eliza smiled. "Of course, I'll keep Thea. You have to follow your young man wherever he plans to go."

Clarissa finished packing and then searched out Rev.

Chapman. Technically she had to secure his permission to go since it would mean leaving her class. It was unlikely she would be back in time for the start of school. But in her heart, she knew she would go even if it meant being fired from the mission.

She needn't have worried, however. Rev. Chapman may have been hesitant to agree to her plan, but Rachel quickly said, "Of course, you should go. I only wish we could send more people to help."

"I hate to delay the start of school," Chapman said.

"There will be no need to. All of us can step in and keep the girls occupied," Rachel countered. "Sarah has already been working with them on needlepoint and Amanda could offer some cooking lessons. Phoebe and I can work with them on art and music and domestic studies. We'll make it work."

Clarissa gave Rachel a look of gratitude. Then she hurried to take her valise to Marcus and Daniel Austin who were loading the mission wagon.

"I'm going with you," she stated firmly when she approached the men. Marcus turned to look at her in astonishment. The grin that spread across his face told the teacher she had made the right decision.

"Are you sure?" he asked, pulling her aside and speaking quietly. "Don't do this because you feel an obligation to me. I don't want you endangering your health on my account."

"My place is by your side," Clarissa said with a certainty that she had rarely felt about anything. "We are partners now . . . or soon will be." Then she took on a teasing tone. "I have to help you get the folks at Pappinville well so we can get married. I'm not letting you out of it."

"I don't want out of it," he said with another smile.

The wagon pulled out of the yard as dawn broke the next day. Streaks of pink tinted the clouds as the mission family had gathered around the wagon and offered a prayer for safety and healing. Clarissa rode in the wagon bed while Mr. Austin drove the team of mules. While their oxen were stronger, they were also slower so the mules were called into service. Marcus and Star rode their mustangs beside the wagon.

At Hopefield, Harriett and Montgomery joined them. Harriett sat next to Clarissa and her husband joined Daniel on the wagon seat. They kept a steady pace to reach the ford at La Saline by midday.

The journey was hampered twice as heavy rains fell, making the road slick and muddy. The women huddled under a canvas tarp in the wagon and the men pulled on rain slickers while they waited out the downpour in a thicket of trees. They were weary and sore when they reached Harmony Mission nine days later.

The Harmony director greeted them with what seemed a sense of relief. "It is so good to see you here," he stated as they dismounted. "Come get something to eat. You must be terribly tired."

Clarissa found that she could hardly move after climbing down from the wagon. Marcus took her arm and helped her walk to the mission dining hall.

While they ate, Marcus inquired about the health conditions in the affected areas. "Has the disease abated yet?"

"It seems to for a time and then a new case will start the spread of it all over again," Dodge stated. "Fortunately, we have only one new case here at Harmony. But it seems like every school child in Pappinville has contracted the smallpox. We have not heard anything from Pawhuska's town."

"Dr. Belcher is still there?"

"Yes, with Black Dog," Dodge nodded. "Black Dog can enforce a quarantine of the Osage village. I don't think anything will spread from there. But the folks at Pappinville seem stubborn about following the same rules. They have little in the way of law enforcement and no doctor to serve as an authority. Mrs. Belcher has been working there but they won't listen to a woman. We are hoping they will listen to your advice, Dr. Palmer."

The doctor's face was grim. A populous that was unwilling to take medical advice always made the job of stopping a communicable disease difficult.

"We'll all need a good rest before we can go in," he said looking around at the group planning to work in the nearby town. "And there is one thing more I will need, Brother Dodge."

"What is that?"

"A wedding," Marcus said looking at Clarissa. She felt a blush spread across her cheeks.

"A what?" the director asked, not understanding.

"I promised Miss Johnson I would marry her this coming Sunday and I intend to do so," Marcus explained. "Can we be wed before we drive over to Pappinville?"

"I think we can arrange that," Dodge said with a smile.

The sisters at Harmony, led by Harriett, took charge of the impromptu wedding and made it a special day for Marcus and Clarissa. In a borrowed dark navy dress, the bride stood with her groom before the minister following the morning worship service. The vows were simply said; there were no rings to exchange. Marcus had assured Clarissa that he had a ring for her, but had left it at Union, not realizing when he packed that she would accompany him to Missouri.

It didn't matter to Clarissa. The ceremony was perfect and she would never forget this day. She knew their bond of love had been forged with patience and strength and that would see them through whatever the future held. Though she felt some trepidation about walking into the midst of an epidemic, she had faith in her Lord and her husband that all would be well.

CHAPTER TWENTY-SIX

Hopefield Farm
September, 1824

The rains were welcome at Hopefield until the creek began to rise above its bank. Usually a shallow and lazy stream, Pryor's Creek became a muddy torrent that spread across the cornfields and into the large communal garden. Many of their not-yet-ripe pumpkins were torn from their vines and made an odd sight as they floated down to the river.

Fortunately none of the homes were flooded. Will and Susan stood in their yard watching the water. Susan held her sleeping baby in a cradleboard made for her by Teresa. She held tightly to Mary Montgomery's hand to keep the curly headed girl from getting too close to the fascinating flood.

They were joined by Teresa and Turtle. "The pumpkin harvest will not be good this year," the Osage woman stated.

"Afraid not," Will agreed. "But since we made such a good profit from selling the corn, we can buy pumpkins at Three Forks if they're available."

Colonel Nicks had purchased every barrel of meal that the Hopefield Mission had brought to Cantonment Gibson. When he counted the money out to Monepasha for his clan's share, the elderly man had seemed astonished. He was even more pleased to learn that the green paper could be used to purchase goods at the Nicks and Rogers mercantile.

While the Requas visited with Teresa, the clan leader made his way along the muddy path through the little settlement. Saying nothing at first, Monepasha joined them in simply watching the water that was even now slowly retreating back to its rightful place.

His gaze moved slowly over the silt covered cornfields and tears filled his eyes.

"The earth restores what we have taken from her," he said. "I see hope for us in these flooded fields."

Will smiled. "That is why we chose the name Hopefield for this mission."

Monepasha nodded. "When we came to this place, I was not sure it was the right choice. I did not want to disrespect our elders by leaving the old path. But I know that the old path will not keep the *Wahzhazhe* well."

"So you plan to stay?" Will asked.

"We will follow the buffalo at the Hunter's Moon," the Osage said. "But we will return and we will be field makers again. This is the best path for us now. The future is uncertain and we cannot be like the turtle." He tweaked the nose of Teresa's son and brought a smile to the little boy's face.

"We cannot pull our heads inside ourselves so we cannot see the danger that is coming," he went on. "I know what the great father in Washington wants for us. We must show him that we belong to this land or it will surely be taken away."

"I'm afraid you are right on that, Monepasha," Will said with regret in his voice. "But you have been a wise father to your clan. We will ask *Wah-Kon-Tah* to bless the *Wahzhazhe* so that you will be on this land a hundred years from now."

Only days later, the fever struck Union Mission once again, as heat and mosquitoes followed the rain. Rev. Chapman took to his bed as did Mr. Howard, the farm hand. Both Amanda and Stephen were sick as well. But most alarming to the family was the ravages of fever against the babies. Charlotte Vaille, Jane Redfield and the Osage twins Moses and Miriam were all very ill.

"Oh, why did Dr. Palmer leave us?" Asie Vaille wailed to Martha as the midwife tended to her child in the Vaille cabin.

"He could hardly know that the fever would strike us

while he was away," Martha countered trying to keep a calm tone.

"The fever comes every summer," Asie cried. "He should be here, not saving savages in Missouri."

"Asie," William Vaille spoke sharply. "Such words are uncalled for."

"I don't care," the woman cried all the more. "I hate this place where my children nearly drown or may die of fever."

Martha looked at the minister. "Dr. Palmer left the quinine with me," she explained in a low voice so only he could hear. "But I am afraid to give it to one so young. I don't know if it might do more harm than good."

"Perhaps we should send for Dr. Baylor at Cantonment Gibson," Vaille said. "Or at least seek his advice as to administering the quinine." The look of concern on his face seemed almost as much for his wife's state of mind as for his daughter's health. The woman had been distraught since Charlotte's birth but had become quite morose after the incident with Billy and Joey at the river.

"I think it would be wise to consult Dr. Baylor," Martha agreed with a nod toward Asie who had taken up the baby and rocked it in a tight grip.

Abraham and Paul were dispatched to Three Forks that day. Paul was always quick to volunteer to ride to the trade community because it gave him an opportunity to visit with Tassie at the Nicks' store. Sallie Nicks was a much more sympathetic chaperone than was Tassie's mother.

Abraham left Paul at the mercantile and then rode the quarter mile up to the fort.

At Cantonment Gibson, Lieutenant Summers was the officer who welcomed him when he dismounted at the remuda where the fort's horses were kept.

"What brings you our way, Mr. Redfield," the young officer asked as the men shook hands.

"I came to see Dr. Baylor," Abraham explained. "We've had an attack of the fever at Union and our Dr. Palmer is away in Missouri. We hope that Dr. Baylor might be able to call upon our sick ones."

"I'll take you to Dr. Baylor, but I'm afraid he's quite busy here," Summers said as they walked toward the tent that served as the fort's hospital. "We have several men down with the fever as well."

"It happens every summer," Abraham nodded. "But we have babies suffering and need his advice on their care."

"It hasn't affected Miss Cleaver, has it?" Charles asked.

"Not so far," Abraham replied. "But she was very ill two summers ago."

"Yes, she told me about that," the lieutenant said. "I've meant to call upon her, but Colonel Arbuckle sent me to Cantonment Towson for several weeks. Then when I arrived back at Gibson we had too many sick men to spare me for a trip to your mission."

He pulled back the flap of the hospital tent and they stepped inside. Dr. Baylor sat at a camp table, making notations in a ledger. His half glasses perched at the end of his nose and his graying hair looked as if it hadn't been combed in days.

He glanced up when the two men entered the tent.

"What can I do for you, Lieutenant?" he asked.

"Mr. Redfield has come down from Union Mission," Charles explained. "They've been struck with the fever, too, and need advice on caring for the babies."

"Babies?" the doctor responded. "Oh, yes, I forget. You have several young families there, haven't you? Is Dr. Palmer ill as well?"

"No, sir," Abraham explained. "He was called to assist Dr. Belcher with a smallpox epidemic in Missouri. Our midwife is quite competent, but is uncertain about giving quinine to the babies."

"How old are they?"

"Various ages," the mission superintendent said. "All the sick ones are under two years. The youngest is but a month old."

Dr. Baylor removed his glasses and rubbed his eyes while he gave the question some thought. There was regret and caution in his voice when he finally spoke. "I know too little about this infernal fever," he sighed. "My advice would be not to give quinine to anyone under two years old. We simply haven't enough study to know what effect it might have. I wish I could offer an alternative, but aside from willow bark, I know of no other remedy."

Abraham nodded and sighed himself. His own one-year-old daughter Jane was suffering.

"Well, I thank you, doctor," he said. "Should you find it possible, we would be grateful for a visit to Union."

Looking around at the hospital full of cots with sick men, the doctor nodded. "I'll see what I can do. My wife and daughter might be able to attend you at Union, if not me."

"Thank you, Dr. Baylor."

The two men stepped out into the August sunshine and walked back to Abraham's mustang. Seeming distracted, Abraham mounted his horse and nodded his thanks to the lieutenant.

"Will you tell Miss Cleaver I hope to visit soon," Charles asked.

"Certainly," Abraham agreed, but his mind seemed to be on other matters. He started toward the ferry below the fort and had almost boarded when he remembered Paul.

"Sorry," he said to the young private manning the ferry. "I forgot someone. I'll be back shortly." Then he trotted his horse back to the Nicks' store.

Paul and Tassie were sipping cider on the front porch of the wooden structure.

"You ready to go, Paul?" Abraham asked, not dismounting, though Sallie stepped outside then and invited him to take some refreshment.

"We need to get back to Union," he explained and nodded to Paul who jumped up to untie his own horse.

"I'll see you soon, Tassie," the nineteen-year-old told his sweetheart. "Don't forget what we decided."

"I won't," the girl said with a slow smile and a look up at him through her lashes.

Sallie smiled at the two and they both waved at the men until they were out of sight.

They arrived at Union late in the day to find the mission family saddened at the death of the Osage twins. Moses had passed first and Miriam breathed her last only a few hours later. They had never been strong in their sweet young lives and could not fight the fever's grip.

Compassionate Leah Chapman was crying quietly in the dining hall with her mother as she tried to console her. Little Moses had become her baby brother and she had loved carrying him around like a doll.

Sarah was equally sad at the loss of Miriam and she wept in George's arms. Though they were expecting their first child together, little Miriam had been taken into their hearts as if she were their own.

Rev. Vaille's task to try to offer comfort to the grieving family was made all the more difficult in the knowledge that his own precious daughter would likely join the twins in death. As he prayed with the group following their evening devotions, his voice caught and for a moment he could not continue.

"And now, our heavenly Father, we pray that you will comfort our grieving hearts. Help us to bear our loss and find solace in you. Amen."

"Amen," echoed those who were present in the dining room. They each left with heavy hearts to retire for the evening.

Rev. Vaille dreaded taking the news of the twins' deaths to Asie. She had barely allowed Mrs. Woodruff to check on Charlotte that last time the woman had visited their cabin.

"It's pointless," Asie had said and so she continued to rock the limp and fevered little girl, her voice hollow and her eyes blank. The child was too weak even to nurse and William knew it was only a matter of time before she too left the bonds of this earthly life.

The following morning, the minister and the other Vaille children stepped out of the cabin to go to breakfast. Martha and Rachel were waiting in the yard to check with him on Charlotte's condition. He sent the children on to the dining hall.

"There is no improvement," he said in answer to their questions. "I do not expect her to recover."

"We are so sorry, Rev. Vaille," Rachel consoled. She had been fighting a battle too with Moses and her husband ill with the fever. Thankfully, Chapman now seemed on the mend.

"Is there anything we can do for you?" Martha asked. "For the baby or Mrs. Vaille?"

"I fear much for Asie's mind if she should lose this daughter," William said. "She has somehow twisted this fever into being her fault. She says she is a terrible mother and God is taking her children from her. She says they would be better in heaven with him and it would have been better had Joey drowned."

Rachel gasped in horror. "I did not know she suffered so. Forgive me, Rev. Vaille, for being so preoccupied with my own grief."

"Please don't feel any guilt over this Mrs. Chapman," he replied. "I would only ask that you help me keep an eye on Asie. I believe I will ask the Requas to take in the older children for a few days. I dare not remove Joey for long from the cabin. She gets nearly hysterical if he is out of her sight for any length of time."

"Is there anything more that can be done?"

"I plan to send for her sister Ella who lives in Ohio," the minister said. "She has expressed an interest in serving at a mission post and I believe it would help Asie to have her here. Ella can help with Joey and cheer Asie as well. With steamboat travel I think she can be here within just a few weeks. In the meantime I will try to stay very close to my wife and would ask that you watch her as well."

"We certainly will," Martha agreed. "And please send for me if you need me for anything – day or night."

"Thank you, Mrs. Woodruff," the minister said. Then they walked in silence to the dining hall.

No one saw Asie slip out of her cabin only a few minutes later. With a bundle in her hands, she made her way toward the river.

BOOKS BY JONITA MULLINS

The Missions of Indian Territory
1. Journey to an Untamed Land
2. Look Unto the Fields
3. Come to Lovely County (Coming in 2016!)

Glimpses of Our Past
1. A Look Back at Three Forks History
2. Life Along the Rivers

Haskell: A Centennial Celebration

Jonita Mullins is a popular speaker on topics of history and inspiration. She also offers history tours in and around her home community of Muskogee, Oklahoma. More information is available on her books, gifts, tours and preservation projects at her website: okieheritage.com

Made in the USA
Columbia, SC
10 August 2017